A Heart with Five Parts

By Kathleen Willett

Chapter 1

There were people who thought that Trish was cold and unfeeling. They had watched her bury her wife and the mother of their child with quiet grace and dignity. Then they whispered behind her back when she had instantly hired a nanny for her child and made the attempt to carry on with her life. So, where were they all now? The talkers, the gossips, the speculators? Trish was here at Robbie's grave site, crumpled up next to the stone marker that Robbie's parents had selected from a picture in a slick brochure. She was here because she couldn't move. She couldn't put one foot in front of the other anymore. That required the energy and willingness to move forward. To go on with life. To go on without the love of her life.

Lisa came into the kitchen in her usual breezy manner. Josh was asleep. Rose was at the kitchen table. Max and Silver were at the hardware store, their favorite home away from home. Lisa had reported for nanny duty and although Rose wasn't warm to the idea, at least she wasn't still ice cold. It was all a matter of degrees as Lisa saw it.
"Where's Trish?" Lisa asked Rose. She hadn't seen her since she showed up, having gone directly to Josh when she first arrived.
"She isn't in her room?" Rose answered with her usual question. If one question could be answered with another question, Rose usually did it. Particularly when she thought that the information wasn't any of the person asking the question's business.
"No, she's not. Anyone check the spooky room?" Lisa asked back.
Ever since Trish and Robbie had bought their old house, there had been a room in the basement that was considered haunted. Recently, the remains of a female skeleton had been unearthed and an investigation worthy of TV crime shows had ensued. That was still pending. What wasn't pending was that Trish had arranged to have the remains buried properly. There had been no further hauntings, but it was still early in the game.
"No," Rose answered. "Do you think we should?"
"I'll do it."

1

"You're not going down there alone."

"So, come on then. If she's not there, she's got to be somewhere else," Lisa said it like she was going to file a missing person's report sooner rather than later. She didn't like it when people she cared for went missing. They went downstairs single file and found nothing. No ghosts, no Trish, no nothing.

"Do you think we should call the police?" Rose asked.

"No," Lisa replied quickly. "I think I know where to begin looking. Can you watch Josh for a while?"

"Sure," Rose always volunteered for that duty readily. "But where are you going?"

"I'll let you know if I find her," was all that Lisa would say. She knew exactly where to go. She was at the cemetery in about ten minutes and had located Trish. At first she was concerned at her crumpled figure but when she saw that she was conscious, Lisa did the only thing she could think would be helpful. She called Mitch from her cell phone.

Mitch rolled over in bed. It couldn't possibly be the phone. She and Reb were still asleep. They were back in Denver, but were still sleeping off the effects of having recently buried Reb's sister BeBe. Grief had taken a long time to process, particularly when they both knew that they would need to continue to keep track of the remaining family. Henry was still drinking heavily and Miranda was becoming heavily pregnant. So while Mitch and Reb were back in Colorado, neither one of them knew for sure how long they could stay. The situation had created a tenseness new to their relationship. And it hadn't helped matters that on her deathbed, BeBe had professed her love for Mitch to Reb. Talk about skeletons in closets.

"Hello?" Mitch answered the phone, expecting Henry to answer back.

"It's me," Lisa said.

Lisa said that whenever Mitch answered the phone. It's the kind of thing that one lover says to another lover and they both know who "me" is. Just because they had been lovers a while ago didn't change tradition.

2

"Hi," Mitch answered back. She would've said "Hi, me," back but Reb was now awake and listening and it would've been a tip-off. A too-familiar greeting too early in the morning.

"Did I wake you up?"

"Does it matter, Lisa?"

"Only to me, I guess," Lisa replied like she didn't like the idea that Mitch was grumpy with her when she had a situation on her hands and Mitch wasn't psychic.

"What's wrong?" Mitch asked. Like she was psychic after all. What she was able to do was to read Lisa's voice inflection. Even in her sleepy state of mind.

"It's Trish."

"What's going on?"

"She's at the cemetery and I'm going to need some help. I don't think I can get her to move."

"Okay. I'll be there."

"How soon can you get here?"

"Soon. Like as in right now. Give me a minute or two and I'll be on the way."

Mitch hung up the phone and looked over at Reb. Reb had an unreadable look on her face and Mitch didn't want to hear about it. That never stopped Reb.

"So, things haven't changed much in that regard, I see."

"What are you talking about?"

"Lisa calls and you run."

By the time Mitch had fallen head-over-heels in love with Reb, Lisa was historical in terms of being her lover. She was still present in their everyday family dealings, only because Lisa had shown the good sense to begin a relationship with Reb's daughter, Mary. It gave an added meaning to the term, "in the family" around their house.

"Yeah," was all that Mitch said as she headed to the bathroom. She took a few minutes to get ready and then looked at herself in the mirror. She was quietly admonishing herself, "You almost told the woman of your life to step off. Keep things in check."

It was a nice, compact pep talk. She walked out of the bathroom and went to change into something suitable for rescuing friends from cemeteries. Reb was up and out of bed by that time, not content with a simple "Yeah," from Mitch.

3

"What did Lisa do now that she needs your help?"

"She called me. That's what friends do when they need help," Mitch didn't want to worry Reb with the details, sketchy as they were about Trish, until she knew more.

"I know she called," Reb's voice was approaching that danger zone where she was beginning to sound more like a prosecuting attorney than a significant other.

"If I call, will you answer the phone?" Mitch asked.

"Are you going to need bail money?"

"If I do, I'll let you know," Mitch knew that she had entered the realm of being childish. But it still sounded better than telling her off. She didn't like her fidelity being questioned first thing in the morning.

They sat looking at each other for a moment. It was that same moment that people experience on a first date. To kiss or not to kiss. How could things be this awkward after everything they had shared in their years together? Mitch gave in first, kissing Reb softly, more along the lines of an apology than passion.

"You'll call me?" Reb sounded like she really wanted to be called, bail money or not.

"The minute I know anything."

Mitch drove carefully to the cemetery and then wound around the curved roads until she located Lisa and Trish. They were both at Robbie's grave site. Trish was still on the ground and Lisa was standing guard like a sentry. It was a nasty cold day. They would be lucky if all three of them didn't come down with pneumonia. Especially Trish. Mitch walked over to them.

"I found her here. She wasn't at the house."

"Do you know how long she's been here?"

"No. Nobody saw her leave the house. I didn't think I could move her on my own. Should I call for an ambulance or something?"

"No. Let's just get her to the car. I think if we both take an arm, we can get her moved, don't you?"

"We can sure try."

Mitch looked at Trish. She was awake, just not responding clearly to questions. Mitch's biggest worry was that Trish would resist their effort to take her away from the grave.

4

"Let's go get some coffee, or something, okay, Trish," Mitch said it like it would be just another outing.

Trish didn't say anything back but nodded her head slightly. Mitch got her under one arm and Lisa took the other. She was willing to walk the few steps to Lisa's car and Mitch followed them back to the house. Rose was frantic, ready to call the hospital, the doctors, anyone who would be able to help. Mitch talked her into putting that off for now, at least until they could assess the minor damage. Trish was wet and cold, so they changed her into something warm and put her to bed.

"Does your doctor make house calls?" Mitch asked Rose.

"He'll come out here if I tell him he's coming out here!" she replied in mother bear tones.

"Why don't you give him a call," Mitch said gently. Then, at the word "call," Mitch remembered she had a call of her own to make. She dialed Reb. Reb picked up on the first ring.

"It's me," Mitch said.

"Hi, me," Reb answered. "What's going on?"

"What are you doing today?" Mitch asked.

"What do you need?"

"I was hoping you could come over to Trish's."

"Why?"

"I could use a little support."

"Moral or immoral?"

"Probably both before the day is out. Trish is feeling under the weather. Almost literally."

"Give me an hour."

"See you then."

Mitch disconnected the call and then went back in to check on Trish. Lisa was standing guard. Again.

"Why don't you go and see how Josh is doing?" Mitch suggested kindly.

"Good idea."

"The doctor will be here in a little while. So will Reb."

"We'll have a whole house full of experts," Lisa commented.

Mitch didn't say anything back. Lisa deserved a break after bringing Trish safely home. Besides, she rather liked the fact that her ex-lover and her current lover were more or less at loggerheads. At least they weren't attracted to each other.

5

Lately, the current of attraction between Lisa and Mary and Trish was enough to confuse even the best electrician. Hopefully, that wouldn't come into play today. They had to concentrate on getting Trish better.

Judging by his suit, the doctor who made house calls for Trish charged a lot of money. If he had introduced himself as Dr. Armani, Mitch wouldn't have been surprised. Except that he didn't look Italian. He shooed everyone out of the room and took his sweet time with the diagnosis. Which wasn't as dire as they had predicted. At least at first.

"She has a viral infection. As to the other," he stopped and looked around for Rose.

"What other?" Mitch asked.

"I need to speak to a family member."

"We're all Trish's family."

"Where's Rose?"

"I'll get her," Lisa offered, realizing that nobody was going to find out anything until they got Rose in the loop.

The doctor and Rose huddled for a minute. To distract herself, Mitch tallied up the bill like she was going to pay it herself. Whatever the doctor was saying, Rose didn't look too surprised. She didn't look too pleased either. The doctor left without further comment, leaving Rose with a prescription in one hand and a referral slip in the other.

"What did he say?"

"He said that Trish needs a psychiatrist. And these pills," Rose handed the prescription to Mitch like she was a pharmacist. Which she wasn't. But she recognized the medication. A popular antidepressant. With about a dozen very nasty side effects.

"Can you get this filled for me?" Rose asked Mitch.

"I could. But is this what you really think is best?" Mitch asked back.

"It's what the doctor prescribed..." Rose said like she took every pill ever prescribed for her.

"After a ten minute house call," Mitch answered back, feeling oddly defensive on behalf of Trish.

"You know more than he does about medicine?" Rose quizzed.

"I know that some participants in the clinical trials who took this stuff killed themselves. It's one of those side effects that never made it into the final report."

"How do you know that?"

"I read up on this stuff. Particularly with Reb's health in mind."

"The Senator takes this for what? Depression?"

"No, she doesn't take anything for depression. I mean, she doesn't have depression. And even if she did have depression, I wouldn't let her take this stuff. And you don't have to keep calling her the Senator. She's not one anymore."

"They call presidents president after they aren't."

"Don't give her any more ideas where politics are concerned."

"So, what are we going to do for Trish?"

"Let's try and find her a good psychiatrist. She doesn't have to go alone. I'll take her. You can take her," Mitch was about to add that Lisa could take her, but that just didn't seem like a good idea.

"What about the one that the doctor recommended?"

Mitch just looked at Rose. That's all it took. "Let's ask the Senator when she gets here," Rose said like Reb was her personal version of the Yellow Pages.

"I have a better idea," Lisa piped up.

"What?" Mitch looked skeptical.

"What's that look for?" Lisa was put off by the fact that she had been ignored up until now. "I know a little something about therapy. I went through enough of it when I had the accident. Mary and I had enough therapy to qualify for green stamps." Everybody over fifty years old in the room knew what Lisa was talking about. How Lisa knew what she was talking about was anyone's guess.

"You know about green stamps?"

"They were in my history book at school. Would you just let me share some advice about therapy?"

"Okay, go right ahead."

"Whatever you do, get a lesbian psychiatrist."

"Why?"

"Because, it saves you a lot of time and money, that's why!"

"How does it do that?"

"You don't spend four or five sessions discussing *why you're gay*. Straight psychiatrists tend to just drag that part out, no pun intended."

"I hadn't thought about that."

"That's because you've never had to spend five-hundred dollars explaining your gay self to anyone."

"Well, okay, so how do you go about getting a lesbian psychiatrist."

"Are you putting me in charge of this task?" Lisa wanted to know up front her role in the planning.

Mitch looked at Rose who shrugged her shoulders. It seemed to be as sound of an idea as anything Reb would come up with. And indeed, when Reb arrived, she agreed. Wholeheartedly. Mitch felt the Earth move. Reb and Lisa agreeing on something.

Trish resisted at first. Something in her background made going to therapy seem like a sign of weakness. Maybe not the same kind of weakness that had made her incapable of walking away from Robbie's grave. But still profound and instilled from childhood. Only kooks went to shrinks. Isn't that what people said behind your back? And sometimes to your face? Finding a lesbian psychiatrist was the easy part. Getting Trish in the car was the hard part.

"You're going," Lisa was practically pushing her down the hallway. At this rate, they would need to go to a real doctor. "You're coming with me."

"I'm staying here. I'm watching Josh."

"Rose is watching Josh. If you don't come with me, I'm not going at all."

The parade came to a screeching halt halfway to the car.

"I don't know why you want *me* to go?" Lisa said carefully.

"I don't think I need to explain everything to the person who is orchestrating this entire process. If you want me to go to therapy so much and have everything all arranged, then it seems to me that it's the least you could do to come...with...me. Please?" Trish's words died off. She sounded plaintive by now.

"Okay, but I get to drive."

"You always get to drive."

"I'm driving. Take it or leave it."

Trish didn't complain further. She had gotten her way, after all. Again.

They waited a whole entire ten seconds in the waiting room before Trish was ushered in. Or at least, that's what they thought was going to happen. Those silly receptionist/office manager types.

"My friend is coming as well."

"We don't have you down for couples counseling? That's a different fee schedule."

"This isn't couples counseling. We're not a couple," Trish sounded impatient.

"Then we think it's best if you go in alone."

Trish looked around the office in a very mocking attempt to find the "we" to whom the woman was referring. Maybe she was the Queen of England in a past reincarnation.

"Look, I'm paying the bill. I'm calling the shots."

"But Dr. Carlson-"

"Don't 'but Dr. Carlson' me. Either we do this my way or I'm finding another psychiatrist!"

As Trish made her opinions clear at a tone above conversational level, the door to the doctor's office opened up. Even Dr. Carlson wanted to hear more about this.

"Good morning. Are you Trish?" she asked with a genuine smile.

"Yes."

"And are you here to see me?"

"Not by myself."

"Who else do you want to bring with you?"

"My friend here," Trish motioned to Lisa.

"Well, that sounds fine to me. Why don't the both of you come in and we'll talk."

"I'll pay extra. There seems to be an issue about that, maybe?" Trish seemed well enough to negotiate.

"I have a friends and family discount," Dr. Carlson smiled that engaging smile again.

"Sounds like a phone company," Lisa muttered under her breath. Trish heard the remark and tried valiantly to hide a smile of her own.

"I like her," Dr. Carlson said to Trish. The woman had grade-school-teacher hearing.

"A lot of people do."

"Do you?" the doctor asked, apparently beginning the session before they were even seated.

"That's not what I'm here for."

"Okay, well then, let's find out why you're here."

The furniture in the room was modular. It was easily arranged for a solitary client, couples, or group therapy, depending on who showed up on any given day. The three of them sat around like it was the living room. Nobody had to lie down on a couch. That was the first major relief for Trish. She didn't want somebody making faces at her comments that she couldn't see.

"Well, I recently lost my wife."

"And you are here to sort through the grief issues of that event."

"That's part of it. I suppose."

"And what's the other part?"

Trish looked over at Lisa. Might as well be honest. This was costing too much to hem and haw.

"And I'm in love with Lisa and I need to sort that out as well."

"And this lovely young women is Lisa, I take it."

"Yes, right."

"So, you really are here because a lot of people like her but you love her."

"Right."

At the first sign of the direction this conversation was taking, Lisa looked puzzled. Now, she appeared to be confounded totally.

"So, that's why I'm here?" she asked Trish.

"You don't think I brought you along because of your driving skills, did you?"

"Don't you listen to her," Lisa turned to face Dr. Carlson. "I'm a good driver no matter what she says."

It was beginning to sound a lot like couples counseling to the good doctor.

"Before we go any further, here's what I propose," the doctor now took control of the session. "First, I'm going to talk to each of you privately for a few minutes and then we'll come back together for a few minutes and then we'll probably schedule another session or two. How does that sound?"

Everyone nodded. Like bobble-head dolls.

After their first therapy session, Trish and Lisa were facing each other over a cup of coffee at the local one-on-every-corner coffee bar. The place where they charge four dollars for a cup of coffee because frankly there's about four dollars' worth of coffee in every cup.

"You could've at least warned me," Lisa said after a long pause in the conversation. A pause that had started when they left the doctor's office and stretched up until now.

"I warned you. Up in Montana. I figured that was fair warning enough."

"Oh, right. Montana…"

When Trish and Lisa had finally figured out about the haunted house, a kindly old woman had given them a lead about a recluse in Montana who knew enough about the history of the house to tell them a secret about a body buried underneath the basement flooring. But while Trish and Lisa were in Montana, they were secluded by a snowstorm for a couple of days. Enough time to discover their mutual attraction to each other. Something that they ignored once they were able to leave. After all, Trish had Robbie, and Lisa had Mary. Until the terrible news had arrived about Robbie. As events unfolded, Trish knew that Lisa had reconciled with Mary. For now, at least. And Trish had taken herself on a guilt trip all the way to the gravestone of Robbie. If she could've buried herself alive, it would've been easier. But she had her son Josh to think about. And though she knew it was wrong to hire Lisa to be his nanny, she had done it anyway. Dr. Carlson was good. She was worth every penny. She had all that out and on the table for Trish to see in about ten minutes during their private session.

"So, what did you talk about?" Trish asked Lisa through the coffee fumes.

"That's why they refer to them as *private* sessions."

11

"So, you're not going to tell me."

"It's your punishment for making me go in the first place."

"This was your idea, remember?"

"It was Mitch's idea," Lisa stretched the truth. "I just helped with the details."

"You call this help?"

"Well, at least you didn't spend four hours explaining why you're gay."

"What are you talking about?"

"Never mind. That's not important. What is important is how you're going to explain to Rose and Max why it is that you and I are going to couples counseling!"

"I'll listen in when you explain it to Mary. See if I can pick up some hints."

"I'm not laughing."

"Neither am I."

They looked at each other. Maybe it sounded like sniping from another table, but when they looked into each other's eyes, they knew it was nothing more than trying hard to be defensive when it was the last thing they wanted to be. The kind of defensiveness that masked the kind of affection they felt for each other that had inevitable written all over it.

"I guess we'd better go," Lisa said. Life was beyond the four walls of the coffee house.

"Yeah. One more thing."

"What?" Lisa was still trying to sound peevish.

"You don't have to be Josh's nanny if it's awkward for you."

"Are you trying to get rid of me?" Lisa asked back in a way that sounded more like a dare than a question.

"I'm just saying-" Trish started to explain.

"You're not getting rid of me. Josh is still the most important person in this big mess that we're in and he shouldn't have to suffer just because the adults in the house can't figure out how to solve their problems."

"Was that a yes or a no?"

"What was the question again?" Lisa challenged.

"The question was, do you feel awkward?"

"Honey," Lisa made it sound tough like in an old movie, "It takes a lot more than someone being in love with me to make me feel awkward."

"Well, then, how does it make you feel?"

"You've already been in therapy *way* too long."

"It was an hour. How does it make you feel?"

"It makes me feel like we need to get back to the house. Rose will have the phone in her hand ready to dial 911," Lisa said as she stood up to leave.

Trish wasn't moving. Lisa could drive home by herself if she had the desire to. Trish just sat still and refused to move.

"I'm leaving without you."

"Go ahead. You have the car keys."

"You really want to know how I feel?"

"It would be a start."

"I feel like you're on the rebound. I think that you haven't even gotten a good start on grieving for Robbie and I'm not about to get in the middle of that. You work through those issues and then you'll have the right to ask me how I feel."

Trish pondered the answer. It was sensible. And honest. And somehow full of love. It would do for now.

"That's all I wanted to know."

Maybe it was just Trish's imagination, but everyone in the coffee house looked relieved when they left. Especially Lisa.

"It was the least you could've done," Reb had informed Mitch after she realized why Lisa had called the morning of Trish's breakdown. They had put off talking about it until now. Mitch sat silently. These conversations never did go very well and she hoped secretly that if she just nodded and agreed, that it would eventually go away completely. Which it didn't.

"Why didn't you tell me outright that Trish was in trouble?" Reb followed up.

"I didn't know all the details."

"You knew some of the details."

"You're right. I knew some of the details."

"And what? You didn't think that I should've known some of the details?"

"Yes, you should've known some of the details," Mitch stuck to being agreeable. It was her atonement for being passive aggressive with Reb. Is this what all husbands went through? "And now you're being this way with me?"

Mitch sat silently again. That must've been what she was referring to. Mitch wasn't taking the bait. That was the passive part, she guessed?

"If I asked real nice, would you please tell me what's bothering you?" Reb finally said quietly.

Mitch hated this. Not the part about Reb asking nicely. She liked that part a lot. What she hated was sounding whiny.

"Please tell me?" Reb asked again.

"Okay. Are you sure?" Mitch just wanted to check one more time. Just to be sure.

"Anything would be better than this."

"I don't like it when you question my fidelity to you."

Now it was Reb's turn to remain silent. Not for very long. Silence and Reb weren't usually known to keep close company.

"Is that what you thought?"

"That's how you made it sound that morning."

"And you're probably right. No, you are right. You're right. And in turn, I resent it when anyone takes you out of my bed on any given morning. I resent the bloody hell out of it."

"Okay, but when it's Lisa, you resent it just a teeny, tiny bit more. And it shows. It's in neon."

"Is there more?"

"And I don't like it that somehow everything is always Lisa's fault."

"I never said that," Reb defended herself.

"You don't have to. Remember, it's in neon. It radiates out of you all the time. It's so much a part of you that you don't even see it anymore if you ever did at all."

"Can I tell you something?"

"You know the answer to that."

"One of the things I love about you the most is how you stick up for your friends."

"And my lovers?"

"Old lovers. Past lovers. Way past in your history lovers."

"Then can I make a logical extension for you?"

14

"Sure."

"If I stick up for friends and old lovers that way, imagine how I stick up for you when you're not around."

Reb couldn't say anything in return so Mitch just scooted over closer and held her.

"I know what you've been through with BeBe. When you find your voice again, we really need to talk about that."

Reb nodded and then proceeded to cry on Mitch's shoulder.

Mary had chilled champagne waiting for Lisa when she got home from work. After Lisa and Trish had gotten back home from the therapy session, Lisa had busied herself with nanny duties to the point where she and Trish had no further significant contact the rest of the day. So when Lisa left a little early, even Rose noticed the tension level begin to go down. Being a wise woman, she didn't ask and Trish didn't tell. Now that Lisa was home early for a change, hoping to compose herself after the revelations at the doctor's office, she was caught off guard by Mary's spontaneous celebration.

"What's this?" Lisa asked.

"I know you've seen champagne before," Mary went over to Lisa and stood waiting for a response from her.

"Well, maybe once or twice."

"Oh, come on now," Mary laughed and took her in her arms. "Just once or twice?"

"Well, maybe three or four times," Lisa pulled Mary close so she wouldn't have to kiss her just yet. It was a stalling technique that was working just fine until Mary caught on.

"What's wrong?" Mary asked.

"Nothing's wrong."

"We haven't celebrated our twenty-fifth wedding anniversary but I can tell when something is wrong."

"It was just a long day, that's all."

"You got home early."

"So did you."

"Now that we've both established that we can tell time, I want you to come over here and sit down and I'll get you a drink and then you can tell me what's wrong."

Mary guided Lisa to the spot on the couch where when she sat next to her, she would be facing Lisa's scars. She used to sit on the other side. Now, she didn't. It was part of her wanting to show Lisa that the scars from the fire didn't bother her anymore. At least not like they used to.

"Sit. Get comfy. Get ready for champagne."

Lisa did so. Mary was back with a glass for both of them and they toasted being home together at the same time.

"So, what's new in the world of nannydom?" Mary asked as she stroked Lisa's arm softly.

"Nothing, really."

"Well, if it's got nothing to do with being a nanny, why are you so tense?"

"I'm not tense."

Mary looked at Lisa. "I know you too well. You're tense."

"Maybe it was just the drive home? You know how people drive these days."

Mary poured another glass of champagne for her.

"Maybe this will help then. If that's all it is?"

"It couldn't hurt. You haven't explained why you're home so early by the way!" Lisa changed the subject. Enough of the hot seat for her for one day.

"Well, I know it happened earlier than I expected, but I got a promotion today."

"You did!" Lisa was genuinely happy. "Good for you and good for them!"

"It's just a small promotion. More of a lateral move actually. A little more money, a lot more responsibility."

Lisa heard what hadn't been said. More hours. You don't usually get more money and more responsibility in a job like that without being expected to work more hours. Hence the champagne.

"Congratulations."

"I know what you're thinking," Mary said.

"You do?" Lisa asked with as innocent a voice as she could muster under the influence of this truly fine champagne.

"You're thinking that I'm not going to have any time left over for sex."

"I wasn't thinking that at all, exactly."

16

"You weren't thinking about sex?" Mary teased.

Lisa began to blush in spite of the day's events. Or maybe because of them. "Why just think about it?" she made direct eye contact with Mary.

An hour later, Mary was asleep and Lisa was downstairs in the kitchen. They had skipped dinner to make love and when Mary had fallen asleep, Lisa went down to see what was in the refrigerator. Actually, she just went downstairs to keep from looking at herself in the mirror and asking herself why it was that every time she closed her eyes for the past hour, all she could see was Trish's face in her mind. And it wasn't even the most beautiful face that she was remembering. It was the defiant one that had looked up at her when they were talking in the coffee shop. The one that was daring her to drive home alone. It wasn't even a sexual image and it had still burned hot in her brain cells like peeking at the sun. Lisa was rubbing her eyes, trying to erase the image when Mary came around the corner.

"Great minds think alike?" Mary said.

"Huh?" Lisa looked up, startled.

"I got hungry too."

"I'll fix you something."

"Oh, no you won't. I'm taking my best girl out to dinner."

"You want to eat out. Again?" Lisa asked with just one eyebrow raised.

"You keep saying things like that and we're never going to get out of the house."

"But then we'd go without dinner and neither one of us would go to work and then imagine how life would be."

"Yeah. Imagine how life would be. Don't make me do that without you."

"Are we dressing for dinner or making reservations at Robes Are Us?"

"Sounds French when you say it."

"French is my specialty."

"I know. Believe me, I know."

"You just go and get dressed. Before the next meal served around here is breakfast."

"Yes, ma'am."

Mitch had finally made a decision. This didn't happen very often. When it did, even Reb took notice.

"I'm sorry. Wait a minute, I need to clean the wax out of my ears so I can hear you correctly," Reb said.

"You want to borrow a Q-Tip?" Mitch replied, hearing loud and clear the sarcasm.

"Run this by me one more time."

"I think we need a new house," Mitch repeated, more for the comic effect by now.

"Are you sure?" Reb looked astonished.

Get out the Academy Awards. Now *this* was acting.

Mitch gave it a couple of beats. One second. Two seconds. "Maybe?"

"I can't imagine why? The floors aren't level and the plumbing leaks and the windows are loose enough to make it look like Kansas in the 1930s on the inside. Other than that, it's a mansion."

"But it's got sentimental value. Remember when you and I were holed up in here with the FBI?" Mitch sounded like she was all set to talk herself out of her decision.

"A dream come true," Reb wasn't convincing. So much for her Oscar.

"We could use a little more space as well."

Red flags began to go up in Reb's mind. She knew that Mitch had something else going on in her mind.

"What kind of space?"

"What kind do I get to choose from?"

"I asked first."

"Space, the final frontier?"

"Sorry. Wrong answer. What are you really planning for?"

Mitch looked at Reb without answering. They both knew what she was thinking about. They had both been thinking about it since they had gotten back from Kansas. They just hadn't taken the time and energy to discuss it. Because that meant that they would have to face some serious decisions. Like, for instance, building a new house. Or at least improving the old one. So, they sat for a long time and then they decided to hug for a long time. Finally, Reb broached the subject, "Are you sure about this, Sweetheart?"

Reb hadn't called Mitch Sweetheart in a long time. It sounded so good.

"The only thing I'm sure about is that Miranda can't raise a baby in prison."

"I agree."

"I mean, even if they allow that and I really don't know if they do or not, is that where you want the baby to live? Miranda can't even take care of herself emotionally let alone a child."

"I don't want you to get your hopes up. The courts might think differently."

"I know. And I love you for helping me to come to terms with that. But this is your flesh-and-blood relative. It's your decision totally. If you want to pursue adoption, I'll support you a hundred percent. I'll even build you a new house. Either way."

"Gee, lady, you sure drive a hard bargain," Reb realized that Mitch had figured out all the angles before even entering into the discussion.

"I'm an old toughie."

"Let's see about that," Reb touched her gently where she knew she would get an immediate physical response.

"Some parts are tougher than others."

"Not when I get through with them."

Mitch surrendered. She got what she wanted in every respect. And Reb knew it, too.

Chapter 2

The next time Trish went to the psychiatrist, she went alone. It
was just easier that way. Everything that the psychiatrist needed
to know from Lisa she already knew. It was Trish who had the
most work to do.

"What do you want to talk about today?" the doctor asked as
they sat facing each other.

"I'm not sure where to start today," Trish said honestly.

"We covered a lot of ground last visit."

"Yes we did," Trish answered, not necessarily irritated by the
vernacular use of the term "visit." However, it made it sound
like they were at a garden party instead of in therapy.

"Do you want to talk about the deciding factor that made you
come in the first place?" the doctor wasn't fooling around after
all.

"The proverbial straw that broke the camel's back?"

"Something like that."

"I, uh, I don't know."

"You don't know the deciding factor or you don't know if you
want to talk about it?"

"Have you ever lost someone?"

"Yes."

"Then you'll understand how hard it is to talk about it."

"That's why I love my job. I help people deal with difficult
issues."

"You put someone in the ground and part of you wants to be
there with them. To stay and guard them. To keep them away
from harm and keep them company. Is that the sane part or the
crazy part?"

"I think that it's the loving part. And we all know how sane and
crazy that part is."

"I didn't think you shrinks used the word 'crazy.'"

"I'm old enough to be a Patsy Cline fan."

Trish finally smiled. She felt more at ease than she could've
imagined. "You remember Lisa?"

"She's unforgettable."

"Yeah. She is. She thinks I'm on the rebound."

"What do you think?"

20

"I think I'm a terrible person to even be needing to discuss this."

"Why?"

"Decent people mourn their loved ones."

"Did you mourn Robbie?"

"Well, yes."

"In fact, according to the facts, you were found camped out at her grave site, correct?"

"Right," Trish admitted it like she was embarrassed by the event.

"So, how much more do you expect of yourself in terms of mourning?"

"Oh, gee, well, I guess I could pitch a tent in the cemetery."

"I suppose so. You'd be the only person to do so in the history of cemeteries and mourning."

Trish became silent. Thoughtful.

The good doctor moved things along. "What else do you expect of yourself?"

"I guess, time. You always hear about a *period* of mourning. I feel callous. I feel like I haven't given Robbie her fair share of mourning."

"Did you grieve *before* she died?"

"I'm not sure I understand the question?"

"When people have depression like Robbie, they change. Did you grieve the loss of the old Robbie during that period?"

"Even before her death?"

"Right."

"We had our problems."

"What kind of problems?"

"I don't feel like talking about it."

"Why not?"

"I don't think it would be helpful."

"How serious was your estrangement?"

"I said I didn't want to talk about it."

"And that's why it's important to talk about it. People don't come to therapy to talk about easy issues."

"You have to earn your pay?"

"You deserve to get your money's worth."

Trish closed her eyes to remember any details that sorrow might've blurred. In the same way that tears blur vision.

"It was different after the baby was born…but it could've been different before as well."

"Different in what way?"

"It was like she changed after we bought the house. Just in minor ways. Things that wouldn't be significant unless you examined them under the therapy microscope."

"The *therapy microscope*?"

"You know. Look at every detail in 20-20 hindsight. Read something into things that really weren't there at all."

"If they weren't there at all, how would you see them?"

"Well, maybe it's more like blowing things out of proportion."

"What things?"

"Robbie was sort of taken over by the house. And believe me, I've heard of stupider plots in movies."

"How was she different after buying the house?"

"She was just a lot quieter. A lot more circumspect. And it might have been something else. I don't know. But the day we first saw the house, it was like she connected with it in a way that was, well, it wasn't anything that I felt. But she did."

"And then what happened?"

"You want to hear all about my haunted house?"

"Just the parts that you feel are important."

"The only part that's important was that when we found out why the house was haunted was when Robbie killed herself."

Now it was the doctor's turn to remain silent.

"What does it mean?" Trish asked. This was costing too much to sit here.

"Some people feel that we die when we have accomplished what we were put on Earth to do."

"And this was Robbie's goal?" Trish asked skeptically.

"There are people who believe that we are all preordained to do certain things in this life. And when we get those things done, then we are called to the next existence. People who have had near-death experiences have reported this anecdotally."

"They come back from the dead with a to-do list?"

"In a way. They just know that there is something left undone. You and I are sitting across from each other because we have not yet done what we were put here to accomplish. Robbie has.

And now she is at peace and maybe you can be too if you look at it that way."

"Unless the only thing I was put here to do was to mourn her death for fifty years."

"That may be true, but do you feel in your heart that that's the correct answer?"

"How will I know?"

"Can you honestly not know after everything that you said at our first session?"

"How many more sessions do you think I'll need to sort this out?"

"I think you're done. Unless you want to come back. You're always welcome. I can always use the cash. But I think you know what you need to do with your life. And I don't think it's sitting around in a cemetery for the rest of your existence. After all, don't you have a child to raise?"

The whistling tipped off Lisa that therapy had gone smoothly for Trish.

"Having a good day?" she asked when they crossed paths in the hallway.

"Yes, a good day," Trish nodded.

"Therapy going okay?"

"I don't have to go back."

"You're kidding, right?"

"You don't believe me?"

"Two sessions and you're...done?"

"She said I could always come back if I wanted, and as tempting as that is, I thought I'd go it on my own for a while."

Lisa didn't say anything. Trish noticed.

"What?" Trish asked in the special way that one friend asks another.

"You're not on your own. Just don't forget that."

It wasn't what Trish expected to hear. "I won't forget."

"Okay."

"Isn't it about quitting time?"

"I hadn't noticed."

"Trying to get overtime pay?" Trish said with a smile.

"You pay me too much already. I'm just not in a big rush because Mary is working late."

"Then, stay and have dinner with us," Trish tossed out the casual invitation.

"Oh, I don't know..."

"How late is Mary working? Do you need to still get home to cook?"

"Uh, I really don't know, and so probably not necessarily."

"So, you're all out of excuses then," Trish summed up quickly.

"Well, maybe."

"What else can I say to convince you?" Trish kept her distance physically but it felt like they were tentatively moving closer together emotionally every day. A little like inching out on thin ice. Only warmer.

"I'm watching my diet. Eating really healthy, you know."

"Rose's cooking makes Pritikin seem sinful."

Lisa smiled at the humor. "With an offer like that, how can I refuse."

When Trish exhaled, she realized that this felt exactly like asking someone out on a first date. All she had to do now was explain it all to Rose and Max.

"So, what is Mary going to do for her dinner if Lisa doesn't go home to cook for her?" was Rose's first question.

"She usually grabs a bite or orders something in."

Rose didn't approve. It was hard to tell whether she disapproved of Mary's eating habits or Lisa's staying for dinner. They took their seats for dinner after Trish carefully steered Lisa away from Robbie's cherished place at the table. Thank goodness the table was still big enough for all of them. A couple of heads of state could've attended as well.

Trish hadn't fibbed. Rose served one squeaky clean healthy meal. Off in the distance, they heard Josh stir awake. Both Trish and Lisa stood up at the same time.

"You sit," Trish put her hand on Lisa's forearm.

"But I'm the nanny."

"I know. And I'm the mommy. And what the mommy says goes as house rules."

"I'll fix a bottle. At least let me do that much."

"Okay. Bring it to us when it's ready."

24

"Will do."

Trish went to Josh's room to do diaper duty. How one tiny baby could soak things up so good was a question only Mother Nature could answer. At least that part functioned perfectly. She got everything changed and dried out on baby Josh and was about ready to begin changing sheets when Lisa showed up.

"Here, you feed him and I'll take care of everything else."

"You don't mind?"

"Of course not. This is my forte."

"I think you're pretty good at everything."

"You would," Lisa deflected the compliment.

Trish sat in the rocking chair and began feeding Josh. He was hungry. Lisa took care of the mundane tasks and then turned to leave.

"Where are you going?" Trish asked.

"You two need some time alone. Besides, I need to get this bundle to the laundry room," Lisa gathered the wet bedding and walked out the door.

Trish leaned close to Josh's ear and whispered, "Do you like her?"

Josh, being so newborn, kept his opinions to himself.

"Yeah, me too," Trish agreed for the both of them.

When Josh had finished his bottle and had fallen back asleep, she tucked him in for the night and went back downstairs. Lisa was nowhere to be found.

"She went home to be with her family," Rose answered the unasked question.

"That's good," Trish was agreeable. She hadn't wanted Lisa to stay the night. Okay, she did. But she didn't want to give that impression to Rose. It didn't really matter at what time Lisa got home. Mary didn't roll in until midnight and fell asleep immediately.

Lisa was all business the next day when she got over to Trish's. Which didn't go unnoticed by Trish.

"Everything okay?" Trish asked when they were alone.

"Yes," Lisa answered unemotionally.

"You had already gone home by the time I came back downstairs last night."

"Thank you for inviting me to dinner."

"It was nice to have you."

"Thanks."

"Did I get you in trouble at home with Mary?"

"Do you think you could?"

Trish thought about it. She had been talking about the dinner. It was hard to tell what Lisa was talking about.

"It wasn't my intent."

"Mary didn't miss me. She got home at midnight."

"So, it didn't disrupt your life?"

"It was nice to have dinner with someone."

"You are welcome every night."

"I'm not sure that's such a good idea."

"Why?"

"You know why."

Trish looked at Lisa until she made eye contact. It took a few seconds. "We'll always have a chaperon. It's a simple dinner invitation for when Mary works late. Just consider it to be a selfish move on my part."

"Selfish in what way?"

"I'd have you to talk to at the dinner table and you wouldn't need to cook dinner for yourself after a long day."

"I usually just pop a frozen meal into the microwave."

"Those things are full of chemicals that aren't good for you."

"I can't shake the feeling that this is about more than artificial colors and flavors."

"I enjoy your company. Is that enough to the point for you. I like Rose and Max, don't get me wrong. But I'm getting tired of talking about arterial health all through dinner. Day after day after day."

Lisa smiled, just a little.

"Is that a yes? Please tell me that's a yes."

"Well, Mary is working a lot of evenings."

"What is she doing that takes so much overtime?"

"She's in charge of a lot of people now so she stays late to get her paperwork done."

Trish didn't say it out loud, but to herself she mused that it would take one helluva huge important bunch of paperwork to distract her from Lisa. Particularly at night.

26

"But she likes it," Lisa added.

"I'm sure she does," Trish tried to hide the fact that she'd rather get successive root canals than wade through paperwork for a living.

"It couldn't be every night for dinner."

"Maybe only the evenings that you wouldn't be missed?"

"I'll think about it."

"Is tonight one of those nights?"

"How soon do you need to know?"

"Just soon enough to send Rose to the store for more broccoli."

"Um, well, okay. I'll let you know. When I know, you'll know."

"Okay."

Trish walked away from the conversation with a vague feeling that somebody was going on a broccoli run sooner rather than later.

"We could just flip a coin," Reb said to Mitch.

"We could," Mitch answered back.

The great debate had boiled down to this. To flip or not to flip. A coin.

"Got a quarter on you?" Reb asked.

"Is it official if you use a quarter?"

"What do you want? A silver dollar?"

"I just want to do this the most official way that you can do this."

Reb reached across their small kitchen table and took Mitch's hand.

"What's really on your mind?" she asked gently.

"I'm really torn between taking the necessary time to fix this place up versus the time constraints we're under with Miranda's due date."

"I don't want you to give up this place. You know that, right?"

"I know."

"So, let's forget about tossing quarters or dollars and really throw some serious money at the problem."

"How serious?"

"Let's do both. Let's buy something big enough for three people and at the same time renovate this place. It can be our vacation home."

Mitch pursed her lips together in thought. It was a logical solution to their housing problem.

"You look so serious," Reb observed.

"Do you find it sexy?"

"You're incorrigible."

"You want two homes."

"What do you want?"

"I want you to be happy."

"I'm already there."

"I wish I still knew someone in the real estate business."

"Maybe Trish does?"

"We could call her."

"We could."

"First one to the phone doesn't have to cook dinner," Mitch dared.

Reb let Mitch win the race to the phone by simply not participating at all.

"You won anyway," Mitch said when she hung up from the call.

"How so?"

"We got invited to dinner."

"That's nice of Trish."

"Particularly on such short notice."

"Maybe she's ready for some company."

"That's a good sign."

Max didn't complain, but he didn't exactly look overjoyed when asked to put the leaf in the already big-enough table. Rose had more fun buying bags of broccoli at the store. So when Reb and Mitch arrived at the appointed hour, they were greeted by both Trish and Lisa.

"I didn't know she was going to be here," Mitch said to Reb quietly as they sat having a before-dinner glass of wine.

"Maybe she's working late?" Reb replied.

Mitch didn't know to which "she" Reb was referring, so she kept her mouth shut. Which worked out nicely because about that time, Rose sat beside Reb and engaged her in conversation. Mitch escaped to the kitchen to find Lisa refreshing her own wine glass.

"Seems like nanny hours are pretty long."

"Some days are longer than others."

"Don't tell Galileo."

"You came all the way to the kitchen to tell ancient jokes?"

"Where's Mary?"

"Same as me. At work."

"So, everybody in your household is working overtime."

"You remember being a member of the working class a long, long, long time ago, don't you?"

"I tried to help you with that, didn't I?" Mitch felt defensive. Lisa looked puzzled.

"I gave you money."

"Oh, that."

"Yeah, that."

"Mary took it away. She put it in some account. An escrow or something. She doesn't want us using it."

"I didn't know."

"Well, I didn't tell you. I didn't want to sound like a complainer."

"Why doesn't Mary want you to use the money?"

"For obvious reasons. She wanted to be the bread winner. And now I'm making more money than her and she's killing herself at work to keep up," Lisa's story wandered to a halt.

"Could you use a hug?" was all that Mitch could think to say.

"I couldn't hurt."

"Come here," Mitch pulled her into an embrace, patiently waiting for her to relax. It took a moment for that to happen, during which Reb rolled into the room. Lisa saw her first and broke off the hug. Mitch looked over.

"Is this where you get refills on wine?" Reb asked calmly. Lisa looked at Mitch. "I'm going to check on the baby before dinner."

It was a very successful attempt at deserting Mitch.

"So, what did I interrupt?" Reb asked point blank.

"I don't suppose I could answer that later?"

"How much later?"

"When we are alone in bed together later?"

"That works for me. Now, how about that refill?"

Dinner was interesting. If you liked broccoli. But what was even more interesting was all the eye contact that was and wasn't made. Max was easy. He looked mostly at his broccoli like he wished longingly that it was lemon meringue pie. Mitch didn't get much eye contact from Reb. That would come later. The real obvious lack of eye contact was between Trish and Lisa. You could hum along to the tension it created. They managed to steal a glance or two when Rose and Reb were occupied in deep conversation and Max was praying for deliverance from anything else green on his plate. Mitch was convinced that everyone else was oblivious to it, too, until she had that appointment with Reb later in the evening.

"It's pretty obvious, isn't it?" Reb said as they lay together in bed.

"What is?" Mitch feigned ignorance. Usually it worked. Usually.

Reb didn't say anything, but gave Mitch that famous "You know what I'm talking about" look.

"There's more to it," Mitch finally said.

"I'm not sure I'm ready to hear more."

"I didn't mean *that* more."

"*That* more?"

"They're not sleeping together."

"How do you know that?"

"People who are sleeping together usually don't create that much tension by not looking at each other."

"Okay, so if it wasn't *that* more that you were referring to, then *which* more were you talking about?"

"It's financial."

"As in money financial?"

"Is there any other kind?"

"What about their finances?"

"You remember when I gave money to the kids?"

"You've done it so often, I've lost track."

Mitch ignored the tone of the remark and forged ahead. "Mary took the money away from Lisa and put it in an escrow account."

"And so what?"

"And so Lisa jumped at the chance to try and earn some bill-paying money so Mary wouldn't need to shoulder all the burden," Mitch explained it as carefully as she could to avoid

30

bringing up the obvious power struggle going on below the surface.

"And therefore, Lisa needed a hug?" Reb followed along.

"She's out-earning Mary. There's tension at home."

"You're saying that it's Mary's fault?"

"I'm not assigning blame. I listen. I hug."

"I noticed."

"But if Mary would make the money accessible, neither one of them would need to work overtime."

"Mary is a proud woman."

In the back recesses of her mind, Mitch heard Tina Turner and tried vainly to block it out.

"Okay, fine. But if you had a choice, would you want to have your pride or your happiness?"

"Sounds as tough as choosing between sex and romance."

Mitch didn't say so, but Reb was closer to the real issue than she knew.

"I'll talk to Mary if you want me to," Reb offered.

"Don't do that. She'll know that Lisa talked to me and I blabbed to you. That will just make things worse."

"I guess so."

"But you could find out why she has to work so late every night. If it's just her drive or ambition, you could impress upon her the joy of home life."

"You think Lisa would come home if Mary was there?"

"A person can only eat so much broccoli."

"Sounds like a saying you would find inside a fortune cookie."

Mary sat back and pondered the view from her new office. Compared to the broom-closet-size office she was assigned to a few short weeks ago, this one was spacious. Still, it felt tenuous. Like it could all be pulled out from under her with one mistake. She was surrounded by college-educated kids who were true Type A personalities. How she ended up managing a team of them was precipitous and unexpected. It took all her energy to keep up with their various stock reports. They brokered all day and then went home. She stayed behind at work to catch her breath, check their work and prepare for the morning meeting

31

that kept them all on the same page. It was numbingly-detailed work. The phone rang, jarring her out of her reverie. It was her mom.

"Hello?"

"Hi, Honey," Reb practically chirped into the phone.

"Hi, Mom. What's up?"

"Does something have to be up for me to call you?"

Mary thought this over. To herself, she said "yes." To Reb, she said, "No."

"I was just wondering if you had time to have a drink with your old mom?"

"Right now?" Mary asked.

"Is now a bad time?"

Mary looked at the stack of papers on her desk. "No, this is an okay time," she lied.

"You're sure?"

"Yeah, but can you meet me downtown?"

"Okay. How about that trendy rock and roll bar across the street?"

"I guess it would be okay if you don't mind shouting to be heard."

"You have a better idea?"

"There's a nice quiet lounge two blocks away in the lobby of the Centennial Hotel."

"I'll be there in thirty minutes."

"See you there."

Mary hung up and tried to concentrate on work but after finding her mind wandering around the various reasons why her mother might be wanting to meet with her, she gave up on the pile of paperwork and headed over to the hotel. She was one drink ahead when Reb arrived.

"Hi, Dear," Reb accepted a kiss on the cheek from Mary.

"What's going on?" Mary asked without preamble.

"Honestly, does something have to be going on for me to want to get together with you?"

"You're not sick or something? Something isn't going wrong physically, is it?" Mary probed.

"Sweetie, I'm fine," Reb patted Mary's hand.

If you didn't know better, you would've thought they were a May-September lesbian couple.

"Okay, well, after what happened to Aunt BeBe, I was worried."

"I didn't mean to worry you."

"How are you doing, you know, after BeBe?"

"Mitch thinks I haven't grieved enough yet."

"Mitch is wise in that regard. She really tunes into people's feelings."

"I didn't tell you about your Aunt's deathbed confession."

"What kind of confession? She didn't rob a bank or anything. Did she?"

"No, she didn't rob a bank," Reb took Mary's hand in hers.

"It's worse than that?" Mary sensed big news.

"Not worse. Just unexpected."

"How unexpected?"

"Your Aunt BeBe was gay."

"You shouldn't joke about the dead."

"I'm not joking. There's more."

"I think I'm going to need another drink."

"You might need a whole bottle by the time we get done with this conversation."

Another round of drinks arrived soon after Mary signaled the cocktail waitress.

"Okay, what's the other news?"

"She was in love with Mitch all these years."

Mary sat without speaking for a long moment. "Does Mitch know this?" she finally asked.

"I told her. We haven't talked much about it."

"Why not?"

"I don't know what to say and neither does Mitch."

"I guess I can see why. Aunt BeBe was so homophobic."

"And so hard on Mitch all the time."

"And probably so very jealous of you, no doubt."

"Because I had Mitch."

"That, and you decided to live your life as an openly gay person."

"Well, I wouldn't say exactly that."

"What do you mean?"

"It took a while."

"I was there, remember?"

Reb smiled. "I know."

"Does Henry know?" Mary asked.

"I don't know. He wasn't in the room when BeBe and I talked and I haven't told him anything."

"It would be a hard secret to keep all those years."

"Which probably explains her hostility toward us. Mitch was right all along. As usual."

"Right about what?"

"She kept at me about getting everything talked about before BeBe died. I guess she knew something was going unsaid between us."

Mary only nodded.

Reb continued, "Mitch understands people. What they say. What they mean. What they don't say."

"Is that why we're having this drink? Has Mitch sent you here with a message for me?"

"I guess you could say that."

"What's the message?" Mary was ready for anything.

"A person can only eat so much broccoli."

"That's the message?"

"That's the most important part."

"I don't get it?"

"When you do get it, you'll know what to do."

"Anything else?" Mary was slightly perturbed to be taken away from important work for this gibberish.

"Just don't mention this conversation to anyone."

"Believe me, I won't."

"I'd better get home to Mitch. You know how she worries about me when I'm out alone at night."

"Thanks for the drink."

"Remember—broccoli's the word."

"Uh huh."

After Reb left, Mary had another drink. It had been a long day and the conversation with her mother confounded her to the point where returning to work would be useless. Her aunt had been a homophobic gay woman and there was a password status where the word broccoli was concerned. She must've looked sultry.

34

No less than three men offered to keep her company. She politely but firmly turned them away. The fourth offer came from a female.

"I noticed you have a pattern of turning the gentlemen away. Does that mean what I think it means?"

It must be riddle night, Mary thought to herself.

"I saw you here with another woman earlier. She's a little old for you."

"She's my mother."

"Lucky me."

"Actually, I was just leaving myself."

"Well, I'm sorry I'm chasing you away."

"You're not chasing me away."

"So, you'll stay and buy me a drink."

Mary wasn't used to this. It hadn't happened in a long time. In fact, she couldn't remember a time when it had happened. And by a redhead with green eyes. She checked her watch. One more drink would still get her home by nine.

"Have a seat."

"Thanks. I was getting tired of standing."

"So you try and pick up women every night?" Mary felt she had the right to ask since she was buying the drinks that were already at the table by now.

"I'm new at this. Does it show?"

"Why are you new at this?"

"You're just full of questions, aren't you?"

"I'm a curious woman."

"A curious woman all by yourself at a bar."

"It was a long day at work."

"What do you do?"

The question gave Mary pause to think. This was, by her way of thinking, a one-drink deal. No need to go into detail.

"I work downtown."

"Not telling, I guess," her guest replied.

"Nothing much to tell."

"You're a spy or something like that, right? Otherwise, you would've blurted out the truth."

"Hey, if you want to believe that I'm a secret agent, that's okay with me."

"So, what do secret agents do all day at work?"

"Secret stuff."

"I like my women to be mysterious."

Mary noticed the proprietary nuance in her statement.

"I'm really not mysterious."

"Everyone is mysterious in their own way."

"There's nothing special about me."

"You were in debate club in high school, weren't you?"

"Look, I'm due home. As interesting a person as you seem to be, I need to be on my way."

"That's okay. It was nice meeting you."

"Same here," Mary left enough money on the table to settle the bill and left without turning around. It wasn't easy. There was just something about redheads.

Lisa was home when Mary wandered in.

"Hey, you're home early!" Lisa looked happy.

"Hey, so are you."

"Have you eaten?"

"I had a bunch of alcohol calories."

"Bad day?"

"Not bad. Just weird. You want to go out and grab a bite?"

"Sounds great. Can it be something indulgent?"

"Sure. I guess so. Why?"

"I've just had my share of broccoli for one week. I could stand something salty and greasy."

Mary smiled. "Me, too."

They ended up at the local Mexican dive that had green chili that could peel wallpaper off the wall.

"So, why did you try and drink your dinner earlier this evening?" Lisa asked with a Margarita in one hand.

"My mom wanted to get together. Knock back a few."

Lisa raised her eyebrows like this was a little hard to believe.

Mary noticed and added, "She also wanted to talk about Aunt BeBe."

"Oh," Lisa still sounded puzzled.

"It isn't easy for her."

"I guess not."

"How was your day?"

36

"Quiet, actually. Everyone left me alone so I could get my work done."

"I wasn't so fortunate. I'll probably need to work late to make up for leaving early."

"Okay. I'll adjust."

"I'll make it up to you on the weekend."

"I'm holding you to that."

"Holding will be just the beginning."

"Go ahead and make the call," Reb said to Mitch.

They had remembered amid all the hugging and broccoli at Trish's house to get the referral of a real estate agent. It wasn't the same one who had sold the Livermore house to Trish. She had left the state shortly afterwards. But another name had surfaced in Trish's memory and Reb and Mitch were now in a standoff over who was going to make the call.

"You don't want to make the call yourself?" Mitch asked.

"Dial the number," Reb intoned.

Mitch did so. A secretary answered and immediately put Mitch on hold. "Things must be busy," she said to Reb.

"That might be a good sign."

In a minute, after listening to some soft pop music, the secretary got back to her.

"How can I help you?"

"I wanted to see about making an appointment with a Ms. Collins-"

"Her first available time is..."

Mitch waited while the secretary accessed a computerized appointment scheduling program.

"We can fit you in three weeks from next Wednesday."

"Uh, okay."

"Name?"

"Mitch."

"First or last?"

"First."

"Last name?"

"Does it matter?" Mitch figured a first name would be good enough for a three-week wait.

"What's that, Italian?"

Mitch had to mull over what she was talking about.

"I guess so," Mitch realized that she had just changed her last name from Tanner to Dosimater.

"Okay, you have an appointment Wednesday the 23rd. We require 48 hours prior cancellation."

"What a coincidence. So do I."

On that note, Mitch hung up and looked at Reb. "Three weeks."

"Three weeks!?" Red was incredulous.

"I guess they're busy," Mitch shrugged her shoulders.

"Give me the phone."

"Why?"

"Just give it to me!"

Mitch handed it over without argument. Reb hit the redial button. The same secretary answered and the first words out of Reb's mouth were, "Do NOT put me on hold."

It must've worked. The conversation continued.

"This is United States Senator Rebecca Fairbanks. I would like to speak to Ms. Collins."

Two seconds went by.

"Ms. Collins? Yes, this is Senator Fairbanks."

Another second ticked by.

"It's a pleasure to speak with you as well. I'm in the market for a new home. I'd like to meet with you as soon as possible."

Another second ticked by.

"Tomorrow will be fine."

Another second.

"10:00 a.m. Fine. See you then." Reb disconnected the call.

"Gee, I guess I'd better cancel my appointment," Mitch said flatly.

"You never told me you were Italian," Reb teased.

"You never asked," Mitch didn't sound her usual self.

"You're upset?"

"No."

"Yes, you are. Your face betrays you."

"I'm Italian. I can't help it."

"Do I have to play guessing games with you or do you just want to tell me?"

38

"Doesn't it ever bother you that you get in line ahead of everybody else?"

"It never has before."

"Really?"

"We know that we're serious about buying a new house, right?"

"Right."

"And all those people ahead of us in line might just be thinking it over or not quite as serious about it as you and I, right?"

"Maybe."

"So, I'm doing Ms. Collins a big favor by letting her know that I'm a serious client. Someone who will put money in her pocket faster than anyone else."

"Okay."

"Besides, real estate agents are like doctors. They always set aside a couple of hours each day for emergency appointments. Believe me, we haven't bumped anybody out of line."

Mitch thought this over. It still didn't sit right with her democratized world view, but she didn't want to fight about it either. "It wouldn't have killed us to wait three weeks," was Mitch's quiet response.

"Okay then, give me the damn phone. I'll cancel the appointment," Reb held out her hand. Mitch gave her the phone and sat silently to see what would happen.

"You really want me to do this?" Reb said.

"You do what you think is right."

They sat looking at each other for a moment.

"You didn't seem to mind using your influence to arrange a prison visit with Miranda."

"The circumstances were different. There weren't people in line waiting to see Miranda."

"That's your rational? When you do it, things are different?"

"That favor was for your sister. I didn't know how long she had," Mitch spoke the truth gently.

"I'm sure that there were other times when you used your wealth to get something for yourself."

"Name one time and I'll go with you tomorrow willingly. Otherwise, I'm going to take a walk."

"It's chilly outside."

"I'll wear a coat."

Mitch shrugged into her coat and left the house. It was chilly. Cold, in fact. She walked without thinking and eventually ended up at the tiny diner that was about two miles from home. It was strictly a meatloaf and gravy kind of place, so Mitch settled in for a cup of coffee to start. Ever since she had changed her eating habits, places like this had few choices for her. The coffee, however, was great. After about ten minutes, Reb wheeled in.

"Hi," Mitch said.

"Mind if I join you?"

"Plenty of coffee to go around," Mitch caught the eye of the waitress and she sauntered over to get, hopefully, a better order. It didn't happen that way.

"I'll have coffee as well."

"Fine. I'll bring another cup."

It got quiet again.

"You want to talk?" Reb asked.

"You followed me. What's on your mind?"

"I canceled the appointment."

"We could use the extra time to sort this out."

"Sort what out?"

"We haven't even talked about what kind of house we want."

"How about one that isn't falling down around us,"

"Okay. That's good. Maybe we should make a list."

"A wish list."

"Right. List what you want and what I want and what we both think the baby will need."

"Sounds like we might need a pretty big piece of paper, and some pie."

Mitch smiled. "Pie?"

Reb looked relieved. "I was beginning to think that you were never going to smile at me again."

"Why would you think that?"

"Because we've both been on edge lately and whatever I do doesn't seem to be helping."

"I know you're trying to be helpful. But having an object lesson in how to throw your weight around just doesn't help. I don't know why? It just really jangles my nerves."

"You're the most unique person I've ever met."

"I like the sound of this, I think."

"You should. You have more money that the Pharaohs and it hasn't changed you one iota. Other people become insufferable. You've only become more loving and generous as time goes on."

"Stop it before I blush."

"I'd like to see that!"

"First you wanted pie, correct?"

"I'll start with pie, but I'm ending with you."

Pie was ordered. One slice. The waitress wasn't impressed.

"Why do you suppose BeBe took so long to come out?" Mitch went on to other subjects.

"It was like lancing a boil," Reb answered bluntly. "She nearly squeezed my fingers off my hand when she told me."

"I didn't know."

"She was so full of fear and regret and loathing that I didn't really know what to say in return. I offered to go and get you but she couldn't face you after all that had happened."

"I probably wouldn't have said the right thing anyway."

"I'm sure you would have said the right thing. You always did. You were always so nice to her no matter how she treated you."

"She was easy to be nice to."

"Did you love her?" Reb asked.

Mitch looked at Reb. "As one friend loves another. No more. No less. And not even close to how I love you."

"So, how do you love me?" Reb pressed for details.

"Your pie is on the way," Mitch indicated over Reb's shoulder. "Should I get it to go?"

"Absolutely not. I want to watch you sit there and savor it."

"You're going to help me eat it. You know that, don't you?"

"I love it when you talk pie to me."

"It's my pleasure."

"Thanks for coming to get me. I know I'm not always easy to deal with."

"Everybody needs a solitary walk once in a while."

"It's not you I walk away from. It's the reactive part of me that I need a break from once in a while."

"All of your emotions are safe with me," Reb promised as she attacked her part of the pie. The girl had an appetite and she hadn't even been the one who had walked two miles.

41

Chapter 3

It took a whole week before Mary wandered back into the lobby
of the Centennial Hotel for a happy-hour drink. The work day
had been grueling and she wanted a quiet place to have a quiet
drink all by herself. At least, that's what she told herself.
Consciously. And her conscious self was getting its wish. She
had one drink and then another and was seriously contemplating
a third when she caught a glimpse of the red-haired stranger
across the proverbial crowded room. It took a moment for her to
look over at Mary, like she was teasing with those green eyes.
They made eye contact and then politely looked away. When
Mary checked again, the woman was at her table. Sitting down.
Making herself comfortable and making Mary uncomfortable.
"Didn't come here with your mom?"
"I'm all alone."
"You don't need to be."
"I'm on my last drink."
"How many have you had?"
"Two."
"You were waiting for me, then?"
"I was having a quiet drink after a long day at work."
"Oh right. You're the secret agent."
"I'm not a secret agent."
"So, what do you do?"
"I work at a company with stockbrokers."
"Well, no wonder you're drinking. Why didn't you say so in the
first place."
Mary wondered the same thing now that they were chatting.
"Because...it's not a very glamorous job."
"I think that people who deal in financial matters are very sexy,
in a disciplined sort of way."
"That's an *interesting* way to look at it."
"All those numbers have to go in all those columns in just the
right way or everything gets all screwed up, right?"
"It can happen if you don't stay focused. Did you want a drink?"
"You don't even know my name."
"Okay, what's your name?"
"What's your name?" she countered.

"Mary."

"Fawn."

It sounded like a fake name to Mary, but she wasn't ready to frisk her for an ID.

"Go ahead and make a joke. See if you can come up with something original."

"Like sin?"

"Sin?"

"Original sin. It's a catholic thing."

"I guess every sin is original when you do it for the first time."

"I guess so. Now that we have that out of the way, what will you have to drink?"

"I'd like a brandy alexander."

It sounded very feminine next to Mary's scotch. Fawn handled the drink when it arrived with all the culture of an heiress.

"What do you do for a living?" Mary got around to asking even though she dreaded hearing the answer.

"I'm a student of the human condition."

"You can actually get a degree in that?" Mary couldn't believe that she was asking this.

Fawn smiled. "You're very cute. Has anybody ever told you that?"

"I'm sure someone has," Mary was beginning to be affected by the scotch. Three wasn't her limit, but it was close.

"Girls as cute as you shouldn't be drinking alone."

"I rarely do."

"Should I be jealous?"

"I should be going."

"Are you okay to drive?"

"I'm fine."

"I could give you a lift."

"You would be too difficult to explain."

"That's how it is?"

"That's how it is."

"Well, thanks for the drink. It was lovely. Really it was."

"You're welcome."

Mary walked steady although her knees felt liquid. It was either the drinks or the red hair. Or a combination of both. She mentally toyed with the ratios. Fifty-fifty? Sixty-forty? Forty-sixty? Even now she knew that she was fudging the numbers. A shameful activity for a financial auditor. Okay. Twenty-eighty was her final offer to her conscious.

She stopped to window shop at a jewelry store a block away from the hotel. They were open late, a rare thing in downtown. Fate was at work. Mary wandered in. She must not have looked like a serious customer, men were waited on ahead of her. Whatever. It gave her more time to browse. Finally, about time, a female clerk approached her as she was looking over a series of necklaces.

"May I show you something?" she asked professionally.

"I'm in the market for a diamond necklace."

"We have these in the case," the clerk pointed out the obvious to Mary. The necklaces in the case were paltry one-diamond necklaces. Not much more than a few hundred dollars per necklace. Mary did the math in her head. She was making decent money. She didn't have a house payment. She always had Mitch's millions to fall back on if need be.

"Do you have one with diamonds all the way around?"

"We have a room set aside for viewing those."

"May I see them?"

The clerk seemed reluctant, like Mary was a looky loo instead of a serious buyer. Mary stood her ground, quite a feat considering all the scotch.

"One moment please."

The clerk disappeared into some sort of back room and then reappeared in a moment with a set of keys and motioned for Mary to follow. They entered the room with an air of reverence, which was fitting since so many people worship the sparkling bits of hardened carbon.

"Would you care for a drink?"

"Oh no, thank you anyway," Mary said. She was already drunk enough for her own good.

"Coffee?" Maybe the clerk sensed something about the lack of true and total sobriety.

"Um, no. It might keep me awake."

"Okay, well then, have a seat."

It would certainly help to sit when spending this kind of money. These diamond necklaces were thousands and thousands of dollars. And thousands. After looking at several, Mary had it narrowed down to two. She knew Lisa would love either one. Lisa would have loved the hundred dollar ones in the front room of the store.

"I can't decide between these two," Mary indicated the two that she liked the best.

"You could always get both," the clerk smiled sweetly. Perhaps she meant the remark in jest. But it sounded like a splendid idea.

"Okay," Mary nodded matter-of-factly. It would only make a tiny dent in the million, after all. And all for a good cause.

"How do you want to pay for them?" the clerk knew that this was the real reason for her prior hesitation. Mary didn't look or smell like she was good for the money, frankly.

"I'd like to buy this one tonight," Mary pointed to the necklace on the left, "on my credit card and I would appreciate it if you would hold the other one for a day or two. Can you do that?"

"Of course. Just let me do the paperwork."

Which meant, in code, check the limit of Mary's credit card. It was good to go, thanks to Mitch and her mother. However, Mary knew it would also be a good idea to transfer funds before going deeper into the platinum. She was happy just to be able to take something home to Lisa.

Lisa was folding the last of the laundry when Trish checked up on her. Snuck up on her was more like it.

"Hello," Trish said.

Lisa jumped a mile.

"I didn't mean to startle you," Trish apologized.

"It's okay. I guess I was just engrossed in laundry."

"I guess you were. Are you staying for dinner?" Trish stepped closer to Lisa, more or less to peek over her shoulder. Lisa turned around.

"I don't think so," Lisa said quietly.

"You haven't been our dinner guest lately. Was it something we served?" Trish asked like she already knew the answer.

"Mary hasn't been too late this week."

"How late is too late?"

"Too late for dinner, I guess."

"And what about tonight? It's already six."

45

"Wow. I guess I better scoot."

"Okay. Well, thank you."

"For what?"

"For everything. For being such a big help around here. For being easy to talk to. For being you," Trish was whispering by now because they were just that close and besides, she didn't want to be overheard.

"You're welcome," Lisa whispered back conspiratorially. It was all very cute until it turned serious. Slowly. Deliberately. Especially on Trish's part. "I want you to stay. I know it's wrong to want that. But knowing it doesn't make it go away."

"I know. But I need to go."

Trish nodded and was behaving herself just fine until her hands took on a life of their own and gently caressed Lisa's face. "I know you can't stay," Trish agreed in word but lingered in deed. Lisa stood still physically even though she was wavering on the inside. Trish was so gentle and tentative when she touched her that she instinctively craved more. In her mind, she was reaching up to pull Trish's hands away. In reality she leaned into the touch.

"See you tomorrow," Lisa said without making any attempt to leave.

"I've behaved myself for weeks," Trish defended herself.

"Yes, you have," Lisa couldn't argue. It was true. Both of them had behaved themselves.

"Okay, well, I guess I'll see you tomorrow then," Trish leaned in for a goodbye kiss on Lisa's cheek. It lasted longer than the usual perfunctory peck that most people share. When she pulled away, Trish saw the ambivalence in Lisa's expression.

"Now I *really* have to go," Lisa pulled away.

"I understand."

Lisa gathered up her coat and keys and headed out the front door. Trish's brief kiss still fresh in her mind. She didn't remember much of the drive home, but was drawn back to reality when she saw Mary's car. She was home after all. Lisa congratulated herself on coming home when she did.

"I'm home," Lisa called out as she let herself in.

"There you are!" Mary came to greet her.

Mary kissed the same spot on Lisa's cheek where Trish had bussed her less than an hour ago.

"I ran a little late," Lisa sounded guilty.

"You're not too late," Mary smiled broadly.

"What's going on?" Lisa could smell the scotch.

"I ran a little late, too," Mary admitted. "I made a stop."

Lisa knew that much. Mary had made a stop alright. At the bar. It must've been another tough day. "You want me to cook dinner?"

"No. I want you to come over here and open your present," Mary led the way to the couch and handed the necklace box to her.

"What's this?"

"It's a box with a present in it," Mary was smiling.

Lisa knew it was jewelry. She was savvy where gifts were concerned.

"What have you gone and done?"

"I've gotten something nice for a fabulous lady."

When Lisa opened the box, she was speechless. Utterly and completely speechless. She had known it was jewelry. She didn't know until now just how much jewelry. Mary was waiting for a critique.

"Oh, my," was all Lisa could muster.

"Do you like it?" Mary noticed that Lisa hadn't even touched it.

"It's dazzling. How do they make them look so much like the real thing?"

"Sweetie, they are the real thing."

"That can't be. We can't afford the real thing with this many diamonds."

"Sure we can. I figured it was about time you had something nice to wear."

"This is way past nice. I can't even imagine..." Lisa's voice trailed off.

"What can't you imagine?"

Lisa just shook her head.

"Do you know what I want you to do?" Mary was still smiling.

"What?"

"I want you to take everything else off and put this on."

"You are a rogue, aren't you," Lisa smiled back.

"I'd like to think so."

"That must have been some raise you got at work."

"Uh, yeah, well," Mary hedged. She didn't want Lisa to know that she had decided to dip into the million that Mitch had given to them.

"This had to cost thousands. All these real diamonds. Did you get a bonus as well, Sweetie?" Lisa questioned gently. She hadn't heard the truth yet and still instinctively knew it. This was her way of giving Mary the chance to come clean now, rather than later. Mary gave Lisa an odd look. So many questions. "Don't you like it?"

Lisa felt the sudden shift of conversation as one would feel a minor earthquake and question whether it was the earth or them who had just moved.

"Of course I like it. I love it. It's just so stunning. I've never been given anything as beautiful as this before."

"So? You'll put it on?" Mary nudged.

"Would you help me? I'm a little shaky right now."

"Of course."

Mary helped with the clasp and then admired the necklace. It was superb.

"Now, I want you to make me a promise," Mary said, a slight slurring of words was still evident.

"What kind of promise?"

"I want you to wear it always."

"Always?"

"All the time."

"You don't wear something this expensive all the time. It's something you wear once in a while to a special event."

"ALL THE TIME!" Mary emphasized each word like she herself heard the slurring of her own words. "I want you to think of me each and every moment of the day and I want everyone around you to know how deeply I care about you."

Lisa now understood what this necklace business was all about. They had gone past the realm of gifting and entered the kingdom of possession and ownership. Mary wanted Trish to know that Lisa belonged to her and her alone. Suddenly, the chain felt heavy around her neck. And rightly so, for it was a telegraph device as well.

"It's lovely," Lisa stated the facts.

"Now, about the other part?"

"What other part?"

"The part about you taking everything else off."

"Oh, *that* part. Are you sure that you don't want dinner first?"
Lisa felt totally unromantic at the moment and needed a little
time. Like a spare millennium or two.

"I forgot that you work on your feet all day," Mary kissed her
hand. "Come on, I'll take you out."

"Isn't tomorrow the doctor's appointment?" Rose asked Trish at
dinner. Yes, there was broccoli.

"Right. Ten o'clock."

It was going to be Josh's checkup day.

"And Lisa will go too, right?"

"Absolutely. She needs to hear instructions firsthand as well."

"She didn't stay for dinner, then?" Rose must have known
somehow that Trish had invited her.

Trish looked at Rose. Rose had a different tone of voice. Softer,
or maybe just less critical.

"I tried to talk her into staying," Trish felt strange apologizing
for her failed attempt, especially to Rose.

"It's okay," Rose conceded the point.

"What are you thinking about?" Trish asked when she realized
that Rose's questions were coupled with a diminished appetite.

"I just worry about the baby."

Trish looked over at Max, who was keeping out of it. Silver as
well.

"You think we're going to find out something tomorrow that we
don't already know?" Trish needed clarification.

"Knowing doesn't stop me from worrying about it."

"Of course not," Trish stood up and walked over to Rose. She
hugged her as she cried at her place at the table. "We all worry
in our own way about Josh."

"I guess I'm the only one who cries about it."

"No. You're just the only one who's crying right this minute
about it."

Rose nodded and sniffed and then excused herself to the kitchen to busy herself out of her sorrow. The dishes had better watch out. When Rose got in this mood, there would be no grime left behind.

Trish went to check on the sleeping Josh and then toyed with the idea of calling Lisa. Mostly just to warn her about Rose's fretfulness about tomorrow. It was in the nature of her employment to be kept abreast of such developments. Wasn't it?" She dialed the house. Mary picked up.

"Hi, Mary. It's Trish."

"Hi."

"Is Lisa available to talk about Josh?"

"She's undressing right now. Can I take a message?"

"It isn't all that crucial."

"You do have four competent adults over there anyway, right?"

"Yes, actually, we do. Just please tell Lisa that I called."

"Okay."

"Thanks."

Trish hung up the phone feeling a mix of irritation and embarrassment. By the time the phone rang, irritation had the upper hand.

"What's wrong?" Lisa asked, sounding panicked.

"Nothing is wrong," Trish said, trying in vain to quell the annoyance she felt toward Mary.

"You called about Josh."

"Right. I forgot to remind you about the appointment. Tomorrow."

"What's really going on?"

"You know me too well."

"Uh huh. And what else?"

It dawned on Trish that Mary was monitoring Lisa's side of the conversation.

"Okay, well, Rose broke down and cried at the dinner table."

"That's not a good sign."

"And I don't know if she's worried about something specific."

"I'll be right over."

"You don't need to do that."

"Give me thirty minutes."

"Is this going to be okay with Mary?"

Lisa hung up without answering the question, or for that matter, any sort of a goodbye. True to her word, she was back at Trish's within the half hour. Trish greeted her at the door.

"I feel foolish making you come all the way back here."

"It's my job. Josh's well-being is crucial so we need to keep everyone in a positive frame of mind."

Trish nodded. The speech sounded well-practiced. Maybe she had already used it on Mary.

"Where's Rose?"

"In the fireplace room."

"Does she know I was on the way?"

"Yes."

Trish and Lisa went in together like a couple. They looked good together. They really did.

"Hello, Rose," Lisa went right over to her and sat down.

"You shouldn't have come all the way back here," Rose scolded with love in her voice.

"It's okay. Trish told me you were upset about tomorrow. Do you want to talk about it?"

"I'm just afraid what we're going to hear."

"What frightens you the most?"

"What if Josh is never going to be well. Or healthy. His whole life. However long. You know what I mean?"

Lisa knew exactly what she meant. They sat quietly for a moment. Lisa looked over at Trish. "Got any coffee?"

"I can make some."

"Take your time."

Trish left them alone together for a long-enough interlude that when she returned, she could tell that they had both had a good long cry. Rose was ready to retire for the evening and did so. Lisa wanted her coffee. Trish took Rose's place on the couch and put her arm around Lisa. She could smell the salt water tears.

"Thank you for coming on such short notice."

"You're welcome," Lisa said and then started to cry again, so Trish just held on to her while she did so. It took a few minutes to subside. Trish figured this was about more that Josh.

51

"What's going on?" Trish asked the only question she could think of.

"You've seen my necklace."

"I thought I'd need an eye exam. It nearly blinded me."

"I don't need your sarcasm right now," Lisa tried to move away but Trish held on gently.

"I'm guessing that the necklace is a problem?" Trish turned serious.

"I know you can't see it, but it has 'Lisa belongs to Mary' written all over it."

"Everyone needs a sense of belonging."

"Is that your version of sympathy?"

"You want my sympathy because your lover gave you a $50,000 dollar necklace?"

"Forget I asked."

"Well, I guess I should let you get back home. You were undressing when I called, after all."

"Mary said that?"

"Uh huh. You can imagine what went through my mind."

"It affected you?"

"Every night, when I go to bed, that image goes through my mind. One diamond necklace isn't going to change that."

"Every night?" Lisa asked, just to be sure she heard right.

"Every night."

"Tonight as well?"

"Tonight as well."

"I still have to go."

"I know."

Trish walked Lisa to the front door like they were in first-date mode. Hadn't they already gone through this once today?

"We've got to stop meeting like this," Trish said quietly.

"Maybe you shouldn't walk me to the door?"

"Maybe not."

"Well, we're at the door. Why don't you just wander that way," Lisa pointed to the fireplace room.

"And you can go that way," Trish indicated the front door.

Nobody moved.

"We could count to three," Lisa suggested.

"You start."

"One."

"Two."

The counting stopped.

"You forgot what comes after two?" Trish leaned closer.

"I know what comes after two," Lisa wasn't backing away.

"THREE!" a voice boomed out. It was Silver. Trish nearly had a stroke.

"I'm waiting to secure the premises for the night. Three comes after two." Silver had her arms folded across her chest. She meant business. And she wasn't backing down.

"I told you that three comes after two," Trish said to Lisa like they were in junior high.

"No you didn't. Silver said it," Lisa said through the night air as she scooted out the front door.

Trish looked at Silver. "Well, what are you waiting for. Secure the premises."

"My mother had a saying about this," Silver still had her arms crossed. She still meant business.

"About what?" Trish wasn't excited about more advice.

"You don't swing on someone else's playground."

"I'll keep that in mind."

Trish went upstairs to bed. Images floated through her mind. Mercifully, she fell asleep.

At nine forty five the next morning, Josh's entourage took up half the chairs in the pediatrician's waiting room. It was a small office. Few clients. Exclusive clients. At first, only Trish went back with the baby to the examination room. After tedious minutes had ticked by, Rose was called back. Max, Silver, and Lisa were left to wait and wonder. The time crawled by.

Finally, Lisa was summoned. She felt oddly faint, like she could feel in her bones and beyond that the news wasn't good. She took one look at Trish and knew that her bones were telling the truth.

"We thought you should be involved in the discussion," Trish said flatly, "since you are Josh's primary care giver."

"I'm just the nanny," she gave herself a demotion, "and you'd better send someone out to talk to Max and Silver before they climb the walls."

"I'll go," Rose volunteered.

"Are you sure?" Trish checked.

"I'll be fine. You two talk."

Trish was holding a happy, contented Josh. He seemed fine on the outside. As fine as he could be without arms. Lisa sat next to Trish. The doctor patiently explained about the complications of bleeding in the brain, the major problem of babies with TAR.

"So, there's brain damage," Lisa surmised.

"Right. We just don't know and can't predict how much damage and whether or not it will accelerate over time."

"I'm sorry. What will accelerate?" Lisa felt foolish for apologizing and also for not understanding what exactly they were talking about. She was in an emotional blur right now.

"The bleeding. The bleeding could accelerate. That's the main concern."

"What can we do to stop it?"

"Nothing."

"What do we look for?"

"You mean, what symptoms will occur if the bleeding gets worse?"

"Right."

"Changes in habits. Sleeping. Eating."

"Okay."

"We're done here, unless you have more questions?"

The doctor couldn't help it. There were more patients to see. Maybe not in his waiting room. Maybe kids who were even more ill in the adjacent hospital. Imagine, kids sicker than this. Lisa looked over at Trish, who now seemed to be in total shock.

"Let's go," Lisa patted Trish's knee. They packed up the baby gear and drove back to the house in silence. Trish and Lisa put Josh down for a nap and then sat down together to talk.

"I had the option of checking Josh into the hospital to monitor his condition," Trish admitted finally.

"It's really that serious?" Lisa was stunned.

"I didn't want to do that."

"Why not?"

"Would you want to live in a hospital?"

"It doesn't matter what I think."

"Yes it does! Your opinion is the most important one."

"Why?"

"Because Josh is emotionally attached to you and likewise. I want him to thrive and he does that around you. If we put him in a sterile environment with a bunch of strangers coming and going every day, I think he would withdraw. You are so good for him."

"But I'm not a professional. What if I miss something important? What if I'm tired or distracted or something and it has a detrimental effect on me?"

Trish looked at Lisa. "Are you tired right now?"

Lisa remained silent.

"I'm sorry. It's none of my business."

"I slept on the couch last night."

"I got you in trouble at home."

"Mary was asleep when I got home. I didn't want to disturb her by crawling into bed."

Trish didn't say it, but she would have been overjoyed to be disturbed like that. Instead, she said, "Just tell me what you need and I'll get it for you. You need to sleep, I'll get you the best mattress. You need a massage, I'll arrange it. I'll hire a chef to prepare all your favorite foods. Whatever you need to make you the happiest nanny on earth, consider it done. Just help me make Josh's life the best it can be for as long as he has..." Trish's voice trailed off.

"That's always been my goal," Lisa filled the awkward silence with the truth.

"And you've done a great job. Let me make it easy for you. That's all I'm asking."

"Don't hire a chef. Or a masseuse. And no new mattress."

"What can I do?"

"Just be patient with me."

"Okay," Trish promised, not knowing if she had recently been impatient. "Why don't you go and take a nap as long as Josh is asleep. I'll take care of things for a while."

"You talked me into it."

Lisa used the guest room to take a nap. This mattress was as good as any. When she woke up, Trish was feeding Josh his bottle.

"Hi, Sleepyhead," Trish smiled.

"Hiya. I really slept hard."

"We should have a change of clothes here for you. And maybe something more comfortable."

"Like, pajamas?"

"Something you can lounge around in when you get tired."

"I don't think today is a good day to go home and pack a suitcase."

"That isn't what I had in mind."

"What did you have in mind, exactly?"

"You could go shopping. Pick out a few things. Charge it to employment wardrobe."

"That's a very sweet idea."

"Well, it's not exactly a diamond necklace, but it's a whole lot more practical. Take Rose and Silver with you."

"You don't want to go?"

"I'll watch Josh. You really don't want me picking out lounge wear for you anyway, do you?"

"You watch Josh. I'll take Rose and Silver."

It was like they were picking teams. At first, Rose wasn't sold on the idea of a shopping spree, but once she was out of the house, her mood lifted, and she warmed to the outing.

"I'm thinking of just buying some sweats," Lisa said when they arrived at the mall.

"Sweats?" Rose crinkled up her nose at the thought.

"They are comfortable."

"But they're not pretty."

"You think I should buy something pretty?"

"I don't want Josh surrounded by drab colors. We need to stimulate all his senses."

It didn't take any more arm twisting than that to persuade Lisa to select gorgeous silk lounge wear. Afterward, they went to a music store and selected a wide variety of music that they would play in Josh's room to stimulate his hearing. Sights and sounds designed to delight their favorite boy were tucked away in the trunk of the car and hauled home. Trish was pleased. She hadn't thought about the importance of music and was glad someone else had. The rest of the afternoon passed with music and meditation.

At the end of her shift, when Lisa went to find Trish to check out for the day, she found Trish in bed. She looked exhausted.

"Long day, huh," Lisa said from the doorway.

"Yeah," Trish agreed, her voice void of any enthusiasm. The reality of the doctor's report was finally hitting home. Lisa came in and perched on the end of the bed.

"You want to say anything about anything?" Lisa asked.

"Not without holding you."

It was a suggestion that Lisa knew would be unwise. "Take my hand and tell me what you haven't told me yet."

"The doctor was pretty brutal. Before you came in, he talked in very explicit terms about retardation."

Lisa nodded. She couldn't think of anything helpful to say. She understood why Trish would want to be held and felt foolish at her reluctance to do so. Without speaking, she gently gathered Trish in her arms. It took a moment for the tears to flow. So much for leaving work on time.

Mary dialed the house five times before giving up on talking to Lisa. She had seen her on the couch when she left for work. It puzzled her. Irked might be a better word. Mary took care of some sensitive banking, stopped by the jewelry store to pick up diamond necklace number two and then went to the Centennial for her after-work scotch. It was becoming a habit. She really didn't give a damn. The cocktail waitress didn't need to ask anymore. She just brought the usual and started a tab. Mary hadn't even taken a sip before she spotted her familiar friend, minding her own business on the other side of the bar. They made eye contact, but the lady kept her seat. Twice she had come to Mary. It was time for Mary to come to her. Mary picked up her drink and went to her.

"What took you so long?" she teased.

Mary smiled. Every once in a while, sass was sexy. This was one of those times.

"Do you know a better place to get a drink?"

"I thought you'd never ask."

Mary paid her tab, swallowed her scotch in one gulp and followed her escort outside.

"Where are we going?" Mary asked.

"My place."

"Okay."

The walk felt exhilarating, mostly because Mary's brain was floating. As apartment buildings go, this one was nondescript. The apartment even more so. Mary looked around the room.

"Looking for something?" her escort asked.

"I've just never been in a prostitute's apartment before."

"I guessed as much. You still want that drink?"

"Sure."

"Have a seat," Fawn indicated the love seat and followed soon with drinks in hand. Mary took a sip of the scotch. It was about one hundred times better than the stuff she had been drinking. She studied her hostess. "Did you buy this just for me?"

"I knew you drank scotch."

"Yeah, but not this expensive."

"I asked the guy at the liquor store for the best."

Mary put down the glass. "I don't know why I'm here," she confessed.

"Do you want to talk about it?"

"Like confession?" Mary was still in Catholic mode.

"Do you have things to confess?"

"Doesn't everyone?"

Fawn smiled. "So, talk!" she encouraged.

"People don't come to your apartment to talk, do they?"

"You'd be surprised."

"Is there one rate for talking and another rate for everything else?"

"I'll let you know when the meter's running. Right now, just relax and enjoy your drink and tell me what brings you to my modest abode."

"I never thought I would say this, but I'm having a hard time figuring out women."

Fawn smiled and nodded. "Go on."

Mary took another drink of the scotch. It was smooth like pure water in Death Valley.

"Don't women like diamonds anymore?"

"I guess it would depend on the woman. And the diamond, of course."

"Of course," Mary echoed.

Mary now knew why she had bought two necklaces. Her indecision wasn't over the necklaces themselves at all. It was a deeper indecision that had fostered her splurge.

"So, tell me about diamonds," Fawn encouraged.

"I already have a girlfriend."

"I gathered as much."

"It shows?"

"Around the edges."

"What does that mean?"

"That's all you've let me see so far. And from what I've seen, you act like a woman in a relationship. You're not at the bar all night every night like some women."

"I do go home occasionally."

"Compared to some, you're a real homebody."

"You don't talk like any prostitute I've ever met before."

"How many have you met?"

"You're my first, come to think of it."

"Should I be honored or flabbergasted?"

Mary chuckled. She couldn't help herself. This was all so absurd.

"I'm really not here for sex," she tried to make sense of this while thinking out loud.

"Then I guess I need to be flabbergasted," Fawn narrowed down her feelings.

"And I didn't mean that in a way that would hurt your feelings," Mary hurried to assuage any reaction Fawn might have had.

"You're not hurting my feelings by talking about yours."

"I wouldn't objectify you for the world. You are just too nice for that."

"So, you came here just for the drink?"

"Actually, I wanted you to have this," Mary produced the box containing the second diamond necklace.

Fawn opened it without question.

"These are the real thing."

"Of course they are. You didn't think I'd give you a cheap imitation, did you?"

"I don't think you ever do anything on the cheap. I can't accept it. It's too much."

"And so now you can see why I don't understand women anymore. It's my way of thanking you."

"For what?"

"For this drink."

"And what else?"

"You want an itemized list?"

"I like hearing nice things about myself."

"Okay. Thank you for listening to me make absolutely no sense."

"You're making perfect sense. You give diamonds to girls and that's a nice thing. And you don't ask for anything else in return and that's an even nicer thing. I wish everyone made no sense like you, but I still can't accept it," Fawn closed the box.

"Then give it away to someone else. You have a mother?"

"Everyone has a mother."

"Then give it to her. Or an aunt. Or a gay uncle. Just, whatever you do, don't give it back to me."

Mary stood to go. Fawn followed her to the door.

"You are one amazing woman," Fawn noted for the record.

"So are you."

The door opened and Mary stepped out. She waited a moment on the doorstep. Fawn waited a moment as well on her side of the door. Then they both went their separate ways.

When Mary got home, Lisa was sitting on the couch in the dark. For all Mary knew, Lisa had been there all afternoon. Mary stood before her. "You're in the dark."

"I guess. It got dark. No use putting on the light."

"Been here long?"

"Heavens no. I went to work."

"I only asked because you spent the night down here."

"I didn't want to wake you up."

"You want to tell me about it?" Mary ventured a question.

"Which part do you want to hear about?"

"Which part do you want to talk about?"

"Are you wearing perfume?" Lisa asked out of the blue.

Mary had to think fast. "We have this lady at work who drenches herself in this stuff. It's gaggy, isn't it?"

"Actually, I kind of like it. Come sit with me."

60

Mary did so. And waited.

"It was a long day at work," Lisa said.

"What happened?" Mary usually made a point of remaining oblivious to Lisa's day-to-day employment realities and knew next to nothing about any of it.

"Josh went to the doctor."

"The routine appointment?"

"There isn't such a thing as a routine appointment where Josh is concerned. I went over last night to get Rose calmed down and today it was Trish."

"Trish needed your attention?"

Lisa didn't know why she even bothered to talk to Mary about this. She inhaled and then exhaled deeply. "Now I know what else I smell. You've been drinking. Scotch?"

"I'm over 21."

"I'm not the police. You don't need to pull out your ID."

"You're not the only one who had a long day at work."

"I understand."

"I'm going to bed."

"I'll be up in a little while."

"Whatever," Mary said and then left Lisa where she had found her. On the couch. In the dark. Alone.

Lisa checked the time and then dialed Trish. Trish answered in one ring.

"Hello?"

"Are you doing okay?" Lisa asked.

"I'm still moping around. Feeling sorry for myself."

"You have every reason to."

"How about you? How are you holding up?"

"About the same," Lisa managed to say before her throat closed up with emotion. Trish heard it even through the phone line.

"Are you crying?"

"Yeah, a little," Lisa managed to say.

"We had a rough day, didn't we?"

"Uh huh."

"I wish I could be near you to comfort you. Where's Mary?"

"She went to bed already," Lisa answered quietly.

"Where are you?"

"On the couch, again."

"For the night?"
"I don't know yet."
"Why don't you know?"
"I haven't made up my mind where to sleep tonight."
"Wherever you end up, I wish you sweet dreams."
"You, too."

Chapter 4

Mitch fidgeted so much that Reb finally reached over and held her hands still. They had waited three whole minutes for their appointment with the realtor.

"Are you nervous?" Reb asked.

"No. Why?"

"You're fidgeting."

"Not anymore."

"But you were."

Further banter was interrupted by the appearance of Ms. Collins. "Please follow me back to my office," she marched away without pleasantries. After some maneuvering, everyone was situated around her desk. Only then did it come to her attention that the former governor of the state was seated across from her. "I could've seen you sooner had I known."

Mitch looked over at Reb, who said, "I didn't mind waiting. It gave us time to discuss what we wanted."

"And it would have been helpful to know that you were in a wheelchair ahead of time," she said with a bluntness that even Mitch took note of.

"I don't spend time thinking about it."

"Well, anyway, so that means that you," she pointed to Mitch, "must be Ms. Dosimater? What is that, French?"

"Actually, it's Tanner. Mitch Tanner."

"Well, then, who in the hell is Dosimater?"

"Must be a typo?" Mitch offered lamely.

"Okay. Let's start from scratch. No stairs?" Ms. Collins looked at Reb like Mitch had disappeared through the floor.

"As few as possible."

"That's a tough call in the city. They don't call it a 'Ranch' for nothing."

"Or we could do an elevator."

"Do you know how many houses have an elevator?" she snapped.

"How many?" Reb asked like there was an actual answer.

"Not many. The correct questions is, do you know how few houses have elevators."

"We could retrofit," Mitch interjected.

"You want to buy a house just to tear it up?"

"It would give me something to do."

"Let me plug a few parameters into the computer and go from there."

Ms. Collins virtually ignored Mitch (no surprise there) and Reb (a bit more of a surprise) as she performed the search. Mitch started to fidget again and Reb calmed her once again. It felt good to hold hands.

"Okay. We are in luck. There are three properties we can begin with. Everybody who needs to take a bathroom break should do so now."

"We'll need to take our van." Reb announced as they were exiting the building.

"Who's driving?"

"I will," Mitch raised her hand like she was in school. At least it would keep her from fidgeting.

Each house was special in its own way. By dinnertime, Mitch and Reb were seated across from each other at the diner two miles from home. They were both too tired to cook.

"I think you have Ms. Collins worried." Reb said.

"Why?"

"Besides your driving? I think she thinks that you don't like the houses."

"I don't care what she thinks. What do you think?"

"About your driving?"

"About the houses!"

"I like all of them."

"Did any one of them stand out in particular?"

"Each had its own charm."

"Do you want to see more?"

"And drive around all day with you and Ms. Collins? Let me think about it. No."

"So, you want to choose between the three we saw today. Am I understanding you correctly?"

"Yes, you are. Although it will be a tough choice."

"Okay," Mitch got out her cell phone and dialed Ms. Collins.

"What are you doing?" Reb asked in vain. Mitch was concentrating totally on the call.

"Yes, Ms. Collins? This is Mitch Tanner. Right. We'll take all three houses we saw today." There was a slight pause in the conversation. In fact, there were two pauses as both Ms. Collins and Reb reacted to the news in stunned silence.

"Right. No. Don't make offers or counter offers or anything like that. We don't want to negotiate. We just want to buy. Okay."

Mitch disconnected the call and took a bite of salad.

"You bought all three?" Reb asked just to be sure she had heard right.

"We can take our time deciding which one we want without anyone pushing us into a decision or having them go off the market. Then, at our convenience, we can sell the other two." Reb didn't say anything in response. Mitch noted the silence. "Unless you want to spend another day or week or month looking?" Mitch checked Reb's eyes for agreement or disagreement.

"No, I'm okay with your unilateral decision."

"If I had bought a house that you hadn't seen, that would be a unilateral decision. This is just plain logic."

"I'm sure I could have made my mind up pretty quickly."

"Well, let's not do it over dinner."

"You think we're going to argue about it, don't you?"

"I think that we're both suffering from pre-baby jitters."

"And we're not even the ones who are pregnant," Mitch made eye contact with Reb.

"I guess it's time to make another visit to Kansas."

"That's a good idea."

"I come up with one once in a while."

They decided to drive rather than fly and had everything packed and ready the next morning. The long drive was punctuated by conversations about houses. To say that the debate was on would be an understatement. Reb couldn't honestly tell if Mitch was argumentative or simply playing Devils' advocate.

"So, you can't live without Italian tile in the foyer?" Mitch asked after an extended silence.

"I didn't say that, exactly," Reb clarified.

"We can put Italian tile everywhere if you want."

"In all three houses?"

"Sure. Why not? It might help the resale value. Of the two you don't choose."

"You're making this sound like it's my choice entirely."

"Well, isn't it?"

"No. I want you to like out new house as well."

"I like them all. I just want you to be happy."

"God, we sound so married."

"We do, don't we," Mitch laughed.

"I'm crazy about you."

"Don't tell me that when I'm driving seventy miles an hour down the highway."

"Should I wait and tell you when you're only going sixty?"

"You should wait and tell me when you have me all alone in a hotel room!"

"There's a town up ahead."

"You are so bad."

"You wouldn't want me any other way."

"So, which house are we going to live in first?" Mitch changed the subject before her desires took over and did the thinking for her.

"You decide."

Mitch knew instinctively that this was a ploy to have her divulge which house she liked the best. She had to think fast. "Why don't we just try them out in the order that we viewed them?"

"We could do that. Are you sure that's what you want?"

"Do you have a different preference?" Mitch used Reb's tactic on her.

"No. That's fine. That works for me."

Mitch smiled to herself. It wasn't just any day that she could outmaneuver Reb in the thinking department.

Although they had teased about stopping at the first hotel in sight, they drove straight through like responsible adults and pulled up to Henry's modest house by late evening. Things were quiet. Eerily so. And dark.

"He doesn't own a gun, does he?" Mitch quizzed Reb.

"Everybody here owns a gun. Don't you read the news?"

"Not that section," Mitch eased out of the van and went around to Reb's side.

66

"You want me to check first to see if he's even home?" Mitch asked through the open window of the van.

"Sure. Unless you don't want to go up to the door alone."

"I'll be fine."

Mitch put on her brave face while the ick factor was churning around in her stomach. She walked up to the front door. It was open as in unlocked. No wonder everyone around here owned a gun what with leaving all the doors unlocked and such. There was no noise coming from the house. No light either. Things smelled funny and not in a hilarious sort of way. What wasn't covered in dust, dirt and grime had been baptized by vomit. Mitch located Henry in the bedroom. He was a sickly shade of gray. The gray you turn when your body revolts against the abuses of hard living and harder drinking. Mitch didn't hesitate to think about fingerprints or foul play. She picked up the phone and dialed 911. After giving the operator all the pertinent information, she went out to the van to warn Reb of the impending sirens.

"I called an ambulance."

"Why? What's wrong?"

"Too much whiskey for one liver to handle would be my first guess."

"Damn," was Reb's reply and she shifted to prepare to get out of the van.

"Don't even think about going inside."

"Why not?"

"Well, for one thing, we'll just get in the paramedic's way."

"And the other reason?"

"You don't even want to know."

"It's that bad?"

"It's a holy mess. It might just be easier to burn the place down and start over."

"Don't joke like that."

"I'm not," Mitch looked at Reb with truthful eyes.

"We could hire someone."

"To burn it down?"

"No. To clean it up."

"Not without paying them triple overtime."

"I'm not going to have you in there cleaning up after my in-laws."

"I don't mind. We're going to be here a while anyway."

The argument was suspended when sirens punctuated the otherwise quiet evening. Curious neighbors wandered out of their houses to see whose luck had turned bad. Whispers carried Henry's name quickly and efficiently up and down the block. While most of the emergency personnel streamed into the house, one stayed behind to interview Mitch and Reb.

"You're the ones who placed the call?"

"I am," Mitch replied.

"Do you know how long he was in there in his condition?"

"No."

"Do you know if he's on any prescription medication?"

"No."

Mitch was suddenly feeling perturbed at herself that she hadn't kept better track of Henry after BeBe's death. It was now painfully obvious how he had chosen to assuage his grief.

"We've just arrived from Colorado. Henry is my brother-in-law," Reb hoped to shed some light on their ignorance of the situation.

"Visiting?"

"Right."

About that time, the rest of the group trundled Henry out of the house. From the rush, Mitch guessed that they weren't kidding around. Life and death was getting into the ambulance and nobody was taking bets on the outcome at the arrival at the hospital. At least they knew where it was. The hospital, that is.

"We'll meet you there," Mitch told the interviewer in charge. Mitch climbed back into the van, resisting the urge to break the land speed record to their destination. Getting the both of them killed wasn't going to improve Henry's chances of survival.

The waiting room brought back memories of the many hours they had spent keeping vigil over BeBe. They were restless memories not conducive to compliant behavior. Reb became demanding as soon as she determined that some doctor knew something about Henry's condition. It was grave. They didn't call it that by accident.

"Do you think you should call Mary?" Mitch asked.

"Would you do it for me?"

"Sure."

Reb rolled down the hall to be by herself. Mitch dialed the house and, of course, got no response. People did work for a living, after all. Not wanting to wait for an okay from Reb, Mitch called Trish's house, hoping to connect with Lisa. She was still there, despite the late hour.

"It's me," Mitch said.

"Hi, me. What's up?"

"We're back in Kansas. Do you know where Mary is?"

"She's not at work?"

"I don't have her work number."

"Doesn't her mother have it?"

"She's preoccupied at the moment."

"What exactly is going on?"

Mitch was stuck about how to respond. Mary should be the first to hear the news. But she also wanted to respect Lisa's role as significant other in the relationship.

"It's her Uncle Henry."

"I'll give you her cell number. The switchboard closed down after hours at work."

"Thanks."

Armed with this information, Mitch connected with Mary in two rings. Mitch went over the story with her. It didn't take long considering the paucity of the information.

"I can't get time off from work again so soon."

"We know. We just wanted you to know. You don't need to come out here. Yet."

"Keep me posted."

Mary hung up like the phone was on fire. Mitch pondered this abruptness for a moment. Then, she shrugged and went off to find Reb. She was sitting alone in the family waiting room.

"I got hold of Mary."

"What did you tell her?"

"I told her that her Uncle Henry was ill and that I'd keep her updated."

"You need to call her back and tell her that her Uncle Henry is dead."

Mitch studied Reb. She seemed awfully composed. In the space of a few short weeks, Reb had lost her sister and brother-in-law. Miranda, had become a member of the orphan's club. Now, with every living relative deceased except Reb, future total custody seemed to be straightforward.

"I think we should notify Miranda first, don't you?"

"Just take care of it."

"Okay."

Mitch really didn't mind being treated like a secretary in situations like this. It had been a rough time for Reb lately. After making two difficult calls, it was time to begin the conversation about funeral arrangements.

"Do you know what Henry wanted in terms of his final disposition?" Mitch asked quietly.

"I haven't a clue."

"The legal papers are probably back at the house. I could go back and look for them."

"I don't want you going back there all by yourself."

Mitch didn't want to argue about it. Reb had every right to go back to the house. Besides, there was nothing left to do here but call the mortuary. The same one they used for BeBe. Talk about repeat business.

By the time they got back to the house, the neighborhood crowd had gone to sleep. It was after midnight. Mitch took a deep breath and then wheeled Reb as far into the house as they could before encountering too much clutter to continue.

"If I were filling out a police report, I'd say there was evidence of a struggle," Reb commented.

"That's what happens when you pick a fight with whiskey and lose."

"Can you at least clear a path to the table so we can have a place to sort through paperwork?"

"Sure. And I'll open a couple of windows as well."

"Thanks."

This took all of five minutes and thankfully, the smell began to disperse. It went from horrid to tolerable. Mitch started a pot of coffee to sustain their energy and then brought out stacks of unsorted papers. Two or three stacks soon grew to ten or twelve. This chore hadn't been done in quite a while. By two in the morning, they had located the will. It gave absolutely no instructions as to burial. Although this find made their eventual tasks easier, it still gave the impression that Henry had lived an apathetic existence that stretched clear to the grave.

"This is all my fault," Reb said after folding up the documents and placing them back in their unmarked envelope.

"What are you talking about?"

"I was a pretty absent sister-in-law."

"Why do you say that?"

"I didn't do enough for him after BeBe died. I didn't call. I didn't visit. I just left him here to drown in grief."

Instead of offering a platitude, Mitch substituted a hug. "We should get some sleep," she suggested gently.

"I don't think you can find a hotel room at this time of night."

"Let me give it a try."

Mitch had a room lined up in three minutes and within the hour, they were resting side by side in bed.

"What did Miranda say?" Reb asked.

"Not much," Mitch strained to remember the conversation for specifics.

"What about Mary?"

"She can't come for the funeral. Something about no vacation time left to take off."

Reb was deathly quiet for a minute. "This is depressing," she finally summed it up.

"I agree," Mitch nodded.

"It's like he was never alive at all."

"Maybe we could try and make his death meaningful in a way that he would've liked."

"How do we do that?"

"We could donate some money to a cause that he supported. Or something like that."

"I suppose we could cut a check to Alcoholics Anonymous."

"I was thinking more along the lines of a hobby. What did Henry like to do in his spare time?"

"I don't have any idea."

"We'll figure something out."

They fell asleep at dawn and didn't wake up until late afternoon. Breakfast was lunch and then they went back over to the house to continue the cleaning and sorting process. Since Mitch had left the windows open overnight, the place seemed fresher if not any cleaner. Certain things could be tossed immediately, like soiled sheets, pillows and dirty torn clothes. Not even the poorest of the poor would have use for these things. Mitch did the physical work while Reb concentrated on the paperwork. She also called the mortuary to make an appointment for first thing the following morning.

"Find a good carpet cleaning service, would you?" Mitch requested.

"What about a painter as well?"

"Couldn't hurt!"

By nightfall, they were both ready for a hot meal and a hotter bath back at the hotel.

"I forgot how good you look naked," Mitch remarked.

"I forgot how you have a way with words."

"I'm a real smoothie."

"Parts of you certainly are," Reb teased.

"It's the soap," Mitch laughed as they soaked together.

"Are you sure?" Reb's wandering hand checked for suds in the most interesting places.

Mitch breathed in quickly.

"I thought you were tired?" Mitch asked.

"I was tired of paperwork and phone calls. I'm never tired of you."

"We have a long day tomorrow."

"Then it would be good to get some deep sleep, don't you think?"

The term "deep sleep" was one of Reb's euphemisms for sex. Or, more accurately, the perfect sleep you get after engaging in rousing, satisfying sex. A promise she could deliver on no matter what the circumstances.

It felt more like being unconscious than sleeping to Mitch when she awoke the next morning. It was funeral-planning day. Hadn't they just done this? It was something that a person just didn't want to repeat too often. Mitch looked over at Reb, who was still asleep. Or faking it. Maybe she didn't want to get up either. Mitch wrestled herself upright and made enough noise taking care of morning prep to roust Reb out in the process. A pall had descended over them and they arrived at the funeral home without much conversation. The appointment didn't take too long. Select an urn and some gospel readings for the service. Promise to think about music selections. Write a check. Accept the condolences of a total stranger. They were back at the house by noon. Curiosity had finally gotten the best of the neighbors. Normally, folks in a town as small as this would have been right over when the news was fresh. Why this hadn't happened was anyone's guess, but Mitch had chalked it up to the small town stigma toward outsiders in general and gay people in particular. Anyway, two neighborhood ladies rang the doorbell five minutes after Mitch and Reb had arrived back at the house. When Mitch offered to perk some coffee, one of the women insisted on doing it just to help out. They were there, after all, to be helpful, not to mooch. They made that clear right up front. Once they realized what a true mess the house was, they set about like generals to right the ship. So what if the metaphors were mixed. They knew what they were doing. One of them looked vaguely familiar to Mitch and the feeling nagged at her memory for so long that she finally gave up and asked outright, "Have we met before?"

The woman seemed to be embarrassed by the question. It was then that it dawned on Mitch where she had seen her before. This was the woman whom Mitch had discovered in the barn with Henry a few visits back. In a rather compromising position. Quite literally.

"I knew Henry," she answered meekly.

Her humility kept Mitch from making any smart aleck reply. "I'm sorry for your loss."

At the simple words, the woman broke down in tears. Mitch escorted her over to the couch and sat with her until she calmed down enough to talk.

"You were in love with him," Mitch said with compassion.

"We were in love."

"He was a nice man," Mitch was quickly running out of small talk on the subject of Henry.

"He was a good man. When he found out that BeBe was ill, he did everything he knew to help."
"And then afterwards?"
"He just folded up with grief. It killed him."
Mitch had an inspiration. "Would you do me a favor?"
"If I can."
"Could you help us write something to say at the memorial service?"
"I could," she hesitated, "but why don't we let Henry do that for us."
"I don't understand?" Mitch was puzzled.
"Henry wrote poetry. You could read some of it to honor his memory."
Mitch tried to hide her astonishment. Apparently, she failed.
"You look surprised."
"I guess I am. A little."
"You know, Henry was more than just BeBe's husband."
"He was a good man," Mitch was once again unable to come up with something more original.
"Do you want to go through it today?" she asked.
"It isn't mushy or anything, is it?" Mitch just wanted to know at the outset.
"It's majestic and heartfelt. You're thinking that it's 'roses are red and violets are blue' stuff, but it isn't. This is manly poetry."

Which was okay as far as Mitch was concerned, but getting the idea past Reb was a tough sell. At first.
"You want to do what?" she asked with a hint of exasperation. Putting up with the sudden influx of still more helpful neighborhood busybodies was wearing on Reb's last nerve. The house had gradually filled up with people and casseroles.
"Unless you'd rather come up with something else. On your own," Mitch summed up the situation. Succinctly.
Reb looked at Mitch. "You made your point."
"You can still pick out the music."
"I already have."
"And the flowers."
"I have them ordered."
"So everything is taken care of?"

"Except, I guess, for the *poetry* reading."

"It's going to be manly. And majestic."

"Uh huh," Reb said blandly.

After a blur of activity punctuated by fitful sleep, it was time for the funeral. The house had been transformed from a veritable shambles to a home fit for a reception following the graveside service. Mitch recognized almost everyone from BeBe's funeral and fought against the feelings of familiarity. She wanted to forget everything about this place the moment they headed home. Panic crept in when she overheard a conversation Reb was having with the minister about staying on for a while. Mitch didn't have a chance to chat with Reb until everyone had finally gone home for the night.

"So, we are packing up first thing in the morning, right?" Mitch asked like if she said it with enthusiasm, that that alone would make it all come true.

"We can't leave tomorrow," Reb practically scoffed at the idea.

"We can't?" Mitch suddenly felt like a plaintiff child.

"We need to talk to the lawyer about the estate."

"Can't we do that over the phone? Like, on the cell phone during the drive home?"

"You are really anxious to go, aren't you?"

"I'd leave tonight if you'd let me."

"You're free to leave anytime you want. I need to stay and work on the legal issues."

When she said it that way, Reb sounded so much more adult than Mitch.

"If you think I'm leaving you here all by yourself, you'd better think again."

"Oh really. Why?"

"Because there are just too many eligible widows on this block. Did you see the crowd of them at the funeral?"

"You think I'd be fair game?"

"I'm not taking any chances."

"And then, we'll need to visit Miranda," Reb reminded.

"I know," Mitch nodded, resigning herself to the reality that they were going to be in Kansas for a while. Panic evolved into depression. Darwin was once again vindicated. Right here in Kansas.

As knocks on doors go, this was unexpected. It was the police. Very unexpected. Since everyone else was gone, Trish answered the door and recognized the officer who had overseen the tearing up of her basement.

"No bulldozer?" Trish tried to make a joke. He wasn't laughing.

"May I come in?"

"Of course."

They stood awkwardly for a second or two in the foyer before Trish figured out that this was going to be an extended visit.

"Please follow me."

They walked into the kitchen. There were chairs and a table and a relatively fresh pot of coffee. Everything they needed for an extended visit. Trish remembered, though she had no idea why, that he took both cream and sugar in his coffee. The memory is a funny thing.

"Are you hungry? Rose makes these delicious cookies and then tortures us by rationing them out. But visitors can have as many as they want."

"No, thanks."

Trish could hear the desire in his voice. He wanted cookies more than anything else. His wife probably had him on rations as well. Everybody was watching their cookie intake nowadays.

"Not even just one?" Trish tempted.

"I shouldn't."

"Okay," Trish smiled.

He didn't smile back. "I wanted to update you on the progress of the discovery in your basement."

So, it was a serious visit after all. "Okay," Trish became somber out of respect.

"It took a while to do the investigation, collect the evidence, take the depositions."

"Particularly on what's referred to as a cold case?" Trish half asked, half stated.

"Exactly. There weren't too many people left to question. The lady in Montana was particularly challenging."

Trish smiled and then the detective smiled.

"So, you found her?"

"We're detectives, Ma'am. We find people. It's our specialty."

Trish nodded. "Are you *sure* you don't want a cookie?"

"Maybe just one."

Conversation halted while Trish fixed a plate. Apparently, whatever he wanted to say had to be said while they were face to face. Eye to eye.

"And, of course, you chatted with that sweet lady in the nursing home as well," Trish picked up the conversation after putting a plate with no less than a half a dozen cookies on it in front of him, and warming up his coffee.

"Mrs. Wrightwood."

"She's pretty spry for an old woman."

"But not the most reliable witness."

"Right. So between the two of them, you've solved the case?"

"Oh no, Ma'am."

"Please, you don't need to call me ma'am all the time. Or ever. Call me Trish."

"Okay, Trish," he took a cookie with great deliberation and broke off a small piece to eat.

"Good, aren't they," Trish smiled.

"Best I've ever had."

"So, you haven't solved the case yet?" Trish got back to the main topic.

"Oh, we've solved the case."

"I thought you said you hadn't?"

"What I should have said was that it took more than the testimony of those two women to solve the case."

Trish thought quickly. What other lead was there? And then it came to her. "The lawyer!"

She remembered the frustrating five minutes she had spent with the man. At the time, she felt it would take a court order to get any information out of him. Apparently, she was correct.

"You've met the man?" the detective asked like he already knew the answer.

"Of course. I bought the house from him."

"But you also made another appointment when you began to get curious about the true seller, right?"

"Let's not play guessing games, Detective," Trish met his eyes. "Lisa and I met with him once. He was not forthcoming. We were definitely out of our league at the time and had no idea there was foul play involved."

"I'm beginning to think I'm a little out of my league," he answered quietly.

Trish had no clue what he was talking about and they studied each other's eyes to discern where next to take the conversation.

Lisa came to the rescue. "Are you two having a stare-down or something?" she asked from the kitchen doorway.

Trish turned and smiled, like she always did when Lisa showed up. "You remember Detective Green, don't you, Lisa?"

"It's hard to forget someone who's torn up your basement. I'm still coughing up cement dust from your last visit."

Trish heard a definite hint of hostility in Lisa's voice. It happened so rarely that it was absolutely noticeable. To her anyway.

"Frankly, so am I," Detective Green answered in a conciliatory tone. He heard the defensive tone loud and clear. It was part of his profession as well to correctly perceive human behavior and attitude.

"So, what are you here to tear up next?"

"Actually," Trish started to explain the purpose of his visit, but was interrupted by him.

"Actually, I was just leaving. Thank you for the hospitality and the cookies," he directed a look at Trish that seemed to suggest that whatever he had to say, he wanted to say it to her privately. Trish nodded.

"Did you want to take the rest of the cookies with you?"

"Oh no thank you. I'm already in enough trouble with my doctor."

Trish laughed. Detective Green laughed. Lisa didn't. They exchanged polite goodbyes and he hadn't even left the front porch before Lisa made her opening volley.

"What the hell was that all about?"

Trish was stuck for a reply. She really didn't know much and felt that what she did know, she shouldn't be discussing just yet.

"He was just updating me on the case."

78

"What did he say?"

"Not much."

"What do you mean by not much?"

"We were just getting to the good part when you interrupted."

"I saw that for myself. I'm not supposed to hear what's going on in the case? I'm the one who helped figure all this out."

"Maybe it was your demeanor that had an effect."

"My demeanor?"

"You seemed a little defensive."

"He was undressing you with his eyes."

"He was not."

"Yeah. *Right.*" Lisa made her emphasis plain.

Trish shook her head. "It's not what you think."

"Then why the secrecy?"

"There are no secrets. From what he said, the break in the case came from the lawyer."

"The one who sold you the house?"

"Right."

"And that's a secret...why?"

"I don't know. He left before he explained it."

"He just wants an excuse to see you again. Alone."

"I'm sure that's not it."

"Well what else could it be?"

"It could just be that I'm the one who owns the house and I'm the one who is entitled to the information!"

"And I'm just the hired help. Of course. I'm glad we got that all cleared up. Will there be anything else, Ma'am?"

Great   Just great. Trish had two people calling her Ma'am.

"You're jealous," Trish guessed correctly.

"I'm not jealous."

"You go home to Mary every night and I'm not jealous."

"Really?" Lisa wanted point-blank confirmation.

"Really," Trish lied. Badly.

"So, the next time you meet with Detective Bedroom Eyes, I want to be there."

"Fine. I'll insist, in fact."

"Okay. I'm glad we have that figured out. I wonder what that slimy lawyer had to say for himself."

"I guess we'll know soon enough."

"I know we will. Detective Green can hardly wait to see you again."

"Please don't start that again."

"So, you're never jealous when I go home to Mary?"

"Do you want me to be?"

They stood facing each other. Arms crossed. Each not wanting to verbalize the true answer to the question, even though they knew it.

"I was going to ask for a day off," Lisa adroitly changed the subject.

"You look tired. Are you still sleeping on the couch?"

"You're just full of interesting questions today."

"I'm just concerned for your well being."

"I'm sleeping just fine. I need to get my driver's license renewed."

"Okay. Good. Take the day off. Whatever you need. Anything you need," Trish's voice trailed off.

"It shouldn't take more than half a day. Unless the DMV has gotten slower since the last time I did this."

"Take a book. A big book."

"I will."

"So, are you going now?"

"Are you trying to get rid of me?"

"I'm just trying to plan a schedule," Trish didn't want to start another argument.

"Sure. I'll go right now. It's still early. I should be home for dinner."

"Okay."

Trish didn't ask if she meant dinner with her or with Mary. They had talked around that issue long enough for one morning. Lisa was gone a whole ten minutes before there was another knock at the door. It was a good thing the baby was still asleep.
Detective Green was on the back porch.

"Hello...again," Trish said.

"I wanted to finish our conversation. In private."

"You were watching the house?"

"Yes. I was waiting to see if you would be alone again soon."

"And what if Lisa had stayed all day?"

"It wasn't a stakeout."

"What was it?"

"More of a break from paperwork."

Trish was torn now. She had promised to have Lisa present during this meeting. But she hated to recall her from her duties as a vehicle operator. She stepped aside to allow the detective in.

"I thought you would want to know the rest of the story."

"I was curious about the private part," Trish blurted out before thinking.

Green had the good sense not to make an off-color remark. But his ears turned red. Trish didn't offer refreshments this time. She suddenly wanted this meeting to be over and done with.

"So, have you made an arrest?"

"No."

"I thought you said you solved the case," Trish felt like she was in some mental echo chamber, where only she was the one who was repeating everything.

"I said we made progress."

"But no arrest?"

"I don't think there's going to be an arrest."

"Why don't you just tell me what you've found out."

"We interviewed the seller of the house. He admitted to knowing about the disposal of the body."

"Who was the seller?"

"One of the Livermore sons."

"And it was his sister's body?"

"Yes, it was. According to him, his sister committed suicide. The body was buried secretly, not an uncommon thing that many years ago."

"There was abuse, wasn't there?"

"I'm not sure we'll ever know and frankly there's no way we can prove it even if we suspected it. The son didn't mention it."

"Maybe he didn't say anything about it, but he sure tried to hide behind the skirt of his lawyer. Not exactly the actions of an innocent man."

"Unfortunately, hiding behind the skirt of one's lawyer isn't ground for prosecution. We can't proceed without more proof or a confession."

"I guess we shouldn't hold our breath."

"I'll file the paperwork and the case will remain open, but unless there's a new development, we're at a dead end."

Trish nodded. He had the dead part right. "Thank you for stopping by," Trish stood up and walked to the front door without looking to see if he had followed. He had. He knew he was being summarily dismissed. Trish's mood had shifted dramatically in the past minute. A young girl had died in despair and no one would ever be brought to justice. That was enough to shift anyone's mood.

After the detective left, Trish checked in on Josh. He was awake and doing well. They were bonding beautifully despite all the obstacles life was putting in their way. A peacefulness filled Trish as she held him for his feeding and then they coo-cooed at each other until he began to get sleepy. It was with reluctance that she put him down for his afternoon nap. She went to her own bedroom and stretched out for a brief rest. Lisa peeked in, back from her DMV visit.

"You're back so soon?"

"It was a quiet day there."

"Detective Green came back the minute you left."

"I know," Lisa came into the room and was at the side of the bed.

"How do you know?"

"I watched. The police aren't the only ones who keep their eyes open."

"And you didn't come back in to hear what was going on?" Trish felt guilty now that she hadn't called Lisa. She didn't want another argument. Life was too short to argue it all away.

"I figured that he was bound and determined to see you alone. If you had called me to come back, he would have clammed up again. And if I came back in on my own, well, I thought that that would have looked childish. And that's the last thing I want to be. Especially in front of you."

"I never thought you were being childish."

"Well, when you finish resting, you can tell me what he said."

"Have a seat on the bed and I'll tell you now."

"No. You rest and then we can talk later."

Lisa left her alone. Trish tried to rest. For about two minutes. Then she got up and went to find Lisa. She was downstairs in the kitchen, stirring sugar into a glass of tea. She didn't start up a conversation, so Trish cast around for small talk.

"Slow day at the DMV you said?"

"In and out."

"Maybe I should run down and renew my license as well."

"Are you due?"

"In four years. From October."

"This October or last October?"

"I'd have to check."

It was then that Trish remembered that you usually renewed your driver's license around the time of your birthday. If you followed the law. Lisa's birthday must be coming up.

"Let me see your new license," Trish requested.

"Why?"

"I want to see your photo."

"I'm not showing you my license. I take a terrible picture."

"That's not possible. You would never take a bad picture."

"Where is everybody, anyway?" Lisa asked, changing the subject.

"Everybody is on a short vacation."

"No kidding!"

"No kidding. I sent the trio up to a resort for a few days. I figured they needed a break."

"And you were here *alone* with the baby?"

"Millions of mothers all across America are alone with their babies every day. You don't think I can handle it?"

"Of course I think you can handle it. I just wouldn't have taken time off. That's all."

"What would you have done?"

Maybe it was all in Trish's imagination, but this small talk was sounding more stilted with each passing sentence.

"I would have stayed here and started dinner," Lisa said as she opened the refrigerator to take stock.

Trish closed the door gently.

"You don't need to cook for me."

They were face to face now, each feeling the heat in spite of the cold air that had escaped from the fridge.

"We can't go out. Not with the baby," Lisa said quietly.

"I don't want to go out," Trish answered. "I'd have to share you with everyone else."

"You have to do that anyway."

"That doesn't mean that I want to be constantly reminded of the fact."

"So, what are we going to do? Stand here and stare at each other and starve to death," Lisa whispered. They were close enough now that whispers were in order.

"I've been hungry for you for so long that it feels like starvation." Trish put her hand on Lisa's face.

Lisa breathed in deeply and then said, "It's the baby."

"What?"

"Listen. It's Josh. He's awake."

"I don't hear anything,"

"Shhh. Listen."

And then, Trish heard him as well.

"You have good hearing."

"I'm the nanny. It's part of the job."

Lisa removed Trish's hand from her face and headed to Josh's room. Left alone to her own devices, Trish started dinner. Enough for two, just in case. In twenty minutes, wonderful aromas were wafting from the kitchen. Lisa couldn't resist checking it out.

"Smells good."

"Are you staying? Or have I made things too uncomfortable for you."

"I had planned to be home for dinner."

"That's probably a good idea," Trish agreed.

"But you can call if you need help."

"Thanks. I will."

"It's your first night alone."

"I'll manage."

Lisa headed out early, feeling guilty for a number of reasons. Hopefully, having a hot meal ready for Mary would assuage some of her unease.

Mary had been good all week. She had worked hard and resisted the temptation to frequent the local watering hole. Two of her

84

sales group had gone on vacation, which meant more work for her. She didn't need to review their sales files, but she was doing so anyway just to get some idea of their previous sales production. As numbers danced across the computer monitor screen, she knew she had been working too hard. The data didn't look right to her tired eyes. Chalking it all up to fatigue, she shut the files and closed down the computer for the night. One quick drink would be her reward for doing the work of three people. The place was busy with wall-to-wall executives who had the same idea. Celebrate the end of the day the liquid way.

"Long day at work again?" Fawn came out of nowhere.

"Imagine meeting you here," Mary said blandly. She was too tired for enthusiasm.

"You're not happy to see me?" Fawn seemed genuinely hurt.

"Of course I am. It's just, well, like you said, a long day at work," Mary felt a twinge of remorse at the thought of hurting her feelings.

"It must have been horrible. Buy me a drink and tell me all about it."

Mary pondered the offer. Fawn seemed truly interested in hearing all about it. For the price of a drink, it was a bargain Mary couldn't pass up. They chatted about all sorts of things for an hour. The latest headlines, about which Fawn had a deep breadth of understanding. This was a woman who didn't dwell on the financial pages, but instead perused all the other major topics. She even knew her sports. Baseball season was upon them. Diamonds meant more to this woman than being mere jewels. Speaking of diamonds, Mary asked, "You're not wearing your necklace?"

"Of course I am. Just not where you can see it."

Fawn was wearing a button-down shirt with a cute tie.

"Do you want me to unbutton myself so you can see me?" Fawn said quietly.

"Not in front of all these people," Mary answered deliberately.

"Or would you rather do it yourself?" she followed up.

She had a way of asking questions that jolted Mary like a carnival ride. When Mary couldn't think of a reply, Fawn stood up. "Come with me."

The phone rang. Trish had just settled Josh down for the night and caught the phone on the second ring. "Hello?"

"Hi. How are things going?"

It was Lisa. The mother hen of nannies checking in.

"I don't pay you enough."

"You pay me plenty. What's going on?"

"I'm pooped. This is hard work!"

"Are you going to be okay? Do you need me to come over?"

"No. I'm fine. I don't want to interrupt your home life with Mary."

"You wouldn't be. Mary's not home yet."

"She's not?" Trish tried hard to keep any judgment out of her voice inflection. Just simple curiosity. "Really?"

"I guess she's working late?"

"Have you had dinner?"

"Yeah," Lisa lied.

Trish could hear the dishonesty clear through the phone lines.

"Okay," she said, giving Lisa a pass.

"We never did talk about your visit with Detective Green with Envy."

At this quip, Trish laughed. "You are so clever with words."

"That's me. I'm a barrel of laughs."

It was painfully obvious that Lisa was upset about Mary's lateness.

"I wish you were here," Trish admitted before she could stop herself.

"I could be."

"It wouldn't be a good idea though. Would it?"

"I'm growing weary of trying to discern between good ideas and bad ideas."

"There really wasn't much to tell about the detective's visit," Trish returned to the topic of the day.

"Is an arrest pending?"

"No. Everyone who might have been guilty of a crime is dead. I guess."

"You guess?"

"It's all a guess. The girl's death was supposed to be a suicide. If there was abuse, it will go unpunished."

86

"I guess it's not a crime to not prevent a suicide," Lisa said without thinking.

A long moment of silence followed her remark. "I didn't mean that the way it sounded," Lisa said.

"I know. I understand. So, I'll see you tomorrow?"

"Of course. Bright and early."

"Whenever you get here will be fine."

They both hung up reluctantly from the call.

"You don't need to always have my favorite scotch," Mary said as Fawn sat down next to her on the couch with a drink in her hand as well.

"Of course I do. You're a special guest."

"There's nothing special about me."

"Why do you say that?"

"I shouldn't be a guest at all, let alone a special one."

"Why not?"

"Because there's someone waiting for me at home."

"Does that mean that you can't visit a friend once in a while?"

"It means that the visit shouldn't have the prerequisite of suggestive dialogue."

"Nobody's naked yet," Fawn laughed as she drank her wine. It was a beautiful clear sound.

"You haven't even loosened your tie yet," Mary found herself smiling.

Sensing that Mary was ambiguous about this entire situation, Fawn steered the conversation back to a safe topic. "So, you said that it was a long day at the office?"

"Right. A long day. Two of my people are on vacation."

"So you had to do their work as well as your own, I take it?"

"It's not as bad as it sounds."

"Your eyes look tired."

"I spent the day looking at numbers on a computer screen."

"Why don't you close your eyes and let me massage your temples."

"Oh, I'm not sure that I need you to do that."

"I'm very good at it. I promise it will be relaxing."

Against her better judgment, Mary agreed. Fawn's fingers were simultaneously gentle and probing and before long, Mary was relaxing. She still saw numbers in her mind, but they were organizing themselves into patterns out of chaos.

"What are you thinking about?" Fawn saw the stressful facial expression.

"I'm thinking about numbers that don't make sense."

"Sounds like my checkbook," Fawn teased. "Numbers rarely make sense to me."

"They don't?"

"When it comes to finances, I'm all thumbs. People like you who understand money and accounting and all that complicated stuff fascinate me. It's a special kind of genius."

Mary began to blush from the praise.

"You're getting warm. Are you feeling okay?"

"I'm fine," Mary took Fawn's fingers into her hands. Her mind was relaxed enough. Too relaxed. "I have to go."

"Was it something I said?"

"No. I'm just way overdue for dinner. At home."

It seemed rude in retrospect, but Mary stood up and walked to the door without saying so much as a goodbye. She was home in thirty minutes and sequestered in the study without even checking in with Lisa. Sitting alone in total silence, she began to write what looked like random numbers down on a sheet of paper. The more she wrote, the clearer the situation became. A cold feeling crept into her bones and it made her shiver with a mixture of anger and dread. A feeling 180 degrees from the warmth she had experienced at the talented touch of Fawn's massage. There was a reason that they made people who work with money take vacations. A soft knock on the study door startled her out of her deep thought. It was only Lisa.

"I thought I heard you come home. Are you hungry?"

Mary set the paper she had been writing on into an unmarked folder on the desk. "Maybe just a little."

"I cooked dinner. I'll reheat it."

"I can eat it cold,"

"Why do that when we have a microwave. I'll fix you a plate."

"Okay. Thanks."

It was more than she deserved. She shoved the unmarked file folder into the front of her filing cabinet and went to the kitchen. Her plate was ready. Still, mentally sifting through the numbers, she was halfway through her meal when Lisa said, "You're very distracted tonight."

"Huh?"

"You're a million miles away."

"I'm sorry. It was just a taxing day at work."

"Is that auditing humor?" Lisa smiled.

Mary didn't smile back. The word "auditing" distracted her again. Those numbers began to drift in front of her eyes.

"I guess I'd better keep my day job," Lisa noted the non-response to her humor.

"What about your job?"

"I'm not going to become a comedian."

"Why would you?" Mary was confused.

Lisa gave up on the discussion entirely and set about cleaning up the kitchen. Mary knew that she should have pursued the conversation. If it had been Fawn, she would have. The reason, she realized, was that because with Fawn, the conversation would've been uncomplicated. And once in a while, uncomplicated conversation was a blessed relief. To be able to say anything without having to explain or defend it was preferable to challenge and debate, particularly when you weren't sure what you or the other person was talking about.

"Mary?" Lisa said.

"What?"

"I said I'm going to bed."

"Okay. I'll be up in a little while."

After Lisa left the kitchen, Mary rinsed off her dinner plate and put it in the already-running dishwasher. Then, she went back to her study to digest both dinner and the revelations of the day. What seemed to be going on at work was the oldest trick in the stock trade. Two brokers were selling and buying stocks with client funds, no doubt without the client's permissions. She was pretty sure that's what was going on. Books had been written about it. Movies had been made about it. People's lives had been ruined by it. Why these two brokers thought they could get away with it was anyone's guess. Mary considered her strategy as she nestled into her comfortable chair. She would proceed slowly and carefully until she knew whom to trust. She was still too new at the company to know whom to confide in. Mary fell into an uneasy sleep. For a variety of reasons.

Prison hadn't changed much since the last visit. But Miranda certainly had. What a difference a few weeks had made. She was showing big time with the baby.

"How are you feeling, Honey?" Mitch asked when they finally allowed Miranda into the visitor's area.

Miranda didn't answer. She sat morosely twirling her hair.

"Are you eating?" Reb asked.

"Do people have to die before you come to see me?" Miranda's tone was nothing short of hostile. Frankly, Mitch could see her point. But it wasn't like they could drop in at any time. Mitch wasn't a psychologist, trained or otherwise, but she knew instinctively that it didn't make sense for a prisoner to be this hostile against the only lifeline they had to the outside world.

"Are you frightened?" Mitch asked.

Miranda didn't say anything else for a moment. And then, she nodded.

"Is anyone else bothering you?"

"You mean raping me? Is that what you want to know?"

Mitch only nodded.

"No. Nobody else is raping me right now. I'm not very desirable right now."

Mitch could have filled a journal with all the thoughts that came flooding to her right now.

"So, is it the pregnancy that has you scared?" Mitch asked the only other question that made sense right here and now.

"Wouldn't you be scared?" Miranda echoed the substance of the question right back at Mitch.

"Me? I'd be petrified," Mitch admitted readily.

The blunt honesty mollified Miranda. She dropped her defenses. She broke down into tears. Mitch took this as a positive sign. At least Miranda had a human side. No longer a spooky, robotic person, but a flesh-and-blood young woman facing a life-altering situation. Mitch looked over at Reb. Tears were on her face as well. Now that she had the whole family crying, Mitch didn't know exactly what to do. So she waited in silence until she could think up a more mundane line of questioning.

"Are you taking your vitamins?"

"I don't have much choice, do I?"

"I guess not. I guess you don't have a lot of choices here."

"I have at least one choice. I want you to have my baby."

"You mean, adopt," Reb clarified.

"I didn't mean deliver," Miranda's tone became snide, a familiar sound to Reb.

"That's not going to be as easy as it sounds."

"I'm not going to fight you for custody. It's up to you to decide how hard you want to fight everyone else."

With that challenge put forth, Miranda stood to leave. In profile, she looked as beautiful as any other pregnant woman Mitch had ever seen.

"What are you gaping over?" Miranda snapped when she saw Mitch's expression.

"The future," Mitch answered back.

"At least you have one."

When Miranda left the room, the tension dissipated. Which wasn't a good sign as far as Mitch was concerned. All those negative feelings couldn't possibly be healthy for the baby.

"We're going to need to stay here, aren't we," Mitch spoke slowly, deliberately.

"You mean, you think she's coming back in?" Reb was unclear.

"No. I mean that we're going to need to stick close to this prison. She can't feel like we're deserting her. Especially now that there's nobody else."

"So, just to make it clear, it's now *your* idea to stay in Kansas indefinitely."

"Well, not indefinitely. The baby will be here before we know it."

"Not soon enough for Miranda."

"But she does look healthy. At least as healthy as someone can look in jail."

"You're terribly worried about her, aren't you?" Reb asked, but it was more of a statement really.

"Yeah."

"How could someone not love you?" Reb asked the Universe.

Mitch answered, "Beats me?"

"I guess we can stay in Henry's house. Unless you want to do something different?"

Mitch thought it over. Henry and BeBe's house resembled something closer to gingerbread than Mitch had ever lived in before. It was small-town, white-picket fence Americana. And the porch was screened in. Summer was fast approaching. The fresh air would feel good in the warm evenings. They could sit outside and give the neighbors something to gossip about. For months.

They left the prison and began the long drive home. To the house.

"Maybe we should just buy a plane," Mitch said about a hundred miles into the trip.

"Along with all those houses you're buying back home?"

"Oh yeah. I forgot about those."

"You forgot you were buying three houses?"

"Just temporary. Like insanity."

Reb chuckled.

"How often can we visit Miranda?" Mitch asked.

"Once a week, I think?"

"So, it's going to be like fifteen or sixteen weeks back and forth."

"It would give us something to do to pass the time. I wouldn't want to do this with anyone but you."

"Leave it to you to sweet talk me going down the highway again," Mitch smiled.

"I need to keep your interest up somehow."

"My interest is up, believe me!"

Reb patted Mitch on the thigh. "And they say driving through Kansas is boring."

"They've never driven through it with you."

Chapter 5

Mary showed up early to work. She usually did anyway, but today she had a purpose. Checking through various files took time away from normal work and she wanted this to occur as surreptitiously as possible. After double-checking the files she had viewed earlier, she got curious as to just how widespread this fraud was. Peering intently at the screen, she blocked out the rest of the ambient sounds of the world.

"Hey!"

Mary jumped at the greeting and struggled to make light of her startled reaction.

"Good morning, Susie!" Mary replied to one of her team members.

"You're in awfully early," Susie commented back.

It wasn't Susie's file that Mary had been studying, so she felt more comfortable chatting with her. "I'm still learning the job. I spend half the day lost in details."

"You'll catch on soon enough."

Mary nodded meekly. She had already caught on to something serious, but couldn't let Susie know. She went about the day as usual, spending blocks of time here and there checking for more accounting irregularities. By the end of the work day, she was ready for a drink. This was becoming a habit, but she didn't care anymore. The stress was taking a toll. She walked to the lounge where she knew Fawn would be. Not even bothering with pretense, Mary walked up to her.

"You're late."

"I'm here."

"You certainly are. And with an attitude as well."

"I'm sorry."

"No wait. Let me guess. It was a long day at work."

"Maybe you're too young to know what that entails."

"Do I look like I'm in middle school or something?"

"You're much better looking than that."

"So you like your women pretty and mature!"

"I think I like my women sassy!"

"Well, I already knew that," Fawn had that inviting look in her eye.

"I shouldn't go to your apartment for a quick drink."

"And I shouldn't ask you?"

They looked at each other and stood to leave. Their ritual of walking in silence was upheld and even after arriving at Fawn's place, they were awkwardly quiet for a few moments.

"What are you thinking?" Fawn asked when Mary had brooded far too long for her comfort level.

"I guess I'm looking for a confidant?"

Fawn seemed surprised. "You have something that you need to get off your chest?" she asked with a deadpan expression. No hint of humor accompanied the question.

"Not like a confession or anything like that."

"So, what is it?"

"Maybe it's a confession of sorts?" Mary was now wondering just how good of an idea this was. All of a sudden, in fact, it seemed like a terrible idea.

"You're being very mysterious."

"It's work."

"Oh, so it's a work thing."

"What did you think it was?"

"I thought maybe it was a personal thing."

"You wanted it to be personal?"

"I don't care what it is. I just want you to talk about it so we don't keep having these moments of silence. It feels like we're in church or something."

Mary smiled at Fawn. "Thank you for being patient with me."

"Tell me what's going on at work that has you all tied up in knots."

"It's nothing, really. I shouldn't be discussing it."

"You're special to me," Fawn made it sound like Mary didn't trust her.

Mary looked at her. She was serious. Very serious. "I guess if our positions were reversed, I'd be worried about you as well."

"Are you into reversing positions?" Fawn asked with a none-too-innocent inflection in her voice.

Mary knew better than to lean closer to Fawn, but she did it anyway. A pull stronger than gravity took hold and she was kissing her before the clearer part of her mind regained control.

It was a deep and personal kiss, familiar and yet unique. Then, it was over. Reluctantly.

"Wow," was Fawn's first full sentence.

Mary remained silent like she was waiting for her lawyer to show up.

"Are you okay?" Fawn sought eye contact.

"I'm okay. I'm beyond okay. I need to go."

"You always do."

"I do."

"You're a good woman."

"I don't feel like I've been good."

"We're friends. Friends kiss once in a while. Everybody still has their clothes on."

"I'm going."

"Of course. Drive safe."

"You're working late again?" Trish found Lisa in Josh's room, fussing over details that she didn't need to be fussing over.

"Don't worry. You don't need to pay me overtime or anything."

"That wasn't my concern."

"What was your concern?"

"I guess it was that I worry that you are working too hard."

"I'm not."

"Or that there's nobody at home yet?"

"Mary's not home yet."

"You called?"

"And she's not at work either."

"Maybe she's somewhere in between?"

"Maybe she is."

Trish thought this over. "So where do you think Mary is?"

"She's somewhere where there's scotch and perfume."

"Sounds like a bar?"

"The perfume is strong. And expensive."

"You think she's with another woman," Trish deduced.

"She's with the same woman. It's the same perfume every time."

"Have you asked her about it?"

"Not really."

"Why?"

"Because then I would be obligated to tell her about you and me."

Trish moved closer. "What would you tell her about you and me?"

"That's why I don't ask. I wouldn't know what to say about you and me."

Without thinking about it, Trish pulled Lisa into an embrace. Maybe physical touch would help out the emotional pain they found themselves in together. It was a long embrace.

"I want you to come to dinner tomorrow night," Trish said quietly.

"Why?"

"Because it would be nice."

"Why tomorrow?"

"Is tonight better?" Trish got in on the question game. She had it figured out, finally, that Lisa's birthday was the following day and wanted to celebrate it with her. But if they were going to play twenty questions over it, she was willing to go along.

"It's short notice."

"How about the day after tomorrow, then?"

"That's the weekend."

"Oh, yeah. I forgot."

"You're the only person I know who can forget about weekends."

"Normally, I don't," Trish looked into Lisa's eyes. "They are the time that I spend without you. I try not to think about them."

"Maybe we should wait until next week?"

"I don't want to wait," Trish admitted adamantly and against her better judgment, kissed Lisa. Neither could claim surprise, especially Lisa, who kissed back with passion. For being ignored at home for so long, she didn't seem out of practice. And then, Lisa pulled away.

"I should be going," Lisa explained her disengagement.

"Not before I get an answer about dinner. Tomorrow. Here."

"I'll let you know."

"When?"

"When I've decided."

"If we end up eating tuna sandwiches because you didn't give me enough notice, you'll only have yourself to blame," Trish joked. Mostly to ease the tension between them.

"Tuna sandwiches are my favorite," Lisa said.

"They are not."

"Are too."

"Then why don't you ever order one when we go out to eat?"

"Because they're inexpensive."

"So?"

"So, when *you're* paying the bill, you think I'm going to eat on the cheap!"

Trish laughed and then held the door open for Lisa. "You'll let me know?"

"I'll let you know."

Mary and Lisa arrived home within five minutes of each other. They prepared dinner side by side although neither one was particularly hungry. Getting Mary to talk about her day proved to be such a challenge that Lisa soon gave up entirely. It was easier to eat dinner, clean the kitchen and then retreat into a novel.

"I have to work late tomorrow," was Mary's version of "goodnight."

So much for birthday plans. Lisa waited fifteen minutes and then called Trish.

"Is that offer still open for that tuna sandwich?"

"Absolutely!"

"Does it include pickles?"

"Sweet or dill?"

"Both."

"Gee, I might need to go to the store on that one."

"I'll go with you."

"Right now?"

"Are you going right now? It's nighttime."

"I could wait and go tomorrow, with you. After you come to work."

"But I'd be neglecting my nanny duties."

"We could take Josh with us. He could use some new scenery."

"Are you sure we should take him out of the house?"

"I don't want him to spend the rest of his life stashed away in his bedroom."

"Okay. We'll do a pickle run tomorrow."

"A pickle run. I like that!"

"Tomorrow, then."

What started out as a pickle run soon turned into a full-fledged shopping extravaganza. They must have been hungry. Between the two of them, they soon filled up an entire buggy with food goodies. Josh slept through the trip, as many a man could hope to do.

"You are so good with Josh," Trish remarked as they put groceries away.

"He's a good baby. He makes my job easy."

"You have a way of coping with things that makes you always seem so competent. So sure of yourself."

"It's all an act."

"It is not," Trish called her bluff.

"I have an easy life," Lisa explained. "It's easy to look good when you have an easy life. And you're the one making my life so easy."

"One of these days, I might try and make it hard for you."

Lisa didn't know quite what to make of the comment. She stole a glance at Trish, who was still concentrating on the task at hand. When it seemed like Trish might look her way, Lisa averted her eyes and searched the shelf for room to put more canned goods. They played eye tag until Lisa looked over to find Trish watching and waiting.

"Did I embarrass you?" Trish asked.

"No. Of course not. Why?"

"I sometimes say things..."

"That you don't mean?"

"No. I meant what I said. It's just that my timing might be a little off."

"That does seem to be our problem. Timing."

"Why don't we go out to an early dinner instead of eating here at home."

"What about Josh? And the tuna fish sandwiches?"

"Josh has Rose, Max and Silver to keep him company. As for the tuna fish, you can order what you like."

"With pickles?"

"Uh huh."

Lisa should have known there was indeed something fishy going on by the time they got to the restaurant. The parking lot was nearly empty.

"Maybe it isn't open today?" Lisa wondered.

"Let's see," Trish got out of the car and waited for Lisa to join her. There was a sign on the door that read, "Closed for private party."

"That explains it," Lisa shrugged her shoulders. "So what do we do now?"

Trish answered, "Let's see who's having a private party." Then, she pushed open the door and waved Lisa inside.

"We shouldn't be doing this."

"Why not?"

"We're barging in on someone's private party."

"I'm sure they won't mind."

They were approached by the hostess. "Ms. Sullivan and Guest?"

"Yes," Trish answered.

"Right this way, please."

Trish took a couple of steps but Lisa wasn't budging. "What have you done?"

"I thought a quiet dinner would be nice."

"So you rented a room?"

"No. I rented the entire restaurant."

"What? You didn't buy the place?"

"I could. You want me to buy the place for you?"

Lisa turned silent and remained un-budging. Trish glanced and the hovering hostess. "Give us a moment, could you please?"

"Of course."

Trish looked around. There was a small bench convenient for waiting patrons. "Can we sit down and talk about it?"

Lisa didn't say anything, but she did sit down. It was a start.

"So, how much trouble am I in?" Trish decided to get right to the heart of the matter.

"You're not in trouble. It's not you. I just can't believe I'm even doing this."

"Doing what?"

"I don't know. I can't explain it."

99

Trish breathed a sigh of relief. "Take your time. Just let me know how I can help."

"You just caught me a little off guard. A lot off guard."

"How?"

"We went from tuna sandwiches to a whole restaurant all to ourselves."

"We can go back to the tuna sandwich plan," Trish reassured gently.

"Are there people in there waiting to jump out and yell 'surprise'?"

"Well..." Trish hesitated.

"There are, aren't there?"

"Just the restaurant staff."

"Don't tell me there are balloons and hats..."

It was Trish's turn to remain silent.

"You went all in, didn't you?"

"I thought it would be fun. Did I guess wrong?"

"No. You didn't guess wrong. Normally, I like pleasant surprises as much as the next person."

"But what?"

"I just expected...I didn't think that you would be the one doing the surprising."

"We can go if you want. No one will be disappointed."

"Not even you?" Lisa quizzed.

"You could never disappoint me. Don't you know that by now?"

Lisa smiled. Finally. "Suddenly, I'm in the mood for a surprise party."

"Are you going to be able to act surprised?"

"You just watch!"

Lisa was one of the most gracious and genuine recipients of a surprise party that the restaurant staff had ever serenaded. Trish didn't get the party girl all to herself until coffee and dessert were delivered with flourish. The tuna sandwiches had been replaced with tuna steak, garlic bread and steamed asparagus. Now, they were settled over espresso and cheesecake.

"This is fabulous," Lisa savored the first delectable bite.

"Maybe we should've started with this course," Trish mused.

"No. Some things are worth the wait."

"Yes, they are," Trish agreed.

100

The silence could've been awkward, but at the tipping point, Trish produced a small, beautifully-wrapped gift.

"What's this?" Lisa asked.

"It's a present. You get them on birthdays."

"You're bad."

"You haven't even opened it yet..."

"How bad have you been?"

"How bad do you want me to be?"

"It's a little late to be addressing that issue, don't you think?"

"Go ahead. Open it and remove all doubt."

Lisa did so. It was a modern necklace fashioned after a military-style dog tag. Her name was engraved and an exquisite diamond was placed offset. The clarity was stunning. Thousands of dollars worth of stunning."

"This is too much," Lisa demurred.

"Actually, I thought it was pretty underwhelming when I saw the finished product. I hope you like it. The salesclerk said that they were all the rage."

"It's gorgeous."

"Well, you're stuck with it. They don't take back engraved items."

"Pretty sneaky on your part."

"I thought so, too," Trish laughed.

Things were quiet as they drove back to Trish's to deliver Lisa to her car.

"Did I wear you out?" Trish asked when they pulled up to the house.

"No. I've been practicing a speech in my head."

"A long speech?"

"No. Just a serious one."

"How serious?"

"I've been thinking."

"About what?"

"I enjoy our friendship."

"Me, too."

"And I know we have this attraction that we're been dealing with."

"Okay."

"I don't want you to be attracted to me just because you don't have anyone else in your life right now."

"You mean, like a rebound?"

"Right. Or maybe a challenge."

"That's an interesting thought."

"I just think we should stand back and think about things. Things like repercussions."

"I agree."

"You're not upset?"

"No."

"Do you want me to return the necklace?"

"No. It's just a present. That's all."

"Okay. Well. See you next week."

"See you Monday."

Trish watched Lisa leave before she went inside. Rose had everything under control except her curiosity.

"So, how was your date?"

"It wasn't a date."

"So then, how was your special dinner out with a woman?"

Trish looked at Rose, mostly to decipher the tone of the questions. She appeared genuinely concerned. After all, you didn't need to be a mind reader to decode Trish's mood.

"Pour me a cup of coffee, could you?"

"You look like you could use some brandy in it as well?"

"That sounds even better. In fact, let's just skip the coffee part."

Rose nodded. She brought two brandies back from the liquor cabinet and settled in a chair opposite Trish.

"Cheers," Trish toasted.

"To love. The only thing worth living for," Rose intoned solemnly.

They sipped and then looked at each other.

"So, what happened?" Rose started in again with the questions.

"Lisa said that I'd better know what I'm doing before we get any more involved."

"Sounds like good advice from a smart woman."

"It isn't like I haven't thought about it."

"Tell me what you've thought about so far."

"Well, I've thought about how good she is with Josh."

"It's her job."

102

"But she sees it as more than that. She's really bonded with him."

"And you think that's a good thing?"

"I know she's not Josh's mother. I know she's not Robbie," Trish felt her throat begin to tighten. She was not good at talking about her feelings concerning Robbie. "Nobody knows that better than me. But Lisa is a positive influence on Josh. And that's my number one priority."

"And it doesn't hurt at all that you're also head over heels in love with her."

"I didn't mean for it to happen."

"Nobody ever does."

"You sound like you don't approve."

"Don't live your life worrying about whether or not I approve."

"Do you like Lisa?" Trish asked, suddenly curious.

"She's a nice girl. I didn't know at first but now, I do."

"Would you be able to put up with her being here all the time?"

"She's already here for most of my waking hours. Why should I care what happens when I'm asleep?"

"So, what else do I need to consider?"

"Rocks tossed into ponds make a lot of ripples."

"Meaning what?"

"Mary has family who are your friends. If that fact changes, can you live with that?"

Trish drank the rest of her brandy without answering.

Chapter 6

Mitch was comfortable on the porch. In fact, she was way past comfortable and drifting toward nirvana. The transition had taken a little while, but the sensation of arrival, the feeling that you were settled in a place for the time being had descended on Mitch. Not without complication, of course. Although the neighborhood ladies and gentlemen had done a decent job of cleaning and repairing Henry and BeBe's house, when the dust settled, both literally and figuratively, Mitch hired professional help. The kind that takes the stench of dead bodies out of hotel rooms type of help.

"Is it mint julep time yet?" Reb rolled out to enjoy the heat and humidity.

"Yeah, except it's iced green tea with lime because we ran out of lemons."

"You want me to start a shopping list?"

"Sure."

"Okay. Let's start with a couple of tons of chipped ice. Gee, it's hot out here!"

"Didn't you grow up here?" Mitch knew the answer.

"Your point?"

"I figured you were used to this."

"You *never* get used to this!"

"Okay. So. A couple of tons of ice. Lemons. What else?"

"How about some baby furniture?"

Mitch wasn't fazed in the least. "A crib. A carriage. Hey, you know who would know all about this! We could call Trish."

"I've reared a baby before," Reb had *that* tone in her voice.

It was folly for Mitch to ignore it. "Well, that's been a little while ago. Maybe there's some new-fangled equipment we need to know about."

"Like a car seat? I do keep up with the modern world, you know."

Okay. They were having their first baby argument. And neither of them was even pregnant so they couldn't blame it on hormones.

"You don't want to consult with Trish?" Mitch asked cautiously.

"*You* can if you think *you* need to."

"Or we could just go to a support group for expecting lesbians. I'm sure they have plenty of those to choose from here in Kansas."

"Your sarcasm has not gone unnoticed."

About that time, a couple of neighbor ladies came to Mitch's rescue. It was that special time of twilight when folks escaped the stifling heat of their houses only to become the mosquito's best friend. Mitch called out a neighborly hello to Cora and Vera. Sisters. And they called back a similar greeting.

"That's a relief," Mitch remarked once the sisters were out of earshot.

"What is?"

"It doesn't feel like we're in a zoo anymore."

"A zoo?"

"For a while, it felt like people would just walk by to get a look at the lesbians. Like an exhibit."

"I guess I hadn't noticed."

"Well, you politicians are used to it. Being gawked at. The rest of us get a bit unnerved by it when it happens."

"You're in a strange mood tonight."

"I'm not the one who doesn't want to talk to Trish about baby furniture."

Silence descended with the remains of the sun and threatened to stay until morning. For all the heat, things seemed chilly.

"Your *friend* Trish is going to take Lisa away from Mary," Reb finally broke the silence.

Mitch didn't care for the insinuation that accompanied the accusation.

"You can't take someone away unless they are willing to go."

"All that money is the temptation."

"Is that why you stay with me?" Mitch asked the question more out of anger than curiosity.

"I stay with you because you're a genuine idiot!" Reb answered in a huff as she wheeled in for the night. Mitch nodded. The woman had a point. She gave Reb a five-minute head start and then went into their new bedroom. Actually, it looked a lot like their old bedroom, except that it was in someone else's house. Mitch did what she normally did when she knew that she was at fault. She sat facing Reb and waited patiently for eye contact. Which happened in a couple of heartbeats.

"I'm sorry," Mitch started with a safe enough declaration.

"Keep going," Reb said flatly.

"Uh, okay," Mitch said, fully realizing just how much trouble she was in. "Could you give me a small clue as to which of the eight or nine things I need to apologize for first so I can expedite this matter."

"I think you should go and expedite things on the couch. Preferably overnight."

Mitch thought this over. When was the last time she had gotten kicked out of the bedroom. Oh yeah, never. Never before had this happened. No wonder she didn't know quite how to react. In the movies, people, usually husbands, yelled and stormed out with a blanket under one arm and a pillow under the other. This wasn't the movies. This was two people whose lives had inexorably gotten a lot more complicated in a relatively short period of time with no end in sight. And now, they were making the colossal mistake of taking it all out on each other. As if hormones were truly dominating the scene, a sudden sadness engulfed Mitch as tears welled up in her eyes. She stood to leave and didn't hear Reb calling her back as she made her way to the front porch. It was still, except for the occasional cricket. Mitch sympathized. True to their usual five-minute lag, Reb was back on the porch before Mitch had time to totally compose herself.

"I'm really sorry," Reb said gently.

"I really am, too," Mitch echoed. "Do you want to sit next to me?"

"Will you hold me if I do?"

"You've got yourself a deal."

They rearranged themselves comfortably next to each other as if the last fifteen minutes had vanished from time. Except for the topic of babies.

"What kind of mother do you think you're going to be?" Reb asked.

"Probably a scared-to-death one."

"Why do you think that?"

"All that stuff I don't know. About babies. I've never done this before."

106

"Nobody does until they do it."

"I think that being an only child has something to do with it. I've never mothered anyone."

"You've done a pretty good job of mothering me."

The statement gave pause to Mitch. Reb wondered silently if it was time for argument number two of the evening. "Did I upset you again?"

"No. At least, I don't think so."

"You don't think so? Don't you know what you are feeling?"

"I don't feel upset in the way that you are thinking. But something about that mothering statement is unsettling to me."

"In what way?"

"I don't want to be your mother. Too many people think that lesbians are looking for a mother figure in their relationships."

"There's a fine line between mothering and nurturing."

"And nursing," Mitch added bravely. If they were going to get issues out on the table, might as well get all of them.

Meanwhile, two more neighbors passed by on their evening escape from a house too hot for human comfort. Greetings were exchanged. Mitch was beginning to really enjoy this custom. Once she had gotten over the notion that people were walking by just to get a glimpse of her, she appreciated this alternative to the summer misery index. Especially when she also realized that these folks were equal-opportunity busybodies. They nosed about in everyone's business equally.

"Is that a new shirt, Luke?" Mitch called out.

Luke blushed and nodded.

"Lookin' sharp!" Mitch gave the thumbs-up to him.

Luke's wife, Matilda, didn't know quite how to react. Imagine! A lesbian flirting with your husband. She assumed it was safe...

"You really need to stop flirting with Luke," Reb admonished.

"I'm not flirting with him."

"As long as his wife thinks you are, then you are."

"She probably thinks I'd make a pretty terrible mother as well. Does that make it true?"

"That's different."

"How?"

"Because she's never seen you in a mothering capacity."

"I doubt seriously that it would change her mind."

"But you won't know for sure until it actually happens."

"Which won't be long from now. How do I prepare?"

"The only thing you need to do to prepare for a baby is to trust in yourself and the world."

"I had hoped the answer would have been a little simpler. Like, have diapers and blankets."

"You need those too," Reb smiled, "but you know all about spending money, so I'm not concerned about those details."

"Does that mean I can go to the store tomorrow?"

"Don't you think it would be a good idea if we first decided where we were going to rear this child?"

"We haven't done that yet?"

"Not to my knowledge."

"Okay. Where do you want to raise this child?"

"Rear."

"Huh?"

"Rear. You rear a child. You raise vegetables."

"Okay, then. Where do you want to inculcate this offspring?"

"I think Colorado would be best. We have four houses there. Not counting the one you bought for Mary and Lisa."

"We need to keep mother and child close."

"I don't think that's such a good idea."

Mitch considered these two schools of thought. Each had benefits. Each had pain. A lot like life in general. It didn't matter what she and Reb thought best. It only mattered what the Universe thought best. And as far as Mitch could discern, the Universe hadn't made up its mind yet.

"I could still go shopping and then ship whatever I buy across the country if necessary."

"What's with all this 'I' stuff? *We* go shopping!"

Mitch smiled. "We go shopping. First thing tomorrow!"

For all the money they had between them, Reb and Mitch didn't ascribe to the theory that shopping solves all problems. But it rarely created more problems for them, which was good enough at this crucial time. It was morning. They were getting ready to go out.

"You're wearing that?" was Reb's version of "Good Morning."

"Is it on my body?" Mitch countered without petulance.

It was plain to see and well known in general that Mitch didn't dress fancy to go shopping. Reb only shook her head. It was an exercise in futility to argue.

"You've never looked lovelier."

"You want me to change?"

"Never."

"What should I wear?"

"You're good. Don't worry."

"I'm changing. I'll be right back."

Right back translated into fifteen more minutes of waiting. Reb was now very sorry that she just hadn't said "Good morning" and left it at that.

"How's this?" Mitch reappeared in slacks and a cotton shirt. A definite upgrade from the sweat pants and t-shirt that she had first modeled.

"Splendid," Reb hurried to remark in the positive before any doubt could creep into the inflection.

"You're just saying that."

"Of course I'm saying it. Do you see anyone else in the room?"

"Are we going somewhere fancy for lunch?"

"We just had breakfast."

"You know me. Always thinking about my stomach."

"I'd argue the point, but then we'd be late."

"Late for lunch, I suppose."

"Dinner probably as well."

"In your dreams," Reb looked at Mitch. "We couldn't possibly shop that long."

Mitch let Reb drive. It was always in the back of Mitch's mind to both allow and push Reb to remain as independent as possible. Besides, Reb was the better driver.

"I assume we are going to the mall?" Mitch asked.

"You make it sound so big."

"There's a Sears there."

"Not exactly boutique shopping."

"We could do boutique if you want. I could charter a flight."

"To where?"

"I heard Paris is nice this time of year."

"You want to shop for a baby stroller in Paris?"

"People in Paris have babies, right?"

"It's been widely reported."

"So, they must shop somewhere for baby stuff."

"Let's see what Sears has first."

"Okay."

They were both quiet for a moment.

"You're serious about Paris?" Reb broke the silence.

"Let's see what Sears has," Mitch said thoughtfully.

The mall, or perhaps a better description, the strip mall, had a
Sears, but it was more of a catalog outlet than anything else.

"Well, at least we'll know where to come if the baby needs a new
set of tires," Mitch looked on the bright side.

"And the tools to change the tires."

"Yeah, this is gonna come in real handy in about sixteen years."

"Who's going to teach the baby to drive?"

"You!" Mitch was more than happy to hand over the keys, both
now and in the distant future.

Reb shook her head. There was plenty of time to argue about it.
At least sixteen years. Maybe even longer. She glanced up to
see Mitch watching her intently.

"What?"

"Where to now?" was Mitch's sole wonderment.

Reb took a small sip of wine. It always helped to calm the
nerves while flying. After their less-than-successful shopping
spree in rural Kansas had yielded no items of interest, they went
back to the house and packed a small bag apiece while Mitch
arranged the charter jet.

"Wouldn't it be funny if we actually got to France and they were
all out of baby stuff?" Mitch laughed at the thought.

"You have such an interesting sense of humor."

"In that case, we can take a tour of the wine country instead."

"Just don't get the brilliant idea of buying the baby a vineyard."

"At least not one that's so far away. Imagine the overhead
expenses."

"Also," Reb set about changing the subject, "We could go to
those places where famous painters lived. As I recall, you have a
budding interest in art."

Budding. Such a tactful word. Reb could, when motivated, be
so wonderfully kind. The last thing Mitch had painted was a

naked man. It had been mistaken for a woodpecker by discerning art buffs.

"I remember doing a little brushwork."

"With some success?"

"The story of my life."

Reb took to her wine again. With any luck, it would relax her enough so that she could sleep during the long flight. It worked. She was out like a light in fifteen minutes. Mitch slept as well.

One of the best things about having money was that it just made some things easier. Having extra cash to throw around arranged for hotel rooms in places that would have otherwise been "completely booked." There was always a suite or two available at an exorbitant rate. The City of Light was no exception. Mitch and Reb settled into the Four Seasons Hotel George V Paris just in time for a room-service snack and another nap. This time, lying down. Next to each other. Really close next to each other.

"This sure is an upgrade from the Super 8, isn't it," Mitch said when she fully woke up.

"You're not going to be the epitome of the Ugly American, are you? Reb asked sleepily.

"The Ugly American in Paris. Wasn't that a movie?"

"Don't even go there."

"So, tell me what it means to be an Ugly American so I can tell you if I will or won't be one."

"How much French do you know?"

"Besides the kissing kind?"

"No comment."

"I know yes, no, please and thank you."

"The please and thank you will serve you well."

"They always do, no matter what country I'm in."

"We decided so quickly to come here that I don't even know where to start."

"I think it depends on what you want to start doing?"

"There are so many fun things to do that I feel guilty."

"Guilty?"

"We left responsibility behind. Miranda is in maximum security. Henry's estate is still pending. And here we are in Paris."

"Once we start rearing the baby, aren't you proud I remembered the right word?"

"Yes, I am."

"Anyway, once we start that, we won't have many opportunities to travel. At least, not in a spontaneous way. So let's take some time and see what we want to see and stay as long as we want."

"We didn't pack enough clothes."

"Sweetie, we are in the shopping capital of the Universe. People from Pluto come here to shop for clothes."

"It just seems a terrible extravagance."

"We spend money on everybody else. It's no crime to spend a little on us."

"Did you know that they have shops here dedicated to lingerie?"

"They do?!" Mitch was instantly energized.

"I thought that would get your attention."

"Where is it?" Mitch asked playfully.

"I distinctly said 'shops' and there are several. I'll have to look up the addresses."

"Is it just me, or are the streets in Paris just a little confusing?" Reb chuckled. Mitch had procured this lovely suite in the perfect hotel that afforded views of the Eiffel Tower and also had them within walking distance of the Arc de Triomphe. Traffic up and down the Champs-Elysees was just a lot more crowded than Kansas. Orders of magnitude more crowded.

"We will need a lot of patience and good humor to get around town."

"I hadn't given it much thought," Mitch admitted.

"You never do," Reb smiled. "It's one of the things I love most about you. You've never treated me like an invalid."

"I'm not about to start now. I do think, however, that it would be best to have a limousine service take care of the driving. If," Mitch paused for effect, "that's okay with you?"

Reb scrunched up her eyebrows as if in deep thought. "Well, let's see...being driven around in Paris in a limo...I guess I can live with that."

"And then, we can rent a car when we tour wine country."

"You are planning on being here for a while?"

"I've never been here. It would be nice to see the sights."

"I've never been here either."

112

"That surprises me."

"Why?"

"I know you've traveled."

"I was raised on a farm. I've been on a few trips. I wasn't exactly part of the jet set crowd."

"Well, we've jetted to Paris. Where to first?"

"What would you like to do first?"

"Can we go to one of those charming coffee places and sit outside and pretend we are writers or painters or something like that?"

"Probably every day for a whole year and not go to the same place twice."

"Well, then, we had better get started."

"I guess we'd better get started."

But neither one moved. They were next to each other, the most perfect place in the Universe for both of them.

"You first," Mitch said.

"No. You first. You need to get a limo."

Mitch reached for the room phone.

"You probably would do better arranging that in person," Reb commented.

"You're just trying to get me out of bed."

"Considering how long it took me to get you in bed, I rather doubt that."

"Yeah, I bring you all the way to Paris and all you want to do is see the sights."

"Call me unpredictable."

Mitch laughed. Humor was always best with the one you love.

"And then, after you get that limo arranged, we can chat about French customs."

"Didn't we already do that at the airport?"

Reb sighed. It was going to be an interesting vacation. She got out of bed and began to prepare for going out on the town in the most glamorous town in the world. Meanwhile, Mitch went downstairs to the concierge desk to inquire about transportation. Knowing that she was going to be asking for a lot of extra help due to Reb's wheelchair reality, she had her wallet handy. Perhaps that was just another one of those Ugly American giveaways, but she would just have to take that risk. If the

113

concierge was offended by the proffering of cash, it didn't show. Not one bit. Apparently, scads of wealthy people chose limos over driving in Paris. The only real question was how large and fancy were they planning to go.

"Will you be going to the club circuit?" seemed to be the deciding factor. If one was going to go clubbing, and this sounded so cave-mannish to Mitch, one would need to make a certain impression upfront. Emerging from a huge limo helped with that certain impression. The concierge was waiting patiently for an answer.

"Might as well cover all the bases," Mitch replied.

"Is that a yes?" asked the baseball-challenged gentleman.

"Yes, please. And it needs room for a wheelchair as well." If the concierge had wondered why anyone in a wheelchair was doing the dance-club circuit, he kept his wonderment to himself. Mitch opened her wallet and generously rewarded the gentleman's discretion.

"If there is anything else you need, please ring me at this number," he presented Mitch with a business card.

"Merci," Mitch practiced one of the four words she knew in French. He smiled. Maybe Mitch wasn't so hopeless after all.

"Is that you?" Reb called out from the bathroom when Mitch came back to the room.

"No, it's the Hunchback of Notre Dame," Mitch pronounced it like it was a position on the famous football team.

"Dame," Reb corrected her.

"What's wrong?" Mitch called back.

"Nothing's wrong. What are you talking about?"

"I thought you said 'damn.'"

"I said 'Dame.'"

"Dom? Like, Dom Perignon, the champagne? Sorry, I didn't bring any upstairs. But it will be in the limo."

"You got a limo with champagne?"

"Is there any other kind?" Mitch asked unpretentiously.

Reb thought it over. Mitch never spent much money on herself. Most millionaires lived a life of self-indulgence. And why not, after all. Spending money was America's number one pastime. Spending money on goods and services meant that your neighbors could have a job. Even if you argued that most of the goods were imported, some American still had to unload it from a boat, stock it on a shelf and ring it up at the cash register. Jobs that were hard to do still gave people pride in their abilities and work ethic.

"You've become very quiet," Mitch remarked.

"Just thinking."

Mitch was afraid to ask. How often unspoken was the issue of Reb's paralysis between them? Mitch would've preferred to see the town on foot and trolley. But that wasn't possible. No use brooding about it.

"Are you too tired to go?" Mitch traveled to the area of safe ground. Anyone could claim to be too tired to do something without losing face.

"You just try and keep up!" Reb replied.

"Can we start with coffee and donuts in some cafe?"

"There are about 20,000 cafes from which to choose."

"How about that one Hemingway used to go to write?"

Reb stopped wheeling. "What do you know about Hemingway?"

"You ask that like I've never read a book," Mitch replied evenly. "I'll have you know that I've read at least two books...on how to change the spark plugs in a car."

Reb shook her head and continued her educative travel monologue. "Instead of coffee and donuts, they call it cafe au lait and a patisserie."

"Whatever they call it, it sounds yummy."

They continued their trek downstairs to the awaiting limo. The driver looked very formal and very French. As if Charles De Gaulle had taken up driving in his next life. The limo was huge. Not your ordinary run-of-the-mill limo. It was one of those that looked like it could carry heads of states.

"Bonjour," Reb greeted the driver.

"Bonjour, Madam," he politely answered back.

Reb looked up at Mitch, giving her some sort of teacher look like something was expected of her in the way of a greeting. A voice in the back of her head said, "Say 'bonjour' to the nice man."

"Bon-jur," Mitch hit the j sound a little too hard and gave the word an overall jagged edge.

"Bonjour, Madam."

Mitch wasn't used to being referred to as a madam, but before she could remark, she got another one of those teacher looks from Reb.

"Let's get you settled," Mitch made herself useful. Reb, to her credit, had always kept her arms strong and toned so that she was as helpful as possible in the many transfers they made from wheelchair to vehicle and back again. De Gaulle put the wheelchair in the trunk and then inquired as to their first destination.

"We want to go to where Hemingway went," Mitch spoke.

"There are several places from which to choose," De Gaulle spoke very good English. Better than any French that Mitch would attempt.

"So, he spread his favors around then?"

This remark was met by puzzlement from De Gaulle and another one of those schooling looks from Reb.

"What?" Mitch asked.

"Hemingway was no Henry Miller," Reb explained.

"Huh?" Mitch replied, thoroughly lost.

Ignoring Mitch, Reb gave De Gaulle an idea where to start.

"Please take us to the Cafe de la Paix."

De Gaulle nodded and carefully nosed the limo into traffic. And so the Paris adventure was underway. Not quite like the beginning of a roller coaster, but every bit as unnerving to Mitch. Maybe it would help to scream. Or chatter.

"What did you mean about Arthur Miller?" Mitch asked Reb.

"I didn't say Arthur Miller."

"You said somebody Miller and since we were talking about writers, the only one I could remember was Arthur."

"From your lack of literary background, I'm surprised that you came up with anything at all."

"So, remind me again of which Miller you were referring."

"Henry Miller," Reb repeated.

"Henry Miller," Mitch took her turn repeating, mostly for purposes of remembering.

"You know. Tropic of Cancer. Tropic of Capricorn."

"Was he an astronomer?"

Reb looked at Mitch. For a long moment. "You're joking, right?"

"Astrologer?" Mitch tried to right her otherwise sinking ship of literary awareness. Could they just please already be at this famous coffee shop before Mitch lost all respect in front of Reb. "What are you going to have when we get there?" Reb abruptly changed the subject. Probably out of mercy more than anything. "You said something about coffee and donuts having a sophisticated name here."

"Everything sounds more sophisticated in French," Reb smiled. It was then that Mitch noticed Reb's smile. There had been an absence of that beautiful smile lately and Mitch was aware of how she missed it when it wasn't present.

"Why are you staring at me?"

"Sorry."

"What are you thinking about?"

"You've seemed a little tense lately."

"I've never been to Paris."

"It's just a city."

"It's so much more than a city," Reb went back to her unsmiling ways. Elucidation would have to wait. They had arrived at the cafe.

"When I was a kid, I pronounced the word 'café' phonetically," Mitch confessed. "Like cafe with a long a and a silent e. I felt so worldly when I learned the correct pronunciation. Cafe. I kept saying it over and over like I was some young Audrey Hepburn."

"I'm sure you were charming."

"You'll help me with the menu, won't you?" Mitch suddenly sounded like that plaintiff eight-year-old girl again.

"Don't I always?" Reb replied.

"Not at McDonald's," Mitch defended her hamburger-ordering skills.

"Hemingway probably didn't come here for hamburger, fries and a Coke."

"He didn't know what he was missing," Mitch mused.

"How are you going to be a vegan in Paris?"

"I'm not. I'm on vacation. So is my diet."

De Gaulle was great. He had the wheelchair at the ready and they were discreetly observed by the passersby as they made

their way to the table. In Paris, everybody observes everyone
else. It was a national pastime. American had baseball. France
had people-watching. Fair enough. Reb had requested outdoor
seating so that they, too, could watch the world go by. After
settling into her chair, Mitch watched Reb for every behavioral
clue. Aware of this, Reb asked, "What do you want to drink?"
"Coffee's fine."
"If you want milk in it, it's called cafe au lait. Cafe is the coffee
part and lait is the milk part."
"My dad always said that anyone who drinks milk in their coffee
was a sissy."
"Did he serve in France during the war?"
"No. He was in the Pacific Theater. First time I heard that, I
thought he was in an acting troupe, like South Pacific or
something."
Reb just shook her head, but Mitch was on a roll now. "So, I'm
sitting right where Hemingway sat, huh?"
"Does your butt feel any more literary?"
"Maybe I'll be a famous writer when I grow up."
"If you grow up."
"My child-like innocence has gotten me this far," Mitch studied
the menu like it was the Magna Carte."
"Did I mention that you shouldn't make eye contact with
people?"
"How am I supposed to join in with all this people watching and
still avoid eye contact?"
"Especially with members of the opposite sex."
"You mean, men?"
"That's right. I don't want to spend my vacation wrestling you
away from every eligible and not-so-eligible man in France."
"I don't think I'm the one we need to be worrying about."
"What are you talking about?"
"You already have an admirer, and he's handsome," Mitch
gestured in a direction behind and a little to the left of Reb.
"I'm not turning around to get a look."
"You won't have to. He's on his way over."
"Look busy planning our vacation!"
"Too late," Mitch smiled as the gentleman descended.

118

Although he knew that there were two women at the table, as the old song goes, sort of, he only had eyes for Rebecca.

"Bonjour," he sounded nice enough and then he added, "Mademoiselle," for good measure. Without even knowing much French, Mitch could tell that this was shameless flattery. Although not ready yet for the nursing home, neither Reb nor Mitch were kids anymore. Reb sat silent. Maybe that was the wise course of action. Something that Mitch rarely ascribed to. So, she answered the nice fellow.

"Bon Jor." Once again, hitting the j a little too hard.

"Are you American?"

"Yes!" Mitch replied, all surprised. The way he pronounced the word American made it sound so much more romantic. And although Mitch had done the talking so far, she could have just as easily been an apparition. A voice without a body.

"Are you a movie star?" he directed the question to Reb.

"No," she said flatly.

"Then your Hollywood is full of fools to ignore your obvious beauty."

This guy was beginning to grow on Mitch, even though she was being totally ignored now that Reb had spoken.

"We are just about to order," Reb thought this might give him the message to leave them alone. He was one step ahead.

"Please allow me to buy lunch for both of you. Consider it a, how do you say, welcome here present?"

"That would be lovely," Mitch said eagerly.

"How do you know that it's our first visit to Paris?" Reb was direct and a little suspicious.

Other people wouldn't have heard the suspicion in Reb's voice, but Mitch picked right up on it.

"You make me sound suspicious, like some tall, dark stranger!" he smiled.

So much for Mitch's monopoly on Reb's subtle nuances.

"Just curious what you meant by a welcome here present."

"I simply meant, welcome to my friendship."

Mitch had never met someone who had an ego as big as Reb's. Until today. This could get interesting.

"What's your name?" Mitch asked.

"Je m'appelle Jacque."

"Jock?" Mitch repeated, mangling the pronunciation. Hopefully, not every French word had a j in it.

"Jacque," he repeated beautifully.

Mitch smiled. Who wouldn't like this most charming man. He was friendly, gracious, generous and damned handsome.

"I'm Mitch."

"Mitch. How wonderful to make your acquaintance."

"And this is Rebecca," Mitch figured that they might as well go all in.

"A goddess named Rebecca," Jacque would have kissed her hand had she offered it. At least they all agreed on something. There was a goddess at the table. Now, because even goddesses get hungry, it was time to order lunch.

"I don't suppose I could get a ham and cheese sandwich?" Mitch asked the experts.

"Gee, when you fall off the vegan wagon, you tumble all the way, don't you?" Reb remarked.

"What are you going to have, Jock?" Mitch was curious as to how the expert would handle this.

"Today, I'm going to have the truite."

"What's that?"

"In English? Trout."

"Sounds wonderful. How about you, Reb?"

Jacque looked puzzled. "Reb?"

"It's short for Rebecca. A nickname."

"Nickname?"

"Nom de plume," Reb offered by way of explanation.

"So, you may be a writer, then?" Jacque looked excited.

"The next Gertrude Stein," Mitch gave it her best literary shot. This got a withering look from Reb. "Thank you, Alice."

"Alice?" poor Jacque was getting more confused than before.

"Never mind, Jacque," Reb soothed him. "And, no, I'm not a writer."

"But, somehow, you are famous or important, correct?"

"Yes, she is," Mitch happily bragged about Reb to anyone who would listen.

"So, you're not an actress or a writer. How are you famous?"

Reb was hesitant to discuss this. A moment passed, but Jacque was patiently waiting for the answer. A puppy awaiting kibble. At least, that's how he looked to Mitch. Adorable. American men could get a clue from this guy on how to charm a woman. "I used to be a Senator."

Mitch watched for Jacque's reaction and saw something that she found unexplainable. Confounding, in fact. It was both recognition and confusion. It was as if he knew what a Senator was, but couldn't understand how a woman could be one. An attitude not at all unfamiliar, even in America, unfortunately.

"You seem surprised," Reb asked Jacque, more to challenge him than to have a discussion.

"Why are you still not," he followed up quickly. "A Senator."

Wow this guy was smooth, Mitch thought as she tried to suppress a smile.

"Events happen," Reb answered curtly.

"The chair with the wheels?" his question hung in the air. He sure cut right to the heart of the matter.

Reb studied Jacque. Mitch knew that they were at a crossroad. Reb would either become friends with this man or treat him like an extinct species. Maybe there was a coin handy that Mitch could toss, so unsure was she of the outcome.

"The wheelchair had nothing to do with it," Reb answered calmly. "But rather than ruin this lunch by discussing American politics, we should decide which wine goes best with trout."

"And ham sandwiches," Mitch added, more or less to break the spell of mutual admiration that was beginning to form between Reb and Jacque.

"You might consider a beer," Reb said to Mitch.

The suggestion felt like Mitch was being sent to the children's table at Thanksgiving.

"No, I'm sure I want wine. I'm thinking red wine. How do you say that? Rouge vin? Vin rouge? A whole bottle of vin rouge, please?"

"Une bouteille de vin rouge," Jacque helped out when the garçon showed up. "And une bouteille de vin blanc, also."

Fine! They could share their bottle of wine and Mitch could have hers all to herself and get good and falling down drunk before happy hour even got underway. As the wine was being

poured, a half glass apiece, Mitch's mind raced to come up with an appropriate toast. She raised her glass, "When in Paris..."
Reb looked puzzled.

"You know," Mitch followed up. "When in Paris, do as the...Parisians do."

"That's Rome, Darling," Reb corrected.

"It is? Well, I'm not in Rome right now, so Paris will have to do."

Jacque joined in, "Paris will have to do."

They all took a sip of wine. Reb and Jacque stopped there, but Mitch drained her serving. It was, after all, only half a glass. For some reason, Parisians felt that this was a polite amount. It seemed skimpy for a country that grew a lot of grapes. Ever the gentleman, Jacque refilled her glass, again, halfway.

"Merci!" Mitch practiced her pronunciation. It was morphing ever so slowly from "mercy" to "merci" but it was still going to take a while.

Whether or not a whole carafe of wine would help or hinder the cause had yet to be determined. She drank half again as much as before and then, feeling settled, looked around at her surroundings.

"Nobody's writing," she remarked.

"What do you mean?" Reb asked.

"I thought that we would be surrounded by writers, like present-day Hemingways."

"You are engulfed in tourists, rather," Jacque explained.

"Where are the writers, then?"

"In less famous places with less expensive food."

"Where would that be?"

"One place would be the university."

"Students always do find the cheapest food," Reb edged her way into the conversation.

"Where is this university?" Mitch asked.

"It's in what we call the Quartier Latin. La Sorbonne."

"We'll have to put it on our list of places to see."

"You cannot actually get into the University, but the neighborhood is alone worth the visit."

"You speak really good English," Mitch complimented him as she drained her wine glass again.

"I started young," Jacque was on the verge of a blush, so he quickly changed the subject from himself. "What is on your list so far?"

"Our touring list?" Reb asked.

"Oui."

"We haven't started one yet," Reb admitted, looking at Mitch like it was all her fault for being so impetuous.

"That's the best way to see France," Jacque smiled.

"It is?"

"One sees so many tourists with a list of things to see and they are like generals with a small army marching here and there conquering France without enjoyment. It would be like hurrying through a meditation garden to keep a schedule."

Mitch was beginning to appreciate this guy. Where could his girlfriend be? Honestly. Mitch scanned the area again. She felt something.

"Does anybody have the feeling as though we are being watched?"

"Of course we're being watched. I told you about that already."

"The eyes of Paris are upon me," Mitch remarked harmlessly enough. At least she didn't sing it to the tune of "The Eyes of Texas are upon Me." That would have drawn even more attention.

Jacque had become quiet. Still. Almost guarded.

"So, will you help us?" Reb directed the question to Jacque.

"Help you?"

"Make a list. The kind of list where we would be less of an army and more of a respectful tourist."

"Did you know that when the German army marched to the Louvre, they found the museum empty?" he inquired.

"Empty?" Mitch echoed. She remembered from Trish and Robbie's (God love and rest her soul) art adventure how voracious the Nazi appetite for art had been.

"You didn't think the people of France would allow the Nazis to just help themselves to the greatest art treasures ever assembled, did you?"

"I don't remember reading anything about it in the history books."

"You also didn't expect to have your American history books
have anything complimentary to say about the French!"
Mitch contemplated both this and her empty wine glass. Jacque
refilled it. Again.
"I distinctly remember in one of my history classes way back in
grade school where the teacher talked in ridiculing tones about
how the French had put their canons into concrete at the border
with Germany and so all the Germans had to do was to go
around the border guns and attack from behind. A lot like
terrorists today, don't you think?"
Mitch's history lecture had created silence in its wake. Jacque
had lost his blush and Reb looked at Mitch like she had been
nothing but offending. To Jacque, she said sweetly, "So, do you
recommend the Louvre for our list?"
"I put the Louvre for anyone's list," he smiled. He was a little
less pale by now and seemingly recovered from Mitch's alleged
earlier rudeness.
Reb pulled some paper and a pen from her purse. At last! Some
writing would be done at one of Hemingway's old haunts. She
started a one-two-three priority list. "The Louvre," Reb said as
she wrote.
Mitch would have needed another bottle of wine in her to have
blurted out "lingerie shopping." Reb would never know how
proud she should be of her.
"Before you go about creating your perfect list, you might
consider whether you are going to limit yourselves to Paris, or if
France is to be your canvas."
What an artistic and romantic way to say this, Mitch thought to
herself. Honestly. Where was this guy's girlfriend? Or wife?
Or both??
"We're not quite decided on that yet," Reb was still stuck on the
suddenness of the visit.
"You really did just decide to hop a flight and come to Paris?" he
said.
"They didn't have what we were looking for at Sears," Mitch did
her best to explain.
"Seers?" Jacque looked confused.
"Never mind. We actually came here to do some shopping."
"Some baby shopping," Reb added.

124

"Baby shopping?" he had to know they weren't into human trafficking. "What is this baby shopping?"

"Shopping for baby clothes. And a crib. A stroller. You know, a layette?"

"You are having a baby?"

"It's a long story," Reb really didn't want to go into the details right now.

"Don't ask. Don't tell," Jacque nodded like he understood.

"Something like that," Mitch agreed as she shifted restlessly in her chair.

"Are you okay?" Reb noticed.

"Yeah," Mitch opted out of further explanation. She didn't know the root cause of her restlessness. Maybe it was the wine, or just the long flight, or maybe just the nagging feeling that people were watching them without making eye contact. It was a lot like those first few days on the porch at Henry's house.

"You may want to add the exotic Monte Carlo to your list," Jacque continued to play tour guide.

"Ah yes. To Catch a Thief!" Mitch smiled.

"A thief?" Jacque asked.

"Cary Grant. Grace Kelly. They don't make movies like that anymore."

"People like to see things blowing up instead," Reb stated.

"Or spy movies with car chases and crashes and shootouts," Mitch made her own list.

"Not at all resembling real life," Jacque joined the lament.

"So, you recommend the French Riviera, then?" Mitch double checked

"With all my heart!" Jacque couldn't have been more profuse.

"And where would you go to nourish the heart of an artist?" Reb directed the question to Jacque, but held Mitch in her gaze. It was for moments like this that Mitch lived and breathed. Reb might have all this time been making pleasant chatter with a drop-dead gorgeous guy half her age, but at this single splendid moment in time, only Mitch and Reb inhabited this place and everything else was just sparkly dust. Jacque waited to answer until he could be sure that they were actually listening to what he said. "Many artists and writers made France their home."

"Why?" Mitch cut him off mid-speech.

"Well, for artists, it was the soft light of the rivers and the beautiful countryside."

"And the writers?"

"They were escaping Puritanical America."

"That's totally understandable," Mitch nodded in agreement. On any other issue concerning criticism of America, Mitch would have been irked. Being defensive was a talent, not just a gift. But Jacque was on to something important here with this Puritanical business. In America, sadly, there was no shortage of sanctimonious people telling other people how to conduct their sex lives, and it was all full of stricture, scripture and reproach.

"And the cost of living was much more reasonable in Hemingway's time," he added.

He was right about that, judging from the prices on this place's menu. Paris was not a city either for the faint of heart or pocketbook.

"You will be able to see some of the France that inspired Picasso and Matisse in the area of the French Riviera, so you could, how do you say it in America, kill two pigeons with one rock?"

"Close enough," Mitch smiled. It seemed odd that Jacque would have known the phrase "Don't ask, don't tell" but got tripped up on birds and stones. She shrugged it off.

"I think," Reb was speaking to Jacque, "you have convinced us that the Riviera should be a part of the tour. But how difficult is it to get there?"

"I can always help with that," Jacque was boastful. Right in character. Mitch was getting the gut feeling that this was just all too convenient. All this help.

"You wouldn't mind helping us?" Reb was gushy now.

"I have a big vehicle," he explained.

So, what, did this guy own a tank? Mitch wondered only to herself.

"How big?" Reb was asking.

"Big enough for the wheelchair and yourself."

Reb was all ready to agree to the road trip from hell when she caught Mitch's subtle shaking of her head and silent mouthing of "no!"

"Can we think about it?" Reb asked awkwardly.

"Of course."

If Jacque was put off, he showed no sign. "I must go for now."

"Thank you for lunch."

"It was my pleasure."

He paid the bill and departed in a whirl. Mitch almost expected to see someone coming along to chase him away, so quickly had he made his escape.

Reb, the woman who would have never gotten in a car with a stranger at home, now lamented, "We didn't get his phone number. We won't be able to contact him."

"I don't think we'll need to worry about that," Mitch said flatly, still mystified that Reb would have traveled with him to places unknown without a second thought.

"Why not?"

"He found us once. He'll find us again."

"It's a big city," Reb reminded.

"And if we're going to see any of it, we should probably get going!"

They stopped back at the hotel only long enough to change clothes before visiting the one place that was on everyone's list, the Eiffel Tower. Even from a distance, Reb summed it up best, "Magnifique!"

"Not too bad for a temporary structure," Mitch agreed. Sort of. They queued in a long line and enjoyed an elevator ride up to the viewing platform. Now, they could really see Paris from atop this tall building.

"Do all cities look alike from far above?" Reb mused.

"I went up in the Stratosphere once in Las Vegas."

"And how was that?"

"I'd never seen so many swimming pools from that far up."

"So, then, not every city looks alike," Reb had her answer.

"Can you see any cafes from up here?"

"What is with you and cafes all of a sudden?"

"I'm beginning to like the idea of sitting around enjoying a cup of coffee or a glass of wine and watching people go by and not feel the ache of isolation that so often occurs in our lives."

"You can be surrounded by people and still feel isolated."

"Yes, but it takes extra effort to do so. We've already made one friend at our first cafe experience. And because you are so beautiful, we may not have to buy lunch the whole time we are here."

"Are you jealous?" Reb had to know.

"No."

"Then, why did you have me turn down Jacque's offer to take us to the Riviera?"

"The guy with the *big* vehicle? Because something is not quite right about it."

"Right, morally?"

"Morals had nothing to do with it. It's just all too coincidental. Why aren't you suspicious. You're usually the suspicious one."

"I'm not always the suspicious one. I just didn't see any reason for suspicion. Haven't you ever felt that things were happening for a reason?"

"Yes."

"And?"

"Ninety percent of the time, it turns out to be a disaster."

"What about the other ten percent?"

"We're still together, right!"

"I'm tired. How about you?"

"I think the day is catching up to me. Or maybe jet lag. Or the bottle of wine I drank."

"Let's go back to the hotel."

"Always my favorite thing to do in your company."

"You are beginning to sound more French already."

"You mean, romantic?"

"Romantic, poetic..."

"I've never been poetic. Never written a poem that didn't start with 'Roses are red.'"

"Maybe you could give it a try one day. You might surprise yourself."

"I might."

The drive back to the hotel was nonstop sight-seeing for Mitch. No matter what new place you visited, whether you were looking at monuments or slums, it was still all new to your eyes. Le Tour Eiffel, as the French called it, was interesting. But so was all of this as well.

"Did you know that we were able to see one of the famous birthplaces of the French resistance?"

"We were?" Mitch hoped to sound impressed.

"We were," Reb parroted.

"How about that," Mitch couldn't think of anything more intelligent to say.

"You have no idea what the French Resistance was, do you? And don't even think that it's what women tourists have to employ around French men."

"At least I now know that its birthplace was at the Eiffel Tower."

"Actually, I was referring to the Musee de l'Homme."

"The what? Was that in English?"

"The Museum of Man. Just across the Seine from the Eiffel Tower."

"Sounds like you might want to go back at some point and visit it?"

"You would enjoy it, too. There's the Cafe de l'Homme right next door."

"Oh good. Another cup of coffee."

"Without the French Resistance, you and I would both be speaking German."

"No. We would both be dead," Mitch corrected her. Even without an extensive historical grasp, Mitch knew that much to be true.

"After the French were circumvented at the Maginot Line," Reb started the history lesson, only to be interrupted.

"The what?"

"The Maginot Line. You remember, the thing you were discussing with Jacque."

"Oh, the canons in the concrete. Is that what it was called?"

"Maginot. Anything else your teacher told you about it?"

"Well, she said that the French built the Mazjiknow Line," Mitch tried her hand at the pronunciation and was pleased with herself. Had she seen the actual word in print, she would have probably mangled it. The civics lecture continued, "so that the Germans would attack Belgium instead."

"Did you ever think to report this obviously misinformed teacher to the local school board?"

"I didn't. But I heard someone else did when she gave us her own personal assessment of Native Americans."

"I dread asking," Reb said.

Undaunted, Mitch continued. "She said that the American taxpayers spent good money on helping Indians get fancy college educations only to have their generosity repaid by having these same Indians return to the reservation so they could rejoin the tribe and have lice grow in their hair."

Rebecca was rendered silent by this recounting of ridiculousness.

"I had a warped schooling," Mitch explained.

Thankfully, they arrived at the hotel. A bed was finally within reach. De Gaulle had been such a thoughtful driver that Mitch tipped him generously. You never knew how much helpfulness a little generosity could *arrange*. "Buy" seemed too crass of a word.

"Will you be dining out this evening?" he inquired deferentially.

"I think we'll have to," Mitch replied.

"Pourquoi?" he slipped into his native tongue so readily, something to be expected.

"Pork what?" Mitch asked back.

"He's asking 'why?'" Reb explained. Why do you think we'll have to dine out?"

"I'm sure it's too late in the day to get a reservation in the hotel restaurant."

"For you, Madam, it would be possible."

"It might be possible, but it wouldn't be right."

Not meaning to argue, mostly due to recent discussions about this topic, but instead helping to explain things to De Gaulle, Reb said that they preferred to go out to dinner. Mitch added that they didn't want to take seats away from people who might never get the chance to eat at such a fancy place. "We can fly here anytime. Not everyone can do that."

The matter was settled. De Gaulle would be good enough to ask the concierge on their behalf to make dinner reservations at a less trendy restaurant and that he would be more than happy to provide transportation.

"We're in Paris. We're not going to get a bad meal," Mitch summed it all up in her famous logic.

It was good to be back in the hotel room. It was truly a stunning room, appointed magnificently with all that that entailed. Kings could have felt comfortable here.

"Was George the Vth a king?" Mitch wondered to herself. She could always ask Reb the Historian. But if she waited long enough, the answer might stumble forth in conversation.

"You never cease to amaze me," Reb intruded into Mitch's reverie.

"In a good or bad way?" Mitch wanted to know before proceeding.

"Why do you always assume the worst?"

"I don't assume the worst, I merely give it a fifty-fifty chance."

"For the record, this is the good fifty percent."

"I'm always willing to listen to good things about me," Mitch smiled.

"You really do put your money where your mouth is," Reb said. Mitch didn't quite know what to make of the remark. She had a lot of money and it would require a pretty big mouth to handle it all. But she was almost certain that this wasn't the point Reb was trying to convey, so Mitch kept her big mouth shut.

"I mean about the dinner reservation issue."

"Oh that," Mitch breathed a sigh of relief. "Well, it's just common courtesy."

"No," Reb corrected. "It's uncommon courtesy. You have never acquired an attitude of privilege."

Mitch could have said about a dozen things, and probably eleven of them would have gotten her into trouble. So, she just simply smiled and said, "I'm a breath of fresh air in a stuffy world."

"Well, Airy, why don't you take the first turn in the bathroom while I catch my breath."

"Okay."

Mitch gathered her robe and nothing else and headed to the bathroom that was bigger than a lot of people's living rooms. Reb exhaled. It had been many busy hours and her stamina wasn't as good as it once was. Mitch was kind and thoughtful. So what if she didn't understand the nuances of history or poetry. She carried in her heart a song that she danced to and carried Reb right along with her in the intricate dance steps of love. Reb couldn't do everything that she used to be able to do, but she certainly could help out by keeping her clothes and personal items in order. She set out to organize her wardrobe starting with the sweater that she had carried throughout the day. As she

131

folded it to store it in a drawer, she heard a crackling sound. Or maybe more of a rustling noise. Had she subconsciously pocketed money? It wouldn't be the first time that she had secreted something away only to find a treasure later in the day, week, or month. Usually it was tissues. Not exactly a treasure. So, hoping for cash was always her first choice. It wasn't cash. It was a page of paper with something written on it that resembled poetry. What had Mitch gone and done now? Had she decided to rise to the challenge of poetess? What a romantic gesture. Reb read the first line, which appeared to be the title. A Heart with Five Parts. So it *was* a love poem. Reb scanned the paper without reading for detail only to discover that the note was signed with a single initial J. Reb realized immediately that it was a love poem from Jacque. Although not exactly panicked, Reb knew instinctively that she should keep this hidden from Mitch. Placing it anywhere in the hotel room wouldn't be a guarantee that Mitch wouldn't find it. That was just one of the facts of life that came with Reb and her wheelchair. Mitch was a blessing, no doubt about that. She would, without even a hint of annoyance, fetch, reach or extract anything from anywhere, often without even being asked to do so. The down side was that, in reality, Reb had no real privacy. Oh, she could have always just asked Mitch to stay out of her purse, but that would just arouse great suspicion. Then, the child in Mitch would soon become dominant and as Reb visualized the contents of her purse spilled out onto the bed, she heard Mitch rummaging around in the bathroom. What the hell, Reb figured. The note had been safe enough in her pocket before. Reb refolded the paper and slipped it back into the sweater pocket and then prepared for her turn in the bathroom. They soon traded places and when Reb emerged, Mitch seemed very much rejuvenated by the shower and the brief rest. She was ready to do more touristy things, and as she helped Reb get dressed, she asked, "Do you know how much of France we would have to see in order to visit all the famous art places?"
"Other than just the entire country?" Reb tried to look solemn before the twinkling eyes gave her away.
"Kind of like how many cafes we'd have to visit to see where all that amazing writing took place."
"Hemingway alone would keep us busy for a week."

"So I was right earlier when I said that he spread his favors around?"

"He had four wives," Reb answered a different question altogether.

"Well no wonder he wrote in cafes. It must have been pretty noisy at home," Mitch replied matter-of-factly.

"Not all at the same time. He wasn't Mormon, for goodness sake."

Mitch smiled. Just a small smile. The smile that indicates that she had known this all along. Even the Mormon part.

"Why don't we start with Monet?" Reb shifted the conversation back to the original discussion.

"He was a painter, right?" Mitch followed along, happy to know something about this.

"Yes. He was an Impressionist."

"Is that because his paintings made an impression on people?" Reb never really knew when Mitch was teasing her. At least, not in this sense. Could someone really be of a certain age and never have heard of the Impressionist style of painting? "It's my understanding that the Impressionist style of painting came about as a result of painters needing to compete with a new and upstart form of art."

Mitch was listening intently. "You have me on the edge of my seat."

"Photography was beginning to make inroads into the art scene, so artists tried to draw a scene with realism and color."

"I like color," Mitch had the eyes of a child now.

"Then I think you'll like Monet."

"Is he anything like Leroy Neiman?"

"Well," Reb wanted to sound as congenial as possible when comparing a historical painter to a contemporary, "they both used a lot of color."

"Okay."

"So, the problem is, the place where Monet painted doesn't have a lot of his works there."

"I'm sure they had to be moved to museums for safekeeping."

"Right. So, do you want to first visit the place where he painted or the museums?"

"How far away is the place he painted?"

133

"Not far."

"What's it called?"

"Giverny."

When Reb named the place, it was with unmistakable reverence. Mitch didn't even dare repeat it. She couldn't match Reb's pronunciation or tone.

"Should we go to dinner first?" Mitch asked.

Reb couldn't tell if this was another Hemingway and his wives jokes. "Giverny is at least a day trip from here."

"Oh good. We'll be traveling through the country," Mitch was getting more excited by the minute. "Can we stay overnight?"

"I'm not sure..." Reb hesitated.

Mitch heard the nuance in her voice. Not everywhere had handicap-access buildings.

"How far away is this place?" Mitch wanted specifics.

"You're afraid to say it, aren't you?" Reb asked in the way that made the question not a question. Mitch wasn't quite sure what Reb thought she was afraid to say, so she quibbled, "Am not."

"Giverny. Giverny." Reb repeated it for her.

"Gi-ver-ny," Mitch repeated after her and then added, "See. I can too say it."

"You did well."

"Is it a small place? Is that why you think we can't spend the night? Not having a reservation and all?"

"I just don't want you to have to carry me over the threshold."

"People will think we're married."

"One day," Reb said out loud.

"In the meantime, we should make it a day trip to Gi-ver-ny."

"I'm sure we can arrange some sort of early-morning transportation."

Dinner was indeed magnifique. Mitch had remembered hearing Reb say this earlier and was now ready to brag. "See, I can learn at least a few French words."

"What did you do? Study the English to French translation guide while I was in the shower?" Reb asked.

"No. I just remembered you saying it earlier."

"So, you do listen to me."

"All the time."

Dinner had been pretty amazing. For a woman who was impressed with anyone who could fry two eggs, flip them once and not break the yolks, Mitch was the prime candidate to be bowled over by French cooking.

"The only sauce I know about is that special one on hamburgers," Mitch concluded her culinary story.

Reb smiled. This was one of the most appealing things about Mitch. Her easy admittance of surprise and delight. Most people steeped in their jaded attitudes until their outlook on life was as bitter as over-brewed tea. But not Mitch.

"I should bring you to Paris more often."

"Magnifique idea!" Mitch agreed.

Heartburn aside, they both slept well after such a busy day. The early-morning transport consisted of another limo. Not quite as expensive or expansive as the prior day, but it was still a very glamorous way to travel to the countryside. It was a short journey to this magical place of flowers and fields and trees and church steeples and one very famous Japanese footbridge. Mitch and Reb joined the many tourists who had come to see this cradle of genius.

"I'd be inspired too, I suppose, if I was surrounded by all these flowers," Mitch breathed her appreciation of this expanse of nature.

"Monet created a lot of this," Reb explained.

"Created?" Mitch wanted to hear more.

"He worked with landscapers to create all this natural beauty."

"Gee," was all that Mitch could think to say.

"His early paintings, particularly of the footbridge, were very clear and precise."

"You mean, he painted the footbridge more than once?" Mitch was curious. She had come from a place where people avoided painting their houses more than once.

"Monet painted many things more than once. Multiple times in some cases. The footbridge. Water lilies. Haystacks. Poplars." Reb ticked off the list like a museum curator.

"Why would someone do that?" Mitch asked.

"Haven't you ever seen pictures of the same place taken during the various seasons?"

"Sure."

"The coloring is so different. Spring is so different from fall. And so on."

"I didn't think about it that way."

"And, of course, the morning light is different from the afternoon light and the dusk."

"Just how many Monet paintings have you seen?"

"I've seen some in books."

"Even so, I'm impressed. Pun intended."

"And in his later years," Reb ventured on despite the silliness, "between his failing eyesight and whatever damage occurred from inhaling paint fumes, the works became even more abstract."

"I can commiserate about those paint fumes. I get a little light-headed after painting just one room in a house."

In past years, Reb might have made a sarcastic remark. But over time, Mitch's enthusiastic innocence had mellowed her a bit. They enjoyed a lovely lunch in the nearby town of Vernon and then passed the afternoon touring as much of the grounds at Giverny as they could comfortably navigate.

"I am tempted to stay," Reb said wistfully as the afternoon light illuminated the gardens.

"Overnight?"

"Forever."

"You would want to live here?"

"It's so beautiful."

"Remind me to plant a bunch of flowers when we get back to wherever it is that we are going back to."

They both remembered that they hadn't really yet decided where they were going to rear the child for whom they had not scheduled this impromptu shopping spree. Giverny had not been in the running. Until now.

"How many?" Reb asked.

"How many what?" Mitch asked. Her thoughts had drifted away from the conversation and she now wondered if there were many more places from which to choose for a final destination.

"How many bunches of flowers would you plant?" Reb really wondered sometimes as to Mitch's power of concentration.

"For you, a million million."

"How horticultural of you!" Reb chuckled. "And romantic as well."

"I've never thought of myself that way. Romantic, I mean. At least, not in the word-wise way."

Reb glanced at Mitch. Had she found the poem by Jacque and decided to talk around it?

"What's wrong?" Mitch asked.

"What do you mean?"

"You suddenly look very stressed."

"I think I'm just a little tired."

"Does that mean we get to spend a couple of days in bed?" Mitch smiled.

"You wish," Reb deadpanned back.

Mitch continued to smile. She couldn't help it. The spell of Giverny was cast upon her as well. The driver was summoned and they were soon speeding back to Paris. Lunch had diminished their desire for a large dinner, so they ordered a snack from room service and enjoyed an evening of being in each other's company out of the hustle and bustle of the world. This was just as romantic as being at Giverny. Or Kansas. When Mitch decided to wrap up in her robe, she noticed that it had been moved. She didn't think anything about it at the time, but when Reb asked Mitch why she had moved Reb's stuff around, they discussed the issue.

"It must have been the maid service," Reb decided.

"I'm glad we took our money with us," Mitch was a little put out.

"Nothing is missing," Reb soothed her. "She is supposed to clean things, after all."

"My robe was clean right where it was. I have half a mind to complain. We're guests, not slobs."

Mitch rarely got upset about things, so when she did, Reb honored her feelings. "You can always request no maid service."

"That's a good idea. I'll do that tomorrow morning."

Reb didn't know how serious Mitch had been about the issue until now. They could do without maid service. They certainly did so at home all the time.

"So, once we get over being tired, where are we going next?" Mitch asked, now robed and calmer.

"I suppose we could take Jacque's advice and go to the Riviera."

"The playground of billionaires. Do you think we can afford it?"
"We probably couldn't afford to live there. But it would be nice to go and get our jewels stolen."
"Are you going to be Grace Kelly?"
"The better question is, are you willing to be Cary Grant?"
"It would be fun for a day or two, wouldn't it."
"The beach, the casinos, the beautiful people..."
"I'll talk to my new best friend, the concierge, first thing in the morning."

One of the caveats about traveling is that if you don't get your reservations in ahead of time, you need to plan on spending more money to secure a room. More money as in wallets full of it in the south of France. Mitch secured the last suite that hotels like this save just for bad planners like Mitch.

The extremely wealthy had a lot of leisure time on their hands and apparently they spent a good deal of it in places like the Cote d Azure. If it wasn't for the fact that Matisse had favored this area, Mitch would have tried to talk Reb out of this once she heard the final total of the expenditure just for the room. Thanks a lot, Mr. Matisse. Mitch also kept the room at the George V so that they would have a base of operations, so to speak. And no more housekeeping unless they were present to witness the work. Mitch was adamant on this point. The hotel manager was always prepared for quirky guests and quirkier requests. That's why he got paid all that money.

One good night's sleep had fortified them for the journey. They were on the road right after breakfast. They could've flown, but then they would have missed viewing the French countryside. One just couldn't see the sights from the window of a jet. Mitch had been tempted to skip the chauffeur and drive the car herself, but then she would have missed out on this moment. She was sitting close to Reb and Reb was resting her head on Mitch's shoulder.
"You're quiet," Mitch finally said quietly.
"I'm digesting."
"So, you're okay?"

"I'm fine. What's on your mind?"

"I guess I was just expecting edification on whatever it is that we will see when we get to wherever we are going."

Reb had to laugh. "You think I'm some sort of travel guide?"

"Partly."

"And what's the other part?"

"I think there are several parts. Like fractions."

"Like what?"

"Like, art expert, for one."

"I'm no art expert."

"You know more than I do. You know all about Monet and paint fumes."

"That was just a lucky guess."

"And now, this Matisse and Picasso stuff. You actually know where they lived and painted. You are amazing!"

"Have you ever seen any works by Picasso?" Reb took the bait, even though she knew full well it was bait. If she didn't talk, Mitch would just sit there and stew about her silence.

"A couple. They were strange. Like people having noses where their eyes should be. That's the guy who should be tested for way too many paint fumes."

"That was part of his style. Do you know why he might have done that?"

Mitch smiled. She had to answer carefully or else Reb might think that Mitch felt obligated to listen. "I'd love to hear why he painted the way he painted."

"I only know part of the story."

"That's still more than I know."

"When the Germans occupied France during the war-"

"The first or the second?" Mitch interrupted.

Reb thought this over. It was a fair-enough question. German troops occupied parts of France during both the world wars. No doubt more extensively in the second war than the first.

"I was referring to World War II," Reb clarified. "Anyway, painters and writers were seriously affected by the Nazi oppression."

"I always thought that Hitler and Goring confiscated all kinds of art and that they weren't all that particular about what they stole?"

139

"That was certainly the case, but they also labeled certain styles as degenerate and forbid the works to be created."

"And the artists put up with that?"

"They were faced with the reality of being put into concentration camps. If they did what the Nazis demanded, their lives were spared."

"Did the artists just wait out the war, hoping the good guys would win?"

"Artists are as varied as every other group of people. Some left France, some painted in secret, others collaborated with the Nazis and there were a few that resisted."

"Here we are back to that resistance stuff. How on earth would an artist resist?"

"This takes us back to Picasso. You said that some of his artwork depicted people's faces as grotesque."

"I wasn't that eloquent, but yeah, that's what they were."

"It's been suggested by scholars that he was painting the so-called monsters. Hoping that we would know from his works how it was to live under the reign of Nazi monsters."

"I guess I would have never thought about that. That's a pretty clever way to send a message."

"Then, there were the tri-color painters."

"Try color?"

"In native tongue, they were referred to as La Peinture Bleu Blanc Rouge."

"I only recognized the words blue and rouge in that sentence."

"Blue, white and red. The three colors of the French flag. The painters of the blue, white and red."

"Oh, I get it. Three colors of their flag. So they painted pictures of their flag."

"No, that would have been too obvious and would have gotten them sent to the camps. They painted pictures that had a lot of red, white and blue in them to show their allegiance to France."

"This resistance took many forms, but if that's how the resistance worked for patriotic Frenchmen, how did the traitor artists collaborate with the Nazis?"

"Mostly by doing business with them. Creating art following the rules dictated to them by the Nazis."

"So, there was such a thing as Nazi art?"

140

"Yes. It fell into two distinct categories. It glorified Aryans. It denigrated Jews. The so-called poster art that appeared in Paris that was anti-Jew sickened the respectable French citizens."

"And the Aryan art? What did it look like?"

"It had a lot of pastoral scenes. And female nudes."

"Let me see if I understand this. Hitler didn't think that nudie art was degenerate, but he considered Monet's flowers degenerate. Am I understanding this correctly?"

"It all sounds so absurd when you explain it."

"That happens to me a lot," Mitch admitted.

"You are so very wise..."

"Are you chilly?" Mitch changed the subject suddenly.

"The air conditioning has that effect on me."

"I just noticed that you've been wearing your sweater everywhere."

Reb thought about the crinkly piece of paper in her pocket. The love poem she didn't want falling into the wrong hands. "It's like my security blanket."

Mitch smiled. They were comfortable and secure and speeding toward the glamor capital of the world. Life didn't get any better than this. They lunched in a charming town and then took turns napping and chatting during the rest of the drive.

The southern coast of France, referred to as the Cote d Azure, was so named because of the blue color of the water. It wasn't the same word for blue that bleu was. Bleu was blue and azure was, well, azure. Whatever word they might have used didn't even begin to adequately describe the beauty of the water. If heaven had coasts, they would be this color. Some people saw the influence of Italy in the area. Other people saw the influence of Russia in the area. Mitch saw the influence of money in the area. Mitch tried to never complain about spending money or the cost of things, at least out loud. She felt that complaining about prices, even if the words were factual in nature, could give loved ones the impression that they had dollar signs hanging over their heads. Like guilt.

Like, "You cost me too much." It usually didn't happen at the beginning of a relationship. When you're first in love with someone, nothing costs too much. Even if it does. And then,

141

time goes by and life grinds on and for those with limited means, a resentment can bloom like a weed in a once-tended flower garden. Those who never experience this are living paradise on earth and your mailing address didn't necessarily need to be Monte Carlo.

Once again, royalty would have been content in the hotel room that Mitch and Reb were escorted to. Whatever all these fancy furnishings and touches were called, Mitch had never learned. When the usual place you stayed at had a numeral in the motel chain's name, you could guarantee that there wasn't any Louie the 14th tables or chairs around. Mitch hadn't yet read up on the mores of tipping in France. She had hoped that a week's salary would ease the bellhop, or whatever they called them in France, out of the suite so that she could have Reb all to herself for the time being. But as things so often go with Mitch, she accomplished quite the opposite. He was very helpful in explaining the various plumbing and other gizmos included in such an upscale establishment. At last, he left, and Mitch and Reb were alone.

"I'm finally alone with the most beautiful woman in the world," Mitch said.

Reb gave her that patented, "You're such a scoundrel" look. Reb knew that Mitch could have any woman she wanted. She was rich, loving and thoughtful. But she was here.

"What are you thinking?" Mitch had been watching Reb's facial expression.

"I was wondering how much rest you need before hitting the casino?"

"That's not what you looked like you were thinking about."

"What did I look like I was thinking about?" Reb challenged.

"You had a thoughtful expression. Almost like you were meditative or wistful. Not the sort of look you would have if you were just thinking about going to a casino."

"How can you tell all that just by looking at me?"

"Because I look with my heart, not just my eyes."

Normally, this would have been an okay conversation for Reb, but nagging at her in the back of her mind was the love poem from Jacque tucked away in her sweater pocket. It had to go away, the poem, not the sweater. And the sooner, the better. "Let's go."

"Right now?" Mitch was taken slightly aback.

"I'm ready. Are you?"

"Okay, well, let me change clothes."

"Hurry up."

"Are you going to wear your sweater everywhere?" Mitch called out from the bedroom as she dressed for the casino. The casino where the richest of the rich tried their luck at the same tables made famous by Bond. James Bond. Of course, Bond had gambled in Las Vegas as well. And the fact that it was all fictitious didn't diminish the glamor of it all. Still, anyone who knew a damn about craps wouldn't have made all those silly field bets. Real gamblers bet the Come line and backed up their bets.. Flashy gamblers tossed chips all over the table and lost money in the long run. It wasn't how you handled the dice that mattered. It was how you handled the money that counted.

"What's the matter with my sweater?" Reb sounded annoyed. Mitch tore herself away from her mental communion with James long enough to answer. "It's lovely and you are lovely in it but you've hardly been out of it since we arrived in France."

"If it passes the casino's dress code, then I would think that you shouldn't have a problem with it."

Mitch was sure that James Bond never had these kinds of problems. Besides, if anyone needed help meeting any dress code, it was Mitch. Would she really need to go out and rent a tux? As she wondered, Reb took turns reading her mind. "You didn't exactly pack for all this dressy stuff, did you?"

"I can't pack what I don't own," Mitch felt her own annoyance level beginning to push off from zero.

"I'd love to shop with you and help you pick out something." It was a fair offer. They had begun the lark using shopping as an excuse, albeit for baby clothes, but if Reb was willing to do this favor, who was Mitch to be disagreeable.

"Nothing too frilly?" Mitch negotiated.

"Only the bare minimum to get you to the baccarat table."

"Dressing to the nines?" Mitch couldn't help herself.

If Reb groaned, it was inaudible.

They weren't the first, and certainly wouldn't be the last women who found themselves doing emergency clothes shopping on the Riviera. They found something wearable for Mitch and throughout the entire ordeal, Mitch never once mentioned that maybe Reb could pick up a new sweater. For this restraint, she silently congratulated herself. Several times. They were now as ready as they would ever be to lose money. Mitch preferred to think of it as helping the local economy. She knew enough about gambling to stay out of serious trouble. Never bet the field (oh James), don't split tens, and watch roulette from a safe distance. Preferably the lounge.

"Well, aren't you going to bet?" Reb asked after their second glass of champagne.

"Maybe just a little."

"Isn't roulette different here?"

"It can be a bit more in favor of the player. One green instead of two. At least, that's what I've heard."

"Roll me over there. It's still the easiest game to access from my wheelchair and it has all those pretty chips."

As always, Mitch complied. Reb played red for a while. And then black for a while. And then even and odd. An occasional win mixed in with the losses.

"Aren't you going to play as well?" Reb asked.

"I suppose I should, just so that one day, I can tell the grandkids all about it."

Mitch fished out the equivalent of roughly one-thousand dollars and placed it on the table to get chips. She put it all on the number 35.

"That's an awful lot to bet all on one number," Reb remarked. Mitch smiled. First, Reb had all but nagged her to wager, and now she was balking at the amount.

"It's my only bet of the evening."

"All on one number?"

"How much luck did you have with red and black?"

"I didn't lose a thousand dollars."

By now, throughout their banter, the ball had dutifully rolled along the rail and had bounded toward its destination. Of course, it landed on 35. It had no other choice.

"You didn't win \$35,000 either," Mitch said calmly. "How about some dinner? I'm starved." Mitch looked at Reb.

Reb looked back, "Are you buying?"

"Don't I always?"

If it was one thing that Reb could do without equal, it was picking out fine restaurants. Today was no exception. She had a budget of \$35,000 and lobster sounded good. It sounded even better with champagne and fois gras and truffles and some kind of cream sauce and chocolate ice cream with coffee beans mixed in. An entire weeks' worth of calories all in one meal. The good news was that the portions were modest. The bad news was that Mitch was almost seeing double from the sugar buzz. So, okay, the check didn't exactly add up to \$35,000. But they made a dent in it.

"You look like you're all done in for the evening," Reb observed.

"You are correct, as usual," Mitch managed a smile. She was tired. She didn't know whether it was physical or mental fatigue and she really didn't care.

"Ready for bed?" Reb checked to be sure.

Mitch only smiled again. What a silly question.

They were quiet on the ride back to the hotel. Reb wanted to once again take a shower before retiring for the night, so Mitch did everything required to help out and then set about to straighten up the room. She was hanging up Reb's sweater when she felt something in the pocket. Mitch chuckled. It was probably Reb's folding money left over from roulette. Mitch pulled out the sheet of paper and began to read the words.

A Heart with Five Parts

My beautiful lady, I have a heart. A heart with five parts. Not a usual heart, my beauty. A usual heart has four parts. But you are not usual, so it is impossible to love you with a usual heart. My heart needs five parts to love and adore you and protect you because there isn't enough room to hold all my love in a heart with four parts. Please do what you must to make sure that a heart with five parts is not destroyed...J

Mitch scanned the poem again. It sure wasn't "Roses and Red" but maybe the French had a better way of expressing undying love. Jock's sense of rhyme was pretty pathetic, but as Mitch pondered this, she realized that he hadn't much time to put pen to paper. Their meeting had been so brief. Maybe he had a pocketful of poems that he kept handy, pulling out whatever was necessary to impress the ladies. He was a smooth operator, no doubt. But for insistence on Mitch's part, he might have been here in Monaco with them, wooing Reb as Mitch didn't play the field. But she had been too smart for him. She never gave Reb any reason to look beyond what Mitch offered. At least, that's what Mitch's ego told her. It dawned slowly on Mitch that Reb had kept the poem. And she had kept it close to her. In the ever-present sweater.

"Going through my pockets again, I see," Reb had finished her shower and was in the doorway.

"You make it sound like a crime."

The seconds of silence that came between them spoke to the tension of the situation. Was there going to be an argument or a level-headed discussion?

"I don't go through your pockets," Reb said.

"I don't have love notes from puppy-eyed Frenchmen in my pockets. You can go ahead and search. I'll wait."

Another couple of seconds passed. Maybe Mitch had been wrong. Maybe the choice was between an argument and a really loud argument. "You've been carrying it around for a while," Mitch remarked when the silence became chilly.

"I was waiting for the time when I could throw it out without you asking a thousand questions."

"When have I ever asked you even one question about anything you've ever thrown out?"

"Well, there was the bra incident last month."

Mitch was caught off guard by Reb actually having an example. She had to think back. She vaguely remembered something and knew that Reb was ready to go into excruciating detail.

"I threw out a bra and you fished it out of the trash."

"I thought you had made a mistake."

"You think I'm senile."

"No, I don't. I throw things out by accident all the time and I'm not senile."

"Like, how many things?" Reb sounded like she wanted an inventory list instead of an example.

"Let's get back to the bra. I was just looking out for you."

"And if you had just fished it out of the trash, I would have understood. But then, when I showed you that one of the hooks was bent, you wanted to get the pliers and fix it."

"And that bothered you?"

"Once you start bending bra hooks with pliers, it's a lost cause."

"A relationship?"

"No! A bra! The minute you need a car tool to fix a bra, the bra is a lost cause."

Mitch fell silent. Reb figured she was brooding. "What?" Reb said finally.

"A pair of pliers isn't necessarily a car tool. A socket wrench is more of a car tool."

It was Reb's turn to remain silent. They had wandered so far off topic that silence seemed to be the wise choice.

"So, what about the poem?" Mitch got back on track.

"I'll throw it out. If I had a shredder, I'd shred it. If I had a fireplace, I'd burn it."

Mitch was far too good of a person to ask what Reb would have done if she had a hammer. Instead, she said, "I want to read it again." Mitch's demeanor had changed in the past minute. She was now impassive.

"Why do you want to do that?"

Mitch now laughed. Reb was truly mystified by now. "You're amused?"

"I want to read it again so I can learn how not to write poetry."

"You think it's not very good poetry?" Reb felt the shift in the conversation away from argument and toward analytical discussion.

"I think it's terrible poetry. It doesn't even rhyme."

"Good poetry doesn't have to rhyme. In fact, the greatest poetry in the world doesn't rhyme."

"So, you think Jock is one of the greatest poets in the world now?"

"I didn't say that," Reb clarified. "Just give me the poem so I can rip it up and throw it away."

"I don't think that's such a good idea."

"What? We haven't argued about it enough yet?"

"It's just that it doesn't seem like what a normal love poem would look like."

"And *you* would know what a normal love poem looks like?"

"I wouldn't be writing about people's deformed hearts getting destroyed."

"Yes, I would hate to think what you would come up with that rhymes with heart."

"I'm not so deep in thought that I didn't hear that," Mitch said as she stared at the words on the paper.

"Okay, so what exactly does bother you about it?"

"It's the last part. I quote, 'Please do what you must to make sure that a heart with five parts is not destroyed.' That line just sucks on every level."

"Why?"

"Isn't the whole point of love poems to make someone feel romantic?"

"I suppose so."

"So, what part of that line induces any romantic feelings? It sounds more like an inner-office memorandum than an invitation to bed."

"Are you sure you're just not jealous because Jacque wrote the poem for me and not you?"

"I'm not jealous. Jock has nothing that I would want, so it's impossible for me to be jealous."

"Let's tear up the note."

"Let's keep it."

"Why?" Reb was trying real hard now to keep the exasperation out of her voice.

"Because something about it puzzles me. And you know how I get when something puzzles me."

"You get irritating."

Mitch nodded in agreement. "Someone has to."

They kissed and made up, but not before Mitch stowed the paper back into Reb's sweater pocket.

148

After all of the fussing of the night before, Mitch and Reb enjoyed the following day on the French Riviera like they had enjoyed no other vacation together. Maybe it was because the ghost of Jacque's poem was no longer. Maybe it was the spirit of Grace Kelly watching over them. Most likely, however, it was probably the specter of impending parenthood that made them appreciate their freedom. Shopping for a layette had been a great excuse to cross the Atlantic. It was now secondary to their adventure. Something that nagged at Mitch.

"We can't forget about the baby," Mitch said as she lazily looked at the Mediterranean. They had decided to throw caution to the wind and took a helicopter ride to St. Tropez. The real miracle occurred when they found a splendid restaurant with a just-canceled reservation. Perhaps the couple had decided to eat in. Gee, Mitch thought, you could do that any old day of the week back home.

"We still haven't decided on where to ship the purchases. I want Colorado, you want Kansas," Reb stated.

"I don't *want* Kansas. I just don't know if we can legally or morally take the baby out of Kansas."

"Which one bothers you more?"

"The morality."

"You worry about the morality of rearing a child of the woman who tried to kill me in another state?"

"Separating mother from child always carried a moral burden no matter who did what to whom."

"I wish the rest of the world was as moral as you."

"Ironic, isn't it?"

Reb nodded. "You have money and morals. A rare combination."

"That's not exactly what I was thinking."

"The day I know exactly what you were thinking, that will probably throw me clear off balance."

"It certainly has that effect on me."

"So, we've decided on Kansas?"

"If you want Colorado, we'll find a lawyer to make that possible. If you want France, we'll find a way to make that possible."

"Gee, think of all the money we'll save on shipping!" Reb teased.

Mitch laughed. "Maybe we should postpone shopping until we decide where we really want to live."

"We never really have done that, have we? We've always gone where we were needed and never really put down roots. It will be nice to finally settle down somewhere."

"Imagine how that will be," Mitch exhaled. "You and me settled down somewhere with a house and a child and a garden."

"You sound like you're becoming much more comfortable with the idea of being a mother."

"I think time is helping me with that. I think of Trish and all she's gone through and it makes my life look so much easier by comparison."

Reb simply nodded. Mitch was telling the truth about a situation that hadn't been easy for either of them to discuss.

"Have you won all the money you had planned to win here?" Reb changed the subject even though she would have changed it no matter what they had been discussing.

"Are you all done soaking up the Mediterranean sun?"

"I don't want to rush you, but if you want to see all the sights of France, we'll need to keep to some semblance of a schedule."

"Which logically means that we should go back to our Paris suite and regroup."

"Do you want to leave right this minute?" Reb was used to checking in with Mitch's impetuous nature.

"I'm sure that we can wait until the morning to leave."

"Which means that I'll just have to put up with one more incredibly romantic night on the Cote d Azure."

"Think you can manage it?" Mitch smiled.

Reb smiled back. She was sure she could.

Mitch was starving the next morning. Blaming Reb was half the fun. Eating a huge breakfast was the other half. Mitch remembered hearing about the Continental Plan when she was a kid. It sounded like a plot for world domination to her typical American kid's ears. Later, when she learned that it was a big fancy term for coffee and donuts, the phrase lost its luster. Not that she had anything against coffee and donuts. In fact, quite the opposite was the case. Usually. Except now, she had a plate of bacon and eggs in front of her. It had been okay to be a vegan

150

for the six or seven minutes that she had adhered to the strict
regime. She absolutely one-hundred percent admired and
respected people who were vegan. Now—where were those
hash browns? And toast? Yes, with butter.
"I guess they needed several trips from the kitchen to bring out
your entire order?" Reb observed as she peered over her oatmeal.
"Are you going to use all that brown sugar?" Mitch asked,
impervious to the sarcasm.
"Why?"
"I thought I'd pack it in my belly button and save it for later. For
a snack."
Reb observed Mitch. There were times when she couldn't tell if
she was kidding or serious. Mitch's expression was deadpan.
Was it residual behavior stemming from the discovery of the
love poem? Or had Reb simply hit a nerve concerning Mitch's
dietary habits. Reb didn't mean to sound sarcastic, but from time
to time, the inflection crept into her voice like an unwanted
guest.
"I'm glad to see you're eating," Reb followed up with kindness in
her voice.
"It all sounded so good on the menu, I couldn't help myself."
"And that's okay," Reb had heard this before.
"How do you do it?"
"Do what?"
"How do you read about bacon and eggs and omelets and crepes
and all sorts of other culinary delights and then choose oatmeal.
Not that there's anything wrong with that. But we're in France."
"I'm planning to live to be a hundred."
"A hundred what?"
"Years!"
"You're going to eat oatmeal until you're a hundred years old?"
"What if somebody told you that you would actually live to be a
hundred if you ate oatmeal every day?"
"I'd say, 'Shoot me now.'"
"You don't want to live to be a hundred, then?"
"Not if it involved eating oatmeal every blessed day."
"Nobody ever lived to be a hundred eating blintzes on a regular
basis."

"Yeah, but they don't lie there on their deathbed wishing they had."

"You are being such a smart aleck."

"I'm not the one who brought up the discussion about food."

"Is this still all about the poem?"

It was quite a reach from oatmeal to Jacque. Mitch prognosticated, "I think he will be waiting for you when we get back to Paris."

"I suppose so. I assume he lives there, after all."

"What are you going to do?"

"I'm going to let him down easy."

"That won't work."

"Why not?"

"He's French."

"Your prejudice is showing."

"It's not prejudice. It's fact. French men pursue women. Especially beautiful women. Like you."

"You're beautiful, too."

"You're the one with the love poem in her pocket."

"Let's just go back to Paris and get this over with."

"You haven't eaten all your oatmeal."

"Are you going to finish that bacon?" Reb helped herself to what she could from across the table.

Dozing through the French countryside had become habit quickly. One day, when they didn't have a thousand obligations to keep, Mitch and Reb would return here and spend quality time looking with appreciative eyes at the same countryside that inspired the greatest artists in the world. Maybe she would even bring her easel next time. They were sluggish by the time they arrived back at the hotel. Mitch didn't honestly know how Reb could stand to be paralyzed in one position day after day without screaming a good deal of the time. The woman was a saint and Mitch gave her a bad time about oatmeal. She should be ashamed.

"We made it," Reb noticed the look on Mitch's face.

"It will feel good to be settled in again, at least for a day or two."

Reb only smiled. She would enjoy stretching out on the bed while Mitch did a thorough body search for pressure points. Reb had never developed a pressure sore. Mitch had enjoyed body search duty way too much for that to happen. All they needed was a few quiet moments. As Mitch opened the door to the suite, hope for that precious time alone evaporated. This wasn't careless maid service. The room had been, as the film-noir cult would say, tossed. Systematically, thoroughly tossed. Upside down by the look of things. Reb was incensed. This sort of thing triggered deep anger in her. Mitch, on the flip side, was relieved that they weren't there at the time.

"Makes me look neat by comparison," Mitch remarked calmly. "Call the police!"

"Right, let's see, would that be the gendarme?"

"Let's go right to the top. Phone the Surete."

"Do you think we should?" Mitch wondered, as she usually did, if it would be just too big of a bother to involve the authorities, whatever they were called here.

"Of course I do!" Reb was angry. Really angry.

"Maybe we should start with the hotel management. Or maybe just look around and see if there's really anything to report."

"If you do that, you're going to disturb evidence."

"It's a burglary, not a homicide."

"So what! Somebody needs to get murdered before you take a crime seriously?"

"I am taking this seriously. I'm just not..." Mitch stopped talking. Too late.

"Just not what? Overreacting? That's what you were going to say. You think I'm overreacting!"

"I didn't say that."

"You didn't have to! It's clear that I'm the only one who is willing to take action."

With that declaration, Reb wheeled over to the phone and called the hotel operator. It seemed like a compromise to Mitch. Contact the hotel personnel and have them decide how best to handle this. No hotel wants a bad reputation, but neither could they choose to ignore the problem. Either choice was bad. What, Mitch wondered to herself, would be worse? She should have known better than to challenge the Universe. Within moments, they were inundated by people. Hotel people, police people, snoopy people. So much for a quiet evening in Paris.

153

Right off the bat, Mitch and Reb were separated, presumably before they could get their stories straight. The questions went on and on. Mitch did her best to answer, but in the back of her mind, she thought this was absolutely ridiculous. This was a simple burglary by folks who knew that they had ample time to complete their task. It was then that the notion dawned on Mitch. Who knew that they would be gone long enough to do such a thorough job and why wasn't anything missing? The detective, or whatever they called them here in France, saw her change of expression. He was sharp.

"You've remembered something?"

Mitch could lie and end up in a French jail until she rotted, or she could tell the truth. She phrased her musing carefully. "They took a lot of time, didn't they?"

"They knew you would not be here," he followed up.

Mitch nodded, "I guess?"

"We will continue talking in the offices of the Surete," he gave the bad news graciously.

"Do you really think that's necessary?" Mitch strained to appear nonchalant. That was a French word, correct? Nonchalant. Like something Maurice Chevalier would say. Anyway, was she a suspect or something? What was really going on here? No police force would ever be this incompetent. Questioning the victim of the crime didn't make sense to Mitch. But she didn't complain or put up a fuss. She was formally escorted to the hotel hallway and then taken downstairs to a waiting car. Reb was nowhere in sight. This was going from bad to worse in an out-of-control way that gave Mitch a cold feeling in the pit of her stomach. Small voices in her head told her to bolt. To run as fast and as far as she could without looking back. For the first time in her life, she understood how someone who was innocent of a crime was tempted to run away. You heard it all the time in the movies. "Please tell the court why you ran away if you were innocent?" Mitch now knew the why of it. Instinct. But she stayed. She stayed for Reb.

The ride to the station was quiet. Mitch wasn't about to blab and give possible evidence by accident. Once at headquarters, she was put in a room all by herself for a long time. It was like Las Vegas in that there weren't any clocks. That was the only resemblance. No clocks. Not much of anything comfortable to sit on. It wasn't gritty dirty or anything like that. But it was hard and cold and you wouldn't want to eat off the floor. No phone call. No visitors. No birds like Alcatraz. What a vacation this was turning into. Finally, after Mitch had felt sleepy enough to doze off for two seconds, a person appeared. Perhaps this was the sleep-deprivation part of the interrogation. This person, without a word, escorted Mitch to another equally-depressing room somewhere down a maze of hallways. Even if she entertained thoughts of escape, she would have no idea which way to go. Shortly after she was seated at a table, a man appeared.

"Mrs. Tanner?" he inquired.

"Close enough," Mitch answered back. She could have corrected the part about being a Mrs. Except that she had the feeling that he may have already figured that mistake out by himself. Mitch had the distinct impression that, in fact, he already knew a whole lot about her.

"Would you like to go over again your statement?" he said. It really wasn't a question. Mitch knew that. He knew that. They were going to go over the statement again.

"I would very much enjoy doing that," she replied. She had lost count of how many times she had gone over this, both out loud and to herself. The nagging question, "What was really going on here?" survived every iteration. Mitch could have asked him that right now, and be considered disorderly. OR she could fully cooperate and hope to be informed. The man, meanwhile, had raised an eyebrow at her polite offer.

"Most of the time, your kind are screaming for their embassies by now."

Mitch assumed that by "your kind", he merely meant American. Nothing else made sense to her.

"I'm not a screamer."

"That will be good news for my ears. Let us hear, once again, your *version*."

He made "version" sound like the linguistic equivalent of "lie". Mitch ignored the inflection. She recounted her memories of the discovery of the room in shambles. It was a pitifully short story. He nodded, not even taking notes. Everything was being listened to by others, recorded somewhere.

"Tell me about the events before then?"

"I don't understand?" Mitch said. What did he want to hear about? The ride up to the room in the elevator? Or maybe her first Christmas? The question was so broadly phrased that it was now a fishing expedition. Mitch knew better than to carelessly offer extraneous details.

"Of course, you don't *have* to answer my questions."

Mitch studied the man. He was serious. Not a kidding bone in his body.

"I would be happy to answer if I knew what you were asking," Mitch smiled. She wasn't about to be painted into the corner with other hostile witnesses.

"It isn't like an American to be dissatisfied with a very expensive hotel."

"That's not a question, is it?"

"You refused to have a maid."

"We were taking a trip to Monte Carlo. We didn't need maid service for those days."

"Is that the only reason?" he asked like he already knew the answer again. It was a transparent ploy. Maybe Mitch should enroll in the police academy when she got back to the states. Even she could do this line of questioning. It was obvious that they had been asking Reb the same questions. Had they found her to be more talkative? Maybe she was the one loudly requesting the American Ambassador? Now that made sense.

"After we returned from a short trip to Giverny, some of the things in our room had been rearranged."

"See now, it isn't so hard to tell the truth," he spoke like a chiding parent.

Mitch pondered how much training interrogators went through in order to quickly find the best and fastest way to irritate people. To Mitch's surprise, he had suddenly and effortlessly angered her. He inferred that she had a hard time telling the truth when, in fact, she had been nothing but truthful and cooperative since she had been unceremoniously perp-marched down here. She tamped down her mood and continued, "I didn't realize that you wanted every detail. I will begin at the beginning. I came to Paris to shop for baby clothes." If he wanted the whole truth, by gum, he was going to get the back story as well. It was his turn now to mask his reaction. Mitch watched in amusement. He was trying to figure out who was pregnant, Mitch or Reb. He hadn't jumped yet to the realization that it might have been someone else entirely. Mitch figured that his best guess would have been her, since she was the larger of the two women and the one not in a wheelchair.

"I don't care about baby clothes," he replied gruffly.

"So, you can now understand my dilemma!" Mitch made her point with a smile.

"What?"

"I'm not psychic. I don't know what details you are interested in and which you aren't interested in."

"I'm interested in anything that sounds suspicious."

"And two women buying baby clothes isn't suspicious?" Mitch asked.

"Not at my house," he countered. So, he had a sense of humor after all.

"Except, that we haven't bought any yet. This is beginning to sound suspicious, even to me!" Mitch sounded gravely serious in a mocking sort of way.

Without notice, he got up and left the room. Mitch wasn't worried. In fact, she made a cradle out of her arms and rested her head on the table. She slept the sleep of the innocent. It was sweet but short. He was back, banging doors and tossing file folders on the table. Mitch guessed that he had asked Reb, or maybe whomever was questioning Reb down the hall, about the baby clothes. The story had matched. He was not amused. Nor satisfied.

"So, you came to France just to buy baby clothes?"

"And furniture," Mitch added. Just for accuracy. Eight minutes worth of sleep had helped her memory.

"Furniture?"

"Baby furniture. Sears just didn't have a wide-enough selection."

"Seurs?"

"It's big in Kansas."

157

"But not big enough for you?"

"Sears or Kansas?"

"What?"

"Seriously, you want the truth?"

"Truth is good."

"I wanted an excuse to visit Paris. Why buy a run-of-the-mill crib in the United States when you could buy a really, really nice one at Prin Temps for ten times the money. Plus shipping?"

"And you wonder why we call you Ugly Americans?"

Apparently, he couldn't afford to shop at Prin Temps on a cop's salary. Mitch wondered if he heard about this fact all the time at home.

"Tell me again why you refused maid service."

"Some of our things had been rearranged while we were out."

"And naturally, you accused the hotel staff?"

"I didn't accuse anybody of anything. I requested no maid service because we were going away for a couple of days and didn't need a maid. I don't have a maid at home."

"You can afford to shop for a baby crib in Paris, but you don't have a maid?"

"I'm used to hard work. Not every American is ugly."

"Who do you think robbed your room?"

"I'm not sure anything is missing, so technically, it's not a robbery, is it?"

"Who do you think rearranged your room, and why?"

"Somebody was probably looking for something valuable enough to steal."

"And what would that be?"

Mitch gave this question serious contemplation. She and her cop friend had bonded. Sort of. Not in a friendship sort of way. It would never be a barbecue-in-the-backyard kind of friendship. But they had a mutual goal. They were both on the same side in the struggle of good against evil.

"I'm really not a jewelry sort of person and money wasn't in the room. No furs. No nothing, really. So what else do people steal?"

"People steal many things. Have you enjoyed your stay in France?" he asked out of the blue.

Mitch felt the hair on her neck go prickly. He was a cop, not a travel agent.

"It's been lovely until now. The room-tossing, I mean."

"Is visiting Paris different than visiting anywhere else?"

"Well, there is the language difference," Mitch answered lamely.

"And the French people?" he continued on this thread.

"What about them?" Mitch asked back, all those warm and fuzzy bonding feelings were skittering away.

"Have you been treated well by our citizens?"

Mitch knew he was going somewhere very specific with all these general questions.

"Can you just ask me what you want to know?" Mitch wanted to cut to the chase. He shifted in his chair. Maybe Mitch had a future in this business after all. She was perhaps forcing him to be on his guard.

"A woman like yourself doesn't often accept the advances of a man."

This short sentence said a lot.

"I don't actively seek men out. I try to be understanding when they seek me out."

"And when they seek out your friend?"

"My friend?"

"Mrs. Fairbanks."

Mitch now knew where the conversation was heading. Did the police think that Jacque turned their room upside down? That didn't make sense. He had wanted to go with them to the Riviera.

"It seems as though you and your friend made the acquaintance of a man pretty quickly in Paris?"

He made it sounds like a threesome. What did the French call such things? A menage a trios?

"You have an overactive imagination," Mitch held her indignation in control, but so much for ever inviting this cop to a party.

"A policeman's life is not easy. We must examine all possibilities."

"Neither myself nor my friend slept with Jock."

"That was his name?"

"That's what he told us."

"I'm not suggesting that *you* slept with him."

"What exactly are you suggesting?"

He shrugged his shoulders and stood up. He left the room. Again. Mitch pondered the possibility of squeezing in another catnap. How long would it take him to confirm the fact that Reb hadn't slept with Jacque either? Probably not long enough to get any decent sleep. Did they suspect Jacque of the robbery? For them, it would make sense. It made more sense than suspecting Mitch of anything. How goofy was this getting.

The door opened again. Her friend was back. He was grim.

"You look like you have news?" Mitch speculated.

"We are moving you."

Moving wasn't the same as releasing. Moving never sounded so ominous.

"To where?"

"Just to another room."

"Bigger or smaller?" Mitch would have a hard time believing there was a smaller room to be in around here, except, of course, for the obvious answer. A cell for one.

He looked around like he was in real estate. "About the same size."

"With or without bars?"

"Without, so far."

Mitch stood up and, under heavy guard like she was considered a flight risk, was escorted from one room to another. She didn't see anything of Reb or for that matter, Jacque, during her journey. This room was bigger and nicer. He had been fooling her. What a jokester! The room was spacious compared to the other one and it even had a coffee pot. They could camp out here for quite a while if there was to be coffee. Hopefully they would brew a pot. It would be nice. Mitch was now either blessed or cursed with constant company. Armed constant company. She asked why. No answer. So much for chatting away the time. This new guard meant business. It was a big gun. Mitch's detective friend hadn't stayed with them. He was off doing Lord knows what.

"Coffee O Lay?" she asked.

No answer.

She thought about asking for a cigarette and a blindfold, but the humor would be lost in translation. Her French just wasn't that good. The door opened and in strode a man in a regular suit followed by Mitch's detective. Looks were exchanged and then Mitch and regular suit were left alone.

"Ms. Tanner, I'm Joseph Delaney. I see they moved you to an upscale room," he smiled.

"Nice to meet you. Are you another French detective?"

"No, Ma'am. I'm from the American Embassy."

"Really?" Mitch was surprised.

"Does this catch you off guard?"

"Well, I'm grateful that you are here, but isn't that just a bit overkill?"

"A strange choice of vocabulary for a person in your situation, wouldn't you say?"

This made no sense to Mitch. Hopefully, all would be cleared up and the sooner the better.

"Do you know why I'm here?" Mitch asked.

"You are suspected of murder. You didn't know?"

"Murder?" Mitch repeated.

"That's correct."

"Who's dead?" Mitch was truly taken aback by the news.

Mr. Delaney studied Mitch. He was one of those people who had an innate lie detector tucked away in his brain. "You have no idea who is dead? What have you and the police been discussing?"

"Baby furniture. Seriously, I have no idea about a murder."

"Sounds to me like you are innocent."

"Who was I supposed to have killed?" Mitch was determined to ask the question in whatever form came out of her mouth until she got an answer.

"One Mr. Jacque Delort."

"Jock? The nice fellow who bought us lunch?"

"Precisely."

"Is Reb okay?"

"Reb?"

"Rebecca. Fairbanks."

"Senator Fairbanks is well."

"Where is she?"

"She's fine."

"Is she under suspicion as well?"

"Not that I'm aware."

Mitch was relieved but puzzled. It showed on her face.

"The alleged motive is jealousy," he explained.

Mitch could only shake her head. This was preposterous. "How did he die?"

"You really don't know?"

"Of course not!" Mitch felt her deep composure beginning to crack. A small fissure.

"I'm not going to go into a lot of detail at this time."

"They haven't told you everything either, have they?"

"My priority is to arrange for your defense, if necessary, and to assist you and Senator Fairbanks in any way that I am allowed to."

"Rebecca needs her rest and a lot more assistance than I could possibly need. Take care of her first, please?"

"I'll do my best. In the meantime, as they say in the movies, sit tight."

"Thank you for everything."

After he left, Mitch didn't feel so brave. A burglary was one thing. Murder was quite another. This wasn't something that she could just joke her way out of. Her detective reappeared. He didn't look like he was having the best day of his life either.

"Did my ambassador give you a talking to?" Mitch sounded sympathetic.

"He's not trying to solve a murder."

"Few people carry that burden. I'm glad you take your job seriously."

"You might not feel that way in a moment."

"Is the real tough interrogation going to begin now?" Mitch asked in all seriousness. She wanted to know what she was up against.

"I need to show you something," he said with just a hint of a grimace. With that condensed introduction, he spread several glossy bright garish photos across the table. It was Jacque. Or, more precisely, what was left of Jacque. Mitch only had to glance before the horror of it all hit her square in the gut.

Clamminess and nausea hit as the same time as what little contents of her stomach lurched upward and all over the floor.
"I assume this means that you recognize Mr. Delort," the detective seemed unfazed by what had occurred across the table. Mitch wasn't the first and would not be the last to be sick in this room.
"I would be throwing up no matter who was in these pictures, but yes, that is Jock."
"It wasn't a simple killing."
"It was a slaughter by the looks of it."
"You're a woman."
"Yes," Mitch nodded.
"Mr. Delort was a young, tall, strong specimen of a man." Mitch nodded. Her head ached and her throat burned from the expelled stomach acid. The detective got some water for her to drink and gave her a moment to collect herself.
"Do you work out? Lift weights?" he asked.
"I used to, but not for a long time."
"Still, it takes a lot of strength to be an aide to Mrs. Fairbanks, doesn't it?"
"I can lift a wheelchair into the trunk of a car. I'm not going to be crowned Ms. Bodybuilder anytime soon."
"But you were jealous of the attention he gave to your companion. This certainly could look like a crime of passion to me."
"Well, I hate to be a stickler for details, but first, I wasn't at all jealous and, second, what other evidence do you have against me?"
"I don't need evidence to hold you as a person of interest in the case."
"I suppose so. But it's you who will need to explain that to the ambassador. I don't envy you."
The detective smiled a rare smile. He had done this before.

Mitch was left alone again. Time ticked away as she reflected on the lost evening. They couldn't possibly hold Reb for too much longer. Maybe she would be Mitch's first official visitor when she was locked up forever in this French prison. The door opened again and her detective was back. This was getting old.

"What's the verdict?" Mitch asked calmly. Calm enough for a person with puke all over her shoes.

"Many Americans have a very bad view of the French. I can live with that. However, I can't live with murder. So, I'm going to have you detained."

Mitch allowed this to sink in. She knew she hadn't murdered Jock. Her instinct told her that the detective believed in her innocence as well. "Are you locking me up for my own protection?"

He tried not to smile. "It would be wise to whittle down the suspect list. If someone else is murdered in this same way, we may suppose that you are innocent."

The logic of the argument was spot on, but still very scary. How long would she be sitting around in jail waiting for another murder to take place? She tried not to think about this and instead asked, "What about Mrs. Fairbanks? Will she be in custody as well?"

"She is being taken care of."

Mitch didn't know if being taken care of and being in jail meant the same thing, but she said, "Thank you for that." She had a gut feeling that the right thing was being done.

"So, now, you will be escorted to your temporary cubicle."

What they called a cubicle in France was still just a very dreary cell as far as Mitch could tell. Not the best, but certainly not the worst. She was alone, perhaps on suicide watch? At least it was quiet. She stretched out on what passed for a bed. It wasn't at all like the bed she had left behind at the hotel. In fact, it wasn't like any bed she had ever left behind. Its only purpose was to take a body from vertical to horizontal. Which, at this point, felt pretty good. Were they really going to hold her here until another person was murdered? How long could that possibly take? And the murder would also need to be just like the murder of Jock. The images floated back to her and a wave of nausea returned.

"You don't look so good."

Mitch looked in the direction of the sympathetic voice. Reb looked great.

"Where have they been keeping you? The Ritz?" Mitch sat up and the nausea subsided.

"Are you okay?" Reb asked her own question in reply.

"Yeah, I'm okay. I suppose everything we say and do is monitored."

"I'm sure it is. But since we haven't done anything wrong, we haven't anything to worry about."

"Sounds good on paper, but I could still be stuck here for the duration of our shopping spree."

"I'm right here."

"Except that they don't suspect you of murder."

"They don't suspect you, either."

"Yes they do. They don't suspect you because they don't think that someone in a wheelchair could commit that kind of murder."

"What kind of murder?" Reb asked, ignoring for now the remark about the wheelchair.

Mitch looked at Reb. What did she know? What didn't she know? What kind of game were the police playing?

"Why don't you tell me how your time has been spent since you were taken from the hotel."

"I just left the hotel to come here."

"By yourself?"

"Of course not. I was escorted by the police. Somebody had to drive the squad car."

"So, all this time, you've been at the hotel?"

"Yes, and it's not the Ritz. It's the George, remember?"

"You've been in the hotel suite all this time?"

"Yes."

"And I've been down here at police headquarters getting grilled like yesterday's dead tuna."

"Oh, for goodness sake, don't make it sound so dramatic. You don't look bruised or anything."

"If that's a pep talk, you need to polish your presentation."

"Come over here," Reb said quietly.

Mitch hesitated. She knew that she smelled. Terrible, probably. No matter how you try and clean up after an incident of the tummy, you never really smell okay until after a bath. Or three. That's why she had remained on the cot so far. But now, she couldn't resist the invitation. She went over to where Reb was. Reb held out her hand and Mitch took hold a bit too forcefully, like it was her only lifeline out of here.

"Your hand is telling my hand that you're scared."

"Number One Suspects have a right to be scared."

"Didn't you meet with the ambassador?"

"Yes."

"You can thank me later."

The image of Reb loudly insisting for him coaxed a smile out of Mitch. "Thank you."

"You're welcome. Now, just exactly why are you still so worried?"

"Because...I'm still on the wrong side of these bars."

"So, how were you supposed to have killed Jacque?"

She really had been telling the truth, Mitch thought to herself. She doesn't know how he was killed. She hadn't seen the glossies of the mutilated remains of him. That pesky nausea returned. Mitch had always thought that intestinal fortitude was an abstract concept. Until now.

"What is wrong with you? You look as weak and pale as skim milk."

"I haven't had anything to eat. I regret not putting that brown sugar in my navel."

"What are they trying to do, starve a confession out of you?"

"Nothing else worked," Mitch smiled weakly.

"You poor thing. I'll arrange some food for you before I leave."

"Where are you going?"

"I'm supposed to remain in some sort of informal custody. Honestly, how far am I going to run in a wheelchair!"

"You got all the way to Paris."

"I had help. Do you need anything else?" Reb checked her watch. There must have been a preset time limit.

Images of Jock's body returned to Mitch's mind. "Yes. Ask them to double your guard. Triple it if you can talk them into it."

"Why? Oh, I get it. You don't want me to leave France without you."

"No," Mitch tried to sound light-hearted, "I just don't want you to sneak out on any shopping trips without me."

"I have to go."

"Come and see me tomorrow?"

"Of course I will."

And then, she was gone. Mitch reclined again. So, she really was the prime suspect. Obviously. Because Reb hadn't been questioned or shown the photos of Jock's body. Mitch, not normally a very religious person, said a quiet prayer for him now. She didn't get on her knees to do so, hoping that the merciful God would forgive her weakness of the flesh. When you are in prison and pray for others, God can't help but cut you some slack, right? Mitch worried about Reb until she dozed off. She slept well. Apparently, God did work miracles in prison. Now, upon awakening, Mitch desperately needed a loaves and fishes sort of miracle. After addressing her human needs, a bowl of porridge arrived. Oh boy! Reb arranged for oatmeal. It was cold like it had sat around quite a while in the kitchen and there was no sugar or cream or anything else other than a paper cup full of water. Wasn't there some long-standing admonition about drinking the water in France? Or in prison, for that matter? Perhaps the prison kitchen staff couldn't decide between themselves which wine went best with gruel. Still, it was better than starvation. Barely. Since every meal in France is considered to be sacramental, Mitch was allowed the courtesy of ingesting breakfast before things got rolling.

She was escorted, again under heavy guard, to the interrogation room. The one with the coffee pot. It was full and smelled like heaven on earth. Would they try to extract a confession via coffee temptation? That tactic would have had the most success, Mitch decided as she inhaled deeply. Then, quite unexpectedly, a cup was placed in front of her and no one stopped her from taking a sip. It was hot and good and felt like oil to her creaking body. One day, she would form better habits. Today wasn't going to be that day. Her detective friend appeared, looking as every bit creaky and disheveled as Mitch felt. Apparently, between the two of them, she had gotten the better night's sleep. "There's been another murder," he grumbled without preamble. Mitch felt her body jolt. It could have been good news in that it should serve to vindicate Mitch. It was bad news because a fellow citizen of the Earth was no longer living. And it would be catastrophic news if somehow Reb was involved. For a moment, there wasn't enough oxygen in the room and Mitch gripped the table to keep contact with something firm while her mind whirled.

"I must show you some more pictures."

Mitch heard what she thought was regret in his voice. This wasn't going to be good. Already her stomach was once again on the point of eruption. He sensed this and moved the trash can within easy reach. Then, when Mitch saw that he was ready to once again cover the table with photos, she closed her eyes. Time ticked by.

Mitch knew that at some point, she would need to open her eyes. She couldn't live the rest of her life with her eyes shut. Some people did. Some did literally. Some did figuratively. She gave this due consideration. Actually, she was stalling. Her stomach was creeping closer and closer to the edge of oblivion. Mitch took a deep breath. It felt good. She took a couple more. Then, she forced her eyes to open. It was the same sensation as trying to open your eyes underwater or trying to wake up from a too-deep sleep. Her eyes darted to avoid looking at the pictures on the table. She looked right, then left, up for a second and then stole a furtive glance at the edge of the photo on her left. Slowly, as her vision settled on the entirety of the picture, her stomach unclenched. As if to retain her anguish, her fist clenched and she resisted with all the will in her body and mind and spirit the urge to punch her detective friend square in his French nose. He noticed her effort and did not goad her but simply sat still. So did Mitch. The last thing Mitch needed right now was an extension of her time here. Days would turn into weeks if she took a swing at him.

"Are you upset?" he asked.

"You knew all along this wasn't Rebecca."

"I never led you to believe it was."

"You should treat innocent people better."

"And I will. You may go just as soon as you tell me about this dead body," he pushed the photos closer to Mitch.

She started to breathe deeply again. This was an experience that she was unprepared for. Nowhere in her life had she ever had to look at the photos of murdered people. She had seen dead bodies. Most grown adults have seen a dead body. At a funeral, most likely. Where dead bodies were supposed to be. And we all looked upon them and stated that they look so good for being dead. But not this. Not this horrible mistreatment of a human being. Certainly, no one was perfect in this life, but no one deserved to be treated like this. And since no one did deserve this, she would do what she could to bring the perpetrator to justice. She looked at the photos with what she hoped could be a more forensic eye. Who was this guy? That was the first thing that she had noticed that had alleviated her panic about Reb being the victim. This was a man. Another man. First, it was Jock, the love poet. And now, this fellow. Who was he? He looked familiar. It was the driver, it finally dawned on Mitch. De Gaulle. What were the odds of that? Two French men who had contact with Mitch and Reb were now dead. It made sense that Mitch was a suspect, and Reb to a lesser degree. For all the police knew, they were a two-woman killing spree. Except that they weren't.

"He was the chauffeur."

"So you know him after all?"

"Only because he drove us around."

"And did he write any love poems to your girlfriend?"

Mitch met his steely gaze. "You would have to ask her."

"I already have."

"Well, did he?" Mitch asked point blank.

"Once I have your answer, we can compare notes."

"I'm not aware of anything."

"From the chauffeur?"

"Right."

"And so Mr. Delort was the only poet that's now dead."

"There was a poem from him," Mitch nodded. Reb must have told them all about it.

"To you?"

"No. Just to the Senator."

"So, a dead man wrote some sort of love poem to your girlfriend and now we have another dead man and no love poem from him."

If Mitch lived to be a hundred, in which case probably no one would comment about how good she looked dead, she would never understand the military mind. It had a logic, or more fitting, an illogic all its own.

"Would you feel better if there were two poems?"

"I would have felt better if you or your girlfriend had been more forthcoming about the first poem."

"Perhaps she felt it was none of your business?"

"Everything is my business when there has been a murder!" he showed a sudden and intense temper. Had Mitch been a few years younger, she might have been intimidated. Now, she was simply bored and anxious to see Reb.

"Are you a man of your word?" she asked calmly.

He didn't answer, fearing a logic trap. Mitch tried a simpler approach, "Can I go now?"

Her request was met by silence. She could only guess at the unspoken meaning. Her short time at the mercy of the French justice system had brought home the realization that nobody got in a big hurry around here. She counted her blessings. The oatmeal wasn't anything to write home about, but it was tolerable. She had been here only overnight. People had been held in foreign prisons for lifetimes in horrific conditions. The worst part for Mitch so far had been the mistaken impression that Reb had been killed. The next worst part was the dried vomit on her shoes.

"We have no reason to keep you here," he answered.

Mitch studied him closely. He looked more like a father figure now. "You are concerned about something?"

"People are dying all around you. You are the one who needs to be concerned."

"I take your concern to heart. Can I go?"

"Your escort will be here soon."

"My escort?"

He didn't elaborate before he took his leave. At least he left the wastebasket behind. Mitch hoped she didn't look as bad as she felt. Before she had enough time to decide whether or not she really needed to use the wastebasket again, the door opened up and Reb wheeled in. Mitch felt immediately better.

"You ready to go?" Reb was all business.

"We can do that?"

"Unless you want to stay for lunch?"

Talking about food wasn't exactly helping right this minute. Mitch thought it best that she not go into detail about what exactly happened with her shoes. Instead, she slipped them off and deposited them in the trash. It came in handy after all. They went down the hallway to sign some significant paperwork. It wasn't her imagination that she felt a hulking presence behind her. Some big guy, roughly the shape of a human cube with legs was hovering. At least, as much as one could hover being that size and dimension. As they made their way out of the police station, the hulk followed. Mitch looked over at Reb. "Is he with you?"

"He's with us," Reb corrected mildly.

Mitch slowed down. He slowed down. Reb slowed down. Then, Mr. Cube started talking into his wrist, which was actually the coolest thing he had done so far.

"Who are you talking to? Who is he talking to?"

He didn't answer, but stood patiently, watchfully, on the balls of his feet, waiting for something to happen. Anything from walking to taking a bullet to further conversations with his wrist seemed to be in his repertoire. Reb spoke up in that soothing tone of voice, "If we don't start moving, the second one is going to show up."

"The second one what?" Mitch asked.

Reb didn't get the chance to answer. Cube Two showed up out of nowhere and imposed himself at Mitch's other flank. Flank was one of those military terms, unless you were talking about steak. If one more showed up, all the oxygen would be sucked out of the area and Mitch would faint dead away.

"How come they're not surrounding you?" Mitch asked Reb.

"I'm wearing a bullet-proof vest. We had thought about putting one on you before we left the building, but I thought it might freak you out."

"And this wouldn't?" Mitch gestured to the bodyguards.

"You can put a vest on when we get to the limo."

"I'd settle for a new pair of shoes."

Cube One started talking into his wrist again and since he could've just talked to Cube Two straight away, Mitch surmised that there was another Cube lurking in the vicinity. She was correct. Cube Three came with gifts. It was like the nativity

171

scene without Jesus. He had a bullet-proof vest and a drawn gun. At least it wasn't pointed at her, the gun, that is. At least, not yet. Maybe she was going to be forced at gunpoint to put this rather ugly vest on.

"Is this new or has a famous person worn it previously?" Mitch wanted to know. She had never worn hand-me-downs, being an only child, and wasn't about to start now.

"Just drape it over your shoulders until we get to the car, okay?" Reb asked nice.

Mitch looked around. She wondered if this was what reality really looked like to Picasso. She was surrounded by human cubes upon release from a jarring jail experience. It all felt surreal.

"Just this once, do exactly what I'm asking you to do," Reb's voice brought Mitch back to the moment. She slipped into the vest and walked within the boundaries of her bodyguards to a really heavy-duty limo.

"It sure looks bullet proof," Mitch said to anyone listening.

"It's bullet resistant, able to withstand IED explosions and hand-held rocket launchers and chemical attacks."

"What are we going to do, recreate the battle at the Maginot Line?"

"We're going to stay alive," Reb answered curtly.

They were all tucked safe and sound into the limo before Mitch resumed conversation.

"You seem on edge," she said quietly.

"I've seen too many pictures of murdered men to be cavalier," Reb replied

So, she had seen the photos.

"I'm not being cavalier. I just feel a little bit pounced upon."

Reb looked over at Mitch. Incarceration hadn't been kind. It rarely was. "I'm just doing what I think is best for you."

"I believe you. I'm just not used to this bodyguard stuff."

"Trish deals with it all the time."

"Yeah. Well, okay. So are we going to be surrounded by these guys for the rest of our lives?"

"At least until we leave the country."

"We're leaving the country?"

"You want to stay? After two dead bodies and a night in a French jail?"

"There were some good times, too," Mitch sounded like she was lamenting the end of a relationship.

"I'm leaving as soon as possible. You can stay as long as you want."

It dawned on Mitch that Reb was lining up a jet. "Is that okay with the authorities?"

"I used to be a Senator. Yes, it's okay."

An abrupt halt to the conversation came with an equally abrupt halting of the car.

"Are we under attack?" Mitch asked.

"No. We're at the safe house."

"The what house?"

"You heard me. Safe. House. Get out of the car."

Mitch decided to follow orders and put off arguing until later. They entered a small damp-smelling room that would make any fallout shelter look like a luxury resort. Which was where Mitch wished she was right about now. The fact that their suitcases were stashed in one corner of this four-corner dungeon didn't give hope for a quick release. There were a couple of chairs, a table, and a bed that resembled something out of Supermax, the famous Federal prison in southern Colorado.

"Did you spend the night here?"

"No. I spent the night with the French police."

"I know the feeling. I'm still surprised we have permission to leave the country."

"You keep forgetting that I'm someone important."

Mitch forgot a lot of things in her life, but she had never forgotten how important Reb was. And frankly, it didn't have anything to do with her title of Senator. It would be awkward to convey this to Reb in front of the Cubist trio.

"So," Mitch looked around again, "We're sleeping here?"

"We are holding here," Reb said as she glanced at the bed.

Mitch did more than glance. She actually went over to it and sat on its edge. It was all too close to the back-wrencher she had slept on last night.

"I've traded one prison for another."

"You're still alive. Stop grousing and get something clean to wear out of your suitcase. I hope you brought a spare pair of shoes."

"I didn't."

"Well, get changed then. The luggage needs to go to the airport."

"I'm not changing my clothes in front of the guys."

"I'll keep guard over that activity," Reb was all business. She was good in a crisis. Always had been.

"Uh huh," Mitch tried to sound as business-like as she could muster. It sounded fake.

"I did the best I could," Reb was now sounding just a tiny bit brittle around the edges. Like peanut candy.

"I know you did."

"I didn't know if or when you were going to be released and I didn't know how soon we would be given permission to leave and I *really* don't know how much danger we're in."

"Do I seem irritated with you?" Mitch had to ask.

"No. I'm sure that it's me who's irritated and I'm projecting up a storm," Reb said calmly and without sarcasm.

"Do you really think that we are the ones in danger?"

"Two dead men. Yes, I think we are in danger."

"Two dead men who may or may not have had anything in common with each other."

"The police think they may have had something in common."

"I'm the one in danger here. The police suspect me of killing some guy in a jealous fit over some badly-written love poem."

"I'm sure that by now they don't suspect that."

Mitch sat for a moment. "It's too bad that you don't have the poem anymore. Maybe it had some significance besides literary."

"I still have a copy the poem," Reb said matter-of-factly.

"You still have the poem?" Mitch couldn't believe it.

"I made a copy of it surreptitiously. The police have the original."

"Probably to check it for fingerprints or whatever," Mitch didn't know what all forensic techniques would be used on the paper. She knew the fingerprints would point to the both of them, but anything else would be exculpatory.

174

It felt good to be off the ten most wanted list, if they had such a thing in France. Things were looking up, except for the part about being holed up in a clammy dungeon. With no food in sight. And no shoes.

"I know you don't like being here," Reb got back to the immediate issue.

"The place is growing on me. In fact, I feel it taking root in my sinuses as we speak."

"They are supposed to let us know the minute the jet is ready and the flight plan is filed."

"I appreciate your effort. Wake me up when we can leave."

Mitch arranged her body on the concrete slab masquerading as a bed and closed her eyes. If she couldn't see the misery, she couldn't be miserable. Isn't it all that simple? She felt Reb settle in next to her and they rested together in detached fashion.

Mitch must have slept. She knew this only because one minute she felt marginal and the next she was wretched. The moldy underbelly of France wasn't agreeing with her.

"Are you awake?" Reb asked.

"How could you tell?"

"You stopped snoring."

"I feel like crap. What's the French word for that?"

"Merde?"

"Something like that," Mitch intoned, all sinus in reply.

"Are you getting sick?"

"I miss Kansas."

"You're sounding delirious. Are you running a fever?"

Reb felt Mitch's forehead with her left hand. Her touch felt good. It always did.

"You don't feel hot."

"Please, dear, not in front of the bodyguards."

"Are you ready to go?" Reb said flatly.

"Is the flight ready?"

"Yes."

"How long was I asleep?"

"About thirty minutes."

"It seemed longer."

"You slept deeply."

That was Reb's nice way of saying that the snoring was particularly obnoxious. They got up, both rather slowly, and were once again escorted to their vehicle. Mercifully, they were airborne within the hour. Mitch's sinuses were already feeling better. The trip to Paris hadn't exactly worked out as planned. There was no crib nor bassinet nor even baby booties stashed away in the cargo hold.

"What are you thinking?" Reb noticed Mitch's silence.

"Can we go to New York?"

"New York? Like, New York City or New York State?"

"Both?"

"Why?"

"We don't have anything for the baby."

"The baby's not born yet. I'm sure it won't know."

"You never know about babies. Babies know things."

"With everything else this baby has to consider, I'm pretty sure that our coming back empty handed from Paris is the least of its worries."

"But it isn't like New York is way out of our way. Hong Kong would be out of our way. If you draw a line from Paris to Kansas, New York is right on the way."

Reb was now the one who stayed silent for a moment. Mitch asked for so little. Shopping in New York didn't seem like such a lot to ask for. Besides, Mitch did need new shoes.

"You have to promise that you'll buy yourself some shoes."

"Is that a yes?" Mitch hoped.

"One of us should inform the pilot of the change in plans. We were refueling in Washington D.C."

It didn't cost too much extra to go up the coast a few miles. Heck, the plane fuel in New York was good enough for her. Philosophically speaking, it was more of a down payment considering the impending shopping spree. Something, Mitch admitted, she was finally getting good at.

Mitch had been to New York before. It wasn't like she was a total greenhorn. From past experience, she did know that the shopping here was pretty good. World class, in fact. This splurge wouldn't go on indefinitely, but she did want to return to Kansas with gifts for everyone. First things first, however. She

176

and Reb reserved a suite in a high-dollar hotel and spent enough time in the bathtub to feel human again. Prison grit, safe-house grime and generic dirt all soaked away down the drain. Mitch was downright wrinkly when she emerged from the bathroom wrapped in one of those inch-thick white robes. The kind where you could fall down in it and you didn't care if anyone came to pick you back up. At least, not for a few minutes. Even her sinuses responded well to all the steam.

"Feeling better?" Reb asked. She had arranged herself on the bed and was studying the room-service menu. In her robe. What a sight.

"Absolutely!"

"You want a $15 cup of coffee?" she asked with a straight face.

"I don't think my stomach is quite ready for that."

"Come over here and tell me about your stomach."

Mitch joined her on the bed. "This feels good."

"Are you hungry?"

"I'm worried, actually."

"About?"

"Look at me. I spend a couple dozen hours in jail and I'm a wreck. I'm worried about Miranda."

"You always worry about Miranda."

"But now that I've been in jail overnight, I can't imagine how people do it. Add that to my amazement as to how a woman endures pregnancy, and I'm now really concerned as to how Miranda is coping with both."

"That's an eloquent statement."

"And there's no good solution."

"Miranda will just need to hang in there."

"I wish I could buy her something or do something nice for her. Are pregnant women treated differently in prison?"

"I could look into it for you."

"That would be nice."

"I'm a nice person."

"Yes, you are."

Mitch blinked her eyes a couple of times. It felt good to close them. The bed was soft. The room was quiet. She was warm and asleep before her stomach could complain about being neglected.

Chapter 7

Mary was so tired. Her eyes felt like they would never again fit
correctly in their sockets. She had heard of churning before.
Even felt it from time to time. For instance, right now. In her
stomach. Mary had been at work early and, almost in a daze, had
left the office about the time that others were gathering around
the coffee pot for their first pick-me-up of the day. She wanted
coffee herself, but didn't want to hang out with the group. She
couldn't trust her eyes. She felt, rightly or wrongly, that she
wouldn't be able to make eye contact without having a suspicious
look. And the last thing she wanted to do right this minute was
to falsely accuse, or perhaps more importantly, tip her hand. So,
without announcement, she left the office and got in her car and
drove to a tony shopping district about five miles away from her
downtown office. Most of the shops were still shuttered from the
night before, but a gourmet coffee house was open and bustling
with activity. Complex coffee orders and croissants changed
hands after serious coin was plunked on the counter. In
Wyoming, you could buy a whole plate full of food for the price
of one bakery item here. And get all the coffee refills your
bladder and kidneys would allow. Mary distracted herself by
wondering why it was that we humans have duplicates of some
organs but not others. We have two kidneys but only one brain.
Two lungs but only one heart. Being lost in thought felt good.
She was so lost in thought that it took about five seconds before
she realized that someone was standing next to her small table.
Mary looked up. It was Fawn. Mary was speechless.
"Buy a girl a cup of coffee?" Fawn asked. She looked beautiful
in the morning.
"Probably not without taking out a second mortgage on my
house."
"You have a first mortgage?" Fawn remarked back.
So, she could be sassy in the morning as well...
"You don't?"
"Don't what?"

178

"Have a first mortgage?"

"Not every girl is poor," Fawn replied. Out of any other mouth, this might have sounded snooty. But from Fawn, it sounded factual.

"Maybe you should buy me a refill."

"Isn't it silly that they charge for that! You get free refills at any old diner all across the country."

"Maybe we should go to one of those and drink our livers to death."

"That's your evening specialty, isn't it?"

Mary had to laugh. "I'm not quite that unredeemable."

"So, are we staying here or going elsewhere?" Fawn was all travel agency.

"What are you doing here in the first place?" Mary asked the question that had formed in her mind when she first noted Fawn's presence.

"Doesn't everyone come here for coffee?"

"You don't live close by."

"You don't work close by."

So, was this going to turn into debate club, Mary wondered. It made perfect sense to Mary that Mary was here. It made no sense that Fawn was here. She could have used two brains to figure this out.

"What are you thinking?" Fawn mocked Mary's serious look in a movie starlet sort of way.

"I'm thinking that people could use two brains, or two hearts, for that matter."

"Don't you think that one heart gets us in enough trouble as it is?"

Mary had to nod. Mostly because she didn't have a witty comeback.

"So, are you ready?" Fawn asked.

"Ready for what?"

"That endless cup of coffee at a real diner, of course."

"You want to have breakfast? Have you eaten?" Mary felt awkward. It was a simple enough situation. It was morning. People ate breakfast in the morning. Humans were the only species that felt it necessary to eat certain kinds of food for different meals. Case in point, who eats oatmeal for dinner? Of course, you could eat steak for breakfast. All of a sudden, Mary was glad that she didn't have two brains. One was doing enough thinking for her.

"Come on. Bring your coffee," Fawn prodded.

Mary followed orders silently.

"Let's take my car," Fawn said as she unlocked her vehicle with a push of a button.

"What about my car?"

"I'll bring you back. I promise."

They both got into the small Mercedes. Even being small, it was not exactly economical. The engine roared to life and then settled into a tamer purr. Fawn didn't talk until they were on the highway heading south with a little west thrown in here and there. Country music streamed out of the six or so speakers in the car. Mary listened to scattered lyrics as they traveled.

"Country music has changed since the last time I listened to it," Mary said.

"When was the last time?"

"I'm sure it was in my teen years."

"Not so long ago, then?"

"Longer that you might think."

"So, how has it changed?"

"It used to be a lot about women and trucks and dogs."

"I thought it still was."

"It probably always will be, to a certain extent. But there's a certain strident element to some of the songs anymore."

"In what way?"

"Well, there's lyrics about putting boots up asses, for one thing."

"Oh, that," Fawn seemed to be unfazed by what others would deem strong language.

"That's the song by Chuck Lee. He tends to get a little stirred up about being patriotic."

"It's patriotic to threaten to put footwear up the behinds of anyone who doesn't agree with his particular brand of patriotism?"

"It sells records. And frankly, plenty of people agree with him."

"Plenty of people agreed with Adolf Hitler's brand of patriotism, but that didn't make it right."

"So you think that country music and Nazis have something in common?"

Mary had to stop and take a moment. The conversation had certainly evolved rather quickly. One minute Mary had been sipping overpriced over-roasted coffee in downtown Denver and the next thing she knew, they were discussing the talking points of Aryan philosophy. Things like this didn't just happen out of the blue. Mary became cautious.

"I believe that people all through the ages have tried to make themselves feel superior at the expense of other people, and that it's ultimately a deeply flawed approach."

"Gee, did you study this in college, or what?"

"Are you kidding?"

"Oh, no. Absolutely not. You sound so intelligent about it all."

"Well, I have done a little reading on the subject."

"There's stuff written about it?"

Mary got that funny feeling again, like the conversation was somehow being shepherded in this direction.

"Where are we going?" Mary changed the subject.

"To Steak and Cake."

"To what and where?"

"I wanted to take you to an old-fashioned diner, you know, pancakes and chicken-fried steak and ketchup on eggs."

"It sounds very charming," Mary held back the urge to gag. Eggs and ketchup should never be in the same sentence let alone on the same plate.

"But you can stick to coffee and pie if you want to," Fawn was mind reading again.

"I'll probably be ready for lunch if we drive much longer."

"Is it okay to be gone from where you work? I guess it's a little late to be asking that."

"It's okay."

"That's nice."

"What?"

"To work somewhere where you can just take off at the drop of a hat without anybody chewing you out about it."

It really wasn't like that at all. Well, maybe a little.

"I don't punch a time clock."

"You must be somebody really important there."

"I'm not."

"Of course you are, you humble thing, you," Fawn smiled like she had universal knowledge.

"I'm the new kid on the block. I work hard when I work."

"Is that why you look like you carry the whole company on your shoulders?"

Mary knew one or two things. She knew that she secretly carried the weight of her new discovery at work. A brooding sort of demeanor, perhaps. But brooding would be natural in this situation. She had no idea that she had broadcast it to Fawn. She had been careful to not do so while in the office. And she knew that she hadn't let this all spill out at home. So how was it that Fawn had honed in on this secret. Maybe she really was a mind reader. Or maybe she was just making small talk and knew next to nothing about Mary's moods.

"Wow, you sure got quiet all of a sudden," Fawn said with just a hint of challenge.

"Why do we always talk about what I do for a living?" Mary blurted out before thinking. The last thing that Mary wanted to hear about was the specifics of what Fawn did for money. Mary quickly followed up with, "Don't answer that."

"Do you always get this way when you're hungry?"

It was an out. Mary took it. "Yes."

"Well then, you'll be happy to know that we are about there."

Mary nodded. She was ready to be there.

Steak and Cake was a diner alright. As in diner with a capital D. It wasn't in Mary's nature to consider herself to be a snob, necessarily. But she wouldn't be being honest with herself if she didn't admit that there was absolutely no chance that she would be dining at this establishment without being dragged here by someone else. Fawn seemed totally at ease. This surprised Mary just a little. A stereotype that all women who made their living the way Fawn did would only eat in the best places might only be true if someone else was paying the bill. They were the only Mercedes in the dirt parking lot. Fawn led the way and they seated themselves in a corner booth. It was all red and the seat was worn and cracked from too much use between remodeling. That ubiquitous country music was playing in the background. It wasn't so loud that you couldn't hear yourself think, but not so soft that you couldn't help but keep time tapping your foot. The menu said that you could order breakfast until two in the afternoon and that lunch didn't start until eleven. They were right on the cusp, ten minutes away from a club sandwich and fries. Or right on time for a western omelet and hash browns.

"It all sounds great," Fawn was enthusiastic.

Mary not so much. "I think I'm going to stick with the basics, toast, maybe a couple scrambled eggs."

"So, you really are a light eater."

They hadn't shared a meal together. Scotch didn't count.

"I just haven't found my appetite yet this morning," Mary explained. She didn't know why she felt the need to explain this. People shouldn't feel the need to explain away their appetites, except to their bathroom scales and cardio-vascular doctors. She, of course, knew full well why she wasn't exactly hungry. Work was stressing her out. Meanwhile, Fawn was trying to narrow her selections down to a dozen or so full meals.

"Are you a waffle or pancake person," she asked nicely.

"I have been known to change my mind," Mary joked. Lamely.

"Huh?" Fawn asked.

"You mean, like, if I was on a deserted island and had only those two choices?" Mary asked.

"You think you could get either one on a deserted island?"

"Even if I could, why do you ask?"

"Well, I was thinking that if I couldn't finish everything I ordered, that I could share it with you."

"You're one of those people who like to try a little bit of everything to see what you like best."

"And in some cases, more than a little bit."

Mary had no immediate comeback. Not anything remotely clever at all. She went back to her quiet mood, having not even answered the pancake question. The waitress appeared, poised to jot down their whims. Mary did as promised and ordered eggs. Over easy. Took all of about ten of fifteen seconds to blurt it all out.

"And you, Miss?"

Fawn then proceeded to order enough food to feed a lumberjack with a hollow leg. Mary was amazed that it all fit on one ticket. Maybe it was all in shorthand. Now, there was a dying skill if ever there was one. Right up there with keypunch operators and buggy whip polishers. Mary kept her mind busy with all of this to avoid thinking about how this reminded her of dining with Lisa. Mary wondered how she managed to attract women who could really eat. And still stay slender.

"You've been thoughtful all morning," Fawn said quietly.

"I guess."

"What's on your mind? I want you to tell me so that we won't have an entire day of awkward silence."

"It's just work. It's not you."

"That still doesn't make it any easier. You're still just as quiet. Just as unapproachable."

"You want to know exactly what's wrong where I work?" Mary put a fine point on the conversation.

"Well, yeah, unless you're like a spy or something and telling me will destabilize the entire western hemisphere."

Fawn had this mock-serious mien that made Mary smile faintly.

"Do I look that important to you?" Mary couldn't help fishing for compliments.

"You don't look that dangerous."

"Okay," Mary mentally weighed what the extent of her reply could entail. "I work with confidential financial data."

"Ooh. I always knew you were, like, super smart."

Mary blushed. She couldn't help it. She hadn't been so nakedly complimented in so long that it felt good. Deep down really good.

"So, stop turning red and tell me more."

It was a cute and innocent remark. Obviously, just doing work with financial data wasn't enough to warrant such a serious and troubled attitude.

"And...some people I work with aren't as, well, ethical as I had hoped they would be."

"Are they your employees and you're the boss and you'll, like, have to fire them?"

Another good question.

"I'm not that important. I don't get to hire and fire people."

"But, you must be some sort of manager to know what's going on."

"I have access to a lot of data."

184

"You find things out on a computer instead of employees just blabbing about it, then, during three-martini lunches."

"I've never actually had a three-martini lunch."

About that time, food started arriving by the plateful.

"This isn't going to be one, either," Fawn smiled.

"More like a three-antacid lunch."

The waitress dropped off what she had and went back for more. "Hope you're hungry," was her parting shot after delivering stacks of toast and pancakes. Mary was secretly pleased. She did prefer pancakes after all. Mary began politely and tentatively to eat her eggs. They had a distinct flavor. They actually tasted like eggs. Real farm-fresh eggs with orange-yellow yolks. Maybe it was just her, but the first time you eat in front of someone could be awkward. Mary had waited a split second to see if they were going to say grace. You just never knew with folks. Fawn might just have been the most spiritual woman for hire that walked the earth. If she said grace, it was to herself with no outward clue like Nazis were ready to pounce. And speaking of pouncing, Fawn did so right into the middle of a four-pancake stack. She had buttered and syruped them all up pretty good. There's just something about carbohydrates and fat and sugar that was about as close to heaven as you could get in a cowboy diner. It took about three forkfuls before she was ready to talk again.

"So, what have you been finding on your computer?"

"I did mention that it's confidential, right?"

"So, who am I going to tell?"

Mary thought it over for about a heartbeat. "There's this thing that stockbrokers do. It's called churning."

"Churning, like, butter?"

"I suppose that's where the term came from? Anyway, there are brokers who buy and sell stocks to earn extra fees."

"That doesn't sound so bad."

"Well, they do it without prior consent of their clients, so that alone makes it illegal."

"I didn't say it wasn't illegal. It just doesn't sound like that much of a money maker."

"It's more like Bonfire of the Vanities than Grand Theft Auto."

"You know, I saw that Bonfire film. They didn't burn one piece of furniture in the whole movie."

Fawn had made quick work of her pancakes and started in on her eggs and corned beef hash, to which she added salt. She wouldn't need to pee for a week at that rate.

"I think that the potential for really salting away the money is to pocket the proceeds of the quick profits and never tell the client what you did with their money."

"But we're still talking about small amounts of money, right?"

"The crumbs from slicing the cake."

"So they don't take the cake like the old saying goes. And nobody is the wiser."

Mary sat very still for a moment. Fawn was right in that there were just small percentages and fees being secreted away. But what could someone do if they really had free rein with some of these small fortunes just sitting around? It was like turning a light switch on and off. You saw the light, but what went on behind the switch was anyone's guess. Unless you were an electrician. Or maybe in this case, a quantum physicist.

"You're thinking again."

"I'm wondering about that cake."

"I only saw pie on the menu."

"Yeah," Mary's mind went back to Denver even as her body stayed put in the booth.

"Something else is bothering you. Something big."

"I just was trying to remember something."

"Did anybody ever tell you that you shouldn't lie for a living because you're bad at it."

Mary felt she was being quite the lady to not point out that she was the only one between the two of them who did not "lie" for a living.

"Okay, let me clarify. I'm trying to logically sort through the things I remember."

"You think that they're taking the whole cake somehow?"

"I'm thinking that they are really stupid or very...brazen."

"Brazen?"

"I don't think they are stupid, and brazen is the best word that I could come up with."

"What were the runners up?"

186

"Sinister and coordinated."

"Wow, you really know how to call people names, don't you."
Mary looked straight at Fawn. She thought she had heard just
the faintest trace of sarcasm. Drip.

"Oh yeah, I'm a real trucker in that regard," Mary responded in
kind.

"Honestly, you think that these nice people you work with are
stealing big piles of money."

"Everything is on paper nowadays."

"What do you mean? Money is made out of paper, right?"

"I meant that conceivably I can send out a printed report every
month that said I invested your million dollars wisely and it's still
only your trusting nature that tells you so."

"Until I try and cash out."

"Yeah and even then, it's still all paperwork. Nobody except
drug dealers carry around a lot of cash money."

"But you're made some pretty big assumptions. Like, everyone
would be in on the take."

"That's why I used those big bad words. Coordinated and
brazen."

"And sinister. Don't forget that one. Why did you use that one,
anyway?"

"It just popped into my head."

"No, it didn't. Look, I don't know you all that well, but from
what I do know, random words don't just pop into your head.
Why sinister?"

Mary weighed her words carefully. "You're going to think I'm
prejudiced if I tell you."

"I'm willing to take my chances."

"There were a lot of funds flowing through accounts with Israel
in the name."

"You think it's some Jewish cabal thing?" Fawn looked more
alarmed than Mary would have expected. Prejudice was like a
weed. It grew everywhere.

"I didn't think any such thing until you put Jewish and cabal into
the same sentence."

"Well, you're the one who deemed it sinister."

"I only meant it in the criminal aspect. Not in who might be
funding what."

"Would it make you feel any better if the word Mohammad was on every account?"

"Why would that make me feel any better?"

"Because then it would mean that your co-workers were funding Muslim terrorists."

"And, again, exactly how would that make me feel better?"

"Because then you would at least know what you were dealing with."

"So, now that you've conveniently determined what I'm not dealing with, maybe you could take a stab at what you think I'm dealing with."

"I haven't a clue. Unless you're working with a bunch of Jews." Fawn didn't say the word "Jews" like she had any as friends or relatives. At the wording "bunch of", Mary had felt herself tighten. It was an instinct. Not that she always felt defensive about Trish, but for entirely different reasons than race or heritage. Any time that Mary heard the words, "bunch of", literally her stomach bunched. Bunch of Jews. Bunch of queers. Bunch of...Mary couldn't bring herself to use the N word, not even silently to herself. Anytime a group fell into the "bunch of" category, discrimination flourished. Let's just keep this bunch of Jews out of the country club. There now, isn't that so much better. I sure wish we could keep that bunch of gay teachers out of the schools. Then my kids wouldn't have to be exposed to that sort of depravity. If those bunch of Black people hadn't moved into Grandma's neighborhood, she wouldn't have to be living with us now.

"I don't think I work with a bunch of any group," Mary kept her voice quiet, her temper restrained.

"You're upset," Fawn the mind-reader replied. She sounded oddly relieved by this, like she was the only one at the table allowed to have prejudice.

"You didn't have to live through the Holocaust to have a knee-jerk reaction to antisemitism"

"It sounds like you're a real scholar on the subject," Fawn seemed to be inviting debate.

"I'm not a scholar of anything, but as a gay person, I've paid attention to the cause and effect of one of the worst, if not the worst, episodes of genocide in modern history."

"Why?"

The question dumbfounded Mary for a moment. Didn't everybody realize the important lessons of history, particularly if people like them were on the receiving end of such cruelty? Mary took a good, long look at Fawn. And then, it came to her. Fawn was one of those who could very easily pass all those Aryan tests. She had the right skin color. Something that had been measured by the Germans who had racial purity on their agenda. And it wasn't just an ebony and ivory, black and white sort of question like in the American slavery criminality. German scientists and doctors developed ways to measure skin color referred to in medical journals of the time as "skin-color scales" that one could use to determine the acceptable amount of white pigmentation of the skin. Kind of like paint strips you take home from the hardware store to see what color wall paint would match your sofa. Except, of course, these color strips were used to send people to the concentration camps and gas chambers. How very easy and convenient for the whitest of the white. The correct shape of the nose. The purest blood. And everyone else? Well, they simply fell into one of those "bunches of" categories. If it had all stopped with the defeat of Nazi Germany, then it would have been one of the few good outcomes of the war. But it hadn't stopped there. We didn't learn our lesson. Well, some did. But far too many hadn't. People still felt it their right and duty and call to arms to purge society of its undesirables. The Blacks. The Jews. The Homos.

"Why not?" was all that Mary could come up with as a response. Everything else running through her mind sounded like a diatribe.

"You're looking at me like you think I'm a Nazi."

Fawn said this so calmly and matter-of-factly that Mary felt on shaky ground all of a sudden. She really couldn't tell anymore where this conversation was heading. She wouldn't be surprised right here and now if Fawn suggested either joining a gay-rights group in the afternoon or attending some cross-burning activity later in the evening.

"I haven't seen you wearing a swastika."

At this notion, Fawn laughed. "You're certainly in a different mood than earlier."

Mary's thoughts shifted back to being away from work. "I should be getting back."

"Of course."

They traveled the return trip in relative silence. It was borderline awkward, again. Before Mary got out of the car, Fawn admonished her, "Promise me that you'll be careful." It sounded like she meant business.

"You think I'm in danger from the Jews?"

"Can I ask you a serious question and get a serious answer?"

"Sure," Mary respected Fawn's sudden and very unexpected request.

"Is there any other word besides Israel that is tied into all this shady dealing that you're investigating?"

Fawn had certainly left the most interesting question until the last. Mary felt a prickle of neck hair and a bit of a shiver. What was going on here? Her body seemed to be imploring her intellect for an answer as well.

"There are a lot of words," Mary found herself stalling, like she wanted clarification for a question she didn't quite understand. She understood the question. She just didn't understand its significance.

"I didn't mean to be vague," Fawn shifted around to face Mary. "I was just curious about the Israel stuff. I mean, if I was a Jew and I was doing something illegal, I sure wouldn't put Israel all over the proof. Would you?"

Mary nodded agreement. "That wouldn't be how I would do it."

"Unless, or course, you were in the business of framing Jews for your ugly activities."

"Sounds an awfully lot like 1930 Germany."

"1930? I thought that the war was in the 1940s?"

"The war was in the 1940s for Americans. Considering all that Hitler accomplished to then, it's a testament to brave Americans that we helped win after such a reluctant start."

"There's nothing wrong with trying to avoid war, but besides that point, what did you mean about the 1930s?"

"That's when the official persecution of the Jews began in Germany. It all just didn't happen overnight. It took a lot of money and policy changes and propaganda to attempt to destroy

190

the Jewish population in Germany. And even that wasn't enough for Hitler. He was bent on destroying every Jew in the world."

"You really do know all about this. But back to my original question. Is there any other word or combination of words that accompany the term Israel?"

Mary had put the question on the back burners of her mind when she heard it for the first time. She didn't have a photographic memory, but words flowed through her subconscious mind like a searchable database. One word finally slipped out. White. It puzzled her. Fawn noticed. "What is it?"

"It doesn't make sense."

"What's the word?"

"White."

"White!" Fawn repeated like she had heard a mistake.

"Yeah. White. It doesn't fit."

"Why?" Fawn was asking the question in a detached sort of way. Like she wanted to hear Mary's reasoning but really didn't. Like when you ask your spouse how their day was and then don't listen to a word of their exposition. Not a good time for a pop quiz in any relationship.

"Well, if you put the words White and Israel together, have you ever heard that combination before?"

"No. But aren't Jews considered to be white?"

"I can't speak for everyone else, but I don't get too wound up trying to figure out who's white and who isn't. I'm not an Aryan, for goodness sake."

"What's a Ryan? Sounds Irish," Fawn mused.

Mary looked at Fawn. Honestly, how can anyone attain adulthood and not read the news. "Not a Ryan. Aryan."

"Aryan? Like it's all one word?"

"Right. It's a specific yet generic term that describes people who believe that the white race is superior."

"How can a term be both specific and generic?"

"Well, because it's a sort of catch-all phrase."

"Like, there's more than one group of these Ryans?"

Mary shook her head and checked her timing. She had blown off most of the morning at work and doubted that the afternoon would be productive.

"If I called in sick, would you like to have lunch or maybe high tea later?"

"You won't get into any trouble?"

Mary resisted the urge to remark that she would be in trouble no matter what she did. She made the call sounding like Typhoid Fever would be preferable to what she was suffering but promised to try and drag herself in tomorrow.

"I'll get my car and follow you."

"Where to?"

"Wherever you go."

No one should be surprised that they ended up at Fawn's apartment. Not that it was the final destination, but it did have a bathroom. Fawn boiled water for tea while Mary settled on the couch. The first visit to Fawn's apartment had seemed like a fog to her. She really hadn't paid much attention to anything but Fawn. Looking around now, she saw the usual tasteful items that one might find in a call girl's apartment. But there was also a tone of study or library as well. Shelves of books, maybe not Plato, but certainly not Jane Moore either. Fawn was back with tea.

"Have you read all those books?" Mary asked politely. At least, she hoped it sounded polite instead of incredulous.

"Those? No. They belonged to the previous tenant."

"Ah," Mary nodded. She had heard of furnished apartments, but this was ridiculous. Who would leave behind or count as furnishings bookcases full of books?

"So, you were explaining to me about these, what were they called again?"

"White supremacists. Aryans. But they go by other names as well."

"You mean like the KKK! Now I've heard about them."

"Are you from the south?"

"If I say yes, are you going to hold it against me?"

"Why would I do that?" Mary sipped her tea. It was overly sweet, a true giveaway of southern traditions.

"Oh, you know about people and their ideas about the south, especially about southern women."

Mary had a vague idea what this might be about, but she professed ignorance. "I'm not sure what you mean?"

"Okay, well you know, like sweet tea. You're being all polite and everything but I could see by your expression that four spoons of sugar in your tea was a bit much."

"Four spoons? Really. I guess I'd consider that a little excessive."

"We call it amateur where I was reared."

"And where were you reared?" Mary asked.

"In the south, silly. I already said that. Pay attention next time." Mary nodded. "Okay, what else do I need to know about southern women?"

"We cook differently."

"Every region of the country has its unique way of preparing food."

"Yes, well, not any other region relies so heavily on can cream of something or the other soup."

"You mean, like green bean casserole?"

"That's for beginners. I'm talking about gourmet soup recipes."

"You'll have to fix me that one of these days," Mary tried to sound open to the idea. It came out sounding like she'd also be interested in hitting her thumb with a hammer.

"So, I guess everyone has their prejudices and discriminations."

"It's when you set out to hurt people, that's when ideology meets destruction."

"Like radical whites-only groups?"

"It's dangerous and distasteful stuff. Hitler set out to destroy every Jew. It wasn't a secret. It was Germany's national policy. Today, white identity groups are everywhere. We kid ourselves and think that it's isolated in the south with the KKK so that we northerners can feel superior."

"Yankees."

"Baseball?"

"NO! Damn Yankees. If you're going to refer to yourselves, at least use the right terminology."

"Yankee?"

"Damn Yankee."

"Damn Yankee," Mary had it finally.

"Now, continue."

"Where was I?"

"Condemning the entire south for being prejudiced."

"I was not."

"Condemning the entire country of Germany for being prejudiced?"

"I'm merely providing historical background. Didn't I say that these groups are everywhere?"

"I don't recall."

"Well, they are. Think about Texas."

"That's still in the south."

"Okay. How about Idaho? Is that far enough north for you?"

"Yankee enough for me."

"Ruby Creek, Idaho."

"Ruby Ridge," Fawn corrected.

"So, you've heard about it then?"

"Who hasn't heard about Ruby Ridge? Somebody got shot and killed there, right?" Fawn sounded awfully vague for someone who knew the exact location of the shootings.

"Somebody sure did get shot and killed. Three somebodies got shot and killed."

"Yeah, some white supremacist was killed."

"Not exactly."

"What do you mean, not exactly?"

"The wife and son of a white separatist were killed along with a Deputy U.S. Marshall."

"So, there are white supremacists in Idaho."

"And right here in Colorado."

"Here?"

"Meetings in Estes Park ring a bell?"

"No."

"I imagine not. It wasn't exactly broadcast to the general public, but a bunch of supporters of the Weaver family-"

"The Weaver family?"

"The people in Ruby Ridge were the Weavers."

"Ah."

"Anyway, there was a meeting in Colorado among supporters of the Weavers. And then, there was a group in California that was into something called Identity Christians, I think?"

"Christian Identity?" Fawn reversed the words as she tried to keep up.

194

"Something like that," Mary nodded. "Anyway, there are groups in Oregon, Michigan, Nebraska..."

"So I was right. It's not just the south."

"And really not true Christians either. Christian Identity groups believe that the Anglo-Saxons were the Lost Tribe of Israel and that Jews, Blacks, and other people of color were inferiors sent to earth as a scourge of God."

The conversation paused while they both sipped their tea.

"Will you call me tomorrow?" Fawn asked quite out of the blue as she checked her watch.

A phrase like this along with a gesture like that usually signals an end to the day's activities. Mary didn't know whether to answer now or on the way out the door.

"When tomorrow?"

"After work, of course. I'll be sleeping in so it won't do any good to call early."

"Of course," Mary all of a sudden understood. Fawn had another "appointment."

"I'd better be going."

"You haven't finished your tea."

"My insulin receptors can't take any more right this minute."

"You always sound so clever. Are you sure you're not a doctor or a lawyer as well as an accountant?"

Mary blushed again. Fawn was the true professional in the room.

Chapter 8

New York City was different than Paris. Mitch hadn't felt any
sudden urges to get down on her hands and knees and kiss the
ground, but it sure was good to be back in the States.
"Hello?" a distant voice rudely interrupted Mitch's mental
communion with the good ole U S of A. It was Reb.
"Huh?"
"I said that we should call the kids and let them know that we're
out of jail."
"You were never in."
"I was busy bailing you out. That's close enough for me."
"Did I say thank you?"
"No, you ungrateful lout, you didn't."
"Well, thank you."
"You're welcome. I wonder if anyone's home."
"I wonder that a lot myself."
"Make yourself useful and dial the phone for me."

Mary picked up on the second ring, sounding quite under the
weather, "Hello?"
"Are you okay, Honey?" Mama Bear Reb pounced on the
situation.
"Oh, it's only you. I'm fine, really."
"Yes, it's only me. What's going on? You sound sick?"
"I thought you were work calling."
"And why would I be work calling?" Reb didn't let up.
It all sounded both strange and usual to Mitch. A contradiction
to be sure, but it was, after all, a mother-daughter conversation.
"Because I'm playing hooky and using Typhoid Fever as an
excuse."
"Very droll."
"Yeah, so what's going on?"
"Mitch is out of jail."
"Was she visiting Miranda?"
"No, she was actually an inmate."
When Reb said it, it sounded ominous.
"How did Mitch end up in jail in Kansas?"
"She didn't."

"You just said-"

"Mitch was in a French prison."

Now it really sounded ominous. Maybe not as bad as being in a Turkish prison, but still...

"How did she end up in France?" was the only logical question Mary could formulate.

"We were shopping for a layette."

Mary had heard enough baby talk between Lisa and Trish to know what a layette was. Fancy talk for blankets and burp bibs.

"For Miranda's baby?"

"Right."

Mary had finally made one correct guess. "And somehow that's illegal in France?"

"Of course not. I don't know of any kind of shopping that's illegal."

"You wouldn't, I'm sure."

Reb ignored the snark. "And then people started getting killed-"

"What!" Mary was truly alarmed now.

"People, wait, make that men started getting killed. Murdered, actually."

"I'd ask you to start at the beginning, but somehow I'm not sure it would help."

"It's pretty straight-forward, Dear. We went to Paris because the shopping in Kansas can leave something to be desired."

"You could have just shopped in New York."

"Don't get ahead of me, Sweetie."

"I never even hope to anymore."

"So, of course, men in France aren't bashful."

"I've heard that."

"And some nice man who bought us lunch got murdered. It was all ghastly."

"And Mitch ended up in jail, why?"

"It was a jealous lover theory."

"And Mitch isn't in jail now because?"

"Another man was murdered while she was in custody."

"This is pretty confusing. Why would the murder of another man exonerate Mitch?"

"I guess the two men were somehow connected?"

"Do you need me to fly out to Kansas?"

197

"That wouldn't do any good because we're in New York City right this minute."

"Doing what?"

"Washing prison grime off of Mitch, if you must know."

At this, Mitch had to laugh.

"Is that Mitch I hear giggling?"

"The one and only."

"Can I talk to her?"

"As long as my mental capacity isn't called into question."

"Just put her on the phone."

Mitch accepted the phone with some reluctance. She hoped this wasn't going to be one of those conversations where she would have to speak in guarded code.

"Hi, Mary."

"Well, you've certainly had yourself quite the adventure."

"France was really pretty until I ended up in the hoosegow."

"Is that French for prison?"

Oh the younger generation.

"Actually, hoosegow derives from Spanish."

"You went to Spain, too?"

"No. I just grew up in an area with a lot of Spanish influence."

"Especially where jails were concerned?"

"I thought we were going to talk about your mother's grip on reality?"

"I'd be careful if I were you. You are within hitting range."

"So far, it's only been warning glares."

"Men were actually murdered?"

"Yes. Killed and the gruesomely dismembered. At least, I think that was the order of events."

"Have you considered that it might have been the other way around?"

"Like, tortured and then killed?"

"Or maybe just tortured to death."

Mitch hadn't given this a whole lot of thought until now. She wondered only for a split second what the exact difference was between being tortured and killed versus being tortured to death. It wasn't something that ever really entered her consciousness on a daily basis. And in many respects, she felt this was a good thing. People who sit around and dwell upon the finer points of torture need help. Desperately. Not that she was thinking that Mary needed help. There was no notion that Mary was doing anything other than thinking logically through the problem. Which made it now clear that this was something that Mitch hadn't done during her overnight stay in jail. She could see this criticism in her great report card at the pearly gates..."does not use time well..." Now that Mary had brought it forward, Mitch felt it important to continue the conversation.

"You may be right," was her only response.

"How were these two men connected? Mother said that the police thought they were."

Mitch considered choosing her words carefully, but Mary was too smart for avoidance.

"The only connection I know of is your Mother and me."

Mary was quiet for a moment. Really quiet. Like funeral parlor quiet. Then she spoke with conviction, "I'll catch the next flight out."

"Uh, are you sure you want to do that?"

"I can join you for a really late dinner."

"I thought you were sick?"

"I'm pretending to be sick."

"Why are you doing that?"

Now it was Mary's turn to weigh her words carefully. "I needed a little time to think."

"What's wrong at work?" Mitch now pounced, happy to be off the hot seat for the time being. Reb chimed in with those exact words as well, realizing that she had never gotten the entire answer to this question while she had control of the phone.

"It's kind of a long story, really."

"I'll arrange a charter flight for you so we can talk face to face."

"That's really tempting and I would love to do exactly that, but I also need to be at work tomorrow morning early."

"It can all happen. Charter here, have dinner, talk, take a sleeping pill, fly home, be at work by 8 am."

"You would do that?"

"It would be my pleasure."

"Okay, well, I'll head to the airport."

"Go to Clancy Field. I'll make the arrangements."

"Thanks."

"Will Lisa be coming as well?"

"Not this trip. She's way too busy."

"Okay, I'll put your mom back on the line."

Mother and daughter talked for a few moments, mostly an extended goodbye. Mitch didn't listen in. She was on her cell phone making hurried arrangements for Mary's flight. Mitch had never really thought about her wealth until times like this. It was a blessing to be able to afford reunions like this. Bringing mothers and daughters together was a benefit well worth the cost.

"So, where are we going to dine?" Reb was off the phone and excited about seeing Mary again.

"Pick somewhere nice."

"Oh gee, I thought we could eat at some mouse-infested dump instead."

"We're eating at home?" Mitch quipped. "I guess we'd better all get a charter back to Kansas."

Reb chuckled. It was a good sound.

Mary debated whether to call Lisa or just leave her a note. The former would take time. The latter would be cold.

"Hi, it's Mary. Is Lisa there?"

Rose was always glad to hear from Mary. "I'll go and get her."

A minute went by and then Lisa all out of breath was on the line.

"Hi. Everything okay?"

"Why wouldn't it be?"

"Well, I was just hoping nothing was wrong."

"I'm going to see Mom tonight for dinner."

"Is she is town? Are you sure you're okay?"

"No and yes."

"Okay. Isn't Kansas a long way to go for dinner?"

"Actually, Mom is in New York with Mitch."

"You're going to New York to have dinner with your Mother and everything is okay?"

"I know it's last minute."

200

"What it is is confusing."

"I know. I don't have time to explain since I have a flight to catch."

Lisa know better than to bring up the subject of why she wasn't invited. It wasn't that she knew the answer already. It was that Mary wouldn't answer. That's just how things had been lately. And Lisa wasn't disappointed. Frankly, the last thing on her enjoyment list was a dinner in New York with Mary and Reb. Maybe in years past Lisa would have been jealous and felt shortchanged. New York was, after all, the glamor capital of the nation. But missing out on this opportunity that she had never even had a shot at anyway didn't seem to trigger any envy. Trish noted Lisa's sudden change of mood when she got off the phone.

"What's up?"

"Mary's not going to be home for dinner."

"Working late again?"

"Something like that," Lisa didn't care to expound just now, so Trish didn't press.

"So, that means you can have dinner with us!"

"It's pretty short notice, isn't it?"

"Rose always cooks for twelve. Just because it's for twelve people on a cardiac diet..."

Lisa smiled. Rose was out to cure the world, one recipe at a time.

"It's still better than what I would be cooking for myself."

"Microwave macaroni and cheese?"

"On a good day."

"I'll ask Rose to set another place at the table."

"Thanks. I really appreciate the invitation."

Trish knew there was more to the story. If she practiced patience, all would eventually be revealed.

New York City was really something else. "Something else" was a catch-all cop-out phrase, and yet, it was the best she could come up with on short notice. When Reb had made the arrangements to spring Mitch from jail and France, in that exact order, the subject of where to stay in New York had been only briefly discussed. As in, "Let's stay somewhere kinda nice"

discussed. Reb's concept of "kinda nice" turned out to be the
Ritz-Carlton overlooking Central Park. This place definitely fell
into the "kinda nice" category. There were robes and telescopes
and pretty soaps in the bathroom. It was way beyond what Mitch
had experienced in childhood. There were vacations. Vacations
like miles and miles in the back of a station wagon that had
bench seats and cowboy motifs printed on the seats. This was
the epitome of upscale in the family. You traveled all day, lucky
if you got only mildly car sick and would have slept on anything
at the end of the dust-choked day. The soaps in the motels
caused skin rashes and there was no shampoo. You used the
rash-inducing soap if there was enough to go around.

And now, here she was, waiting patiently for Reb to decide
where they were going for dinner.
"Here's a place that has a $14 bowl of soup," Reb mused as she
read through the sample menus in the hotel information.
"How much for a salad?"
"Eighteen."
"Why don't we just eat at this hotel?"
"It's in the top ten most expensive restaurants in New York
City."
"I think that the money we'll save in cab fare will make up the
difference."
"It's French food."
"I'm assuming you don't mean French fries?"
"No."
"How about a good steakhouse?"
"You sure didn't spend a lot of time being vegan, did you?"
"I just figure that any place that has steaks will automatically
have French fries."
"I'd think baked potatoes would be the preference."
"I'll leave the choice up to you. You know what's best for
Mary."
"Children aren't always that easy to figure out."

Mitch knew instinctively that they weren't just talking about
dinner anymore.

202

"What do you think is going on?" Mitch brought up that subject again to avoid silence.

"I'm not sure. Mary is giving the impression that things at work aren't going well."

"I hope it isn't serious." Mitch said.

"Usually, it's Lisa who is at the root of most of the problems." It was a sweeping judgment that irked Mitch. Never mind that Lisa had saved Reb's life. She still considered Lisa to be the blond sheep of the family.

"Maybe we should wait and hear the whole story from Mary."

"How is she getting to the hotel?"

"Limo. I set up everything. You just figure out what kind of wine goes with French fries."

"I already know that answer."

"Really! What kind?"

"The expensive kind, of course."

By the time Mary arrived, everyone was hungry. They were seated in a spacious booth in the hotel restaurant befitting the hundred-dollar gratuity that Mitch forked over to the maitre'd with her usual quiet sophistication. Reb and Mary chatted while Mitch scanned the wine list for a selection that would please Reb's palate. Even at this late hour, the place was full. Back in Kansas, the chickens had long since roosted. Here in the big city, the night was just beginning. Mother and daughter had run out of small talk by the time the first glass of wine had been poured.

"So, what's going on, Dear," Reb was ready to have her presumptions once again confirmed.

"Something's going on at work."

"Is your boss treating you okay?"

"That's not the issue."

"Are your co-workers being problematic?"

"Not exactly."

"I'm all out of guesses," Reb admitted as the waiter refilled her wineglass.

Mary hesitated for a moment. She had practiced the story all the way here and now all she needed to do was to start the first sentence. The waiter finished pouring the wine bottle empty and

Mitch ordered another. It would be her contribution to the flow of conversation.

"I've been monitoring some of the financial data," Mary began.

It was a solid first sentence.

"Okay," Reb nodded.

"And it doesn't seem..." Mary hesitated.

"Kosher?" Reb took a stab at completing the sentence.

The word "kosher" seemed to startle Mary. "That's a strange choice of words."

"What? Kosher?"

"Yes. It implies that somehow this is a Jewish issue."

"I meant it in the most generic sense. You seem a little touchy about it."

"I've just already had an extended conversation about this once today."

"A conversation about what exactly?" Reb pressed. She would wait to know the who part of the story later.

"Another glass of this wine and I'll tell you everything I know. This is pretty decent stuff."

"It should be, at three-hundred dollars a bottle," Mitch noted.

"Only three-hundred dollars?" Reb arched an eyebrow, which made it all worthwhile to Mitch.

Over the course of a thousand dollars worth of wine and appetizers, Mary told a sanitized version of her discoveries at work and her dialogue with Fawn. Sanitized in that Fawn carried no more importance than that of a casual acquaintance. There was no mention of a diamond necklace or the creeping truth that Mary would have done just about anything to woo the woman straight to bed had it not been for Lisa. The other truth was that Mary didn't need to say in words what Mitch understood just by being observant. Reb was too busy listening to hear the truth. Once the story was told, they ate an expensive dinner. It was wonderful food, but Mitch felt distracted.

"What do you think?" Reb asked.

It took a second or two for Mitch to realize that it was her opinion that was being sought.

"I think I want dessert," Mitch did her best to sound relevant.

"Just how long were you in that French prison?" Mary asked. She was tired of talking about herself and was frankly curious about Mitch's detached manner.

"It was the worst ten minutes of my life."

"You were in overnight," Reb reminded.

"Oh yeah. It was you who was there for ten minutes."

"Are you sure you're okay?"

"I'm ready for dessert."

"You're still hungry after all this dinner?"

"I'm not hungry. I just want dessert."

"Like, in a to-go box?"

"No, like on a plate. Who do I need to flag down to see a dessert menu?"

Mary and Reb exchanged glances. Dessert didn't seem an important enough issue to fuss about. The woman had served time. The woman wanted dessert. The psychic waiter appeared and presented the choices to the trio. There were numerous selections so Mitch ordered one of each rather than go through the bother of making up her mind. Mary and Reb exchanged glances again. Mitch caught the looks. "Do the two of you want anything?" Mitch asked pleasantly.

"No," they answered in unison.

"And coffee," Mitch was pleased that she remembered. It would be a shame to keep running this nice waiter back and forth. "How many coffees?" he smiled.

The correct answer turned out to be three. They had to do something while Mitch sat there eating enough sugar to send even the healthiest person into a diabetic coma.

"While we wait for dessert, which will probably take the pastry chef a week to prepare, let's go back to my original question," Reb said peevishly.

"Which was?" Mitch asked.

"When I asked you what you thought it wasn't in regards to dessert."

"Oh, okay."

"I was wondering what you thought Mary should do."

Mitch glanced around the restaurant like she was curious what everyone else was eating. Like maybe she wanted to see the size of one of these fancy desserts so that she would be prepared for the error of her ways.

"It's hard to give an answer when I don't have the whole story."

"I've told you everything I know," Mary was borderline huffy.

"I'm sure you have," Mitch replied blandly, clearly signaling the fact that she wasn't trying to start a fight. At least, not deliberately. "I think the better question is, what were you planning to do when you showed up to work tomorrow? You know, before you thought to consult us?"

"I was going to memorize the names of all the accounts that are suspicious."

"And then what?"

"I hadn't planned past that."

"Do you trust your boss?"

"Do you think he might be the ringleader?"

"It sounds like you can't be sure."

"I've only been there for a few months. It isn't like these people are my college buddies."

"So, you would logically go to a higher authority."

"Like the Feds?"

"I wouldn't even know who to call," Mitch was always ready to profess ignorance.

Reb took over. "I'd start with the Colorado Securities Commissioner. He will know what to do and if he thinks it's a federal case, then the Feds will be brought in."

"And I'll probably be out of a job."

"You think you'll get fired?"

"I think there won't be a company left to work for if I do this."

"Well, Lisa still has a job. She can support you for a change."

The ensuing silence would have been uncomfortable had it not been for the arrival of desserts in the plural. Dessert, like everything else in this place, wasn't cheap. Back home, a slice of pie might set you back a couple bucks. Ala mode was extra, of course. Here, a slice of white cake was twenty-five dollars, and that was the bargain of the selections. Of course, there was cheesecake. It was New York, after all. The slice looked like a quarter of the entire cake and was drizzled with some berry red syrup that cost more per ounce than pricey perfume. And there was chocolate. Some sort of chocolate molten concoction that the menu had bragged about having a dozen or so different varieties of cocoa in the batter. A dozen kinds of cocoa? Mitch had never known that there were a dozen different kinds of cocoa. She had never even assumed that there was more than one kind of cocoa. Then again, there were dozens of kinds of coffee, and not just the various permutations found at the local coffeehouse. Like, coffee with cream didn't count as being different from black coffee. Coffee from Hawaii was different from coffee from Ethiopia. And then, there was key lime pie. Key lime pie was already expensive enough in regular stores. Maybe the pastry chef here grew his own key lime trees? Lost in her musings, Mitch looked up to see Reb and Mary and the waiter looking to her for an answer.

"Will there be anything else?" was the repeated inquiry.

"I don't know," Mitch answered truthfully. The question was so broadly phrased.

"Not at the moment," Reb answered in form that gave the waiter the clue to tend to his other tables.

To Mitch, she said, "I hate to think how you're going to be after the sugar shock sets in."

"I'll be fine. I'm fine now," Mitch said without defensiveness. She was fine. She was just taking in the complete New York City dining experience. Although everyone had protested at the splurge, they all still wanted a taste of everything. Mitch took her sweet time with her own sampling and after a couple of refills of coffee, the cups were small and dainty after all, the bill arrived. Mitch had enough cash on hand to pay and leave a good tip. Now, everybody was happy. Reb had shared a nice dinner with Mary. The waiter had a nice chunk of change that he could choose to share with the IRS...or not. And Mitch? Mitch wanted an after-dinner drink in the hotel lounge.

"You want what?" Reb was trying to decide between irritated and curious. Mitch had her quirks. She could eat plain mustard on crackers and consider it a gourmet treat. She would buy houses and not live in them. She ordered expensive wine for others and then want a simple after-dinner drink. Curiosity won over irritation. Reb gave a look toward Mary that conveyed silently to go along with the request.

"I'm sure I can sleep on the flight home."

"Of course, you can, Dear. It's a charter, after all."

They walked into the hotel lounge. It was money. You could just feel it. Almost smell it. Mitch was used to places like cheap casinos in Las Vegas. That bordered on a contradiction in terms. There was never such a thing as a cheap casino. There were expensive casinos and less expensive casinos, but there's no such animal as a cheap casino. However, there are cheaply-designed casinos. Places where your brain rattles due to the excessive noise. Not one sound absorbing feature was used in these rattle traps. Ever wonder why nice restaurants use linen tablecloths? It wasn't a bafflement anymore. This lounge was quiet and still. It gave immediate calming to all who passed through the portal. Mitch would be content to sip a crème d menthe here and feel that she had experienced about the best that New York City had to offer excepting the Macy's Thanksgiving Day Parade. Maybe they could come back in November. Except that the baby was coming. Would it be too soon to travel? As a child in Catholic school, Mitch had been taught that Catholics didn't take their babies anywhere until they were first baptized. So, if you were born say on January 5th and your favorite parish priest was on a well-deserved vacation after the Christmas rush, you maybe didn't get baptized until late January. So you didn't go anywhere and why was this? It was because if you died in a car accident or something, your baby soul could never go to heaven and you would never see the face of God because, you guessed it, you hadn't been baptized. They, the nuns, didn't seem to be joking. But they couldn't really explain where the babies went other than to limbo. Which was somehow fitting because they also wouldn't explain where babies came from in the first place at risk of being drummed out of the Holy Roman Catholic Church for talking like that to first graders. So, all in all, it was very symmetrical. Dead babies didn't go to hell nor to heaven nor to purgatory. They went to some weird place called limbo. Which, to anyone who has actually read the bible, is a made up place. It was all beginning to sound like the Scopes Monkey Trial, and didn't the Catholics lose that one? Anybody who believed in the strict literal interpretation of the bible was certainly rocked back on their heels by that ruling. If you believed that the world was created in six days and that God rested on the seventh day, and yet days weren't created on the first day, well then, how would you really know how long things took? How could you be fanatically certain that you were right and everyone else was going to burn in hell for not believing the way your bible told you to believe? What kind of merciful God would doom babies to a place of outcast simply because the parish priest was on vacation and a house fire killed everyone in the family on January 10th?

"Are you sure you need a drink?" came Reb's voice out of the vortex.
"Huh?"
"You seem out of it."
"I was just thinking."
"About what?"
Mitch didn't want to say the real answer. Limbo babies wasn't a good conversation staple.
"First-grade catechism."
"O-kay," Reb answered like Mitch was still losing it.
"How about a snifter of some really old brandy?" Mitch came up with a bland yet expensive suggestion.
"And an Irish Cream and a chocolate liquor," Reb completed the order. All of a sudden, this idea was sounding better. They sat and sipped, comfortable in the concept that they had chosen the best course of action for Mary.
"Do you want one or both of us to fly back with you?" Reb offered.
"No, I'll be fine. Honest," Mary was resolute. The first person she wanted to connect with when she got back was Fawn. And she didn't want to go into a whole big explanation about that. Neither Mitch nor Reb pressed the point and Mary gave thanks for small favors.
"You still haven't told me all about France."
"I'm not convinced that we know all about what happened," Reb replied.
"Other than I was accused of killing your Mother's admirer in a fit of jealous rage," Mitch embellished.
"Just how long were you there?"
"Not long. Men move pretty fast in Paris."

"How fast?"

"It was the first time we went out for lunch."

"And this guy appeared out of the blue?"

"Yup. Ready to buy us lunch and writing love poems to your mother. It was all a shock when he turned up dead."

"Love poems?" Mary honed in on what she felt was a pretty important detail.

"Well, just one poem, really," Reb was eager to clarify with an uneasy smile.

"Geez, not even Dad ever wrote you any love poems," Mary was putting way too fine a point on this.

"And just how would you know that?" Reb was defending her womanhood like it all really mattered.

"Because you never mentioned it."

"I don't always tell you everything."

"What else haven't you told me?"

"I'll begin my autobiography tomorrow. Remind me to buy a ream of paper."

"In the meantime, tell me about this poem," Mary got back to the subject of real interest.

"She can probably show it to you. She carries it everywhere," Mitch explained without the slightest hint of jealousy.

"You do?" Mary was now extremely interested.

"I wanted to throw it out, but kept it at Mitch's insistence."

"Now I'm confused."

"You want another drink?" Mitch asked.

"You think it would help?"

Mitch made eye contact with the barkeep and another round was on the way before anyone could come up with a reason why it was a bad idea.

"Good thing I don't have to fly the plane home," was Mary's idea of a toast.

"Show her the poem."

"I'm not sure I have it."

"It's in your purse."

"Pocketbook."

"Whatever."

Reb was reluctant to bring the paper to the table, literally, but all eyes were on her now. She fished the paper out of her pocketbook.

"Can I see it?" Mary asked.

"Well, I certainly wasn't going to read it out loud," Reb was back to being droll.

"That would be awfully awkward," Mitch nodded agreement.

Mary took her time reading the lines. Part of that was probably due to way too much alcohol floating around in her bloodstream. The other part was mostly due to the clunkiness of the ode itself.

"If this guy relied on his writing skills to get women to sleep with him, I'm sure he spent a lot of nights alone."

"The man's dead. All of his nights are going to be alone now," Mitch said quietly.

"You have a lot of sympathy for a complete stranger."

"I had a night in jail to mull it over. A lot goes through your mind when you're locked up with nothing to eat but oatmeal."

"So, how was it that you're still not locked up?" Mary asked.

"The only reason I can think of is that some other man was killed while I was still locked up."

"Who was this other guy?"

"One of our drivers. Same MO. I really don't believe I was ever really considered a suspect, but somebody had to go to jail."

"So you had a brief amount of contact with both of these men and because you were in jail at the time of the second murder, you were exonerated."

"Right," Mitch nodded.

"And Mother, you weren't a suspect because?"

"Because I'm in a wheelchair."

"So, two men are dead and because they were in your orbit and you have this weird poem as the only artifact of the events?"

"Are you getting to a point?" Reb could sense Mary's logical brain working in spite of the excess lubrication.

"Maybe the poem isn't really a poem at all?"

"You can say that again!"

"That's not what I mean. Maybe it's something else."

"Something else? With all the endearments and mushy mush?"

"That could just be camouflage."

"Like, it's in code," Mitch was beginning to see where Mary was going with this.

"Right. I mean, how romantic is it really to talk about a heart in such strange terms. If I were trying to impress a woman, I wouldn't be talking about a heart like I was a medical student. Would you?"

"I've never been very good at impressing women with my writing skills," Mitch told the unvarnished truth.

"She relies on her oral skills," Reb added.

Everyone was beginning to sustain the effects of a little too much alcohol. Mary was oblivious to the back and forth between Mitch and Reb. She was still engrossed by the paper in her hand.

"A heart doesn't even have five parts. What has five parts?"

"A pentagram."

"Like as in devil worship pentagram?"

"You think he was in some cult?"

"He didn't seem at all the type. He was tall and clean cut and very well dressed."

"That doesn't preclude someone from being in a cult. From what you've said about the murders, it was all pretty horrible. It wasn't like someone was shot and left for dead."

"So, you think he was trying to recruit me into a cult?" Reb asked.

"Or maybe he was trying to warn you about one?" Mary took the opposite view, as any good daughter does.

"I don't need any warning about a cult! That doesn't make sense."

"Well, it makes less sense than him trying to turn you into a devil worshiper by writing you a poem."

"So, we're back to square one."

"And running out of time," Mitch checked her watch. Mary would soon need to fly back to Colorado and solve her own predicament.

"You know you have our full support," Reb again reassured Mary.

"I know. When are you coming back?"

It was an opened-ended question.

"From New York to Kansas or from Kansas to Colorado?" Reb wanted clarification before she answered.

"How about west of the Mississippi for starters."

"Soon. I think we need a day or so just to recover from our France experience."

"You won't have many more opportunities to live it up before the baby arrives."

"Babies do change things."

"I'd better get going."

"Do you want this poem to decipher?" Reb offered.

"No. I wouldn't even want to try and explain it to Lisa if she found it in my possession. But I will keep thinking about it."

"That's all we can ask."

Reb and Mitch were upstairs before they discussed the matter again.

"Do you think this poem thing is really a sinister message?" Reb asked.

"I'm not sure about the sinister part, but Mary did make some good points. She had an objective viewpoint, which is something we lacked."

"We got all emotional about it?"

"As much as we ever do."

"I could use some rest."

"Me, too."

They snuggled up in bed together before Reb needed to talk again.

"You seemed very distracted tonight. Are you feeling alright?"

"Something was just bothering me, but I don't know what it was."

"Were you upset about the poem again?"

"No, that wasn't it at all."

"Do you think it was a cult message?"

"It really wasn't in the center."

"The center?"

"It was something about the periphery."

"The periphery? Can a poem have a periphery?"

"Not the poem. The room."

"What room?"

"The restaurant. The lounge. The lobby in between. You didn't sense it?"

"Sense what?"

"We were being observed."

Reb raised herself on one elbow. She was really taking care of herself, which was more that Mitch could say for herself. Reb had her incentive. Since the accident, she had to rely on her arms to do a lot of work that non-paralyzed people never need to worry about. She had to be able to transfer herself from chair to car to bed using upper body strength. Mitch noticed now how toned and buff Reb was and for a long moment got distracted all over again. Fantasies of losing an arm-wrestling contest teased her mind.

"So, that explains it!"

"Explains what?"

"Why you were acting in such a bizarre fashion tonight."

"Bizarre?"

"You haven't ordered one of each off a menu since we were at the diner in Utopia."

"Technically, I didn't order one of each tonight. Otherwise, I could have sampled steak and lobster and quail-"

"Okay, point taken. So why did you order one of every dessert?"

"Because I've spent my life trying to find something sweeter than you."

"And?"

"Failed in spectacular fashion."

"And?"

"I wanted to see if we could outlast all the other diners," Mitch finally got to the truth.

"You mean, you wanted to out eat everyone in the restaurant?"

"I wanted to see how long the people who were watching us would really stick with the task."

"And you think this person or persons were in the restaurant watching our every move because...?"

"I don't know why and it wasn't just the restaurant. Someone was in the bar as well."

"Someone? Like a different someone other than the one in the restaurant?"

"Right. It would have been way too obvious for the same ones to follow us across the lobby."

Reb paused to give this the serious consideration that Mitch had. She hadn't noticed anything out of the ordinary and since she prided herself on being observant, it annoyed her. Perhaps she had been too distracted in her conversations with Mary. For a moment, Reb doubted Mitch. It felt wrong to do so. Like she was somehow superior to Mitch and therefore automatically discounted everything she was saying.

"You think I'm mental," Mitch summed up in four words. Five if you counted contractions as two words.

"I think that maybe your imagination in running at a higher speed than usual."

"We could put my theory to the test and still have fun in the process."

"That sounds...interesting." Reb did her best to keep the panic out of her voice. Mitch's idea of proving a theory usually involved a break from convention.

"Tomorrow, let's take a whirlwind tour of New York City and its surrounding areas."

"How surrounding?" Reb asked cautiously.

"I'm making this up as I go along, just in case *someone is listening.*" Mitch mouthed the last three words.

Reb didn't say anything. It wouldn't do any good to ask for more information as long as Mitch was under the impression that they were being bugged. Whatever she had in store for the morning would just have to wait until then.

Mary rolled in late, even for her. Lisa stirred awake for a moment and then succumbed to sleep again before having a sustained conversation. It would have to wait until morning, which it did. And even then, it wasn't much of a dialogue since they were both due early to work.

"You must be exhausted, going all the way to New York and back all in one night. I've heard of whirlwind trips, but that's really pushing it," Lisa chatted as casually as she could while dressing in blue jeans and a t-shirt.

"I was lucky to sleep on the plane," Mary answered blandly. She didn't want to make the trip sound exciting, which wasn't much of a challenge since it hadn't been. Still, there wasn't any purpose served by making Lisa jealous. The meal had been good, the dessert made the trip tolerable and the liquor had expedited the slumber. A few years ago, a jet flight to the Big

Apple was an exciting lark. Now, it had been almost businesslike. One day, she would go again, when murder and fraud weren't the main topics of conversation. There were lovely places in New York, weren't there? Would Lisa even want to go and see the sights? Would Fawn? Mary shook her head. It didn't help to ask these kinds of questions to herself. She had no answers. Mary got to her office as early as she had planned even though she had jetted halfway across the country and back last night. She had called in sick the day before and now truly did look the part. With tired eyes, she began to study the account activity that had raised her suspicions. There indeed was a lot of reference to White Israel now that she was looking for the exact wording. The numbers involved were staggering once she cross-referenced the phrase with all the accounts in the company. But what didn't make sense to Mary was the fact that nobody in the company appeared to be filthy rich. Mary's assumption was that if someone was bilking money from the company, they were too smart to make a big show of it. It would be the best idea ever to leave this whole mess to the Colorado authorities. Lunch would be the best time to exit the premises. It would be a long morning.

Chapter 9

Mitch woke up first. This bed was great! Lots better than the Surete accommodations. Reluctantly, she got up quietly and took another nice hot bath with bubbles. She never did this sort of thing at home. It would have entailed having a bathtub that was a decent size and design, and, of course, bubble bath. They probably had bottles of bubble bath back home at the general store, but you would have actually had to buy the whole bottle. It wasn't like they allowed you to bring a shot glass and just take what you needed for an individual bath. So, here and now, she was enjoying a squishy bubble bath and wondering if this activity was considered to be overly feminine. Mitch had never given much thought to the issue. She had never been overly feminine during her formative years. It wasn't like she was ever prepping to be in a beauty contest. Being Miss Colorado just wasn't on her list of things to do. Not that she had any knee-jerk reaction against anyone else running for the title, but this was, in some circles, a complicated conversation. The fact of the matter was that beauty was a pinnacle issue in society. You could try and deny it all you want, but we all consciously or subconsciously seek out beauty. All you had to do was to sit in a coffee shop some busy morning and watch people come through the door. Then try and deny that you don't look longer at beautiful people. You do. You know you do. Which is different from staring. Looking and staring are two different things. If an obese person makes their way into your coffee shop, you try not to stare out of decorum. But it happens. Social scientists working on some Ph. D. could probably explain the difference between looking longer than usual and staring, and you'd probably need algebra to understand.

"Wow, you are really deep in thought, aren't you!" Reb was peering around the edge of the bathroom door.

Mitch had jumped at the word 'wow' but not enough to disturb too many bubbles.

"I'm thinking about Miss Colorado."

"Meeting or entering?"

"Huh?"

"Are you going to compete for the crown yourself or do you just want to meet the winner?"

"Neither, actually."

"It must be a very specific train of thought."

"I was the quintessential tomboy as a child. Running in beauty pageants didn't seem to be nearly as much fun as climbing trees."

"Your bubbles are bursting."

"Must be time to get out of the tub and get on the road."

"So, where are we going?"

"I'll tell you once we get on the highway."

"I really don't think all this cloak and dagger is necessary."

"No use taking chances."

Mitch surrendered the bathroom to Reb and they were ready to head out in thirty minutes. The SUV Mitch rented was nice and roomy.

"I guess I'll let you drive since you're the only one who knows where we're going," Reb tried to sound peevish but was now intrigued by the secrecy.

"I don't know exactly where I'm going, but one of these roads has to lead to Yonkers," Mitch was studying the map after she and Reb were seated in the vehicle.

"What's in Yonkers?"

"Yonkerites?" Mitch made her best guess.

"Do you need me to be your navigator?"

"It would be a Godsend."

"Hey, maybe there's a couple of tour books in here as well," Reb started going through the various compartments. "Here we are," Reb produced two books with a flourish. "I wonder what they say about Yonkers."

"Instead, why don't you find us a nice place to eat in Tarry Town."

"Tarry Town?" Reb repeated.

"It sounds like a nice, calm, little place."

"Tired of the big city already?"

"I've just never been to Tarry Town."

"I've never been to a million places. That doesn't mean that I'm going there anytime soon."

Mitch loved Reb's logical mind.

"You did bring the poem with you, I hope?"

"Yes, even though I probably didn't need to. Don't you have it memorized by now?"

"Not really. Just the pentagram part."

"Why don't we find someplace out in the New York wilderness and ceremoniously burn it?"

"And risk starting a forest fire?"

"We'd need to find a forest first."

"You're the navigator."

"Just keep driving."

The ride up to Tarry Town made for a relaxing morning, after Mitch found her way out of the city. No small feat. There were people who lived all their lives in the vicinity of New York City who had never obtained a driver's license. Mitch now knew why. Tarry Town was in the lower Hudson Valley, an area made famous in American history as a shipping conduit and more recently as a tourist draw due mostly to mansions, antiques and Ichabod Crane.

"Please don't tell me that we're doing the cemetery tour," Reb asked.

"You make it sound like I drag you through cemeteries every chance I get."

"Sleepy Hollow wasn't on my top ten list of destinations."

"Headless Horsemen give you the creeps?"

"I'd rather drink a latte on a charming front porch of some Colonial B & B."

"Who wouldn't?" Mitch smiled. "Let's take a break."

Thanks to Reb's quick study of the tour books, they located a quaint coffeehouse that didn't have so many steps that Mitch couldn't get Reb situated in the patio seating area. The establishment had latte and about a dozen other coffee drinks from which to choose. Mitch opted for a triple-shot mocha. That would keep her awake during all the driving they planned to do through the Hudson Valley.

Tourists and locals wandered in and out of the place. It was easy to tell them apart. Locals were recognized by the wait staff and didn't dress to impress. Tourists looked all touristy. There was just no other way to put it. And then, there were the really dressed-up folks who caught Mitch's eye. They had come in not

long after Mitch and Reb had been served and had taken up a
strategic perch so that they could watch all the action and still
make a quick exit. Mitch now knew that last night hadn't been
just her imagination.

"You're not drinking your mocha. Is it okay? What's wrong?"
Reb was full of questions.

"It's fine. I was just wondering where you might want to spend
the night?"

"We're not going back to the city?"

"When there are so many charming places to spend the night up
here?"

"That's such a romantic idea. So how is it that there's no hint of
romance in your voice?"

It was hard to act romantic when you were being watched. How
movie stars did it Mitch would never know.

"I guess I'm just preoccupied," Mitch figured this was a better
answer than once again discussing her intuition that they were
being watched.

"By what?"

"Let's go," Mitch said quickly.

"Now? We haven't finished our coffee!"

"We can take it with us. I want to visit Sleepy Hollow
Graveyard before it gets too dark."

"It's a long time until sunset."

"Good. I wouldn't want to risk it."

Reb shook her head. "You're up to something, aren't you?"

"I'm just ready to roll, so to speak."

Reb let the comment slide. Mitch, for whatever reason, was
done here and it was time to go. They took their coffee and
headed to the car. When Reb checked the tour book again, she
realized that Kykuit, the famous Rockefeller Estate, was
practically right next door.

"Can we make an unscheduled stop?"

"Of course," Mitch replied.

"Let's take a tour of the Rockefeller Estate."

"How long will that take?"

"Hours, probably. Do we have time for it?"

"Sounds like fun!" Mitch couldn't have sounded more
enthusiastic.

"You're not being facetious?"

"Absolutely not. I'd like to see how rich people live."

Reb shook her head. Somewhere in that statement was a rich vein of irony. Reb thought better of discussing it right now. Maybe later she would revisit it. They drove to the entrance and Mitch bought tickets for admission. They wandered the opulent house and ground of Kykuit like the tourists that they were. Art, sculpture, gardens and fountains. It was far beyond anything that Mitch could ever afford. Even so, it was a pleasant way to spend a summer day.

"And now, to the cemetery!" Reb was happy to indulge Mitch after having her wish fulfilled.

"To the cemetery!" Mitch echoed.

Once they arrived at Sleepy Hollow, they sat in the rented car for a quiet minute. Cemeteries tended to foster somber moods.

"That estate place was sure something," Mitch stated.

"It was breathtaking. I think I understand now what you meant about how the rich live."

"There are certainly degrees of wealth. I don't think both of us combined could afford even one roomful of that kind of furniture."

"And yet, when we die, we end up in a place like this with a solitary tombstone."

"I've seen some pretty big tombstones."

"Yeah, but the owner is still dead."

"Did we come here to talk about death?"

"No," Mitch stated quietly.

They had driven to the most remote part of the cemetery and Mitch had vigilantly observed the road for a number of minutes. If you wanted to avoid a traffic jam, all you needed to do was go to the nearest cemetery. Except for Memorial Day. Mitch's grandmother had called it Decoration Day. It was the day when her generation dressed up in their military finest and decorated the grave sites of fallen soldiers and other deceased relatives. Back then, the focus was on war. The war to end all wars was fought and won and didn't end any wars at all. We had bombs we were afraid to use. And still, those weren't really a deterrent.

"Did you come here to see something in particular?" Reb asked.

Neither the Headless Horseman nor Ichabod Crane was

entombed here. There was just the famous bridge over which
they had creaked to get to the far corner of the cemetery. But the
scene made famous by the book was just that, a piece of fiction.
"I'm going to check the tires." Mitch announced.
She got out of the car and disappeared from sight like she had
stepped into a dug grave. A few moments later, she resurfaced
and got back in the vehicle. She handed a note to Reb that read,
"The car is bugged." It probably wasn't the exact terminology.
But if she had written "lojacked" or "GPSd", it might not have
registered as quickly. Besides, there could also be tiny listening
devices in the car as well. Whoever it was that had these finds of
resources could be eavesdropping as well.
"Can I see the tour books?" Mitch asked a logical, innocent
question.
"Sure."
Mitch studied the various bed and breakfasts until she found the
wording that she was looking for. She silently pointed it out to
Reb and Reb nodded silently. Then, Mitch said in a normal tone
of voice, "I wanted to see the grave of Washington Irving. He is
considered to be the first American to earn a living as a writer."
"The author of The Legend of Sleepy Hollow," Reb added.
They found the gravesite, spent a moment in quiet reverence, and
then left the cemetery. Mitch checked the rear view mirror.
Somebody was back there. Somewhere.

Mary couldn't get away for a lunch break. Every time she tried
to leave, something else had come up. It was the price she paid
for taking a day off. Unfinished business from yesterday kept
her occupied until six. So much for getting in touch with a
government employee. It would have to wait until tomorrow. A
drink sounded good. She went to the usual place and ordered the
usual and Fawn was at her table even before the drink.
"Are you okay?" Fawn asked when nobody else was around.
"Sure. Why wouldn't I be?"
"The last time we talked, you were investigating illegal stuff. I
didn't know if you were safe!"
"I'm safe."
"So, are you working with criminals? What did you find out?"

Mary took a sip of her scotch. Fawn seemed overly worried and Mary found it enchanting.

"Can I buy you a drink?" was Mary's response. It always seemed rude to drink in front of someone.

"No, I think I'll wait."

"Until what?"

"What?"

"Until what? What are you waiting until?" Mary was curious. Were they going to end up at Fawn's apartment again? Is that what she wanted? Mary knew that the real reason she drank here in the first place was so that she could run into Fawn. She saw more of Fawn lately than of Lisa.

"I'm just not ready for a drink yet."

"Then, why are you in a bar?"

"I guess that I hoped you would be here sooner rather than later."

"So, you're spying on me or something?" Mary felt suddenly awkward. It was like she was a teenage boy with braces trying to ask a girl to prom and floundering in the process. Badly. It didn't matter anymore whether she was investigating criminals. It mattered that Fawn was here and concerned.

"I'm just following up. Don't get all full of yourself."

Mary laughed in spite of being brought back down to earth. "I did do some more investigating," she said.

"And?" Fawn was on the edge of her patience.

"Are you sure you don't want that drink?" Mary seemed stuck on this point.

"Do you want to go back to my place?" Fawn asked.

"Okay," Mary hoped that she didn't sound overly eager. Fawn made her living dealing with eager people, after all.

"Come with me in my car."

"What about mine?"

"I'll give you a lift back. As usual."

Mary was easy to convince. They rode the few blocks in silence and Mary really didn't get to talking much at all until she was settled on Fawn's couch. It was getting more and more comfortable each time she was here.

"I did find a lot of questionable transactions."

"How many?"

223

"I didn't keep track."

"How about a wild guess?"

"Dozens, at least."

"Dozens of dollars?"

"No, dozens of transactions," Mary succeeded at sounding condescending.

"Oh, so how much money are we talking about?"

"It depends."

"On what?" Fawn wanted specifics.

"On whether fees are being pocketed or entire funds are being redirected."

"Would that make a difference?"

"The difference could be millions."

"You mean to tell me that all along, you've been working at a place that handles that much money?" Fawn seemed overly gushy in her surprise.

"You didn't know that?" Mary asked back. Didn't we all make the assumption that people who handled stocks were working with loads of funds? It was far too simplistic to assume that everyone knew about something just because you knew something.

"Well, I knew you were really important," Fawn went back to flattery as a possible defense. "But, wow!"

"I need to think about getting home," Mary said suddenly. If she stayed much longer, it wouldn't take much to convince her to stay the night. And then, she wouldn't be any better than Lisa. How important was that? Claiming the high moral ground was a sport worthy of medals in Mary's book. How could she possibly disapprove of Lisa's attraction to Trish from the bedroom of a prostitute?

"You just got here!"

"How do you feel about me?" Mary asked the question that was more important to her than all those millions of missing dollars. It all came down to this.

"How do I feel about you?" Fawn repeated the question like she had heard it wrong.

"You heard correctly."

"What does that have to do with the missing money?"

"It has nothing to do with anything, actually. Other than the fact that we've been running into each other and having lots of drinks and doing a lot of sitting on your couch. So I just logically wondered how you feel. About me."

"Feelings aren't logical," Fawn said quietly.

"Feelings are anything but logical," Mary agreed. She regretted bringing the subject up now that it was awkward beyond belief. "Forget I asked," Mary spoke into the void.

"Too late," Fawn said quietly as she faced Mary.

Their kiss was magnetic, the attraction of all earthly forces. They had kissed before and then joked about being just friends. This was no longer the realm of friendly kissing. This was serious affection. Was it love? Was it too early to know for sure? Mary didn't know the answers to the questions that flooded her mind. This felt natural and blessed by the Universe and so why question it now? Mary decided to be clever and keep all these thoughts to herself. It shouldn't matter about Fawn's profession and abilities in that area.

"You're awfully quiet," Fawn stated the obvious.

"I usually stick my foot in my mouth at times like this," Mary admitted the truth.

"Do you still need to go?"

"Yes, I still need to go."

"You're not like anyone I've ever known."

A statement like that can be taken a number of ways. Mary took it as being all good. The look in Fawn's eyes confirmed her assumption. Could she say the same in return and have it sound charming rather than crass? How many ways can you say, "I've never met a prostitute before," and have it sound even close to a compliment? What slipped out instead was, "Would you ever consider leaving your chosen profession?"

Fawn seemed to be giving the question the same serious consideration one would give a proposal of marriage.

"And do what, exactly?" she answered with a question.

The conversation had become edgy. They had gone from a tender kiss to an uncomfortable dialogue in a matter of seconds. Mary could've easily blurted out, "And be my wife," except that she already had one. Not in the strictest sense, of course. And not in any other sense recently, either. Still, she didn't want to

225

go all Mormon and start collecting wives every time it seemed like a good idea.

"What did you do before you became a lady of the evening?"

"I dropped out of high school," Fawn answered flatly.

"By necessity?" Mary probed.

"Everybody is always escaping something, aren't they?"

Fawn's answer hadn't exactly cleared anything up. From the vagueness of her reply, it sounded as though her teenage years weren't ideal. By comparison, Mary had had such a different adolescence that she didn't know what question to ask next. Yet, silence felt so unfeeling.

"Did you need the money?" seemed like the least intrusive and most logical inquiry.

"Yeah, right. I needed the money. Everybody needs money, right," Fawn answered with more than a tinge of bitterness in her voice.

"Yeah, I guess so," Mary agreed. If the fight started in earnest, at least she could declare agreeability as her main defense.

"It's amazing what men will pay you to do," Fawn added.

Mary began to feel squeamish. She didn't want to listen to a litany of what men did to prostitutes. By extension, if she couldn't stomach hearing about it, how on earth did Fawn participate night after night without suffering emotional and physical trauma?

"I imagine so," Mary had no clue.

"You have no clue," Fawn the Mind Reader chided. It was a gentle chide. More gentle than it would've been when they first met. Their relationship had changed. Mostly for the better. What would life be like with a former prostitute? Would sex be a problem at first? Would it be detached out of habit? Would it mean nothing? Or would it mean everything because it finally meant something? No looking at a clock to make sure you gave someone their money's worth?

"You don't have a client tonight?" Mary asked what she really wanted to know.

"I guess you're my client tonight," Fawn said with a softness that caught Mary unaware. She had grown accustomed to the sassy persona of Fawn. This unguarded woman was real and vulnerable and damn alluring. Did everyone secretly believe that they could redeem a hooker and was this the sole basis for the romantic feelings that Mary was now experiencing? Or was it true love settling in for a long stay?

"As nice as that sounds," Mary was once again cautious with words, "I'm not sure that being a client was what I was aspiring to."

"It doesn't take much to make you feel all icky, does it?" Fawn smiled through her decisive surmise.

"Words mean things. They stand for something. The word 'client' means that I'm paying you to have sex with me and since neither one of those things has happened, then I'm not even close to being your client."

"You're forgetting about the necklace."

"Oh that, well-"

"Yeah that! Unless it was paste, I'm figuring it's worth a whole lot of money."

"It was a gift."

"Nobody ever gives something without expecting something in return. I think that's one of those laws of physics, isn't it?"

"I don't know much about physics, but I never expected you to sleep with me because of that."

"Never?"

"Never. I'm just not the bartering kind."

"So, we may never sleep together?" Fawn sounded like she was seeking closure on the question.

"It's really getting late."

"Right. I'd better drive you back to your car."

"Okay."

Mary felt like she had somehow hurt Fawn's feelings or bruised her ego or committed some other unnamed transgression. They drove to Mary's car and Fawn's parting comment was interesting. "Keep your head down at work tomorrow."

"Thanks," Mary nodded.

Chapter 10

One thing about all these cute little bed and breakfasts all along
the Hudson Valley was that it was difficult to find one that had
wheelchair access. Old houses had lots of stairs and steps and
Reb wasn't normally accustomed to sleeping in a lobby.
Fortunately, what was difficult wasn't by definition impossible.

Mitch and Reb had secured a comfortable room for the night and
Mitch was now happily browsing even more tourist information
as she was stretched out on the bed.
"You missed your calling. You should have been a travel
agent," Reb was smiling.
"I do enjoy seeing the sights. Anything you want to see
tomorrow?"
"I didn't wear you out at Kykuit?"
"Not a chance."
"Okay, what are my choices?"
"There are museums, more estates, antique shops, and, hey,
here's something that might pique your interest! How about a
trip to West Point!"
"A military academy? You think that would be on my list?"
"I guess I thought that it might be up your alley?"
"Why?" Reb kept her question short to gauge which direction
Mitch was going with this.
"Uh, because it's one of those military things and you did used to
be a Senator and all."
"So, because I was a Senator, I'm naturally into all that war
stuff?"
"I didn't mean it exactly like that."
"How exactly did you mean it?"
"I was thinking that governments and military institutions work
together in a Democracy."
"Okay."
"And that there's a mutual respect and support between the two."
"That's logical."
"And West Point is the largest military site east of the
Mississippi, next to the Pentagon, of course," Mitch was pleased
that she had remembered all this from her tour book perusal.

"The Pentagon. Of course," Reb echoed.

"The Pentagon…of course!" Mitch was suddenly looking pale.

"Are you okay?" Reb asked, noting the color drain from Mitch's face.

"The Pentagon."

"You've said that several times now."

"Right. Pentagon."

"Are you feeling alright?" Reb hadn't gotten her answer to that query and it irritated her when she didn't get answers.

"We have to go."

"Go? Go where? We just got settled!"

"We need to go to where we can talk to someone about the Pentagon."

"What are you talking about?" Reb was now very concerned. Mitch normally made sense. Sort of.

"The poem."

Reb felt Mitch's forehead like she was searching for proof of delirium. Or maybe just the flu.

"Jacque's poem. It wasn't a love poem. It was a warning."

"A warning?"

"Right. It wasn't a love poem after all."

"You said that already."

"I know. It makes me happy. Except for the panic."

"You're worried about the Pentagon?"

"It's the Heart with Five Parts."

"All pentagons have five parts, or sides, actually."

"So, you were paying attention in geometry class."

"Which means that you don't need to be in such a panic. Terrorists have already tried to attack the Pentagon."

Reb was right. Terrorists had attacked the Pentagon and the World Trade Center.

"Wasn't there an earlier attack on the World Trade Center?" Mitch was fuzzy on the details, but remembered a bombing in the underground garage.

"What's your point?"

"Well, if they mounted two attacks against the World Trade Center, they why is it folly to suspect that they wouldn't do the same with the Pentagon?"

"I never said it was folly. Perhaps a bit far-fetched."

"It's not so far-fetched that two men have paid with their lives."

"You suspect that it's all connected?"

"I think it's all very connected and maybe even more connected than you or I can know. But what we do know is that we need to tell someone. Let's pack up."

"You're kidding."

"We need to drive to Washington D.C."

"Now?"

"You know what! We don't even need to pack. We can come back for our stuff later. Just remember to bring the poem."

Secretly, Reb had always wondered what life would be like living with a mentally unbalanced person. It was certainly...interesting.

"Okay. I'll go along with you this time. But you owe me. Big time."

"I'll make it up to you, I promise," Mitch said fervently.

"A yacht would be nice."

"In Kansas?"

"Negotiations are still open."

They gathered up a few essentials, including the poetic evidence of Mitch's alleged unbalance, and quietly guided their rental vehicle down the road leading to the highway. And then, the action movie started. The black SUV that had followed them everywhere now overtook them and blocked their path. Shifting into reverse would be fruitless, another identical SUV was now behind them. Not even Nancy Drew could get out of this predicament. People, mostly men, exited the vehicles and stood with weapons drawn, ready to die in a gunfight. Mitch had never carried a gun. She had actually shot one once or twice at a tin can when she was a teenager. It hadn't been the highlight of her life. She more acutely remembered being shot in a place crucial enough to the human body to have a permanent disability. Not being able to fully straighten ones elbow paled in comparison to what other gunshot victims endured. Still, it ached at the thought of being engaged in battle again.

"Put your hands where I can see them!" the voice bellowed out. She complied and urged Reb to follow suit. No reason to risk irking the folks with the itchy trigger fingers.

"Get out of the car! NOW!"

"I can't do both," Mitch said back in a reasonable tone of voice.
"If you move slowly, I think you'll be okay," Reb remarked with
total calm, like she had been ordered out of vehicles a dozen or
so times.
"You think so?"
"They haven't shot us yet."

Mitch opened the car door and was pulled out by her bad elbow.
It wasn't pleasant being manhandled by her bad limb, but after a
body search for weapons, she was simply put in handcuffs and
placed in the rear seat of the trailing SUV. They were off and
driving before Mitch could see what was to become of Reb.
"I don't suppose anybody wants to tell me where we're going?"
Silence descended.

Mitch decided to calmly await whatever was going to happen
next. Getting all worked up would just rob her of what energy
she had left. They traveled for a few minutes by car until they
reached an airfield. A huge, black helicopter was waiting and
before Mitch could voice her awe at the sight of the myth turned
real, she was inside and lifting off. It would've been nice to do
this in daylight, and any flying was amazing to her. Just about
the time that she wondered if they were going to copter the entire
way to wherever the hell they were going, they landed. It
happened quickly, not like in an airplane where you took a good,
long descent from the sky. Helicopters didn't need to do that.
After being on terra firma for only a moment, Mitch was
trundled into an aircraft that soon thereafter rumbled down a
runway. East, West, North and South became a jumble as the
plane roared through the night sky. Whoever had arranged this
little jaunt had spared no expense. And if Reb was transported
under separate cover, the tab was double.
"I don't suppose I get a meal on this flight?" Mitch figured she
might as well up the ante.
The heavily-armed person guarding her didn't take the bait.
"How about a drink then? You got any bourbon in those tiny
bottles? Or did the pilot finish them off already?"
Still no response.

"Okay, can I get a tonic water or club soda for my impending airsickness?"

He shifted the gun that he had trained on her, but it was all for show. Mitch didn't know much about rifles, other than they were longer than pistols. From the size of this weapon, it would probably shoot a hole right through the fuselage. And then, they would all be dead. Mitch rearranged herself slowly and carefully into the most comfortable position possible and then closed her eyes. It had been a long day. She slept until she was prodded awake for landing. It had been one of those naps where it was impossible to tell if it had lasted one minute or one hour. It was still dark, so it hadn't been hours, unless they were crossing a lot of time zones. Rifle guy was still there, wide awake, perhaps just a little jealous of Mitch's restful journey.

They landed, rolled to some predetermined spot and then disembarked into another SUV. It felt humid, like they had stayed near water. They drove down roads for a while, down streets for a while and then suddenly turned into a tunnel like a subway system. Only top secret places like the Bat Cave had secret tunnel entrances. Gotham. Bat cave. Maybe next she would meet Bruce Wayne?

The SUV stopped in front of an elevator and Mitch, with new guards, went up two floors to a hallway. She was escorted into a room, released from her handcuffs and left alone. This was all too familiar. Another interrogation room, more sophisticated than the one in Paris, but still unmistakable. If another guy had been murdered, she had an alibi. But where was Reb now? Probably in a similar room, and no doubt raising a bigger fuss than just asking for a drink of water. Mitch made a cradle with her arms and put her head down on the table. Whatever was happening was out of her control. She resumed her nap.

Mary woke up early. She knew it was important to be at work for what was most likely her last day there. Once she turned her fellow co-workers over to the authorities, her job was history.

"You are sure keeping long hours," Lisa said as a conversation starter. They hadn't done much conversing lately. They would soon need to consult a thesaurus to come up with another word for awkward.

"I have a feeling that's about to change," Mary said with none of the joy that normally signals a lightening of work burdens.

"Are you getting fired?" Lisa asked with more than passing interest.

"Why would you ask me that?"

"I have to ask because you don't talk to me about it anymore."

"I'll talk about it tonight. If you're going to be here?"

"I'll have dinner ready if you'll show up."

It sounded exactly like a fight, except without the volume. Mary left before Lisa could expound on the menu selections. She really didn't care what they ate. She wouldn't taste it anyway. Lisa left five minutes after Mary, not even bothering to take anything out of the freezer. If Mary did show up, they could eat takeout. Lisa arrived at Trish's before she had lifted out of the funk of the conversation.

"How are you?" Trish noticed Lisa's mood immediately.

"What are you doing for dinner?" was Lisa's unusual response.

"Besides eating?" Trish wanted clarification.

"As in, is it going to be another broccoli-a-thon?"

"It doesn't have to be," Trish could stand a change as well. "Do you want me to make reservations somewhere?"

"As long as you don't reserve the entire restaurant."

"I won't. I promise. What are you in the mood for?"

"Steak."

"And lobster?" Trish brightened up like it could turn into a real gourmet indulgence.

"Just anything but broccoli."

"Okay. You have a date."

Lisa might have felt ill at ease at the wording, but she was too busy feeling guilty at her actions instead. Was her behavior toward Mary passive aggressive or just pissed off? Only a psychologist would know for sure.

Mary got to work on time, just under the bell, and was at her desk for thirty minutes before she heard the hubbub in the hallway. It wasn't screaming like a bank robbery, but there were

233

raised voices and lots of scuffling around. Before Mary could decide what action to take, her door was banged open and a gun was pointed at her head. For whatever relief it provided, the person holding the gun was in uniform. Some sort of Federal ATF Marshall by the looks of him.

"Put your hands on your head."

Mary did so without hesitation or fear. She had planned to contact the authorities on her lunch break anyway. It was convenient for them to make house calls, or in this case, office calls. What was strange to Mary, as events unfolded, was that she was perp-marched out of the lobby in front of the other employees. No one else was in handcuffs yet, especially the people she knew to be guilty of the embezzlement. It was as if she was the sole guilty party and all the guilty people were innocent. The fear that had stayed at bay until now started creeping into her stomach. Mary was driven downtown to a building that served as the major Federal justice center in Colorado. The room she ended up in was small, windowless, and had a suspicious mirror through which she knew she was being observed. She had seen too many cop shows on TV to be fooled. So much for having a lunch break. Time crawled by. No one came in. Her hands were still in cuffs and her bladder wasn't happy.

When the door finally opened after way too much time had elapsed, Mary looked up to see the last person on earth that she would have ever expected to see.

"Huh?" was all that Mary could say.

"Good morning. I'm Special Agent in Charge O'Neal."

"*Agent* O'Neal?" Mary said as Fawn sat across the interrogation table from her.

"Special Agent in Charge O'Neal."

"Special Agent O'Neal?" Mary felt the burn of embarrassment start to creep up her neck.

"Special Agent in Charge O'Neal," Fawn clarified all business like for the record. Like they had never kissed.

Mary nodded. She was feeling her embarrassment mix with anger now. It was a sickening sensation and she had to force burning bile back down her throat.

234

"And I need to ask you a few questions."

"Well, I need to ask you a couple of things myself while we're at it."

"This will go a lot better for you if I do the asking and you do the answering."

Mary resented the hell out of this. It was a stunning revelation. Wasn't it enough that she had been tricked, almost literally, by this woman? It was dawning on Mary that so far, she was the only one in trouble in this whole plot. No one else had been marched out of her office building, at least to her immediate knowledge. She wasn't in the mood to be nice. They were being watched through the mirror on the wall and every word was being recorded. This bullshit about answering instead of asking questions had a shelf life of zero right about now.

"So, our kisses meant nothing to you?" was Mary's idea of an opening volley. Her eyes were hard. She could play tough, too. If this agent and agency wanted answers, they were going to get them. All of them.

"What kisses?"

"When we spent the night together!" Mary figured she may as well test the limits of this situation."

"Are you willing to take a polygraph?"

"Are you?"

Mary studied Fawn for any indication that this could be anything but ugly. Moments passed. Hell, Mary had all day. She had this day and many more to come now that she was out of a job. As long as Agent O'Neal wasn't in any big hurry, neither was Mary.

"You're not in a very talkative mood, I take it?" Fawn said in that same tone of voice that Mary recognized from their previous encounters. It jolted her to the core. In such a short period of time, she had gotten used to this tone. Gotten used to looking forward to hearing it. Mary had talked to Fawn more than she had to Lisa over the past month and not just talky talk. Real talk. At least, it had been real for Mary. Apparently none of it had been real for Fawn.

"What are you thinking?" Fawn finally asked when silence stretched too thin for an interrogation.

"Was it all a lie?"

Fawn grimaced slightly at the question. "Don't ask what you don't want an answer to."

With that pronouncement, she picked up her case file folder and left the room. She'd be back with more questions soon enough. Mary would be ready…for a lawyer.

Chapter 11

Mitch slept well in the cradle of her arms and would've continued to do so had someone not slammed a door. It jolted her awake, but by no means threw her off her game plan. Some guy named Agent Samuels sat down opposite her.

"Name?"

"Mitch Tanner. No rank. No serial number. Do you want my Social Security Number instead?"

"We already have it."

"Well, if you have that, then you already know my name."

"Just making sure I'm in the right room."

"My dentist made that mistake once. I almost got a crown out of it."

"Do you know why you are here?"

"I've ruled out braces."

"Is that a yes or a no?"

"It's a little of both. I know that there might be an attack pending on the Pentagon. I haven't figured out who would be stupid or foolish enough to attempt it."

"And if you're not the one mounting the attack, then how do you know about it?"

Mitch had been in enough interrogation situations lately to appreciate the logic. "A guy in France was killed after giving us a clue."

"Us?"

"Reb and I."

"Reb?"

"Former U.S. Senator Rebecca Fairbanks."

"You expect me to believe that some guy in France knew that he was giving this alleged clue to a Senator? That's a bit of a stretch."

"You've never been married to a United States Senator, have you?" Mitch smiled. There hadn't been much to smile about the last couple of hours. It felt good to relax. Yeah, she was still under suspicion for sedition or treason or some other crime against the nation, but she felt in no real danger. It was one thing to be shadowed all around a cemetery. That had been spooky. Now, however, she was in a nice, clean room. So even though

237

she was still being questioned, it was all okay. They were all on the same side.

"Not too many people can claim to be married to a Senator, and, technically, neither can you."

"It feels like marriage to me."

"I suggest you start telling the truth."

"The truth about living with a Senator is that people come out of the woodwork to talk to you."

"Is that so?"

"It's amazing, really. After the President, the one-hundred most important people in America are Senators. Some would even reverse that ranking, depending on who you ask."

"But Senator Fairbanks is no longer serving in the Senate."

"In some cases, that makes them even more revered. Don't ask me why. I'm just an ordinary citizen."

"Why were you and ex-Senator Fairbanks in France?"

Not this story again! Mitch figured that he had already studied up on the report of the Surete. Honest to God, it was the last time she would ever go shopping in Paris. Maybe Dublin or Botswana would have baby furniture. Mitch gave her best recounting of events to this agent. He barely nodded as they went point by point down the list of events.

"Okay," he stood up to go.

"One more thing you should know," Mitch intoned.

"What?"

"I wouldn't call Reb ex-Senator if I were you."

He nodded thoughtfully. It was apparent to Mitch that he had been raised right to seriously take advice on how to properly respect people. It was also obvious to Mitch that this was all a lot more serious than a couple of murdered men in Paris. Not that that in itself wasn't serious enough. But murder was murder and terrorism was something far beyond that. Orders of multitude beyond. She put her head back down to rest.

Mitch was awakened again by the door opening and closing. No slamming this time. Her friend was back and seated at the table.

"So you didn't buy any baby furniture in France."

238

"Is that a question or a statement?" Mitch asked. She was very much beginning to regret not having splurged on something, anything, for the baby.

"Just a clarification. You can understand why it makes your entire alibi suspicious."

"Are you married, Agent Samuels?"

"I'm the one asking the questions."

"I'll take that as a 'no' because otherwise you would know that women do a lot of shopping without ever buying anything."

"And you couldn't shop in Kansas?"

"At the risk of getting on your bad side again by asking you another question, have you ever been to Kansas?"

"No."

"It's great if you're shopping for farm equipment. When the baby needs a tractor, I won't even need to leave the county."

"But you left the United States to buy a crib?"

"That's not a crime."

"And then some men got killed trying to warn you about an attack on the Pentagon."

"It sounds farfetched when you say it."

"Have you ever heard of a group called White Israel?"

"No."

"Never?"

"No."

"How can you be so sure?"

"Because if I had heard the words white and Israel in the same sentence, I would've remembered it."

"You would?"

"I'd bet you a thousand dollars that if you asked a hundred people on the street if they had heard the term White Israel, those hundred people would say no as well. It's a pretty unique term."

"It would depend on where you did the asking."

"Why?"

"Because there are certain places in the United States where the words White Israel would ring a bell."

"Places I've obviously never visited."

"Are you so sure?" he asked like he knew something pertinent to this case that Mitch didn't know.

"After ruling out Germany, really, I'm clueless."

"You don't think White Israel would be known in Germany?" Agent Samuel's eyes showed a hint of light.

"I don't know because I've never been there. I predicated my answers on whether or not I had visited the place.

The agent sighed deeply. He was handsome. Handsome men who sighed deeply had no effect on Mitch.

"So you've never heard the term White Israel?"

"Asked and answered."

"Even when you had dinner with Mary Fairbanks?"

Mitch's eyes narrowed. She had been right all along. They had been spied upon.

"You're smiling?" he asked.

"I rarely get credit for being right. Allow me to enjoy this moment."

"You and your friends are under suspicion for terrorism and you're enjoying yourself?"

"Honestly, do I look like a terror cell to you? I can't even find a crib in Paris!"

"People more innocent looking than you have been traitors to their country."

Mitch stopped talking to regroup. She and Reb and *Mary* were all under suspicion? Were they all in custody? If she got one phone call, who was left on the list to contact? Please, Dear Lord, spare me the ignominy of having to call Lisa to arrange bail, Mitch prayed silently. The end would never be heard of this.

"Do I get a phone call?"

"No."

"Oh, good!" Mitch was relieved.

Agent Samuels sighed again. He was so confused.

"It's all just too complicated to explain," Mitch nodded wisely. He just shook his head.

Chapter 12

Mary waited as long as possible before loudly requesting a
bathroom break. It was still the United States of America. They
wouldn't allow her to soil herself, would they? Someone had
been monitoring her. The door opened and Special Agent in
Charge Fawn was back.
"I'll escort you to the bathroom."
At the word "escort" Mary burst out laughing. Which didn't
help her circumstances in the slightest.
"You think something is funny?"
"It would appear that no matter what you do as a career choice,
you're still just an escort."
Fawn didn't find this funny in the least. "Follow me."
"They walked single file down a hallway that was conspicuously
empty. No glass windows or open doorways. Just a hall.
"Aren't you afraid I'll make a break for it?"
"You would be in leg chains if we were worried."
"Leg chains! I thought the handcuffs were just a bit over the
top."
"You're not considered a flight risk."
"I usually charter."
"Your friends sure do."
"My friends?"
"Your New York friends."
"I don't have any friends in New York."
"So are you denying that you recently flew there?"
This was such a clever strategy. Get somebody with a full
bladder on their feet and take them for a walk down a long series
of hallways while you ask leading questions.
"You female agents should sue for discrimination."
"Why?"
"We've passed two men's restrooms already."
"More men than women work here."
"Shouldn't matter."
They arrived at the bathroom and even it was under guard.
"The men's rooms didn't have guards," Mary stated the obvious.
"There are no male detainees wandering the halls."
Mary went in, followed by Fawn.

"Don't tell me that you're going to be in here," Mary looked at Fawn.

"Regulations."

Mary held out her wrists, expecting to be released from her cuffs.

"Make yourself useful, then."

"Sorry. More regulations."

"You're kidding, right?"

"No."

Mary now knew that, one way or another, everyone gets their revenge. She had made a remark about escorts and now she would need to figure out a way to go to the bathroom in handcuffs. Well, at least nobody was in a hurry around here. Except Mary.

"Okay. See you in an hour."

"You need to leave the door open."

"Isn't this against the Geneva Convention or something?"

"You think you're being ill-treated?"

"I'm certain that I'm being humiliated."

"I won't really need to watch. Just go already."

Mary went into the stall and inched her slacks down. This had to be the easy part and she knew she would need to worry more about the tough part after she completed her necessary relief. After christening the bowl she had paid for with her tax dollars, her anger returned. She was the good guy in this story, so to speak. She had found something rotten in Denmark and was primed to tell the authorities and now she was stuck in a bathroom in handcuffs, unable to pull her pants up. This wasn't justice. This was crap.

"I could use a little help here," she called out.

"I promised not to look, remember." Fawn's voice had a twinge of droll to it.

Mary was not amused. "You don't need to look. You just need to help."

"Technically, I can't. Not without a witness. Let me get the guard."

"No! Don't do that. I don't want some guy pulling my pants up."

"Do you want a female guard instead?"

242

"I want you to apologize."

"You're not exactly in a position to be making demands."

Literally, that was true, Mary admitted to herself. But she wasn't going to let reality get in the way of her expectations. "You were dishonest with me. You lied to me. I was one-hundred percent honest with you and for that, I'm being punished."

"You're not being punished. You want to be punished! Believe me, I can arrange that."

"You're angry with me?" Mary couldn't believe this.

"I just don't need to hear any more escort jokes, okay."

Mary allowed this to sink in. It was a fair request. "Okay."

"Okay, what."

"Okay...Sir?"

"Do you want help with those pants or not?"

This was a test, right? Don't make a joke, Mary pleaded with herself. "Please."

Special Agent in charge Fawn did a fairly decent job of pulling up pants with her eyes shut. It was when she opened her eyes and looked at Mary that the real challenge began.

"You meant something to me," Mary spoke the truth with softness.

"Something?" Fawn looked away but didn't move away.

"Do you need specifics?"

"I felt pity from you," Fawn made eye contact.

"Pity? Okay, maybe a little at first."

"No. At first, I felt lust."

"Are you talking about you or me?" Mary was confused.

"I'm married."

Mary was speechless for a moment. "Married?" she finally asked.

"Incredible, huh?" Fawn said with that tone bordering on sassy.

Mary ignored the urge to sass back. Instead, she followed up with her next question, "Kids?"

"Two."

"Since when do they allow married women with kids to do field work?"

"Did you sleep through the women's rights movement?"

"Only in history class."

Fawn smiled briefly and then said, "We should be getting back."

"If you were my wife, I wouldn't let you go on dangerous assignments."

"You think you're a dangerous assignment? You can't even pull your pants up."

"Not in handcuffs. Which means I'm a dangerous assignment, right?"

"You weren't considered a dangerous assignment at first," Fawn sounded like they were taking depositions for court.

Mary flashed back to their original meeting. It had all seemed so accidental. But it really hadn't been.

"You were sent to spy on *me*?"

"At first, we didn't know exactly what was going on."

"We?"

"The Agency. We didn't know whether you needed to be spied on or protected."

"Really? I'm just that mysterious?"

"You were either the ring leader or the patsy."

"The ring leader of what exactly?" Mary was growing impatient.

"White Israel. Christian Identity. Whatever you want to call it."

"So that's why we had that conversation on the way to breakfast that day!"

"I was quantifying your ignorance."

"It didn't take as long as you hoped, huh?"

Fawn ignored the remark and continued her speech. "Christian Identity is a badly-kept secret in America. Though Christian Identity churches aren't listed in the phone directory, still, word of mouth spreads the message effectively. Those who seek it out don't have much trouble finding a group to identify with."

"I thought everyone knew about the KKK," Mary mused.

"Everyone does. That's why they are ineffective as a pro-active group anymore. What we are concerned with are these various groups that are loosely connected, and at the same time, well connected. It's a conundrum. Which is where you come in."

"I still don't understand?"

"Come on. We are due back in the interrogation room."

"Do we have to go back there?"

"You don't want guys with guns storming the ladies' room, do you?"

They walked back single file like an abbreviated parade and settled back into chairs to wait. Fawn took the cuffs off Mary. It was a good feeling.

Chapter 13

Mitch was once again startled by the sound of a door opening. How did anybody ever get any sleep around here! This time, however, it was a pleasant surprise. Reb was wheeled in and situated next to Mitch. The agent was now across a table from the both of them.

"What's going on now?" Mitch asked as she gently squeezed Reb's hand in hers.

"We are checking on a point of information and when we finish that, then we will know how to proceed," the agent replied.

"For a complete sentence, that doesn't make much sense," Mitch said flatly.

She felt Reb squeeze her hand back, kind of tightly for the situation. "It's spy talk," Reb explained. "You're not supposed to understand."

"What point is being checked?" Mitch wasn't satisfied with being kept in the dark.

"The point about Ms. Fairbanks giving certain directions to the second Ms. Fairbanks."

"Certain directions?" Mitch was still puzzled.

"They want to double check that I instructed Mary to go to the authorities with her information," Reb summed it up nicely.

"So, they've been grilling you in another cubicle?"

"I wouldn't call it grilling. Merely a search for the truth."

"And so while we sit here and while away the hours, the Pentagon is in imminent danger?"

"Not exactly imminent," Reb said as she squeezed Mitch's hand even tighter. Her fingers were going to start turning blue at this rate.

"Then, how exactly?" Mitch was irritated.

"More like a creeping danger."

"Creeping? Like snakes or something?"

"Do snakes creep?"

"Now that you mention it, I'm not sure."

"Be patient just a little longer and all will be revealed."

"You know I'm not good at being patient."

"Yes, Dear, I know."

Mitch looked from Reb to the agent and then back to Reb. Then, she put her head back down on her arms to resume her nap.

"I need to ask you a question," Fawn said.

"Okay," Mary shrugged her shoulders. They had been killing time since returning from the bathroom until Fawn had been called out of the room. She was back now, and it felt like something important was about to happen.

"What did your mother and you talk about in New York?"

"We talked about a lot of stuff," Mary answered vaguely. She had never been in an interrogation before and wasn't very good at it.

"Okay. What topics did you cover?"

Mary thought about Fawn's method of questioning her. If Mary had been doing the asking, how would she approach the situation? Would she ask direct questions, hoping for direct answers? Obviously, that's not how the professionals did it. They treated it more like a decision tree, finding which branch the suspect would eventually crawl out on and find themselves stranded.

"The major topics we covered were the murders in France and the fraud at my workplace."

"Did you think they were connected?"

"Not really."

"Then why did you talk about them?"

"It was current events day."

"Why exactly did you have to fly to New York to discuss these current events?"

"Mitch and Mom suggested it."

"Talking on the phone wasn't sufficient?"

"What do you really want to know?" Mary decided to just be blunt.

"Not everyone just decides to jet to New York for dinner."

"You've never met Mitch."

"Can you understand why that might raise suspicion?"

"Only if you have a suspicious mind."

"Which is something you possess. After all, you were the one who uncovered the fraud at work."

247

"And for my trouble, I'm the one who gets marched out the door in front of everyone."

"You're really upset about that, aren't you."

"I was going to go to the authorities on my lunch hour. My mother told me to contact the Colorado Securities Commissioner."

All of a sudden, Fawn smiled. Just a little. Just enough.

"If I told you that we marched you out of your workplace in front of everyone to protect you, would you believe me?"

Mary didn't have a glib answer. She remained silent.

Fawn stood up. "I'll be back in a few minutes."

Mary shook her head. She had heard *that* before.

Mitch couldn't get a decent nap to save her. Reb was shaking her awake. "How can you sleep?"

"Not so well when I keep getting woken up."

"Our agent left."

"Okay."

"So, *something* is going on!" Reb looked concerned. Interrogation didn't become her.

"I wouldn't worry too much. If we were still in trouble, they wouldn't have left us in the same room together."

"I'm not concerned about that."

"You still think the Pentagon is going to be bombed or something?"

"Let's not talk about bombs in an interrogation room. It's like talking about being hijacked in the airport security line."

"I'm sorry I brought it up. Wake me up when you find out what's really going on."

Mitch had no more put her head back down when the agent reappeared. With company. Mitch automatically stood up at her best attention posture. It wasn't every day you met the President of the United States. She didn't know whether to salute or shake his hand. So she just stood there and smiled.

When Fawn returned, she held the door open for Mary. "Please come with me."

"I don't need to go to the bathroom again."

"We're not going to the restroom. Please. Follow me."

Mary stood up. It felt good to stretch. She took her time moving. It had been a long day. They walked a different direction down the hallway to an elevator where they went down two or three more floors. The numbers weren't lit up, so it was difficult to tell how far they descended. This must have been another anti-terrorism feature of the building. Their destination room had retina scanners, so whatever was going on was very top secret at this point. Fawn held her eye steady for the scan and then the door cracked open. Mary glanced around when they entered the room. It was some sort of tactical communications room dominated by a huge TV screen. Mary was guided to a spot in front of the TV and told to wait there. So, she and Fawn stood and waited. People were on the periphery, sitting in front of keyboards, talking into headsets, doing the business of the government.

"How many channels does this thing get?" Mary asked, mostly from nerves.

Fawn didn't answer. Cracking jokes in tactical wasn't what the paid help was paid to do.

Chapter 14

"Senator Fairbanks. It's nice to see you again."
"Thank you, Mr. President. Forgive me for not standing."
He chuckled. "You said that the first time we met."
"I'm flattered you remembered."
"This must be Ms. Tanner," The President held out his hand to
Mitch. A Presidential handshake. How much better was this day
going to get!
Everyone thinks that they will have some erudite comment when
meeting important people. And then, it all flees the mind when
the moment arrives. "Mr. President," was all that Mitch could
muster.
"You ladies have had a busy morning and it's about to get busier.
Please follow me."

Without further explanation, they were taken to a room that
looked suspiciously similar to the one where Mary and Fawn
were waiting in half a continent away, complete with the TV.
Mitch gave a low whistle.
"What?" Reb asked under her breath.
"Imagine what the Super bowl would look like on this."
The President looked at Mitch and said, "It looks great! I'll have
you come to the White House next February and you can see for
yourselves on the one we have there."
Reb only shook her head, outnumbered by football fanatics.

They lined up in front of the TV screen and then people on the
sidelines started talking into headphones. The screen crackled
and then they saw Mary and some other woman they didn't
know. The President, in true Type A fashion, took command of
the dialogue.
"Good afternoon, Special Agent in Charge O'Neal."
Fawn snapped to attention without actually saluting. "Mr.
President, Sir."
"Are we ready for the briefing?"
"Yes, Sir."
"Proceed."

Before she could begin, Reb, the other Type A in the room, started firing questions like she was in charge and they were in some Congressional hearing. "What is going on and why is my daughter in custody?"

"Senator Fairbanks, I'm happy to answer all of your questions, one at a time."

"Okay," Reb got to the point. "Why is my daughter in Federal custody?"

"Technically, she isn't. Mary was brought here ahead of a Federal raid on an entity."

"I'm fine, Mom," Mary piped up. The faster they got this over with, the happier Mary would be.

"I thought you were going to the state authorities?"

"I got interrupted."

"By the Feds?"

"It's obviously a long story."

"Were you being followed?" Mitch wanted in on the conversation now that it was open for discussion. She remembered feeling all the eyes in the hotel restaurant in New York on the three of them during their dinner together.

"Followed isn't exactly the word I would've chosen," Mary wanted to talk around this topic right now. They were in the presence of the President, for goodness sake. If he really wanted to know how his various employees performed their jobs, he could ask the appropriate bureaucrats another day. Mitch sense the awkwardness. Only people who had something to hide acted the way Mary was right now.

"It's my understanding that to some extent, all of you were being observed," the President explained, trying to get the upper hand on the proceedings once again.

"In New York?" Mitch wasn't letting go of this until she had an answer.

"And France," he added.

"So, Jock wasn't just some ambitious gigolo?"

"He was one of our best agents."

"And now, he's dead."

"We're dealing with very vicious, single-minded people."

"Exactly who are these people?" Reb asked, point blank.

"I'm going to leave the detailed explanation to these capable agents. I just wanted to extend to all of you the thanks of a grateful nation and President."

He shook hands all around and then disappeared from the room with his protection detail. Most people would have been too impressed with the meeting to stay on topic. Reb was not most people.
"Which of the two of you are going to explain what's going on?" Mitch didn't know which two Reb was talking about. There were five people in the quorum.

There was no question who was going to do the explaining. The agent who was with Reb and Mitch had seniority.
"There was an attempted bloodless coup on the U.S. Government and with your help, we were able to thwart it."
"So, it wasn't a physical attack, like a bomb?" Mitch asked.
"No. It would be fruitless to bomb buildings. This attempted coup was infiltration in nature."
"Infiltration? What was being infiltrated?"
"The Pentagon was the starting point."
"The Heart with Five Parts."
"Right. Agent Delort was trying to warn you. He knew he had been 'made' like they say in the movies. So he left the only clue that he thought would escape detection."
"A love poem," Reb breathed.
"But why were we being followed? We didn't know anything." Mitch asked.
"You didn't. But the younger Ms. Fairbanks did."
"I didn't know anything about a coup!" Mary protested.
"You didn't know about a coup, perhaps. But you knew something was going on where you worked."
"Right, but how and why did the government get involved in a case of fraud?" Mary wasn't a believer of perfect knowledge.
"We were suspicious of the firm prior to your association with them. When you were hired and promoted so quickly, red flags went up. You were either a patsy or co-conspirator."
"Co-conspirator? I couldn't handle being co-leader of a girl scout troop let alone being part of a criminal master plan."

252

"Which is exactly the same conclusion Agent O'Neal came to."
Mary looked at Fawn like an underlying unspoken betrayal was
still between them. "You didn't think I could manage a girl
scout troop?"
"Your words, not mine," Fawn clipped back.
"So, you were lying when you kept telling me how smart I was?"
"I knew you were smart. This wasn't about being smart," Fawn
was getting tense as the conversation extended.

Even across the miles through the magic of a closed circuit
secure TV link, to Mitch's ears, Mary and Fawn sounded like an
old married couple. What was going on here? Mitch would've
given a thousand dollars minimum to ask just how closely
Special Agent O'Neal had been watching over Mary. The
correct answer to that question would probably answer quite a
few more in the process. She didn't get a chance to ask. The
explanation continued from the senior agent.
"Since we deemed that you were going to be the fall guy, so to
speak, we ordered you to be brought out in front of everyone else
so that you would appear to be guilty."
"You planned for me to look guilty?" Mary asked.
"Yes, in front of the real bad guys. It will help us with what
comes next."

Words mean things. Lawyers know it. Politicians know it.
Secret agent bureaucrats know it. Reb looked directly at the
agent. "What exactly does come next?"
"We live in an ordered society. All manner of legal maneuvers
happen next."
His phrasing sounded like it was all routine. Not casual, but not
glib either. The part of Reb's personality that housed her U.S.
Senator ego once again took center stage.
"Define legal maneuvers," she asked with the pointed tone like
they were all back in third grade and the teacher was miffed.
"In the United States of America, when people commit crimes,
they are given a fair trial."
"I understand that. You needn't be condescending."
"Ms. Fairbanks will be our best government witness."

Uh. Oh. Mitch caught on fast. What she didn't know from book learning, she had filled up by watching TV for too many hours. Being a government witness probably excluded everyone from being able to go home and resume their daily lives at the end of this day.

"I didn't witness that much," Mary protested from half a continent away.

"You witnessed some of the paper and computer transactions," Fawn explained succinctly.

"But I don't have copies of it. It wasn't like I was taking pictures with my 007 spy camera."

The agents looked pained. They probably got tired of hearing all about James Bond. And he hadn't even been an American.

"You weren't the only thing we took out of the building," Fawn answered.

"But we will need her to be a witness at the trial to seal the case," the senior agent explained in a tone of voice that could've just as easily translated to, "Don't make me get the President back in here."

"Don't question my daughter's patriotism," Reb retorted.

"I wasn't doing that," he answered back. "We need her cooperation."

"Stop talking about me like I'm not even here," Mary ignored the logistics of the situation. Everyone stopped talking. She followed up with her announcement. "I'll do whatever you need for the trial."

"You'll need to understand everything this entails," Fawn said quietly.

"I know a little about going to court. You get up on the witness stand and tell the truth. You know, the *truth*. Whole and nothing but."

Everybody may have been listening, but the emphasis about truth was directed at Fawn.

"It's everything leading up to the trial that you need to know about," Fawn talked like she was above criticism, truth-wise.

"You mean, like prepping testimony?"

"No. I mean, like the hiding under cover."

"Hiding?"

"You're going into the Witness Protection Program."

"No, I'm not!"
"Yes, you are."

Oh, gee, Mitch thought, here comes the bickering. Mitch sensed for no concrete reason that Fawn was stepping outside the bounds of normal agent behavior. Agents couldn't demand that citizens go into hiding. They could suggest, cajole and beg. But demand?

"Are we finished here?" Fawn looked at the folks from the Washington D.C. connection.
"I am, for now," Senior Agent replied.
The screen went multicolor patchwork quilt before Reb and Mary could voice their goodbyes. Just when things were getting interesting, like a bickering family reunion, Reb and Mitch were escorted back to some waiting area and left to cool their heels. Why exactly, they weren't told.

Meanwhile, Fawn and Mary set about the serious discussion of the witness protection offer. Mary, always the law-abiding citizen, could only tap the fiction she saw on TV and in the movies for her side of the argument.
"I'm not some mobster who's turning state's evidence!" Mary decided to display her ignorance in the matter. It was charming in its own unique way.
"Yeah, you're about the last person in the lineup who would be mistaken for a mobster," Fawn smiled.
"Which means that I wouldn't exactly fit into your Mobs Anonymous program, right?"
"Are you working from the mistaken impression that we have some big dorm somewhere where we house all penitent mobsters in one facility?"
"Isn't that what we call prison?"
Fawn stopped smiling. Mary was closer to the truth than she imagined. There were stages to witness protection. During the first phase, the cooperating witness, usually a criminal turncoat, had to be available for court proceedings. Anyone who had ever been involved in this system, from fighting a parking ticket to serving on a jury, knew that it was a system that moved at a

lumbering pace. The proceedings that you saw on fictional lawyer shows and read in detective books was just nonsense. Anyone who thought that Matlock could wrap up a murder case in one week so he could go on vacation were themselves on a mental vacation. Which is what TV is all about anyway.

"You stopped smiling," Mary said into the silence.

"You've done a great thing for your country," Fawn said it like it was the beginning of a Fourth of July proclamation. The sales pitch was starting with a bang.

"I still haven't figured out what happened, but if the President bothered to show up, it must have been important."

"You stopped an attempted overthrow of the government." Mary had heard people get more excited when their cat hacked up a hairball, so it still didn't seem like all that big of a deal. They had used the word "coup" and that gave her pause for thought. A coup, by definition, was when the military overthrew the government. That explained the much-relieved President. Mary was still puzzled and in disbelief. Fawn sensed this.

"You don't believe what we've been telling you?" Special Agents like Fawn were trained to observe and perceive. It would have taken no special training to witness Mary's disbelief. It wasn't that she didn't believe in coups in general. But didn't they usually happen in smaller countries with dictators and military-based governments? Not the United States! Not a country that had democratically-elected leaders and a firm control over a voluntary-based military.

"It all seems far fetched," Mary tried to soften her words so that they wouldn't sound like a rebuke. Technically, she was still at the mercy of her merciful government even if they seemed happy with her accidental acts of bravery.

"The challenge was rooted in the fact that this coup attempt was nearly imperceptible."

"And why does that matter?"

"Most coups you can see a mile away. A lot of bluster and tension and bloodshed. Not hard to miss."

"Yeah, I guess I didn't see any of that in this case. So, how did you know what to look for?"

"It's been a long, involved investigation," Fawn became vague.

Part of her ingrained training, Mary surmised. "Who was trying to take over?"

"There are people out there who believe that the separation of church and state is a mistake."

"I'm sure that's the case. But there is still the majority that believes that the wall of separation is what makes this country great. Otherwise, we would just be another oppressive theocracy. It's the reason people left England and established America."

"You see things logically and with historical perspective. Those are admirable qualities. Not everyone thinks like you."

"Most Americans do," Mary reiterated.

"It doesn't take most Americans to attempt an overthrow of our government."

"How many does it take?" Mary wanted the math.

Fawn shook her head. "The tally is still out on that."

"And even if you knew, you wouldn't tell me."

"So, here's what we really need to know from you..." Fawn paused for dramatic effect, "are you willing to help the government that you seem so eager to defend?"

The circular argument had come around to this. It sounded like Mary had enlisted in the service. She considered herself as patriotic as the next person. Maybe not with blood in her eye, but certainly loyalty in her heart.

"Help how?"

"Testify."

What an interesting choice of words. Testify. We testify in court. We testify to the Lord Jesus Christ. The ability to testify spanned the very divide they were trying to protect.

"I can do that."

"Good. So, we will need to place you in protective custody."

"It can't possibly be that much of a risk," Mary scoffed. "It was a couple of stockbrokers. They aren't known for being armed and dangerous.

"This is more than a couple of stockbrokers. This was a nation-wide network of operatives."

"Gee!" Mary tried to sound impressed so that it would make Fawn forget that she was gradually revealing more details about the case.

"So, witness protection happens in stages," Fawn got back down to basics.

"My mother always thought I belonged on the stage."

"The first stage," Fawn ignored the attempt at humor, "is where we need to keep you safe while you make your depositions and court appearances."

"That doesn't sound so bad."

"Usually, we house witnesses in prison."

"Hold on. That doesn't sound good at all."

"It's safe."

"I'm not going to prison. You can forget that. I'm going home."

"Not a good idea."

"Take me home and tell the local police to drive by the house a couple of times a day."

"That won't be enough protection."

"I'll hire a bodyguard."

Fawn shook her head. "You wouldn't have to be in a bad prison."

This had to be, without a doubt, the worst sales pitch Mary had ever heard about anything. "I didn't know there was any other kind of prison besides bad?"

"You need to seriously consider this option," Fawn sounded like her agent veneer was about to crack wide open.

"You need to drive me home. You do it or find somebody else to do it. Get me a car, a driver, and get me out of here now!"

Mary wasn't happy. Fawn wasn't happy. It wasn't happy day at the local Federal Canter after all. The investigation had taken months to come to fruition. Fawn needed Mary's cooperation more than she wanted to let on right now, but she was quickly running out of options. She could drive Mary back to the house. It would give her some extra time to work the leverage of duty to country. Too many Americans balked at the idea of getting involved in Good Samaritan works for fear of backlash, injury or lawsuit. What the country was now asking of Mary could go way beyond this. It was, by its very nature, a tough sell at best. They were in an unmarked vehicle a whole five minutes before Fawn started in again.

"You know, there are prisons and then, there are *prisons*," she sounded philosophical.

"And the difference?" Mary rose to the bait. No use riding in sullen silence.

"Well, there are rock-pick prisons where you would serve hard labor and then…there's the country-club prisons where you would be-"

"Might be. Maybe," Mary intoned for accuracy as well as argument sake.

"Where you could be housed comfortably and protected around the clock."

"It still sounds like the mafia."

"I wouldn't know. That's not my area of expertise?"

"What exactly is your area of expertise?" Mary asked the question carefully. She wasn't out of custody yet and Fawn could always turn the car around and Mary would be back to trying to pee with handcuffs.

"Religious Warfare."

"Doesn't that reek of contradiction?" Mary mused.

"Not as much as you would think."

"I mean, I see the possibility in other places, like the Middle East. But in America? There's no such thing."

"Thanks, in part, to you."

Mary could only shake her head. She fell silent. Religious warfare in America? She wasn't a believer. They were nearing Mary's neighborhood when they had to pull over for a passing fire truck with its sirens and horn blaring. It careened by, but Fawn didn't return to the road.

"Why are we waiting?" Mary asked impatiently. She was ready for this trip to be over.

"Because fire trucks are like nuns. They usually travel in pairs." Fawn was proved right. Another fire truck soon appeared over the crest of the hill and then, another truck behind it.

"Whatever it is, it must be big," Mary said without emotion.

"And close by," Fawn noted ominously.

The vehicle they were in was equipped with emergency flashing lights as well and Fawn turned them on so she could bypass traffic as well. With help from a dispatch system hidden from casual observation, she now knew for a fact what Mary could only speculate about. The final leg of the journey didn't take long. It was Mary's house that was ablaze. Not just a smolder like a barbeque run amok. It was a full-blown conflagration. Flames were leaping heavenward in a super-hot fashion, scorching the house from foundation to rooftop. So many emergency units had responded to save the neighboring homes that it was impossible to park close, and unwise to attempt it. Mary was jumping out of the car before it was even at full stop. Luck was with her that she escaped injury. What she couldn't escape was the grasp of the first fireman who realized that she would have run headlong into the burning structure if not restricted.

"You can't go any closer, Miss."

"There's somebody in there!" Mary had to shout the words in order to be heard over the din.

Fawn had caught up to her and shouted, "What's going on?"

"Lisa is in there!" Mary screamed, wild with panic.

"If she is, we'll find her," the fireman assured Mary as he hastened to begin the rescue.

"How long did you know?" Mary now wheeled and yelled at Fawn.

"Know what?"

"That it was my house that was on fire!"

"Not until the last two blocks."

"You had a dispatch radio?"

"I had an earwig."

"Earwig? That's some sort of bug?"

Fawn didn't really know Mary well enough to discern if she was joking or serious. People reacted differently in panic situations. Not everyone was familiar with law-enforcement terminology and technique.

"An ear piece."

Mary wasn't listening anymore. She was watching the futile attempts of the firefighters as they tried to search the house for survivors or victims. Lisa had been burned once. A second scarring would be devastating. One of the firemen approached them, shaking his head. No luck or bad luck? It was impossible to tell.

Just then, Mary's cell phone rang. The caller ID indicated that it was Lisa.

"Oh my God, where are you!" Mary hollered into the phone. It was Mary's assumption that Lisa was calling from somewhere inside the burning house and therefore, they could divine her location for rescue.

"You don't have to yell," Lisa remained calm despite the loud greeting.

"Just tell me where you are so that they can come and get you!"

"What are you yelling about? I'm still at work. Nobody needs to come and get me. I just called to apologize for not getting home to cook dinner."

"So, it wasn't you who accidently started the fire?"

"What fire?"

Fawn had listened to enough of the conversation to make a few basic assumptions. First, the foremen could call off the search for Lisa's body and concentrate on fighting the fore. Second, it would now be easier to talk Mary into protective custody because she had nowhere else to go. Third, she needed to dispatch agents to secure Lisa as well. Fawn signaled to Mary that she needed to give her instructions.

"Tell Lisa to stay where she is."

Mary nodded, but instead of talking to Lisa, she asked Lisa to put Trish on the line.

"Why?" Lisa asked, put out that Mary had made the request.

"Just do it!" Mary raised her voice.

Trish came on the line, "Hello?"

"Keep Lisa there until the authorities come to pick her up."

"The authorities?" Trish was totally in the dark.

"The Feds. And have Silver do a search and lock down of the premises."

"What are they looking for?"

"Anything suspicious."

"That doesn't narrow it down much."

"Do it!" Mary disconnected without talking to Lisa again.

To Fawn, Mary instructed, "Let's go and get Lisa now."

Fawn shook her head no.

"What?"

"I have agents rolling already."

"But you don't even know where to send them?"

261

Fawn didn't reply. She knew where to send the agents. She knew a lot about Mary's life. The Feds knew just about all they needed to know about Mary and Lisa and Trish.

"We need to get you somewhere safe!"

Mary knew it was inevitable now. It didn't make her any happier about it. Fawn walked her back to the car, turning their backs on the total ruin of Mary's house. Mitch wasn't going to be happy about this, once she knew everyone was safe, of course.

Trish rarely got hung up on and it unsettled her. But even more unsettling was the instructions given by Mary. Battening down the hatches was no small matter in a mansion. There were a lot of hatches to batten. It wasn't just a matter of bolting the front door. Besides, maybe the boogie man was already inside, which would make locking doors a folly. By the time the Feds arrived, sirens and all, the task was only half done.

"Which one of you is Ms. Beaumont?" the one leading the charge asked in a no-nonsense tone of voice.

"I am," Lisa stepped out from behind Silver.

"Please come with us."

"Where am I going? Where's Mary?"

"Ms. Fairbanks is in an undisclosed location."

"Where?"

"That's why we refer to it as undisclosed. Please come with us."

"Where are you taking me?" Lisa asked as she edged closer to Trish.

"To an undisclosed location."

"The same one where Mary is?"

Either they didn't know or they couldn't tell. They weren't going to answer anyway, so it didn't matter.

"I think I'd just rather go to my house."

The agents exchanged looks. The leader spoke plainly, "You no longer have a house to go back to. It was destroyed."

"Was that the fire Mary mentioned on the phone?"

"Yes."

"Why are the Feds involved in a house fire?" Trish asked the question that had piqued her interest from the start.

"It's a Federal matter."

The best non-answer in the history of non-answers.

"How did a house fire become a Federal matter?" Trish tried again.

"We're not at liberty to discuss the matter," the senior Fed went from obtuse to stonewalling.

"I'm not going anywhere until I get some answers," Lisa began to assert herself loudly.

"I think you should go with them," Trish said in soothing tones.

"You do?" Lisa seemed to be more upset by this than she had been over the loss of the house.

"Look, the Feds don't show up on your doorstep unless they have a pretty good reason. Maybe you should find out what it is."

"Okay," Lisa said, a little calmer. "When I know something, I'll let you know."

The agents looked at each other with an expression that indicated this wasn't going to happen. Lisa didn't see the silent exchange, but Trish did.

"Just give me a hug for now."

Trish hugged Lisa and didn't want to let go. She was under no illusions about what was happening.

"Kiss Josh for me," Lisa requested.

"I will. Go along now and take good care of yourself."

Lisa was hustled to the black SUV like they thought there was a sniper in the area. Two agents stayed behind to complete a securing of the property.

"What are they looking for?" Rose asked Trish.

In the old country, a visit from the authorities was never good.

"A fire bug, I guess," was Trish's best answer.

After the house and grounds were searched, the agents left with the admonition to keep on the lookout for anything suspicious.

"When will Lisa come back?" Rose asked.

Trish had no answer.

Chapter 15

Reb was never very good at waiting around. A lot of people don't enjoy waiting. People who don't enjoy waiting are usually those who didn't bring along something with which to amuse themselves, and find the provided amusements to be substandard fare. Other people don't like to wait because it affronts their feelings of importance. Reb was the latter.

Mitch, on the other hand, didn't mind waiting at all. As long as not one was asking her to do chores or making her time unpleasant, it was fine by her to cool her heels.
"Well, I'm not going to sit around here any longer!" Reb announced to Mitch.
"There's no one to complain to," Mitch replied calmly.
"Start banging on the two-way mirror. I guarantee that someone is watching."
"I'm not going to risk damaging government property just to shorten our wait. It would be just my luck to break either the mirror or my hand."
"They have no reason to hold us here. We've told them everything we know," Reb stated the second of her two sentences loudly. Apparently volume does account for something. An agent entered the room. He was new, at least, new to them.
"You can't leave just yet," he said without apology.
"We are citizens and we're leaving!"
"That wouldn't be wise."

Now *there* was a sentence that had an ominous tone to it. It wasn't like they were just being obstinate on purpose. Wisdom was involved.
"What's going on?" Mitch asked calmly.
"There's been an incident."
"What sort of incident?" Reb took over the questioning with the air of importance laced through every syllable.
"Your daughter's house was burned to the ground."
Gee, when he answered a question, he got right to the point.
"Is Mary okay?" Reb shot back.

"She's fine. She wasn't there at the time."

"What about Lisa?" Mitch asked the logical follow-up question.

"She was off site as well."

"So, everyone is okay?"

"The only casualty is the house."

"When can I see Mary?" Reb asked.

"She's in protective custody."

"What about Lisa," Mitch kept up her line of questioning as well.

"She's under protection as well. Which is why you are still here."

"Why?" Reb was puzzled.

"Both of you need to be in protective custody as well."

Reb, who had been full of questions up until this point, was now silent. She knew enough about the subject, having been a student of the law, to know that this option wasn't even close to a desirable lifestyle. Witness protection wasn't as glamorous as portrayed in the movies. It was a grim and lonely last option for brave witnesses and slimy criminals.

"I'm afraid that's impossible."

It wasn't Reb who voiced this opinion. It was Mitch. And it sounded awfully final. No arguing, no quibbling. Just a simple refusal.

"Your best choice right now is WITSEC," the agent began the hard sell.

"The problem is that we can't just be thinking about ourselves."

"I don't understand?"

Mitch looked at Reb. "Do you want to tell him, or should I?"

"We're expecting," Reb announced.

"Expecting what?" he asked.

"A baby."

This fellow was apparently raised right by his mommy. He didn't roll his eyes or anything. In his line of work, he'd probably heard it all before anyway.

"How soon?" was his polite question.

"Pretty soon now," Mitch replied.

"And, you're the mother?" he scanned Mitch.

There is a wise saying that instructs one to never ask a woman how far along her pregnancy is until you actually see the baby emerging from the birth canal.

"I'm not the mother," Mitch answered quietly.

Since it always was and would always be that Reb was more petite than Mitch, the agent did everything in his power to avoid even a hint of a protracted glance at Reb's midsection.

"I'm confused," he confessed.

Imagine the irony of a Federal agent doing the confessing in an interrogation room.

"It's my niece. She's having a baby," Reb said this like it completely explained the situation.

"Well, she and the baby can join you in the Program."

He had subtly shifted from calling it WITSEC to simply The Program on purpose. It sounded like a less intimidating place to whisk a pregnant mother and pending newborn.

"She's in Federal prison already. So, technically, she won't need too much more protection."

"What crime is she doing time for?"

"Attempted murder. And arson."

Everyone sat silent for a moment to reflect on the coincidence of this.

"Are you sure your niece hasn't escaped?" the agent finally asked.

"We wouldn't know. We've been traveling."

"Right. The baby crib shopping trip."

"You've heard about that?"

"Everyone's heard about it. You two are a legend by now."

Mitch's parents would've been so proud. Mitch was a legend in her own time.

"Still we can't disappear into witness protection. We have to be here for the baby."

"We could arrange for the baby to be brought to you when it's born."

"You don't understand. We need to be there to support the mother until the birth."

266

"You could all go to the same prison," he suggested.

He probably had to make the suggestion according to some hidden rulebook. You didn't need to be psychic to know that it wasn't going to fly. Reb wasn't about to go to any prison, especially one with Miranda in it.

"I guess not," he stated the obvious for the record.

"We'll get some kind of protection. It couldn't possibly be that difficult to protect ourselves out in the middle of Kansas."

"We'll arrange for your flight home. You're on your own from there."

Maybe he thought the reality would set in if he just told his plan in tough enough language.

"You got yourself a deal," Reb nodded with finality.

Fawn had driven quite a while before Mary figured out that they weren't heading back to headquarters or Trish's place. The shock of witnessing the fire destroy her home had dulled her sense of attention. All of a sudden, her curiosity came back into play.

"Where are we going?"

"To a safe place."

Agent Fawn's idea of a safe place was the Women's Federal Correctional Facility in the southern region of Colorado. A dismally gray stark building in the hottest part of the state. Not hot as in chic. Hot as in being famous for cultivating watermelons for a cash crop kind of hot.

"Stop the car!" Mary demanded forcefully.

"That's not a good idea," Fawn replied.

"Stop this damn car now!" Mary ordered.

Fawn slowed to a stop but didn't cut power to the engine. It was standard procedure to never get caught flat footed. Even from a distance, the building was imposing and sickening. A knot was forming in Mary's gut that threatened to upend her stomach.

"I'm not going in there."

"It looks better on the inside. It's a PR thing. We don't make prisons pretty on the outside just to assure the public that we are tough on crime."

"You can't convince me that I'll be any happier inside that place."

"Maybe not. But you will be safer. Give me an hour. One hour. If you change your mind, I'll drive you back to the city."

Mary knew there wasn't anything left for her back in the city. No job, no house, and no Lisa. Her circumstances were desolate enough to make prison a reasonable alternative.

"One hour!" Mary held up her index finger.

There's no experience quite like entering a Federal prison building. Most Americans who travel on commercial airlines and citizens who visit various Federal buildings know a little about the drill. But prisons are even more secure. You surrender a lot of your personal possessions right off the bat before you even go through the multi-door system. They take your car keys just in case you were the designated getaway driver in the prison break and your driver's license as well in case you're inclined to steal the previously-mentioned getaway car. And, of course, you leave behind any guns or knives or toenail clippers that you may be trying to smuggle in.

Fawn led Mary through a maze of hallways like she had been here before until they reached what looked like a typical downscale New York City apartment. There were two rooms. One room was a closet-sized bathroom and the other room was everything else. It was depressing.

"Here we are!" Fawn sounded chipper like she was going to make a percentage off some real estate deal if she could close the sale.

"What's this?"

"This is the witness holding living arrangements."

"This is a joke, right?" Mary couldn't tamp down her distaste both literally and figuratively. Stomach acid was inching its way up to the back of her throat, leaving behind a trail of burning sour taste.

"It's not exactly the Ritz, but it's safe."

"I didn't see any other prisoners as we walked in?"

"You talk like you're one of the inmates."

"Well, aren't I?"

"No. Not at all."

"It sure seems like it," Mary took a ten-second tour of the place.

"It isn't like you own a lot of stuff anymore anyway," Fawn tried a new selling point. Good thing she had a government job. Sales just weren't her forte.

"Lisa and I will need more space," Mary remarked.

They were already estranged enough as it was. Sharing such a small, cramped area would really strain their fragile relationship.

"Lisa won't be joining you."

"She won't?" Mary didn't sound quite as upset as she thought she would at the prospect.

"Lisa will be at another location."

"Equally glamorous?" Mary made no attempt to hide her sarcasm.

"Different."

"How different?"

"She won't need to be available for court appearances."

"I wish you'd just stop talking agent-speak and tell me what's going to happen."

Fawn sighed. It was going to be a long story, not to mention ordeal.

Lisa had been a perfectly-behaved escorted person for quite a long time. As her life progressed, she had changed. She hoped that whoever was keeping track of the good and bad deeds would be tallying vast improvement on her part. She had left her life of crime and had made retribution to everyone. Nagging at her conscience was the knowledge that she had been very attracted to Trish. The heart is a strange and demanding creature. Being with someone and wanting someone else is, and always has been, the fodder for countless novels, movies, and TV shows. So, Lisa carried her all-too-common guilt and it had quieted her indignation at being whisked away without having even a moment to gather her spare toothbrush from Trish's. The lowliest Egyptian was buried with more artifacts than she had on her person.

"So, where are we going?" she asked when curiosity got the best of her.

Nobody answered. Like it was such a deep, dark secret that even they didn't know. Except that they would have to tell her after a while. For now, it was silence on the drive down the interstate south, and then they headed west for a while and then they turned onto rural highways meandering across southwest Colorado. It had been a long journey and Lisa needed a bathroom break. The male agents looked at each other like their biggest curse in life was the female bladder. They stopped at a tiny rest area that looked like it could be infested with snakes and guarded Lisa like she was going to sprint off into the wooded darkness. Had it not been under such tragic circumstances, it would've been comical. Lisa knew enough about the geography of Colorado to know that they were somewhere close to Durango. Durango would be a nice place to be relocated. When millionaires grew weary of the social scene in Aspen or Vail, they moved to Durango with their millions. It was a bit more authentic than the resort areas. A little bit less ski town, a little more western.

Alas, the driving continued. They were in and out of Durango and now traveling south again. Lisa lost track of her whereabouts when she nodded off to sleep. The darkness and lolling of the car had been too much to stay awake through. When they woke her up, a smidgen too roughly for her taste, it was to transfer her to a squalid motel room out in the middle of dusty nowhere.

"Where are we?" she asked, still trying to shed the startled feelings of being awakened from a sound sleep.

"Just stay in the room. We have agents surrounding the premises. If you attempt to leave, we will put an armed agent in the room with you."

Lisa knew for sure that she didn't want some guy staring at her for the duration of the night.

"What about food?"

"We'll find something."

270

Gee, did that sound appetizing or what! Based on what the motel was like, she held out no hope that dinner was going to be any great treat. Almost every small town in southern Colorado had a pizza place and a taco place. Lisa pondered it like it was a King Solomon question. Pizza…tacos…whatever. About an hour and a half went by before there was a knock at the door. This had given her a chance to shower, put her old clothes back on and rest her eyes for an hour. She hesitated opening the door. There had been no prior discussion about a secret knock or password or anything on the kind.

"Who's there?"

"Special Agent in Charge Smith."

It all sounded real except for the Smith part. No imposter would be so stupid as to make up such a silly fake name, would they? Lisa opened the door just a sliver.

"You should ask me for my ID," he said.

"I'm new at being on the lam."

"Ask for my ID."

Lisa closed the door and then called out, "Let me see some ID, Smith."

He slipped something under the door. It wasn't easy to do with the carpet and all. What did Lisa know? It looked like an ID. She opened the door.

"How was that?" she asked.

"That was much better," he smiled.

Smith was different from the other agents. His eyes crinkled and twinkled like he was her grandfather and she was his most favorite grandchild. Lisa assumed that the FBI or CIA or whoever had her in custody had a retirement plan. So who was this guy who looked like he should have been mothballed years ago?

"May I come in?" he asked politely.

"You look harmless enough."

He smiled again. Gosh, he was cute for a septuagenarian. And he understood the dynamics of young ladies and older gentlemen. They adored each other across the boundaries that society put up between them.

"It usually isn't the goal of men to be perceived as harmless, but in this case, I shall take it as a compliment."

He entered the room with a gait that suggested that his knees were sore and lacking enough cartilage to make walking as easy as it had been in his youth. As crippled as he was, he waited for an invitation to sit before he took a chair. He selected the most upright one in the room to take some of the strain off of his joints when sitting down. Lisa would've offered him refreshments had she had any. Where was that pizza and beer anyhow. He sensed this.

"The preliminary report is that your dinner will be here shortly."

"I hope we get taper candles as well."

Agent Smith laughed. He was enjoying himself. The other agents who had been on this trip had been dour, humorless men who seemed to feel like they were on punishment duty instead of special assignment.

"I understand a lot more about your circumstances than you might suspect," he said.

"That doesn't surprise me at all. You seem like you might know a lot about a lot of things."

"I do know a lot about a lot of things, but I know more about the Witness Protection Program than any of the other agents assigned to you."

"Probably all added up. They did appear to be pretty short in the tooth," Lisa reversed an expression she had heard in her youth.

"Probies. They do the running around part of the business. I do the thinking part of the business."

As Lisa smiled, another knock came at the door. Agent Smith yelled out good and loud, "Who is it?"

"Dinner," came the timid reply.

"Enter!" Smith yelled back, all smiles.

One of the probies held the door open while the other brought in the food. Lisa had expected brown paper bags dripping with ground beef taco grease covered with chili powder and substandard cheese. What she got instead were pristine to-go containers full of chicken-fried steak, mashed potatoes with gravy and broccoli.

"What did you do? Talk your wife into cooking for me?" Lisa asked Smith.

"Sadly, there's no longer a wife to do the cooking," he said in a way that told the story of a death too soon.

"I'm sorry."

"You don't need to be sorry. I was the happiest man on earth for longer than I ever thought possible. Nothing to be sorry about."

"Will you join me for dinner?" Lisa offered to share her meal.

"No, thank you," he said and then looked squarely at the younger of the two probies.

"Where's dessert!"

It wasn't a question. It was an order.

"Uh, dessert?" he stammered.

"Yes, Son. Dessert. We are entertaining a lady. Go and get dessert."

"Boss, it's the middle of the night..."

Agent Smith was still sitting down, but he gave the distinct impression that if he had to stand up to make his point, the probie would be a washout in agent academy.

"You are a Federal Agent. Go and use all your powers and whatever brain you have to track down dessert. And, so help me J. Edgar Hoover, if you come back here with something like a cupcake, be ready to hand in your badge."

Shaking, the probie left the room, closing the door behind him. Agent Smith cracked another smile.

"Sometimes, I love my job."

Lisa only nodded. She had taken a bite of food and didn't want to be so impolite as to talk with her mouth full. Agent Smith carried on the conversation, mostly because he had the most to say.

"I know you're probably a little bit confused and no doubt a lot angry about what's happening to you."

"I'd rather focus on the former. Discussing my anger won't be productive."

"Your girlfriend is a hero."

"Because somebody burned down our house?"

"No. That was just the end result. Her testimony will help us to put a lot of very bad people in jail."

"How bad?"

"Treason bad. You see, there is this group who want America to be a Christian nation."

"Isn't it already? I mean, gee, every few blocks you run into a church."

"There's a difference between Christian and religious. America is religious, but there's no government-sponsored religion."

"Well, of course there isn't! It wouldn't be constitutional."

"Correct. Mary managed to find something out at her place of work and that will help us untangle this web of traitors."

"I didn't even know she was looking for anything?"

"Neither did she, I'm sure. So, she's heading to court and you are heading to somewhere nice and warm and sandy."

"I like the beach!" Lisa brightened up.

"We're breaking camp at dawn. Be ready."

"That'll probably about the time dessert will show up."

"We can only hope."

Chapter 16

Mitch and Reb were on Air Force 17 or 18 by the unglamorous look of things. The President traveled on Air Force One. Cool plane. Those who watched NCIS or West Wing reruns know just how sweet life can be on that aircraft. The President can run the country from it. Mitch's mother could run the world from her kitchen, so that was really no big deal as far as she was concerned. Mitch didn't know if the Vice-president traveled on Air Force Two and was too embarrassed to ask Reb. Reb would know. Reb knew all that kind of Washington D.C. logistical stuff.

Anyway, whatever plane they were on was strictly bottom of the line. Mitch didn't care. They were out of Federal custody and on the way back to Kansas.

"It will be good to get home," Reb sighed.

Home. It was an emotionally charged word. Not necessarily good or bad emotions, but home was an important concept.

"Yeah," Mitch mumbled distractedly.

"What are you thinking?" Reb knew she was brave to ask this question. She never knew what the answer might be.

"I think we're going to need to sell those houses in Colorado."

"We knew we were going to sell at least one of them anyway. Won't our real estate agent be thrilled at another commission."

"Let's not hold out for the highest price. Deserving families would probably really appreciate a home that didn't require their firstborn as a down payment."

"So, we can busy ourselves fixing up Henry and BeBe's place."

"Top to bottom remodel if that's what would make you happy."

"You make me happy. Houses are just houses."

They both fell silent. The plane flew across the Ohio Valley to their destination.

Mitch and Reb were back on solid ground almost by daybreak and the government had been kind enough to escort them the rest of the way in a bullet-resistant SUV. When they got close to the neighborhood, Mitch sensed that something wasn't quite right. A certain energy was present and it wasn't good. When they pulled up to what was left of the house, it was clear that the long arm of conspiracy had torched Henry and BeBe's house in the same manner that they had destroyed Mary's home.

"Damn bastards!" Reb spat the words out.

Just because it hadn't been her favorite residence didn't get these terrorists off the hook.

"Wow," was all that Mitch could articulate.

"Is that all you have to say!" Reb spoke like it was a criticism.

"This must have burned half the night," was her follow up.

Hopefully, it would fly under Reb's radar. No such luck.

"That's the best you can come up with?"

"It wasn't me supplying the matches and gasoline!" Mitch let her ire be known.

Reb paused to take a deep breath. And then another. "I'm sorry," she apologized.

"It's okay."

"No, it isn't. I'm taking my anger out on you and that's not fair."

"I know. It's just that I don't have an attachment to this place. So it doesn't affect me."

"You have personal belongings in there. Or, at least, you did."

"Nothing that money can't replace."

As this discussion was winding up, the agents who had brought them home were now communicating nonstop with the powers that be at headquarters. Burning down one house was a message. Burning down two houses was a gauntlet. Could they be so foolish as to try again?

Mary felt like the walls were closing in after only two hours. There was nothing to do and no one to do it with. Fawn had left for the day. There were a couple of books provided from the sparse prison library. A TV set had been promised but not delivered and dinner had been inedible. She had inadvertently saved the nation and now was in stir.

"This is my new home now," she said quietly as tears stung her dry eyes.

She had spoken the words out loud to feel less alone. It didn't help. It felt lonelier than ever. The chair was cheap, the bed was hard and without a good pillow, her arms cramped as she cradled her head. Prison books were boring. There were just some things that you didn't want inmates reading. No good purpose would come from romance novels, for instance. People in prison had enough issues with their needs. It was okay anyway, since Mary didn't read romance novels. Page after page of dashing men ravaging nubile ladies wasn't her idea of entertaining reading. And, of course, there would be no action books if they contained a lot of violent images sure to start a prison riot. And you could forget about murder mysteries. At this rate, Pilgrims Progress might be at the top of the request list. The most boring book ever written. The next two books in the most boring list ever were currently in Mary's *apartment*. Maybe after a good night's sleep, they would be more interesting.

Trish had asked Silver how much more they would need in the way of security resources once the government detail had left them to their own devices. They had been down this path before, but now it seemed like they were speeding down the on ramp to the highway of big-league protection.
"Having guards for the perimeter of the property would be a start," Silver had replied.
"Please arrange for that," Trish had answered without hesitation. Silver didn't look at all like Kevin Costner in The Bodyguard. And, truthfully, she didn't much resemble Whitney Houston. Either way, she knew her stuff. She wouldn't ever need to whisk Trish away from adoring fans, so she instead concentrated on securing the house, property, and by extension, the family. New guards started showing up out of nowhere the following morning. There had to be a business advertising rent-a-guard service. Hopefully, they were all properly vetted.
Then, just when things had started to settle down, the authorities showed up again in force. Trish was alarmed, fearing that something had happened to Lisa and perhaps the others as well.
"May I come in?" Agent Jones not only held out his badge, but allowed Trish to hold it for a thorough inspection as well.
"Of course," Trish said after she was satisfied with his credentials.
They walked to the fireplace room where there were plenty of chairs for everyone. The family gathered to hear the news.

"What's happened to warrant another visit so soon?" Trish asked.

"There's been another arson."

"What kind of arson?" Trish didn't know if that was the correct phrasing, but grammar wasn't her main concern at the moment.

"The Fairbanks' residence was burned down."

"I know. Mary's house-"

"No," he interjected to hurry the conversation along. "Senator Fairbanks' residence in Kansas."

"Oh, God. Is everyone okay?" Trish was truly alarmed. There had already been enough fires in the history of the family.

"Everyone is fine."

"I'm sure that's not all you came to tell us though, right?"

"I need you to seriously consider going into the Witness Protection Program now as well."

"As well?" Trish needed the whole truth.

"Both Mary and Lisa are in the program."

"Where are they?"

"That's confidential information, but they are being kept in separate locations for the time being."

"And we would also be in separate locations as well, correct?"

"For your own protection."

Trish thought it over. For about two seconds. "If anyone wants to join the program, you have my blessing. But I'm staying here."

"We can't guarantee your safety here," Agent Jones was a one-note kind of communicator.

"I understand that. But I'm not taking my infant son on some dead-end road trip."

The rest of the family agreed with Trish.

"We will just be extra cautious," Rose affirmed Trish's decision. When the family conference adjourned, and Agent Jones was sent on his way with some cookies, Rose went over to sit with Trish.

"This is going to be very difficult without Lisa here to help." Through her tears, Trish could only nod. Words failed her utterly and completely.

Lisa was expecting her journey to find its next juncture at an airfield. Where would they be jetting off to? The Bahamas? Aruba? The Caribbean? Or just good old Hawaii? Whatever resort area they had in mind for her would be okay in her book. As far as she knew, this was a limited engagement. Mary would do whatever she had to do to satisfy the courts and then they could both spend a little time on the beach. When all danger had passed, they would go back to Colorado and resume their life together. Mitch could buy them another house, Mary could get another job and Lisa could continue her nanny duties. And see Trish again. When this came to mind, a sadness welled up inside her. She missed Josh and Trish already more than she ever thought possible. Agent Smith noticed her glumness. He was either very perceptive or Lisa was going down a predictable path as far as making a quick getaway was concerned. Like the seven stages of grief, the road trip version.

"We're almost there," he said in soothing tones.

"To the airport?"

"He looked puzzled. "We're not going to the airport."

"We're not?"

"No. We're staying here. Right here in the United States."

Lisa had paid attention in geography class. Right now, they were in the middle of nowhere. The desert and prairie fought for control over these barren lands.

"Exactly where are we going to end up?"

"Farmington."

"Farmington?"

"Farmington, New Mexico."

"It sounds…agrarian."

"What were you expecting?"

"My most modest hope would have been Hawaii."

"You think the government is made out of money?"

"Well, they do print it."

Agent Smith got a big kick out of this. He ever slapped his thigh. "If I had a daughter, I'd sure wish she was like you."

"So, now that I know where I will be, how long will I be there?"

Agent Smith turned somber. "Well, if things work out as planned, the rest of your natural born days."

Whatever Lisa muttered, it vaguely sounded like "some beach" to Smith.

Mitch and Reb had taken the time to talk with all the neighbors who had curiosities and condolences concerning the house. The good news was that nobody brought Jello salad due to the fact that there was no working refrigerator to put it in. The bad news was that Mitch had to scout up some food before they half starved to death. They ended up driving to the local diner that was halfway between breakfast and lunch on the menu. Just the two of them and five agents. So much for a cozy meal.

"You fellas want some coffee or pie or something?" Mitch wanted to be polite since it appeared that they were all going to be stuck with one another for a while.

Nobody took Mitch up on her offer, which wasn't exactly endearing them to the diner staff and management. Jessie wasn't thrilled much either. Mitch knew a sizable tip would be in order.

"Is anybody going to have anything since you're scaring away all my other customers?"

Jessie could be pointed when necessary.

Reb ordered a turkey sandwich and Mitch decided on meatloaf. Yes, with gravy. Mashed potatoes? Absolutely! The meal arrived in five minutes due to the sparse crowd. As they ate, Reb asked, "What's our next step going to be?"

Mitch thought it over. "Let's move close to the prison."

"It sure would cut down on the commute."

"And that way, we can really support Miranda."

"How bad could that possibly be?" Reb mused.

Mitch had been wondering that herself. Hopefully, it would turn out to be a rhetorical question.